*Her chin was lifted defiantly,
her eyes narrowed.
"I promised Mallory."*

"You mean it, don't you?"

His throat tightened with fear; Mallory had lived a hard life, and Rachel knew nothing of the details. He'd been frustrated, angry with Mallory. And now the same thing was happening all over again. "She's dead, Rachel. You don't owe her anything. Do what you have to do and settle down to raise kids, join a bridge club or something."

"I . . . owe . . . her. And I loved her."

Kyle's curse boiled out of him. "Hell-bound and determined to do whatever you want, regardless of the danger. You were always like that—a crusader against all odds. It doesn't look like you've changed. But this place cost Mallory." His eyes darkened as they stared into hers.

"And it could cost you, too."

*Avon Contemporary Romances by*
**Cait London**

# CAIT LONDON

## FLASHBACK

**AVON BOOKS**
*An Imprint of* HarperCollins*Publishers*

This is a work of fiction. Names, characters, places, and incidents are products of the author's imagination or are used fictitiously and are not to be construed as real. Any resemblance to actual events, locales, organizations, or persons, living or dead, is entirely coincidental.

AVON BOOKS
*An Imprint of* HarperCollins*Publishers*
10 East 53rd Street
New York, New York 10022-5299

Copyright © 2005 by Lois Kleinsasser
ISBN-13: 978-0-06-079087-5
ISBN-10: 0-06-079087-3
www.avonromance.com

First Avon Books paperback printing: October 2005

Avon Trademark Reg. U.S. Pat. Off. and in Other Countries, Marca Registrada, Hecho en U.S.A.
HarperCollins® is a registered trademark of HarperCollins Publishers Inc.

Printed in the U.S.A.

10 9 8 7 6 5 4 3 2 1

*In much appreciation to HarperCollins,*
*Avon Books Division,*
*for their special attention.*
*With a special thank you to my editor,*
*Lucia Macro,*
*for her care,*
*and to Tom Egner,*
*whose talent is responsible*
*for my unique and great signature covers.*

# Prologue

---

**"NO, HONEY. I DON'T THINK THAT IS A GOOD IDEA." TRINA** Everly knew that her daughter was set to fight for what she wanted. A natural champion of just causes, Rachel was independent, logical, methodical, and determined when she'd decided to enter a fight.

Twelve-year-old Rachel's chin was set and Trina knew the battle was going to be a hard one.

Rachel stood clasping the hand of a girl one year older, a thin, lost and frightened-looking foster child she'd brought home from school. Just looking at the girl caused Trina to ache, but she had her hands full raising her own two daughters and trying to set money aside for their education. She'd just gotten her own life on track, with a steady job and an income that paid the bills, if she watched her budget.

In bib overalls and puppy dog tails that shook when she spoke, Rachel asked fiercely, "Why can't you adopt Mallory, Mom? You haven't even thought about it, have you? It's only logical that you get another daughter. We can all wear about the same clothes and it's not like having a boy or anything. One more tax dependent would save you money. I'd teach her how we run things here, doing our own laundry, vacuuming, whatever. With three girls—

Jada, Mallory, and me—you wouldn't have to do any house- or yard work at all. We'd designate duties, take care of the lawn, wash the car, and you could relax when you come home. You'd have more energy for your work. . . . And it's the right thing to do, Mom. Admit it. 'Many hands make light work,' the saying goes, or something like that."

Trina shook her head. Rachel, as the eldest daughter, was more responsible than Jada, the youngest by two years. Keeping her own two girls dressed and fed and in the home Trina had purchased by working several jobs and playing billiards took every bit of her paychecks.

Trina had been only nineteen when Rachel was born, only twenty-one and expecting Jada when her ex-husband deserted them. The terror of those early years still haunted her, fearing that she might fail her babies . . . that they would be taken from her.

With hard work, everybody pulling, the three of them were living in a nice oceanfront home and the girls had a backyard swing and bicycles. Already Rachel, a high achiever, was determined that she was going to college, and though the expenses terrified her, Trina intended to support her daughter to the fullest.

But her heart went out to Mallory, the girl Rachel wanted her to adopt. With curly red hair and freckles dancing across her nose, Mallory was too thin and pale, her clothing worn and too tight on her budding body. She looked like she needed food and attention—and love, most of all, Trina thought, as she moved to the refrigerator and made the girl a sandwich. "Why don't you eat this, Mallory, while Rachel and I have a little talk? Milk?"

And then, because the girl seemed terrified, afraid to eat the food in front of her, Trina gave her a big slice of chocolate cake. "Here. Rachel made this, and you'll hurt her feelings if you don't eat every bit, okay?"

*Oh, why can't I adopt this poor girl? Where does the 'can't' list stop?* Trina asked herself as she prepared to argue with Rachel, whose mind ran quickly, sharply when she was determined to have her way. *Why can't I? Because I've struggled through years to bring my two daughters, and myself, some kind of financial security, to buy a house, to get a job, and you, my oldest daughter, bore too much of the load.*

In the laundry room, she closed the door and faced Rachel, who had hopped up onto the dryer. Trina recognized her daughter's expression, those brown eyes were dark and pinning in that intense expression, her young body taut. "We can't do this, Rachel," Trina began. "Mallory is a girl, not a puppy for you to bring to the house."

"She's a girl, like me, and she needs us. Would you want someone to turn me away, Mom? You know what can happen to girls like her in foster care? Not all those places are nice, you know."

Trina sucked in her breath and because her daughter went right for the heart of her, she folded towels to give herself thinking room. "Honey, I know you have a generous heart, but I'm a single mother. I don't know how the authorities would see me as a potential parent for Mallory."

"Well, love is the most important thing. Jada and me have got a lot of it to give, and so do you. I know what to do . . . I checked it out before even asking Mallory if she might like to live here. I wouldn't want to promise something we couldn't do. You always say to make certain of what you have before you try to sell it, right?"

Rachel's young face wasn't just excited, it was fiercely determined, a look that Trina knew well. Because of their financial struggles, her daughter had grown up too soon, sometimes her viewpoints too adult, and when Rachel argued, her logic was already in place, rock-solid and bottom line. "You need references. And you've got contacts, good ones, and you go to church every Sunday. So you could have the minister write a letter for you. You've got the room, a nice house—you've almost got the mortgage paid off, and your car is paid for, too. You've got the means to take care of three girls, and with three of us here, taking the housework and yard work on, you'll have more energy to invest in selling used cars and getting customers. Look at Jada and me. Look how healthy we are and how you take care of us. And Mom, no one fights better than you to get what you want."

*My daughter does. . . .* Trina could feel herself start to waver. "Boy, you're really laying this on thick, aren't you, Rachel?"

Rachel leaned forward and put her hand on her mother's shoulder, an old sales trick that she'd just learned while watching her mother put through a used-auto sale. "You can do this, Mom. You're a fighter, that's what they say about you. People respect you, because you fought to keep us together and now look what we have. . . . Details, that's what you're good at. You're smart and you're good. You know how to pressure. Or keeping up the pressure and getting things your way. Why, you're a sterling example of a good mother capable of taking on another daughter," Rachel ended decisively.

*All the details lined up, the sales pitch ready,* Trina thought, her pride in Rachel weighing against the emotional and financial responsibility of another child. Nothing could stop Trina's steadfast determination to give her daughters an education and thus a life better than she'd had, pregnant and married at eighteen, deserted and divorced at twenty-two with two babies in tow.

"Okay," Rachel continued firmly, "so you don't know anything about Mallory. But her foster parents won't care if she stays here for a while. They're okay, I guess, but we've got a lot more going for us. You can get used to the idea gradually. We won't mention that you're thinking about adopting her. Meanwhile, I'll work with her grades. She's behind because of being moved around so much, so you might as well know that up front, but it isn't because she's dumb or anything. Let's see, I'll take care of that and—"

Trina felt like she was in front of a runaway train. "Wait a minute, Rachel. I haven't said this is a go."

"What if that was me out there, Mom? Wouldn't you want someone to be kind to me, to love me and feed me?"

Her heart proud, her mind wary, Trina held the breath that Rachel had just taken away with that last statement. "I'll think about it, Rachel, and that's all I'm promising."

"We can do this, Mom," Rachel said brightly as she hopped down and gave her mother a quick hug. "I know we can. There, now I think that went well, don't you?"

"Don't get your hopes up—or Mallory's. I'm only thinking about it," Trina stated carefully, but already she suspected that if she could manage it, Mallory would be theirs. . . .

# One

**"ONCE UPON A TIME, THERE WERE THREE . . ."**

Rachel Everly had to see where her sister had died. She gripped the handrail leading up the side steps to the second-story apartment. The first step creaked a little, as if warning her not to trespass.

"Once upon a time, there were three sisters, Mallory. Now, damn you, there's only two. I've got a right to be mad."

In late March the first floor of Nine Balls Billiards Parlor was dark and silent in the night. The howling wind swept through the streets of Neptune's Landing, carrying the creaking sound of the business's swaying sign on Atlantis Street. The Oregon coast's salty mist swirled around Rachel, the tide a rhythmic pulse, sounding almost like a heartbeat in the distance, beating endlessly against the jutting black rocks.

With beachfront access to the Pacific Ocean, the town of Neptune's Landing offered business executives and the wealthy pricey oceanside homes. The real estate developments clustered along the beach, containing magnificent homes, or expensive condos with club houses, swimming pools, and tennis courts.

Located away from the town's thriving chic business

center, Atlantis Street lay closer to the older, ocean-front, historic section of town. Trees lined the street, shadowing the turn-of-the-century homes that had been converted into businesses to accommodate tourists. In the mist, streetlights glowed eerily upon the wet bricks of the street, an inheritance from the first wealthy families who had settled in Neptune's Landing. Once, horse-drawn carriages rolled across those bricks, the wheel rims clattering noisily, but now only the dense fog moved quietly through the too quiet streets.

The candy maker's Sweets sign and Natasha the Fortune Teller's pink lighted sign were only indistinct shapes in the fog. The mist hid a variety of less flashy signs for day spas, beauty shops and health food store signs in the elegant two-story homes' front yards.

With her sisters, Rachel had grown up in Neptune's Landing, had ridden her bicycle down these same streets on her way to pick up shells at the beach.

She looked around the parking lot adjacent to the billiards parlor. In the past few years, neglected by the owner, Mallory's billiards business had declined. Empty now, the parking lot was once filled with very expensive luxury cars and SUVs, owned by the patrons of the upscale billiards parlor, Nine Balls. Most of them had very expensive custom-made tables in their homes, and until the last few years Nine Balls had provided a sedate place to relax away from home. Undeterred by gossip, a few women still enjoyed Ladies Only times, where they could relax without a beer-and-guys-tavern atmosphere.

Above the game room was where the owner had lived, and in later years, gossip questioned how many men had gone up those same stairs to bed the owner of Nine Balls and the town tramp, Rachel's adopted sister.

Rachel closed her eyes and saw Mallory as a scared, ragged thirteen-year-old, then later, as a laughing teenager rushing into life.

Today, thirty-four-year-old Mallory had been laid in her grave.

Tears brimmed and slid softly down Rachel's cheek. "Oh, Mallory. I could have helped you. Why wouldn't you let me in?"

She looked up the steps to the apartment's door. Its window was a cold, silvery square, the mist on it glittering, lit by the streetlights.

Rachel rubbed the ache in her chest and forced herself up the stairs, her fingers gripping the handrail, locking to it with each step. At the small platform, she looked down the stairs, and wanted to run away from what she might find.

*You aren't welcome in my home, Rachel,* Mallory had screamed furiously over the telephone just a month ago. *Because it's mine, all mine, a part of me that just might not meet your Miss Perfect standards. Oh, and don't try that Good Samaritan act on me. Your mom took me in . . . she adopted a tramp foster kid who didn't turn out okay, got it? Think of me as a wasted effort. Leave me alone!*

No one had been in the apartment since "the body" had been removed. *The Body, so impersonal, so cold,* Rachel thought. With shaking hands, she inserted the key, turned it, and opened the door. The interior of the apartment was cold, damp, and musty with stale cigarette smoke, the place where Mallory had chosen to take her life. *Why?*

Rachel stepped into the living room, closed the door, and leaned back against it. She listened to the wind, and Mallory's vanilla scent came to curl softly around Rachel, as if welcoming her . . . vanilla, sweet, good . . . just as her sister had been until later years.

"Once upon a time . . ." Once upon a time there had been three sisters, loving each other, sharing secrets—Rachel, Mallory, and Jada. Then Mallory had stepped into the shadows, excusing herself from that bond, appearing only at family gatherings when absolutely necessary. And now she was gone, leaving Rachel without closure for an adopted sister she'd loved. . . . Grief and anger and love weren't a stable mix, and Rachel felt frustrated and helpless.

" 'Mom, Rachel, Jada, I love you' is a hell of a suicide note, Mallory. I'm mad at you. You could have come to me for help. You could have told me anything. But oh, no, you just up and killed yourself, didn't you? Did you think of Mom, who loved you like her own daughter? Did you think of Jada, who's crying at the house right now? In the very same bedroom we shared growing up? Damn you."

Rachel could almost hear Mallory's voice, taunting her in a husky, smoky singsong. *Naughty, naughty. Good girls don't cuss.*

The slight vanilla scent seemed stronger. "Yeah, well, Goody-Two-Shoes does curse, given enough reason, and I'd say you killing yourself is enough, Mallory."

She hadn't been in the apartment for years; Mallory had made it clear that it was off limits. Grief and frustration took Rachel as she went striding around the apartment. The decor was dark and heavy, more suiting a man than a woman. But then Mallory had made no effort to hide the fact that she had gentlemen callers, men who came in the night and left her well rewarded. . . .

"I earned this place," she'd said fiercely. "It's mine, bought and paid for with hard times that you'll never know, Miss New York City girl."

Heavy maroons, trimmed in gold, softened the dark brown furniture, a humidor standing beside a big leather chair.

Rachel studied the entertainment center. Mallory had always been very careful about her music, choosing it to suit her mood. Rachel pushed the On button and whiskey-smooth rhythm and blues music poured into the room, perfect for dying. Like a living heartbeat, the music throbbed through the silence. . . . *I'll be with you forever, till the tides no longer flow, till doves no longer fly and roses no longer bloom, till spring rain comes no more. . . . I'll be with you forever. . . . On the far, still side of tomorrow. . . .*

The song tore at her heart and, unable to bear more, Rachel turned off the music. She passed into the neat kitchen; she took her time opening and closing cabinet doors and drawers. In them, the few unmatched dishes and some cheap silverware and utensils were dusty and unused. Rachel automatically rinsed dried coffee from the drip machine and replaced the pot. The refrigerator held nothing, but there were a few frozen dinners in the freezer.

In the bedroom, drawers had been riffled, a framed painting of the French Louvre Museum tilted slightly. "You missed the Mona Lisa, Mallory. You always wanted to go there, and now you can't. Did you ever think about the rest of us? You see what you've got me doing, Mallory? You've got me talking to no one. And I am mad at you and I don't care if it is irrational."

In her mind, Rachel heard Mallory blow a puff of cigarette smoke and say in a bored tone, *Yeah, well, hard times for everyone, sis. What are you going to do now, come after me?*

"Smart-ass."

In the bedroom, the sprawling bed where Mallory had died was mussed a little where someone had sat, probably the police or an investigator, scribbling on a notepad, listing the circumstances. . . .

"Where are you, Mallory? Where is the girl I knew? This isn't you . . . it isn't," Rachel whispered fiercely, looking around the bedroom.

Mirrors covered the closet doors, and cosmetics layered a mirrored vanity table, the colors stark, flashy. In the spacious bathroom, Mallory's cosmetics ran across a counter, mixed with men's toiletries. *I love you, Kyle. Thanks*, she'd written in red lipstick across the mirror.

*Kyle.* . . . Rachel frowned, her body tensing. Years ago at twenty-two, Kyle Scanlon had arrived in town in a low, hot red sports car that he later sold to buy part interest in a rundown garage. At twenty and in college, Rachel hadn't liked the big, tough-looking, angular Kyle, who wore long hair and sideburns and a lot of mechanic's grease on his tight jeans. That tilt of his head and cocksure attitude said he didn't care what she, what *anyone*, thought of him. Twenty-one-year-old Mallory had found Kyle to be fascinating and they'd begun a long-term open relationship. Kyle was thirty-five now, the sideburns were gone, and he'd settled into Neptune's Landing with an ease that irritated Rachel.

"If you'd never met him, Mallory, things would have been so different."

*I love you, Kyle....* Written in lipstick, Mallory's loopy script remained on the mirror, and behind it, Rachel's reflection appeared. Careful application of cosmetics couldn't conceal the shadows of grief and disbelief in her brown eyes. The wind had taken strands of her smooth shoulder-length hair from the band confining it, pulling it back from an average face, edgy and pale with emotion, lips tight with emotional pain. Rachel's intent expression seemed to peer past the mirror to the woman who had written the note—her sister.

Why had Mallory taken her life? Why had she turned away from her family? The answers all seemed to be twisted into one name—

"Kyle. She wrote to Kyle. What was she thanking him for? For ruining her?" A woman who rarely got angry, Rachel was furious with the man she believed contributed to Mallory's suicide, Kyle Scanlon. "She's dead because of you."

Rachel hurried by the bed again, not wanting to picture how Mallory had sipped her champagne, swallowed her overdose, and had written her brief suicide note to her adoptive family. In the living room, Rachel studied the colorful array of liquor bottles on the minibar, the various glasses glittering from a rack above. She slowly ran her hand over the long black case that held Mallory's cue, a gift from Trina. On impulse,

Rachel opened the case and studied the two-piece custom-made "stick" with the inlaid design. She fitted the cue's pieces together, studying the well-tended wood, the new tip. Mallory had always taken very good care of her cue, if not herself.

"Okay, so I wasn't invited in here for the last few years. You definitely did not want me here. Oh, sure, come see me at Mom's house, or anywhere else, but here? Why not here? You owe me an explanation, Mallory. This is a hell of a cop-out."

*I'm still here, you dope. I'll always be here for you.* Mallory's whisper seemed to echo in the dank, airless shadows, almost so real that Rachel held very still, waiting. . . .

The wind howled, Nine Balls' wooden sign on Atlantis Street creaked on its hinges, and the city's garbage truck was grinding its way down the street, trash cans banging as they were emptied and discarded. The metallic rattling sound said the wind had caught one, sending it rolling down the pavement.

The truck was running late; Tommy James, the owner of the garbage disposal company, had attended Mallory's funeral today. . . .

Anger gave way to pain, and Rachel crumpled into a wide brown overstuffed chair, hugging herself. She kicked away the matching ottoman. "I do not want to think about what happened here, who you were with, or what you did with them. I loved you from the moment you came into class that day. I didn't bring home a stray for Mom to adopt, someone to pity because your parents had deserted you. You were my sister, the same as Jada, and you couldn't trust me with whatever drove you to this? After all we'd been through?"

*She should have come home more, tried to spend more time with Mallory.*

In the last few years, Mallory's drinking had increased, and she'd become a shadow of herself, bitter, cynical, cold.

And desperate and terribly afraid. Fear seemed to haunt her, and at times, she'd stare at Rachel as if she'd wanted to tell some horrible secret. . . .

Sisters shared secrets, didn't they? What did Mallory fear?

Was it so bad that she had to die to escape?

"Too bad, Mallory. I owe you and I'm going to pay you back—somehow. What a crappy thing to do, leaving me owing you," Rachel whispered through a throat tightened by emotion. "I am going to pay you back, and don't you dare leave here until I do."

*You don't owe me a thing, kiddo,* Mallory had said years ago.

"You know I do, dammit, and hell yes, I'm going to pay you back. Damn you."

Her emotions shifted from anger to grief instantly. "You never did play fair, Mallory. I love you—"

Anxious to hurry away, Rachel jerked open the door and a man towered over her. His face was in shadow and his collar was turned up against the cold mist and wind. It could be any one of Mallory's—Then Shane Templeton, the minister who had presided over Mallory's funeral, turned his head slightly and the wind riffled his soft, fine hair. He smoothed it and spoke softly. "I saw you coming here. We haven't really had a chance to talk, and I thought you might need someone to talk to, here—where Mallory lived and died so wrongly."

"I—yes, come in."

"But you were just leaving. I don't want to keep you. We can talk some other time. Mallory came to me for counseling, you know."

"No, I didn't. I'd like to hear more, Reverend Templeton."

"Please call me by my first name. Perhaps that will make this easier. I'm sorry we've never met, though your sister always spoke so highly of your achievements." Shane entered the living room and Rachel closed the door. "Chilly outside."

"It's cold in here, too." She clicked on a lamp and studied Shane's fine-boned face, his full curved lips. "Tell me about Mallory, how you knew her. In the last two years, she—we were a little estranged."

Tall and angular and in his late thirties, Shane Templeton was dressed in a full-length dark coat, a dark red turtleneck sweater showing at his throat. His brown hair slid diagonally across his pale brow, softening his narrow face. He glanced around the apartment and then looked closely at Rachel. "I tried to reach her. I told her of the love waiting for her if she would just accept it. Your sister was a wonderful, rich person, you know. Very strong, until—"

"I know."

"Her biological parents were alcoholic, did you know?"

That fact startled Rachel. "No, I didn't. She was always very closed about her childhood, before Mom adopted her. We knew that she wasn't well tended."

His blue eyes were fierce, his voice hard. "She was only a child, suffering so much, barely enough food to eat, raised in filth. I felt so helpless as I listened to her. I wanted to comfort her."

His tone changed to melodious and calming, his expression gentle. Set in that sharp hawkish face, his blue eyes were kind, and at odds with his angular features, his lips seemed soft with compassion. "I think I gave her something she needed, a little bit . . . I hope I did. She was such a lovely person."

"Mom and Jada told me that Mallory helped at church functions for a time."

Shane was staring at the print of the Louvre. He moved to level the frame. "I gave her that. Something to dream about, to have some motivation to get out in life, to travel. It's a wonderful place, really—France, I mean. . . . I tried to get her involved with the other women in the church. But there was always something she held apart; some dark recess within her blocked off communication. She respected your family, though. She loved you all very much."

He looked around the living room. "Yes, this place is very chilly. She warmed it with her presence. I wonder if you feel that she's still here. Sometimes loved ones say that—for a time, then the grief eases and they are able to let go. . . ."

"I don't think I can ever let go of her. Mallory was my sister. I loved her."

"She was easy to love, so warm and friendly—I gave

her a Bible and I wonder—I wonder if it would be too much to ask to return it. I'd like to keep it as a memory of a woman who tried, and use it as an inspiration for other lost souls."

Rachel touched his arm and found him shaking. "I'm so glad she had you. I haven't really been through her things, but yes, if I find it, I'll see that you get it."

"Sometimes people wrapped in grief need a helping hand in dealing with the deceased's effects. Please let me help. I am rarely surprised at anything, though Mallory did like to play the shock game with me." He smiled and placed his hand over hers. It was soft and pale, a match to his scholarly appearance. "I would welcome the chance to help your family in your time of need. Please do call me."

After Shane had gone, Rachel again caught the slightest vanilla scent, Mallory's favorite before she began using heavier musks. "Mallory?"

Rachel shook her head; her sister was gone, and her senses were probably influenced by emotions and grief as Shane had said happened.

She closed her eyes and heard echoes of a child's delighted giggle. She saw a young Mallory with matchstick legs and arms running across the beach, diving headfirst into the waves, then turning to dare Jada and Rachel to come into the icy water.

One look around the apartment told Rachel that child had gone forever, long before Mallory actually died.

Yet, Rachel sensed that her sister was near. "Don't you dare leave yet. I'm not done with you," she stated angrily.

Then, softer, uneasily, she whispered, "Mallory? You're still here, aren't you?"

*You betcha, kiddo.*

Rachel frowned, chilled by the room. On the day of her sister's funeral, she was too emotional, still attached to Mallory though the last years were difficult. Mallory's voice and phrases were still trapped inside Rachel's head, reoccurring with the memories.

She cursed quietly, though no one could hear but the walls where her sister had led the last bit of her life.

Silence fell around her, stiff and unyielding, because Mallory wasn't coming back. "I need you, Mallory. And you aren't here. That's enough to make me really mad, you know."

Rachel wrapped her arms around herself. "Once upon a time, there were three sisters. Wasn't it always supposed to be that way? Forever?"

Mallory's last words to Rachel echoed around her. "Things change, sugar plum. We're not in fairy land here, you know. . . . We're different, the high achiever/no boundaries/success story girl—that's you, in case you didn't know. Then there's me . . . low class and always will be. You're not changing me, and no one can change your mind, once you set it to something. I admire that, I really do. My sister, the high achiever."

"I loved you. Didn't that matter?" Rachel demanded furiously of the cold, empty room, and her words echoed in the silence. . . .

# Two

AT THE BOTTOM OF THE APARTMENT'S STAIRS, RACHEL wiped her tears with her jacket sleeve. But expensive, trendy brown leather didn't absorb grief very well and she cursed again.

The broody hours following Mallory's funeral had been rough, and she wasn't ready to return to her mother's house until she had given Kyle Scanlon a good piece of the hell she was feeling.

It'd been three days since flying from New York to help her grieving mother and sister with arrangements for Mallory's funeral. Now Rachel inhaled the fresh spring air. She grimly licked away a lingering teardrop, straightened her shoulders, and started walking toward the outskirts of town. Before she left for her four A.M. New York flight, she was going to rip a good chunk off Kyle's backside. All the high board fences and locked chain link gates in the world couldn't protect him now.

Less than a quarter of a mile away, the Pacific Ocean's waves pounded furiously against the jutting rocks and sandy beach. The wind carried the sound to Rachel; it equaled her frustrated anger. Her fingers curled into fists. "Scanlon actually had the nerve to come to the funeral," she said to herself.

*He had the nerve to leer at Rachel when she was glaring at him, warning him that if he didn't leave, she'd—*

But then a man with two ex-wives who occasionally lived with him—at the same time—probably didn't care. Just the same, busy with ex-wives, or the assortment of down-on-their-luck characters who he seemed to collect now and then, he should have done something to stop Mallory.

Rachel tossed back her head, and the wind took her hair flying away from her face, the mist damp upon it. She picked up the pace, cutting across an empty lot that was being cleaned for building. She skirted a heaping pile of upended tree trunks and brush and a bulldozer gleaming like a yellow monster in the streetlights. Her black designer slacks caught on a branch and Rachel stopped to tug free. The branch was sizeable and attached to a tree trunk, the roots stuck out of the ground like an eerie hag's frazzled hair. On her way to serve Kyle Scanlon just what she thought of him, Rachel yanked at the cloth and her slacks tore, freeing her. Unbalanced too quickly, she stumbled backward.

The mud puddle surrounding her backside was cold, and she scrambled to her feet. But nothing could stop her from telling Kyle where to go. Where to burn everlastingly.

The mist carried the scent of the damp spring earth. Mallory's favorite flower, the daffodil, would soon be blooming—without her. . . .

An image of young Mallory, running with a fat bouquet of daffodils in her arms, beaming as she gave them to Trina, her new "Mom," floated by on the wind. Rachel fought the tears brimming to her eyes, wiping them with her hand.

For exactly the two hundredth and second time that day, Rachel braced herself. She didn't want "the man-who-had-ruined-Mallory" to see her crying. She wanted to burn him with curse words, flay him into a repentant, spineless, sniveling—And that would take some doing. That confident male, baby-I've-got-what-you-want curve of those hard lips was always there.

But something else had linked Kyle to Rachel today, and it had troubled her.

Kyle had appeared at the funeral in a navy blue dress suit, a pale blue shirt that set off the vibrant color of his eyes, and a fashionable, expensive tie. For once, his dark brown waving hair was neatly clipped, and he didn't look like the mechanic who spent most of his time repairing classic cars. Tall and imposing in a suit that contrasted his usual careless shirt, jeans and boots, Kyle's narrowed stare had softened as he looked at Rachel, and something she didn't understand had briefly passed between them—and she felt the need to move into his arms, to be held safely.

On the flip side of that quivering emotion, was the sense that perhaps he needed to be comforted, too. . . . With his ex-wives and revolving door of down-on-their-luck strays, it was difficult to perceive that Kyle Scanlon actually needed anyone.

When he'd stood beside the casket, Kyle's big shoulders had tensed beneath the suit, his legs braced apart, and for just a moment, his fists tightened as he looked at Shane Templeton, the minister who stood amid a cluster of mourners. In profile, Kyle's jaw was rigid, his mouth compressed into a hard line.

Shane's eyes had momentarily widened, his head going back as though he'd taken a slap. But then, the two men in Mallory's life—one who played within social boundaries and one who didn't—understandably wouldn't like each other.

When Kyle Scanlon had bent over Mallory's casket, something like tenderness had shifted into those hard-set features. He'd reached to straighten the collar of her dress just as a caring brother would.

Maybe, just maybe there was an ounce of regret that he'd ruined Mallory's life, that he hadn't prevented her suicide. . . .

That ounce of humanity wasn't taking him off Rachel's hit list. Brush tore at her clothing and she'd snagged her leather jacket, tearing a button away, but nothing was keeping her from Kyle. She trudged down the sidewalk of another two blocks, building her anger. "I've never hit anyone, but you, Scanlon, you've got yours coming before I fly back to New York."

The powerful motor of the city garbage truck ground beside her. Tommy James's head poked out of the cab's window, his face shadowed by a baseball cap. "Need a lift?"

"No, thanks. I'm just out for a walk." Tommy had always been nice and was probably eager to get home to his wife and two little girls. He was the same age as Rachel, thirty-three, and he'd gotten married right out of high school.

Most of Rachel's high school friends were married now and had children. But after seeing her mother's struggles, marriage and children had been far from Rachel's plans. She'd wanted an education, a high-paying, challenging job, and independence, and now, as a top human resource officer for a major insurance company, she had them all.

On the other hand, she had lost touch with a sister who needed her. . . . *Mallory—I wasn't there for you . . . I should have been. . . .*

The garbage truck's gears shifted, grinding slightly as it prowled beside her. "Didn't get to say how sorry I was about Mallory. She had a hard time in the last few years. Personally, I mean. No matter what happened, Mallory tried to help kids get off the street with her junior league pool programs on Saturday mornings. She got those kids into tournament play, too."

*Mallory had wanted to give something back to kids like herself, the unloved discarded ones.* "I'm okay, Tommy . . . Just needing to walk it off. I know you want to get home to your family."

Tommy studied her for a moment, then the gears shifted again and the engine revved. "Sally Mae said to call her if you or your family needed anything. She sure did enjoy the ladies' get-together at Nine Balls . . . a night away from the kids and house. Tell Trina and Jada that we're thinking of them, will you?"

The garbage truck rumbled into the night, and Rachel picked up the pace, her face damp with tears and mist. One car passed, headlights spearing into the mist, the heavy sound of rap music pounding through the closed windows. A farm pickup, low in the back as if it was carrying a heavy weight of feed, drove by, and the sound said that it needed a new muffler. Oncoming lights blinded Rachel momentarily as a big SUV passed, splashing a roadside puddle and washing Rachel's slacks and shoes with mud before disappearing into the night.

At ten o'clock at night, Rachel was dirty, cold, soaked with mud, her shoes and suit slacks ruined, and every bit of that fueled the blast of hot hell she would soon serve Kyle. "He should have done something, anything."

Out of breath, but not out of temper, Rachel stopped in front of Scanlon's Classics. The big sign across the old weathered garage was the first thing Kyle had done after taking full ownership of Mac's Garage when the owner had retired. In a prior life, the old building had been a warehouse, and now it was surrounded by a tall gray board fence. A Beware of Dog sign hung on the huge closed metal gates, a hefty length of chain and a padlock preventing easy access.

Through the mist and the metal links of the gate, Rachel noted a big Hummer and, past that, the lights of the shop—and in the rear of that, Kyle Scanlon's apartment home. Country music sounded above the wind, the beat loud and heavy. "And on the day of Mallory's funeral, too. Show a little respect, Scanlon."

Rachel jabbed the buzzer at the big wide gate several times, but the shop door remained closed, and no one came to open it. She took only a moment to gauge the six-foot fence, then she found footing and started up. The pocket of her designer leather jacket snagged on a rough edge and tore. Rachel glanced down at it. "That'll cost you, Scanlon. I paid a mint for this jacket—I wore it my first day on the job in New York City—and I'm going to take it out on your hide."

She was grieving for Mallory, her emotions unsteady, but more than anything she was angry with Kyle. Usually in control, methodically approaching lists and what needed to be done, Rachel's burning anger and need for revenge surprised her. "You started her trouble, Scanlon, initiating her into sex, and you should have helped her."

At the top, she looked the long way down to the ground. Battered garbage cans stood to one side, filled trash bags piled beside them. The big brown Hummer nosed against the gates, facing out and preventing anyone from driving through. But the big rooftop looked like a good landing spot. "Maybe this wasn't such a good idea after all. I could have waited . . . No, I couldn't have. A. Mallory deserves more than a few words at the end of her life. B. I've got an early flight out and if I don't do this now—I'm going to burn your butt, Scanlon."

When Mallory had needed support at the last, she had chosen Kyle Scanlon instead of Rachel and that had hurt. . . . *I love you, Kyle. . . . Thanks.*

"Thanks for what? Ruining her life? He should have stopped her. He should have come to us, at least let me know that Mallory was that low. He could have done something."

*Mallory had chosen Kyle and not her adopted sister. . . .*

She leaped, and on impact twisted her ankle. When it gave, she rolled over the side of the Hummer's roof, hit a garbage can on her way down, and ended amid stuffed trash bags that tore with the impact.

Winded momentarily, Rachel jackknifed into sitting, her hands holding her throbbing ankle. She cursed, tossed away a used dinner napkin from her shoe—and a warm rough tongue licked her face. The hot breath and low growl flipped her back to that horrible night—

She screamed, flattened back against the heap of garbage bags, and terror swallowed her. She struck out blindly, trying to fight her way free, her legs threshing wildly against hands that hurt, her heart pounding with fear. Her hand struck plastic, but she wasn't being held down. She forced herself to breathe slowly, putting her instant panic back into reality: The rough hurting hands weren't there, only the cold rain in her face and the bags of trash surrounding her.

The big boxer beside her started barking loudly and Rachel remembered the Beware of Dog sign. She wrapped her hand around a can and stared at the dog. "You're not stopping me."

"Quiet," the man crouched beside her ordered firmly, then asked, "How bad is it?"

There was only one person who had that deep drawl, raw with power. It was the kind of voice that gripped a person and held them, waiting for the next word, because this man didn't talk unless he had something to say; the deep almost lazy tone said he meant what he said and he'd had the experience to back it up. Rachel sat up to rub her ankle. "Get away from me, Scanlon. Haven't you done enough damage?"

In the night, Kyle Scanlon's eyes were cold silver, cutting at her, the wind whipping at his hair, taking the deep brown waves away from the stark hard bones of his face, those blunt, wide cheekbones.

"Not near enough. Think anything is broken?" He spoke with that same quiet tone; it rumbled over her skin just as it always had since she'd first met him.

"If it was, I wouldn't tell you."

Without a shirt, the light gleaming on his damp shoulders, Kyle was all primitive, scowling male. In their brief meetings through the years, he'd always been smoothly insulting, either with that challenging slight smile or with a terse, pinpointed comment that always set her anger simmering.

Kyle inhaled roughly as their eyes locked once again that day, and something electrifying and unidentifiable shimmered between them. In the rising wind and light rain, Rachel's senses prickled dangerously as she noted the bunching of his shoulders, the cords standing out in relief.

The wind carried the tang of soap and whiskey to her and Kyle's low smooth drawl rumbled through the mist. "Next time, call first. Maybe I'll let you in. Maybe I won't. Dumb thing to do, Rachel. I thought you were supposed to be smart."

He stepped up on the Hummer's running board and at six-feet-four inches easily ran a loving hand over the roof, then cursed and glared down at her. "You put a dent in my roof."

The accusation caused her to sound like a light-brained female. "I'm here to tell you off, jerk. The gate was locked and no one was answering the buzzer. That fence wasn't going to stop me."

That hard, angular face glanced down at her, the light

from the overhead pole catching the slash of Kyle's cheekbones, the shadow of his jaw. He stepped from the running board and frowned down at her, crouching at her side once more. His voice was softer and he touched her cheek lightly with his thumb, swiping it gently, then again. "You've been crying."

She hadn't expected that brief contact, the gentleness of it. "Some people grieve, you know. And you've been drinking."

"Uh-huh," Kyle stated grimly as he placed his hands on his hips, towering over her. "You don't have the right to come here and look down your nose at me. People usually drink at wakes. You're invited. Just don't start in on me, because I'm not in the mood to back up this time. You want closure, someone to blame about Mallory's suicide, but here's a memo for you—tonight isn't the time to choose me. I cared for her, too."

"Then you should have done something."

"You think I didn't?" he asked grimly.

"No, I don't."

"But then, you weren't around much either, were you?" he leveled her own thoughts back at her, cutting down to the naked, guilty truth that took her breath away.

Rachel's ankle throbbed and her heart twisted painfully. She blinked back tears as Kyle crouched beside her. He wrapped his fingers around her wrists and pulled her hands away from her ankle. Kyle's hands replaced hers before she could tell him off and he studied her face. "It's got a little heat. You've twisted it a little, but that's all. You'll be okay, but your hair is messed up.

I've never seen you so ungroomed, Miss Everly. Is the sky falling down?"

One hand remained on her ankle while his other skimmed up her calf, cupping and squeezing gently. Rachel sensed the live, hot need of a man before Kyle's expression darkened. "Like I said, today isn't a good day for you to jump me."

His hand was big, warm, rough, and caressing as he watched her face. Rachel licked her dry lips and tried not to look at his bare chest. She looked at the dog, sitting patiently, watching the humans with a swaying spindle of drool coming from his jowls.

"Mallory's funeral was for family and friends. You shouldn't have come at all. You knew it would upset us. You knew how I felt about you . . . that you led Mallory into the life she led, the men."

"I was her friend and I had a right. Besides, I wouldn't have missed you getting all worked up at the sight of me, like you usually do, ready to light on me and tell me off. I'm sorry about Mallory, honey, I really am," he added softly.

Kyle was studying her too closely, seeing something inside her that Rachel wanted to hide; uncertain and wary it hovered between them.

He was holding a wake for Mallory, probably just to assuage his conscience, like paying a bill, she thought. Still . . . her emotions swerved into grief. She blinked and damned the tear that rolled down her cheek. "I came to tell you off," she repeated unevenly.

"I thought so. You were working up to it at the funeral. Your eyes turn black and sizzling when you're mad. They're usually the color of chocolate, like my dog's. Then, when you're pressing your lips together hard and trying to be intimidating, that cute little dimple peeps out."

He'd never said so much to her in years, and now, it was too personal, treading on the edge of making a pass. . . . Rachel shoved herself into one mad pile, ready to explode. "I'm here on behalf of Mallory—"

Those silver eyes narrowed dangerously. "Uh-huh. Sure. But where were you when she needed you?"

He was enjoying this and Rachel served him the first of her tell-offs. "Mallory worshiped you and you took advantage of her."

"So you say. She wasn't complaining."

Kyle sounded distracted and Rachel realized that he was studying her breasts, his expression hard. A quick glance downward told her that in the fall, her jacket had come open and the top button of her white silk blouse had torn away.

She fought the panic rising in her, the flush that had risen to her cheeks. Kyle's hard, narrowed eyes locked with hers. "Your nipples are hard and dark beneath that lace and silk. You're either cold, or you're worked up and needing sex. Anytime, sweetheart. . . . If you have something to say to me, you'll have to come inside to do it. Otherwise, call someone to come pick you up on that cell phone you're always using. There's a door to the left of the gate. The lock is electronic. I'll unlock it for you. Meanwhile, you're welcome to keep sitting on that garbage sack. I won't charge you for the accommodations," Kyle said as he stood and walked toward the office doorway.

Rachel jerked her jacket closed and struggled to breathe. His intimate nipple notation had momentarily stopped her thoughts, but then, she didn't often associate with men as bluntly spoken—crude—as Kyle had been tonight.

He'd never really spoken to her at all. Their exchanges had been brief and potent, running to "Get out of my way, Scanlon" and "Sure thing, honey." But then on the day of Mallory's funeral, maybe she was too sensitive to what she should have expected—Kyle's very unpleasant reaction to her accusation that his lack of action had contributed to Mallory's death. Was it possible that Kyle actually cared deeply for Mallory, mourned her, his emotions rocked, too?

The big boxer looked at Rachel, then at his master. With almost a sorrowful expression, he whined and trotted after Kyle. It was an odd trot, the kind of a hop and walk that a dog missing one leg would do.

The night was chock-full of oddities, like the blush that remained on her cheeks, the need to rummage her fingers through that wedge of crisp hair on his chest, and the startling awareness of his hands on her body, the stroking of his thumb against her cheek, her ankle, the kneading of her calf.

In the thirteen years she'd known Kyle, he'd never touched her, had never been so close to her. Rachel closed her eyes, shivered, and told herself that she had a mission to level him into groveling rubble.

That image didn't work; Kyle was too big and powerful, a male animal at his height, and he knew it. The office door closed behind him and Rachel muttered, "My nipples are just fine, Scanlon. . . . thank you. I'm not needing anything. If you think that's going to make me back down from telling you just what you are, think again!"

She shivered and realized that only Kyle brought out the worst in her.

Rachel eased to her feet, using the Hummer's running board, and braced herself against the vehicle while she tested her ankle. A banana peel slid down her thigh and caught in the torn slacks at her knee. She flung it back onto the trash bags and tentatively waded through the spilled garbage. The kick to the beer bottle caused her to hop a few feet on her way to the office. Damn him. He'd been right. It wasn't sprained, or broken, merely twisted slightly, enough to make her limp on her way to verbally flay pieces off that fine-looking taut backside.

Kyle had a butt that caused other women to stop and stare, but Rachel told herself that she had never been a particular fan of narrow hips, hard butts, and long lean legs.

She had just reached the door when it jerked open and with a gallant bow, Kyle swept his hand in front of her, indicating she was to enter. His stare slowly took in the length of her body, locking to her breasts, then rose to meet her eyes. Kyle was always there with a smirk and an invitation that lit Rachel's temper.

"I came to talk to you about Mallory."

Kyle's grin was brief and taunting. "Okay, like I said, you were brewing this at the funeral, so get it off your chest. You evidently need someone to lay this on, so it might as well be me."

His slow look at her chest reminded Rachel of how her wet torn blouse was clinging to her breasts.

He tilted his head and those silvery eyes raised to hers. "You were saying?"

"I was about to ask where you get all your money to support your ex-wives. From Mallory?" Rachel asked, her face tight with anger, her fists tightened at her side.

Her question broadsided Kyle. "What did you say?" he asked carefully.

Rachel Everly had always gotten to him; her quick, pointed jabs through the years hadn't taken a chunk of his pride. But now, the feel of Rachel's curved leg remained on his hand, and he thought of a better use of that sharp tongue.

"I know that you were always hanging around Mallory. I never saw what she thought she saw in you. When Mom's boyfriend backed my sister, getting her into a mortgage at Nine Balls, you decided to hang around, didn't you? A little profit involved then, wasn't there?"

Kyle took a slow breath and hauled back his temper. *Rachel Everly had come to make his life hell, to twist that emotional knife in his gut.* "Get your facts straight. I bought out Mac's Garage three years before Mallory got into her own business nine years ago."

"A little extra money never hurts, does it?"

Brooding about Mallory, feeling guilty as hell that he hadn't been able to prevent her suicide, had been a perfect time for Rachel to literally drop in on him. But then she usually picked her moments right on target.

Rachel was pure attitude, in the slanted, edgy way she looked at a man, as though sizing up his worth and his honor, as if seeing straight into what made him tick. She had a tight, athletic body and a way of putting her hand on her hip, shifting her body as if for a fight, of lifting her jaw, that challenged him. She'd done that the first day he'd met her. Mallory had wanted to keep their "get-togethers" away from Rachel, because she'd said she wasn't up to arguing with her older sister. Since a good time and plenty of sex was all Kyle had wanted back then, he'd agreed to the secret rendezvous.

But that one night, when he and Mallory were parked in the Everlys' driveway for that last bit of loving, Rachel had decided to break up the party. She'd been dressed in a red sweater and jeans and sneakers, and as a college girl of twenty, she already had an attitude, walking briskly down the Everlys' driveway to where he'd parked. Rachel had been carrying a flashlight and burned it right into his face, blinding him. Mallory had cursed quietly.

"Who's this?" Rachel had asked as if Mallory had dragged home discarded trash.

At that point, maybe he was just a young tough with a lot of survival time already in his life, out to see what the world owed him. At the time, it was a fast car and all the sex he could handle. With Mallory looking all hot and rumpled in the seat beside him, Kyle just leaned back and let Rachel draw her own conclusions.

"This is my boyfriend," Mallory had said unevenly. "We've been seeing each other for three years, off and on, since I was eighteen. I told you about him, but you weren't listening."

The flashlight had clicked off and Rachel stated quietly, "You mess with my sister, buddy, and I'll have your hide."

"Maybe I'd like that," he'd come back with a leer. "You having it, I mean."

There had been only a flicker of distaste, then Rachel had coldly taken him apart. "I know about you. You do some mechanic work down at Mac's Garage. You're a twenty-two-year-old nowhere guy with no place to go. That's not good enough for my sister."

That had sunk deep, because Kyle had known she was right. He'd never known his mother, who'd dumped him on his father, one Joe Smith of Chicago. As a kid, Kyle had grown up moving from town to town, hauling his drunken father out of messes, and taking his backhand until Kyle was too big, and then it really got rough. But for the family who took him in, loved him, Kyle would have ended in the same gutter as his father, or jail.

Rachel's "You're a nowhere guy with no place to go" comment was enough to make him want to sell that hot little sports car and show Rachel and just maybe himself that he could amount to something. Ex-cop John Scanlon, Sr., then the owner of a small Idaho ranch, had given Kyle a home, pride, and a hefty down payment on Mac's Garage. "You've earned it," John had said when Kyle was too choked up with emotions to answer. "Hell, boy, everyone should have a fresh start in life, and I'm just glad to help. We've got to pass these things around. You like the ocean and watching whales and you think Neptune's Landing feels like home. If you feel that way, do something about it. You're a hard worker. You'll make it. And you say anything about paying me back and we're going to have a real down and out fight. Just fix the tractor when you come back for Irma's cooking," he'd added grinning.

Another attraction in Neptune's Landing had been nettling a high-nosed girl with a mile-wide attitude. Hellbent for her career, Rachel had an attitude that just made a man want to strip it away, to see what she looked like when she was needing him . . . to see what happened when she didn't know what to do next, because Rachel always was in control.

She had a way of lifting her head quickly and meeting a man's eyes straight on, of locking onto him as if she were seeing into what made him tick. She didn't have to speak. With a look, she could cut a man down to the bone, if he stepped on her wrong side. On the other hand, she could look him up and down as if he were insignificant.

Too tough. Maybe. But all the sweet female package was there, in unguarded, soft bubbling laughter, or in a movement of her hand, the looks of love she gave her family.

On the surface, she seemed self-sufficient, strong, single-minded, a career-bound woman who wasn't getting caught in the same trap as her mother—married young, a mother too soon and promptly deserted.

But through Jada, Kyle had an insight into a woman who as a child had moved through that survival struggle with her mother and who deeply loved her family. An older child, Rachel had never forgotten those difficult early years, and Trina had been firm about her daughters being self-sufficient and supporting themselves.

Rachel was definitely that, and though Kyle didn't reveal his fascination with her through the years, she revved him every time he saw her. Her dimple was a killer, Kyle decided savagely, just one tiny little mesmerizing thing set into her smooth cheek. A man wanted to make her smile just to watch it appear; but then, a man wanted to do a lot of things with Rachel Everly . . . like make those brown eyes darken until she went inside herself . . . like feasting on that soft mouth, tasting her. . . .

That fierce face with high-winged eyebrows, those knife-edge cheekbones and firm jaw said she'd come to fight. Kyle had developed a fine respect for her sharp mind and control that he just had to nudge.

She wasn't a quitter, going after what she wanted. He respected that too, her strength and dedication—if it didn't nick him, but tonight he was in no gentle mood. He'd miss Mallory, the warm, loving girl she could be, trapped inside a darkness that rarely lifted. . . .

The sisters weren't alike: Mallory didn't have a temper and avoided confrontation, but Rachel could hold her own, blending brains with fury. Tonight Kyle didn't trust himself with Rachel Everly; she could get to him too easily. But then most women did, he admitted; they reached inside him to the protector someone should have been for him, a kid left to fend for himself most of the time.

He liked his life private and just maybe he enjoyed Rachel thinking the worst of him, her flashing brown eyes telling him where to go when they first met.

And maybe he just liked Rachel thinking about him at all. . . .

At the funeral, her eyes had been puffy, her nose red, and she looked all soft like a little kitten that needed holding. He couldn't imagine cuddling Rachel Everly—his hands would be too busy getting what he wanted.

As a man who appreciated women, Kyle sensed just how that five-foot-seven curved body would fit against his, how she'd feel close and tight.

Now, all flushed with anger, her smooth, shoulder-length hair mussed by the wind, tendrils clinging damply to her cheek, Rachel Everly was all passion and heat—the kind that made a man think of sliding into her, of enjoying bringing her to the edge and then maybe, just maybe because she had tormented him for years, making her wait, maybe asking for it—as if that was likely.

Kyle inhaled roughly. Once inside Rachel, it wasn't likely he could wait. The sight of the damp cloth over her nipples was enough to harden him instantly, but then he was riding an emotional edge tonight—because he hadn't been able to help Mallory; she wouldn't let him and something had finally driven her over that fine edge into death.

He hadn't thought that seeing Rachel again, all muddy and her clothing torn, her hair flying around her in the wind, would get to him. But it had. He should have been laughing at Miss Perfect, as Mallory had called her, but when he saw Rachel rolling off the top of his Hummer and landing on the pile of trash bags, he'd been terrified at first, almost running to her.

She'd been winded and had pulled herself together instantly. But when Pup had licked her face, she'd panicked, arms and legs flailing wildly. She'd been terrified, her eyes huge in her pale face, her mouth opened for a scream that hadn't come.

She'd always been so poised and strong, so complete, but that momentary terror had reached out to grab her, tearing away her shields. *What the hell had happened to her?*

Her accusation that he'd bled Mallory of money and emotions until nothing was left had left him raw and angry. Everyone knew that Mallory kept lovers who paid for her services, because Nine Balls wasn't exactly a profitable gold mine. He'd helped Mallory financially a few times, but when her drug and alcohol use escalated and she wouldn't seek help—or let him help—he didn't want to invest in her habits.

With Rachel Everly ready to take him down, Kyle wasn't exactly certain of what had happened outside—when she'd looked at him, the awareness of a woman close to a man. He hadn't missed her quickened breath when he touched her, the way her eyes had glanced at his chest, the telling blush on her cheeks. . . .

Her first sexual awareness of him had stunned and hardened him.

But then, it was like Rachel to be right on target and find him at his weakest. Tonight, with emotions riding each of them, she just could validate her lowest opinion of him.

"Okay, Rachel. Say what you have to say. Let it all out."

# Three

---

IN THE LIGHT FROM A BALD OVERHEAD BULB, KYLE MOVED TO
a battered, massive rolltop desk. Papers seemed to drip
from the rows of pigeonholes, cluttering the desk surface below. A stack of folded men's jeans rested on a
new air filter box near a computer screen plastered with
yellow sticky notes. Various auto parts topped the clothing stacks, and a hefty, evil-looking semi-automatic lay
on top of a stack of thick catalogs. Kyle followed her
eyes to the gun, lifted it with the familiarity of someone
who knew how to use it, and briskly tucked it into a
drawer. "I haven't robbed anything lately."

He didn't close the drawer, but removed a lacy bra
from a chair as old as the desk; he tossed the bra into a
filled laundry basket on the floor. Kyle sat on the chair,
pushed back on its rollers, and raised both feet to rest
on the drawer. His moccasins were almost worn
through, a leather cord unraveled at the toe.

Rachel avoided looking at that broad chest with a
dark V of hair in the center. Kyle knew exactly how
rude he was, taunting her. "I'm not leaving, if that's
what you think. Crude comments won't work."

"Take your time. I've been waiting for this . . . Miss
Perfect coming to call. Imagine that, you—here with

me. Coming after me, so to speak. Needing me." Kyle reached lazily for a rumpled T-shirt lying on top of the desk's rolltop. He tugged it over his head; the shirt was grimy with oil and torn in several places. "Does that make you more comfortable, honey?" he asked in a rich, sultry drawl that caused the hair on her nape to lift.

"Trying to be your usual disgusting self isn't going to change this, Scanlon," she stated curtly as she looked around the small littered room. She wanted to remember every detail of where she had demolished Kyle.

A dented apartment-size refrigerator hummed beside the desk, adding to the sound of the rain beating the metal roof. A stack of new tires took up one corner near a school bus bench; the upholstery was ripped, the exposed stuffing dirty. Beside it, the cigarette butts that filled a three-pound coffee can overflowed onto the unswept concrete floor. The three-legged boxer was sitting on a rumpled, tattered rug, a big oil-drip pan serving as his water bowl. He studied Rachel with a curious tilt of his head, then seemed to fall into a small mountain of wrinkled brown fur. With relish, he started gnawing loudly on a big knotted rawhide bone.

Out-of-date girly calendars ran around one wall, curled and yellow with age. A girl's mountain bike with pink handlebar grips and missing the front wheel, stood below, propped up on a box marked Auto Parts.

When lightning flashed at the windows, the dog's head raised with one pointed ear straight up; his chestnut brown fur seemed to ripple over his powerful body. His growl was low and dangerous. Kyle spoke softly, almost gently, "It's okay, boy. It's all right."

The dog returned to gnawing noisily and Kyle turned to study Rachel. "Are you ready yet? Or are you just going to stand there, holding your jacket together with both hands and trying to forget that I saw your nipples? You look like you're going to explode, Rachel. You know, I've never seen you really messed up. Gosh, I must be special. You came all this way out here—walking through mud, maybe rolling in it from the looks of it. Did you want me to come take that Caddie off your hands? Be happy to. It's not doing anyone good, parked in your mother's garage."

"You're enjoying this, aren't you?" she managed tightly.

"You always could peg me right, sweetheart," he drawled easily. "That jacket must have cost plenty. Sorry about the shoes . . . and the blouse," he added, but his tone said he didn't really care.

"You need to be sorry. Sorry about Mallory."

"I am," he agreed too solemnly.

"You should have done something."

He nodded, apparently accepting that, and Rachel found the words rolling out of her: "You ruined her life. You were her lover, she said so. You and whoever else she was seeing. People said that you were over at Nine Balls more often at the end. There's probably a paper somewhere that says you'd get Nine Balls if anything happened to her. Think about it, Kyle. Mom's boyfriend, Bob Winters, financed Mallory's start at Nine Balls. They're saying that you just might collect on her hard work . . . that at the end, she wasn't in shape to resist any notions put into her head. You're probably the new owner of Nine Balls, Scanlon."

Those steel blue eyes narrowed and a cord in Kyle's jaw worked rhythmically. "If that's what they say."

Rachel began pacing between the stack of tires and the front door. "She was not only my sister . . . Mallory was my friend. But in the last few years, I couldn't reach her. She blocked me off. She put in whatever appearances at Mom's that she had to for the holidays or special occasions, but she wasn't sharing her life with us . . . she was sharing it with you."

She turned to face Kyle, her hands balled into fists. "You could have stopped her. Correction: you *should* have stopped her."

His silence echoed in the shabby, cluttered office, punctuated by the abrupt roll of thunder. He reached lazily to one of the desk's pigeonholes and drew out a bottle of whiskey. He splashed some of the amber liquid into a pint jar with a handle—the same kind that was filled with apple butter and sold during Neptune's Landing's Oktoberfest, and lifted it to Rachel. When she shook her head, Kyle lifted the glass and drank deeply, his strong throat working. He sat the glass down with a quiet thud.

"You're turning me on, honey." But the words weren't an invitation, they were hard and cutting. He turned the empty jar, studying it, running his thumb over the raised glass logo.

He continued slowly turning it when Rachel bit out the words, "You killed her, Scanlon. When she was eighteen, you started Mallory into what she had become and then you bled her."

"Is that what you really think?" Then the cold blue eyes slowly lifted to her and the room seemed too still, his deep smooth rumble warning her that Kyle wasn't taking her accusations lightly. "Who are you really mad at? Me? Or you?"

The impact took her breath away. "Go to hell, Scanlon."

He smiled tightly at that and stood, resting hip shot against the desk. He patted his thigh and the boxer stood to his three paws. "Is that the best that you can do? Oh, that's right. You work in a fancy New York insurance office, HR for human resources department, wasn't it? All nice and clean and sweet in an executive's office, away from the gutter? You were living with some upscale hot-shot when Mallory flew off to see you three years ago—so you should be getting married, raising kids, focusing on that and leaving me the hell alone."

Kyle didn't like someone else telling him what he already knew, that he'd failed Mallory. He'd tried to fight her battles for her, tried to protect her, but in the last two years, she was straight on the road to self-destruction and nothing could stop her. And now, when she'd barely spoken to him in years, Rachel wasn't soft about laying the blame. "What do you want me to do, say I'm sorry? I am. Goddamn sorry. There. Do you have what you need? An apology from me? Now that does Mallory a hell of a lot of good, doesn't it? Just maybe you should have taken more time with her. That's what's really going on in there, isn't it? That you should have taken more time with your sister?"

Before she could recover from the searing truth that he'd again pinpointed, Kyle added, "Why don't you go on home now, little girl? Flying back to New York in the morning, are you? Back to nice clean offices and a clean conscience? You can buy yourself a pricey new jacket and shoes and forget all about Mallory there, can't you?"

Rachel moved across that short distance before she knew it. He looked down at the fist she'd wrapped in his T-shirt and the dog growled softly, warningly. "It's all right, Pup. Sit."

Pup plopped his butt down, sitting close to Kyle's thigh, but he edged just slightly, protectively, between his master and Rachel. His chocolate-colored eyes stared at her, one of his scarred ears stood up, the other folded over. A long thread of drool escaped his mouth and dropped on Rachel's foot, sliding warmly inside her shoe.

She had a choice: to let Kyle escape, or to find something and wipe the drool from her foot.

"You're going to owe me the time it takes to fix that dent in the Hummer," Kyle stated quietly, watching her as she debated. "Or you could deduct it from the price of the Caddie when you sell it to me."

"I do not think I dented that rooftop, and if it is dented, it happened before I fell on it. I truly do think I need to hit you," she stated, feeling it was fair to give him warning.

" 'Truly'?" he mocked. "Such an old-fashioned word for an uptown girl like you."

Then a slurping noise drew her attention down to the dog. Another long spindle of Pup's drool slid into her shoe and she shuddered.

Above her head, Kyle breathed heavily and murmured a husky, "Any time you want to 'truly' hit me, think about the consequences."

Disgusting and warm, the drool won over any physical or verbal battle with Kyle. "Wait right there."

Rachel hopped to the desk and grabbed something from a folded white stack. She sat in the desk chair and gingerly lifted her foot from the shoe sticky with Pup's drool. "Eww," fit the situation, but she wasn't giving Kyle the pleasure.

She grimly peeled away her black silk kneehigh, dropped it on top of an overflowing trash basket, and mopped her foot with the soft white cloth, taking care to go between her toes. On an afterthought, she lifted her other foot out of the muddy shoe and sat crunched on the chair, with her feet above the floor, wiping desperately.

Rachel didn't like the curve of Kyle's lips as he sprawled across the school bus seat, propping his arms behind him. "You're enjoying this, aren't you?" she asked as she used a new cloth from the stack to wipe out her shoes. She bent, desperately scrubbing at her shoes.

The air was too still and she glanced at Kyle. That long sprawled body had definitely hardened and Kyle's expression had changed, those narrowed steel blue eyes locked to her breasts. One glance down her chest said that he had plenty to see, the open cleavage of her blouse had slipped to reveal the lace of her beige bra. She straightened, tugged her jacket closely around her and stood. "This isn't an X-rated video, you know."

"Ever watched one?" Kyle asked curiously in that low husky drawl.

Her quick comeback, "Have you?" drew a smug smile. Kyle Scanlon probably filmed his own, as the star.

"You're disgusting," she snapped as the desk's telephone began to ring. It continued without the aid of a message machine answering the call. "What kind of business doesn't have an answering machine? Aren't you going to pick it up?"

Pup, sitting beside the bench, issued a low growl.

"He doesn't like it when people use that tone to me. You might want to soften it a little." The telephone stopped ringing as Kyle said, "I'm having too much fun right now with you all looking mussed and hot. It's a good look on you, like you've just been rolled on the sheets. . . . I guess I'll have to throw those shorts away now—you just used my underwear. If it makes you feel any better, you can take whatever you want. As a remembrance of tonight."

He stood slowly, walking toward her. She moved back a step and Kyle's expression said he'd enjoy pushing her. He reached to smooth her hair behind her ear, his finger sliding to trace the pearl stud in her ear before she thrust his hand away. "Don't . . . don't ever touch me."

"Are you finished telling me off?" he asked quietly as he stuck his hands in his jeans back pockets. "Or is there more?"

"I just wanted you to know that I know exactly what you are—a lowlife who caused my sister's death—or at least someone who got her started on a wrong road and who didn't help her when she needed it. If you didn't hand her those pills and champagne, you helped Mallory commit suicide. It's the same as murder and you know it."

He snorted at that. "Honey, Mallory chose what she chose, and it's no good now to look down on her, or to feel guilty."

"I do not feel guilty."

"Sure. Tell another one. Every time you lectured her, Mallory felt worse about her life. You never thought about that, did you? About Miss Perfect telling everyone else how to live their lives?"

"I . . . do . . . did not do that. I only thought I could help her."

"Sure. Every time you came home, Mallory tried to pick herself up. But she just couldn't meet your standards and she sunk a little lower. My God, no wonder you never got married. It would cost a man his spine to live with you. Why didn't you ever marry, by the way?"

"I had college and starting a career and—It's none of your business. I don't need to explain my life to someone like you." *And her ex-fiancé, Mark, couldn't take it when things got rough; he didn't stay long enough to work things out. . . .*

"You do when you jump into my life. Until now, you weren't bothering me. But Mallory's suicide is another issue. You take off the gloves and so will I. A full week of sex would probably do you a whole lot of good."

"Why, you—" she began and then caught the crinkle beside Kyle's eyes, that slight turn of his mouth. He waited, watching intently as she shoved her temper down, controlling it before speaking again. "Stop baiting me. That's what you do, isn't it?"

"Can't you take it? If you can't, then get out, because I'm not putting up with you tonight."

As if bored with her, Kyle started to walk toward his apartment door in the rear of the office. He stopped, turned, and patted his thigh; Pup stopped staring at Rachel as if she were threatening his master, then trotted to Kyle. "There's the phone. Call someone to pick you up, and don't hang around or people will think you're hot for me. Just make sure the door on the outside fence is closed when you leave. I'll lock it electronically after you."

After the door closed behind him and the dog, Rachel considered opening it and getting in that one solid punch. Just one, and she wasn't a physical person, nor one who lost her temper easily.

Rachel looked at the clean clothes and nudged the stack of underwear; it tumbled onto the floor. The neatly folded jeans followed. She stood on them, slid her muddy shoes around for a few seconds, and then considered her choices of next moves. She could A. go after him and battle Pup, who obviously adored him, or B. use her cell phone to call someone to collect her—which could be embarrassing

She hadn't come off well in leveling Kyle Scanlon, but she wasn't leaving until she'd said her bottom line. Rachel picked up a tire iron standing beside the apartment's door and banged on it.

The door jerked open, the tire iron caught in Kyle's fist and he jerked it away from her. Pup angled protectively in front of Kyle, the man scowling down at Rachel. In an odd way, they looked like a comfortable family to Rachel . . . but then the night had been filled with oddities.

Kyle tossed the tire iron to the school bus seat. "What?"

Rachel straightened to her full height. "Just one more thing, Scanlon. Mallory wrote she loved you on her bathroom mirror—"

"I know. The police told me. So?"

"I think you had something more to do with her death—*than just ruining her life,* and I'm going to prove it. She actually wrote 'Thanks' with that message. That just shows how mixed up she was."

He stared blankly at her, then gave a disbelieving snort and closed the door.

Rachel stared at that battered door and wished she had taken that punch. "I am so above this," she muttered finally.

Leveling Kyle into a pile of groveling rubble hadn't been exactly a success, Rachel decided, as she slammed out of the office door in the front of the building. She'd had a glimpse of Kyle that she didn't expect and he wouldn't be that easy to take down.

"There's always another time, Scanlon."

She muttered to herself as she walked to the exit Kyle had indicated. "For your information, not that it's any of your business, but I was engaged five years ago, Scanlon. I lived with Mark Bradburn for two years and then three years ago, something very unpleasant happened to me. Very unpleasant. Two men in ski masks held me down while a third tried to rape me. There were a few slaps in there somewhere, that left my head spinning, my face and body bruised, my clothes torn completely off me. After being attacked, my whole relationship crumbled. I was afraid to leave my apartment. For a time, I couldn't bear for a man to touch me and Mark didn't want to wait and moved on. I had a really bad time of it, but Mallory saw me through the worst part."

\*   \*   \*

In the cold rain outside the board fence, Rachel hitched her jacket up over her head, but kept her arms in the sleeves. She had only walked a few yards when the tinkling song sounded and seconds later, the headlights of the ice cream wagon cut into the sheets of rain.

"I don't know how to turn off the sound," Jada explained as Rachel climbed inside to the passenger seat. In the rear of the Broadway Ice Cream truck, Jada's housecleaning supplies rattled softly as she made a U-turn to return to Neptune's Landing. "You look like the Headless Horseman walking with your jacket up over your head like that. I've been trying to call you on your cell phone. You'd turned it off for some reason, so I left a message for you. Then I tried the garage— because the way you were staring at Kyle today and I know that you think he destroyed Mallory, I thought you just might come here. So I called here and when no one answered, I just started looking, and then you called me. . . . You're all muddy and your jacket and blouse— What have you been doing, Rache?" Jada demanded.

After a battle with Kyle, Rachel didn't feel like explaining herself. "I'm not in the mood for this, Jay. You sound like Mom."

"She and Bob are worried about you. Bob still hasn't gotten over finding Mallory like that when Mom sent him over to check on her. You should have called. And you went to Mallory's place, didn't you?" Jada studied Rachel's face, then said grimly, "I knew you would. You always have to have answers, to make the pieces fit. You're really chewing on this one, aren't you? Well, maybe the pieces won't fit, no matter what you do."

"Scanlon was Mallory's lover. He owed her. He was probably getting money from her. Those first years when Mallory opened Nine Balls were pretty successful. She was so proud of how much she was making and the improvements she'd made, the better equipment she was able to buy. When her money went down, he probably wasn't happy."

"Boy, your opinion of him just sank lower, if that's possible. We already went through this a long time ago. He won't admit it, but Bob had to have given Mallory the down-money. He was always doing things like that. I guess he always liked taking care of us girls because he never had kids, and as a widower, he's lonely. If she was paying anyone back, it would be him. But she'd let her business slide so much in the last years that she probably couldn't pay anyone."

"She had an income, and you know it. It's just not the kind nice people talk about, is it?"

"Hey, don't get all huffy with me. I'm her sister, too."

Rachel studied Jada as the windshield wipers clacked rhythmically and the cleaning supplies rattled. Jada smiled warily, flashing her dental braces.

"Did you know that Mallory wrote she loved Kyle on the mirror of her bathroom?" Rachel asked.

"You're changing the subject, but yes, I knew. She did love him, like a brother."

"Scanlon isn't someone you love like a brother."

Jada grinned and in the light of the dashboard, her braces gleamed. "I do. But I'd jump him if he were interested. Sounds kinky, doesn't it? But he's got it. If my ex-husband, Wussie-boy, only had a quarter of what Kyle has, I might have lasted longer. As it is, I stayed long enough to get our names on the same credit cards and now I'm paying off charges he ran up. . . . Anyway, my future baby could do a lot worse than Kyle Scanlon for a father. . . . Yep, Kyle-sweetie is going to fill the cup for me."

Rachel stared at her sister. "That is so sick and disgusting."

"I want kids and Kyle has agreed to be the donor if I don't get one in four years. My eggs won't be there forever, you know. Just think, your little niece or nephew could have Kyle for a father. Wouldn't it be neat to have a little Kyle running around the house? You could buy him toy trucks and take him to the playground and—"

Rachel knew that Jada was teasing her, trying to distract her. She settled into her damp torn jacket and her dark mood. "Shut up, will you?"

"Just a little torment to ease what we've been going through for the past few days, sis," Jada returned easily. "Bob is at the house, staying with Mom. She's really torn up and feeling guilty. I guess we all are."

Each sat wrapped in their own thoughts, the windshield wipers clacking until the ice cream truck pulled into Trina Everly's driveway. The modest, well-tended home in a quiet neighborhood had been where they grew up, had played in the backyard overlooking the Pacific Ocean, and had loved Mallory. Roses would bloom across the front of the house as they did every summer, the decorative shrubs would need trimming. The spacious lawn with the stone walkway leading down to the mailbox on the street would need mowing. The white shutters on the brick siding would need cleaning. And Mallory wouldn't be sitting at the backyard picnic table this summer. . . .

When Jada and Rachel ran up the steps to the back porch, their mother was waiting with a worried frown and her hands on her hips. Bob Winters' hand rested on her shoulder. In comparison to Trina's tall, slender body, Bob carried weight around his jowls and his midsection. Older than Trina's fifty-two years, Bob was gray and thinning.

It was a scene that had met Rachel often through the years—her mother and Bob, waiting for her to come into the house . . . but this time, Trina's face was pale and etched by grief. At her side, Bob looked grim. Protective of Trina, worried about her throughout the days since Mallory's death, Bob leveled a look at Rachel that said *You shouldn't worry your mother. Not now, when she's so upset about Mallory.*

Within the back porch, Rachel hugged her mother, lingering in Trina's tight embrace. "I'm fine, Mom."

"You're cold and chilled." Trina Everly had that fair, blue-eyed blonde look that still attracted men's admiring stares. Her hair, cut in layers, was soft and shoulder length, adding to a youthful delicate look. But Trina was anything but delicate when it came to protecting her children, Mallory included. Life hadn't been easy for Trina as a twenty-two-year-old divorcée with two babies in tow and an unemployed, disinterested exhusband who had left her responsible for bills. By working days as a waitress and a telephone saleswoman and a bookkeeper at night, she'd scrambled out of a dirty apartment into low-income housing.

Then she'd found that she could play pool with the

best and had brought home extra money from bets and tournaments. Local sponsors backed her, glad for the advertising. A woman who met horrible circumstances with dignity was good for advertising, too. Neptune's Landing pitched in to help the local minor celebrity, and in a few years, Trina found another talent—that of selling used cars. Now she owned her own business, Trina's Used Cars, and this charming oceanfront home into which they had moved.

Dedicated to her children, Trina had dated often, but selectively. Then, when Rachel was just eleven, Trina had met Bob, the new owner of Neptune's Landing's Handy Hardware store. Bob, a widower, had easily become a gentle, stable part of the Everlys' lives. He was often at Trina's home, comfortable in it, contributing little fix-up jobs; a marriage offer was always on the table, but Trina had remained too scarred from her early marriage to accept it.

As a woman, Rachel had recognized the looks shared by her mother and Bob. Though Bob never stayed overnight when the "girls" were home, the couple was in a long-term, comfortable, and definitely sexual relationship.

Trina leaned back from the embrace and smiled wearily, her metal braces glittering around the neon pink rubber bands, the color matching Jada's. "Go take a shower and we'll talk later. Bob and I were just looking at pictures of Mallory. I—"

Bob's arm reached to draw Trina close. Suddenly looking her age and helpless with grief, Trina leaned her head on his shoulder.

"She's tired. You all are. The kitchen is loaded with

food—cakes, pies, casseroles, soups, sandwiches—the whole town seemed to stop by and bring something, and that's a credit to the high esteem that they hold of your mother. Can I get something for you to eat? Warm a casserole or some soup for you?" Bob asked Rachel and Jada as he removed Rachel's torn leather jacket. He studied it. "It was always Jada or Mallory who came home with—"

He paused briefly as if wishing he hadn't reminded them of the day's funeral, of a loved one now gone, then continued, "The other two used to come in scraps, their clothing torn or muddy. This time it's you. Are you okay?"

"I'm fine. Just working off a little of the last three days by walking in the rain." Rachel was grateful for Bob's remark, meant to welcome and lighten the heavy dark emotion of the past few days.

"See? It isn't always me ruining clothes," Jada responded with a slight, sad smile. The brief silence seemed to echo the thought of all: *Sometimes it had been Mallory. . . .*

"I took a walk across that empty lot next to Nine Balls and tripped. The mud was cold and the rubble unfriendly. I should have known better to do that in the dark."

"You could have been hurt. But I'm so glad you're home now, I just wish—" *I just wish Mallory was here, too. . . .* Trina recovered and added, "You need a hot cup of cocoa and some food. You should eat something, Rachel. I don't think I've seen you eat anything during all this. . . . We'll never eat all that food our friends brought. They knew Mallory was having a hard time. But this—"

Bob kissed Trina's blond head. "They knew you loved her and that's why they came to the funeral and visited here this afternoon. They know how hard the last two years have been for you."

Drained by the last few days, Trina leaned against him. "I did love her. Rachel and Jada may have been born to me, but Mallory was just the same. I loved her from the moment Rachel brought her home, a scraggy little frightened thirteen-year-old."

"You fought to adopt her, Mom. She loved you, too."

"I have to believe she did. If only she loved herself as well—" Trina roused and hugged Rachel and Jada briefly. "Go on now, clean up and make that shower nice and hot so you won't catch cold."

Jada kissed Trina's cheek. "I'll make Rachel something she can't refuse. She's been at—"

With a dark look, Rachel stopped Jada from completing her sentence; her mother had enough to deal with, let alone worrying about her brooding at Mallory's apartment or arguing with Kyle.

"I just had to go for a walk, to get some fresh air. I'm okay, Mom," Rachel said again as she moved down the hallway to the comfortable bedroom they had shared once with young, frightened Mallory. Filled with Jada's things now, a divorcée moving back into her mother's home, the room echoed memories of thirteen-year-old Mallory. She'd been fiercely tough on the outside, rudely accepting new clothing and kindness, but her terror that she would be once more rejected or somehow cruelly treated had been evident. She'd gradually warmed to the Everlys, living as a daughter and a sister, but there was always that slight hesitation, that reserve that said she didn't really think she belonged. . . .

"You were my sister, Mallory, in everything but blood," Rachel stated passionately as she kicked off her ruined shoes. "Now look what you've done. Mom looks like she's been through hell—And how am I going to pay you back for—"

Rachel pushed away another time, one in which Mallory had come to be with her, to ease her back from the darkness three years ago. . . . Three men in ski masks had stalked her as she crossed that New York park at night, and they'd caught her, pinning her to the dirty rubble of leaves, hands hurting—

But the man who had prepared to rape her couldn't perform and one of the others had laughed, turning his fury on them—then she'd been alone and naked on the damp ground, too shaken and bruised to move.

On the dresser, a picture of Mallory in an ornate pewter frame caught Rachel. In the later years, when Mallory was getting that hard, knowing look, she'd had the picture taken and gifted each of the Everlys with it. "Don't forget me, Rachel," she'd said quietly as she watched the gift being unwrapped. "I had this taken without makeup, just for you, Jada and Mom. Show it to anyone else and I'll kill you. Maybe someday I won't be around—and maybe then someone will look at my picture and remember me as different than I—" she had floundered before rushing away.

In the picture, Mallory had the wild look of an Irish scamp, feisty, with a mass of reddish gold ringlets and sky blue eyes. Mallory's image stared back at Rachel as memories churned around her—giggling late at night, picking over every detail of Lori Walker's horrible but expensive taste in clothes, their plans to travel to France and hike across Europe. And there was always plenty of boy talk, fads, music, and sex—except Mallory was always very quiet when it came to that topic.

At sixteen and sexy, Mallory had suddenly demanded her own room.

At twenty-one, she was waitressing and saving money for her dream, a business of her own—and she was openly dating a new mechanic in town, twenty-two-year-old Kyle Scanlon. She'd wanted to move in with him—

The thought of Kyle with Mallory fueled Rachel's anger as she stripped for her shower. She used Jada's shampoo and body gel and scrubbed thoroughly, trying to wipe away the way he'd looked at her.

Rachel shoved open the glass door, stepped onto the bathroom floor and toweled dry quickly. "Scanlon hasn't changed at all."

Taking her time, Rachel wrapped a towel around her hair, moisturized her face, and entered the bedroom. In the closet was a stack of "home-clothes," and Rachel selected a faded blue sweatsuit.

She was just tying the strings of the pants when Jada burst into the room, waving an envelope. "It's from Mallory. She must have mailed it just before she died . . . the postmark is from out of town. It's for you," she exclaimed breathlessly. "We didn't get the mail today, so I just went to the mailbox. I was just opening the sympathy cards, you know, trying to keep anything unpleasant from Mom—say Wussie-boy's letter because she knows that upsets me—I didn't tell Mom, because she looks ready to crumble and because Mallory could have put anything into that letter . . . she was pretty—unstable—at the end, and Mom just can't take any more right now, and because—Open it, Rachel!"

Rachel held the envelope tightly, then forced herself to sit on the bed, staring at it. Why had Mallory written to her?

Her fingers shook as she opened the two-page letter, in Mallory's distinctive, big loopy script, written on lined yellow tablet paper. "Hi, Kiddo. I'm already missing you and Jada and Mom. If I had any good going for me, it was you. I'm so sorry I couldn't be more. Well, that's enough of that and life goes on, or it doesn't. That's what I told you once, wasn't it? Don't ever look back, Rachel. What happened to you wasn't your fault. You're the best person I know."

Rachel inhaled and swallowed the emotion tightening her throat before reading on: "I'm going to ask a big favor of you. I worked damn hard to get Nine Balls up and running. I've paid big prices. But it just can't be for nothing, not the way the kids love coming here, kids like me who need to be kept off the streets. Your mom gave me something special by teaching me about love and how to play pool, and I want to give it back. I guess that's about it. By the way, with me out of the picture Nine Balls is officially yours and the bank's. See if you can keep it running until you find someone who wants it and should have it. If you could just manage it meanwhile, I'd appreciate it. Don't let anything happen to Nine Balls, will you, please, Rachel? It's the only good thing I've done in my life. Call Terri Samson, my lawyer, when you can. I know you don't like Kyle, but try to understand that he was my friend, and maybe try to repay him a little for his kindnesses since I can't, will you? And give Mom and Jada a hug for me. Later, Mallory."

"What did she say, Rachel?" Jada's arm had been around Rachel as she read the letter.

Rachel carefully folded the last letter Mallory wrote and eased it into the envelope. She pressed it to her heart where she would keep Mallory forever.

"I guess I'm the owner of Nine Balls now," she whispered unevenly.

# Four

**JUST A MONTH AFTER MALLORY'S DEATH, KYLE SCANLON** leaned back in his office chair and propped his feet on his desk. He glanced outside into the late April sunlight to the board fence where Mallory's daffodils had bloomed and listened to the woman on the telephone. Kyle had been listening very carefully to Jada, waiting to catch any tidbit about Rachel. Gossip had been running like wildfire through Neptune's Landing that Jada's sister, Rachel, was moving back to town and that she was the new owner of Nine Balls.

But Jada's cheerful chatter ran to that of Wussie-boy's damaging credit affecting hers and her spring-cleaning woes, her clients wanting more than the usual.

"Every client I have is on a cleaning rampage and I ache from my butt to my shoulders. Mrs. Johnson over on Pearl Street? She wants her bottom cupboards re-lined, so I squatted all day . . . had to lay on the floor to reach to the far back corners."

"Life is rough. But I bet you looked cute, all laid out like that," Kyle teased. "So what else are you doing with your life, except cleaning?"

"I'm planning my ice cream route. . . . I'd like to let Shane Templeton catch me. He's such a hunk. Mallory had a thing for him once, you know. . . . But, unless I can make Shane come across and make me the local minister's wife and the mother of his future children, you're still on the top of my sperm donor list, okay?" she asked.

He smiled slightly and answered, "Sure. In four years, if your mother-motor is still humming, I'll do my best to fill the cup. So Rachel is back to sharing your bedroom at your mother's?"

"Yeah, we picked her up from the airport this morning and her things are being shipped. Mom is happy to have us all together again. Like most of us, she's wondering where she went wrong and what she should have done for Mallory, so Rachel coming home now eases her a bit. Rachel isn't bringing much. She's going to invest everything she has into building Mallory's billiards parlor back up into what it was. That's going to take some work. There were a few bad scenes there at the last and now people are wary."

Jada sneezed several times and swallowed something before continuing, "I hate cats. The Michaelsons have three long-haired monsters and their fur is everywhere. Rachel brought her cat, Harry. I'm allergic to him and he loves me . . . he's all over me. Shoo! Go away! Get!"

Kyle smiled at the sound of something hitting a wall and a hiss that sounded like Harry didn't like that play before Jada said, "Nine Balls is the only place that is upscale and suitable for women who really want to play and for children to learn the game. The rest of the places with tables are taverns. There are some buyers already lined up for it, if Rachel wants to sell—but knowing her, come hell or high water, she's going to get the whole place back up on its feet. She's going to get those women back, the ones who liked to come to Mallory's to let off a little marital steam and have some time out from kids and husbands and housework. She wants to get the teens programs up and running—the parents wouldn't let them come when Mallory was so—volatile at the end. I'd make a good minister's wife, don't you think? I mean why the hell not? Am I not sexy, or what?"

Kyle's smile widened. Fast moving, fast talking, Jada couldn't be put into the mold that straight-necked Shane Templeton would expect. Meanwhile, the church was getting free cleaning at the parsonage and Shane wasn't complaining. The minister wasn't on Kyle's "friends" list. A regular secret visitor at Mallory's before her decline in the last two years, Shane had deserted Mallory when she needed him most—but then he couldn't afford to openly acknowledge a relationship with a tramp, could he?

"So how is Rachel anyway?" Kyle asked to distract Jada from her pursuit of Shane. Kyle had tried to stop Mallory from falling in love with the attractive minister, from dreaming about becoming his wife, and now he was listening to the same thing from Jada. This time, his warning conversation with Shane would be a little stronger and a whole lot more affective. . . .

"I'm tired. . . . Shoo! Get off me! Rachel's exboyfriend called while she was having dinner with us and things sounded rough. Rachel wasn't putting up with Mark's plans to get her back and she told him off. She just took some food to Mallory's apartment. She's needing to work off some excess energy and decided to pack up Mallory's personal stuff. Hey, by the way, thanks for fixing the ice cream wagon and I'll try not to ride that clutch as much, but that's pretty hard when you have to go slow through the neighborhoods. I'll be over to get it in a couple of days. I'm going to start driving a summer route through town from about four or so until after suppertime, and Saturday evenings. I'll clean houses in the morning. Gotta go. Bye."

Kyle replaced the telephone and took a deep breath. Jada was an information bank about everything, especially about her sister. Through the years, Rachel may have had dates and boyfriends, but she hadn't married. She'd lived with her fiancé, but as far as Kyle knew, now there wasn't anyone in her life.

Her breakup with Mark what's-his-name had occurred around the time Mallory had borrowed money from Kyle to fly to New York.

Mallory never went anywhere and the request to borrow money from Kyle to visit Rachel had been a surprise. When Mallory had returned, she was grim, not talking about her trip or Rachel, and was quietly furious—it showed in how she played pool, fast, hard shots, pitting herself against the balls as if she hated them.

*Something bad had happened during that trip. What was it?*

Outside, the April night was quiet, and once in a while on the road in front of the garage, a truck would pass—sometimes an eighteen wheeler, but more likely a farmer bringing home feed for his livestock, or taking a cattle truck to the stockyards. The old reconditioned oscillating fan on his desk purred softly, and Pup, sensing that his master was in a brooding mood, came to lay his head on Kyle's thigh. Automatically Kyle reached for a length of paper towel, folded it, and slid it beneath the dog's jowls.

The apartment behind his office was quiet tonight; since Rachel's attack on him, Patty and Iris had come and gone as they usually did. This time, they were job hunting in Vegas. Their job hunts, financed by him, usually were unsuccessful, and they'd be back, needing a place to stay. He liked having the sound of women around, and the good cooking was a real plus. All he had to do was the laundry and pay the bills.

Pup's chocolate brown eyes looked soulfully up at Kyle and he petted the dog's smooth fur. "She's got the same shade of brown, but when she's mad, they're black. I like that, when they turn black and she's locked onto me. I get tangled up with Rachel and it would be an all-out war."

He'd almost gotten her out of his system, when she'd torn into him a month ago. It had taken her just one month to quit her job and move back to Neptune's Landing. But then Rachel usually did what she wanted.

"Dammit, anyway. She doesn't know one thing about running a pool hall."

Pup whined softly, his forehead layered with wrinkles, as he seemed to understand. "Mallory used to say, 'one thing about Rachel, she always lands on her feet.' Maybe she will, but life can be pretty boring in a small town. She couldn't wait to get out of here after high school graduation—went to a big college, made a name for herself, and graduated summa cum laude . . . landed a New York hot-shot job straight out of college, too."

Okay, Kyle admitted reluctantly, he'd always been proud of Rachel.

For an entire month, he wondered what would have happened if she'd hit him with that cocked fist.

He would have reacted, of course. . . .

Maybe that was why he had a hard time keeping his hands off her . . . because so far as he knew, Rachel was always in control, except in this same office, a month ago. Kyle didn't trust his own nobility, leaving Miss Perfect undamaged in her perfect life, with her perfect takes on everyone else. Rachel thought he'd ruined Mallory, and maybe he had.

He scratched Pup's scarred ears. When Kyle was twenty-two, he decided to move into Neptune's Landing. At twenty-one, Mallory already knew what it took to please a man. But years before, when he visited the town that first time, she had been eighteen and far ahead of his nineteen years, far too experienced in the backseat of that car. . . .

Restless with the Scanlons' rural life and on his way to a small-time race up the coast, Kyle had come into town during the Neptune's Landing annual summer parade. Mallory had liked his sports car and he was in need of the soothing feel-good a willing woman could give him. After that, when he visited town, she would always be waiting and ready—but his mind was usually on the teenage girl riding the float. Her name was Rachel Everly, and she wore a mermaid outfit, the pink shells cupping her breasts. . . .

Dreams of those pink shells and the soft flesh beneath them had given him more than a few aches through the years. If Rachel stayed in Neptune's Landing, and she would, they would certainly meet and clash.

Rachel had only a surface glimpse of the darkness devouring Mallory's life. The inside picture was even uglier. . . .

Someone had owned Mallory, had made her jump to his call, had beat her sometimes, but she hadn't talked. "Fell down the stairs" and "ran into an open cabinet door" were her usual explanations, but Kyle knew that the bruises were from a man's hands. Through the years, she just drank a little more, took a few more pills, and became a living ghost of herself.

Two things kept Mallory going—Nine Balls, the one thing she considered her "baby," her mark in the world, and now Rachel was the owner; the other thing, the bigger prize in Mallory's life, was a nine-year-old girl who knew nothing about her.

Kyle's job was to keep Rachel from discovering that girl as he had promised Mallory he would do. . . . Exposing the girl could endanger her, and terrified for her, Mallory had given her away at birth.

He rubbed his chest where Rachel had planted that unwanted ache, the need to see her again, to see her light up, to see her eyes darken as they had when she'd looked at his chest, the air simmering between them.

Kyle didn't look forward to seeing another woman settling into Nine Balls, let alone one as determined as Rachel. Would she be as obsessed with Nine Balls as Mallory had been?

"That's a distinct possibility, because Rachel isn't likely to back down from a few little problems." Kyle stood up and stretched. Tomorrow he'd bring home a beauty of a classy Chevrolet, a Bel Air '54. A new breather, a little bit of patching the rough spots and popping out the dents, some sanding and paint and she'd be purring again.

As he went to the stock room to check his parts inventory, Kyle wondered what it would take to make Rachel purr. "Things are going to get really interesting with her around, Pup," he said to the boxer following close at his heels. "She's got a way of stirring things up."

Kyle reached for a used but cleaned breather to match the old Chevrolet's. "She sure did look good in that mermaid outfit. . . ."

"I don't want you staying there, Rachel," Trina said over the telephone. "In the last two years, Mallory had too many—visitors. I couldn't stop her—"

"I know, Mom. I'll lock the door and call you before coming home." Mallory's private upstairs quarters bore a sad tale of drugs, alcohol, and sex. After ending the call, Rachel worked feverishly, emptying drawers of slinky teddies and thong panties, and cheap, flashy jewelry. The bathroom's small plastic trash can was heaped with empty bottles. There were a few legitimate pharmacy bottles, but most bore plain white labels and Mallory's handwriting.

The open windows and fans helped take the over-heavy perfume scents from the rooms and into the chilly night air. Moths, drawn by light, fluttered at the screens.

Rachel tore the black satin sheets and leopard print spread from the round bed, tossed them onto the floor with the jumbled assortment of pillows; she wanted nothing of this Mallory to remain.

"No wonder you never let me come here, Mallory," Rachel whispered as she slid aside the big mirrored doors of the closet. A strong cedar scent, sometimes used to keep moths from clothing, swept out at her.

Mallory's clothing landed on top of the bedding. Her shoes were neatly ordered, which seemed strange, the boxes stacked perfectly. Sitting on the floor, Rachel opened the boxes. The top boxes were shoes, mostly high strappy heels, which she tossed onto the growing stack. A pair of high heels seemed too large, and Rachel compared one to the others—someone with a bigger, wider foot had worn them. Curious as to the owner, she put that box aside.

The other boxes held shoes and surprises—a rubber band circled Rachel's letters, little high school mementoes like the corsage Kyle had given her, a frayed pink ribbon and some teenage jewelry, a tiny worn locket. That box wasn't neat; it seemed as if it had been riffled by a hurried hand.

Another box held business papers, copies of big cash deposits mixed with her pay stubs as a waitress and barmaid. Rachel studied the paperwork and could find nothing but big cash deposits that gradually amounted to the first sizeable "down" money on Nine Balls. Everyone in Neptune's Landing suspected that Bob Winters had helped finance Mallory's purchase of Nine Balls and he'd never denied it.

Rachel carefully folded the papers and placed them into their rubber bands.

Dislodged by her rummaging, purses and folded clothing tumbled down from the closet's shelf. A cedar board ran from the shelf to the ceiling, held in place by heavier blocks on either end. Rachel noted the nails in the blocks at one end of the shelf, and the absence of nails in the other. But slight gouge marks were on this block. Rachel drew up a chair and using a sturdy metal envelope opener, she gently pried at the wood.

It came free and when Rachel lifted it away, there was another box, standing on end. She eased it out and opened the tightly sealed plastic lid. Inside was a neatly arranged, obviously cherished, collection of scrap-booking materials—special design scissors, ribbons, pens, colored paper.

Beneath them was a thick scrapbook.

Rachel held her breath, her heart racing as she opened the scrapbook to find collages of the Everly family pictures, and Mallory's careful notes, love wrapped into every word. In contrast, there were no pictures of Rachel, Trina, or Jada anywhere else in the apartment. Rachel held the scrapbook to her chest. "This is the heart of you, isn't it, Mallory? What you really were? What you loved so deeply that you didn't want anyone to know? Why?"

The other pages contained a vivid collection of Mallory's dedication to Nine Balls, to the youth who came to play there, to the women evidently enjoying themselves while competing. "Oh, Mallory. You were so wonderful. Why didn't you believe that?"

For some reason, Mallory had hidden the loves of her life, wanting to keep them apart and safe. Rachel carefully replaced the scrapbook and eased the box back into the closet. "See you later, Mallory."

She could almost hear young Mallory return, "Later. Keep safe."

The apartment was too quiet and Rachel held very still, listening, waiting for Mallory to speak. "I promised I'd do my best, Mallory."

At the windows, the fringes of the heavy maroon damask curtains moved eerily. "Mallory?"

Rachel let the slight nuances curl around her. "I feel you, Mallory. You're still here, aren't you? You're waiting, aren't you? For me? For me, Mallory? What do you want from me? Why did you choose me to inherit everything?"

The echo of her voice skittered around the empty room, and she was alone. But the room was heavy with the sense of the woman who had once lived there. . . . Rachel ignored the tears burning her eyes. "Dammit, Mallory, you're laying a load on me. I don't know what you want from me. I've promised to do my best, but you're wanting more, aren't you? What?"

Why had Mallory hidden the boxes beneath shoes and deep in her closet? Rachel closed the closet doors, questions running around her as she looked at her reflection. Harry, who had been sulking behind the living room couch, strolled into the bedroom, his tail high and crooked at the end. The big gray striped tomcat had been neutered, and at times, his yellow eyes rightly accused Rachel of the deed.

But now, he leaned against her calf, rubbing himself on her. She reached down to haul him up close, hugging him. Harry dug his claws into her arm and purred loudly. "Ouch! Harry! You're trying to make up after being so horrible on the trip here, aren't you?" she asked as she rubbed her cheek against his fur.

Harry was still peeved and ran into the living room.

Rachel looked at the mess she'd made in the bedroom and decided that feeding the cat might gain her some friendly points.

In the kitchen, she pulled the tab on a can of his food and bent to place it in his favorite dish. At the familiar tap of the can on his dish, Harry came running, tail straight up and crooked at the end, When Rachel stood, watching her cat eat, a beam of light pierced the kitchen window and moved around on the ceiling as a car honked.

"Oh, boy. Mom and Jada would have called first. If that is Mallory's gentleman callers, they are in for a surprise." Harry continued eating, undisturbed by the sound of another car. "I may as well end this now, Harry."

Rachel walked to the front door, jerked it open and stared at the women leaning against the vehicles in Nine Ball's parking lot. "We thought we'd do this right," Terri Samson called up to Rachel. Are you too tired to play? We've been waiting for you to get back. Mallory would have wanted that."

Dorothy Wainwright, the funeral director's wife, Tommy James's wife, Sally Mae, and two other women looked up at Rachel. They looked grim and each held a cue stick case.

They'd been at the funeral and they each had something to say about Mallory that was kind. But Rachel wanted to know more. She hadn't gone downstairs since she'd arrived and braced herself before calling to them, "I'll be right down."

Downstairs, the women moved silently through Nine Balls' front door. "We've done our hugging and sympathy route," Terri stated briefly. "Now we're here for Mallory's belated wake, and just maybe to get a little drunk."

"It's too quiet. It feels funny in here. Mallory was always talking, nervous, sometimes, but she had a lot to say about nothing at the end. She talked about flowers growing—daffodils, I think. She worried if the ones she planted at Scanlon's Classics would come up, if they had enough water and sunlight to do well." The woman who had been introduced as Jasmine Parker, a middle-aged slightly plump woman in an over tight T-shirt and jeans, looked around the pool hall.

Nine years ago, Mallory had returned to Neptune's Landing after an unexpected five months' "vacation to find myself." A few postcards from neighboring states and regular telephone calls said that she was traveling and happy, and that had been enough for the Everlys. It had been her first time to leave town; the next was when she came to stay with Rachel three years ago.

Mallory had never explained the whereabouts of her "vacation," but she came back pale and tired and had purchased Nine Balls immediately. She'd started to work at a frantic pace, building her business with a determination that was obsessive.

"Mallory always liked daffodils," Rachel stated softly. "We used to go cut them for Mom."

"The light switch is over there," Jasmine said quietly as the women watched Rachel take in Mallory's "baby." The varnished floors gleamed beneath the bright lights overhead. Across one wall, opposite from the front window, was a row of tall stools from which the players could be watched. Bamboo blinds at the big front windows had been unfurled; beneath them the potted African violets were dead. Black wrought-iron stands held ferns, untended and brown now, that dripped dead fronds onto the floor.

Someone switched on the lights and the overhead fans began to rotate slowly, eerily. On the cork bulletin board were snapshots of young teenagers, grinning as they held a cue in one hand and a trophy in the other. Some of the pictures had been taken with Mallory, and Rachel forced herself to look away to the twelve empty tables, the balls lying within the V-shaped racks. Eleven tables were the common billiards parlor eight footers, but one—Mallory's special one—was standard tournament size at nine feet.

In contrast to the usual coin operated tables, these tables were commonly arranged by reservations paid in advance.

Rachel walked to the nine-foot table, circled and studied it. The balls were perfectly racked into the diamond shape for nine ball. Everything in the room was too neat, as if it too had been cleaned and prepared by a loving hand. . . . *Mallory, how could you?*

"Haven't you been down here since Mallory—left?" Dorothy asked tentatively.

Rachel ran her hand over the smooth wood, the padded railing, the green fabric, and knew instantly that was what Mallory had done last—come here to say goodbye to her dreams—preparing her "baby" for Rachel. "I'm weak, Rachel. You've always been a crusader, but I'm not you. You could always do anything you wanted. But I can't change. I've tried and each time, I knew I was disappointing you. Do you understand? *I'm not you. I'm what I am.* You want too much. *I can't be you . . . I can't be you. . . ."*

"I haven't had a chance to come down here—okay, maybe I wasn't ready to see it. I can't stand the way she lived upstairs. I've been working up there, cleaning. . . . I thought I'd come down tomorrow when it was light." She'd needed to prepare herself mentally before entering Nine Balls, a place that her sister had loved desperately.

"Mallory used to let the kids play every Saturday morning," Terri stated quietly. "She looked like a kid herself, down here, teaching them how to stroke, how to hold the stick, finger bridges, whatever. She had a lot of patience with kids. Sometimes more than I would with my own two boys. Your mother and Kyle were here, helping to see that the equipment survived and that not too many dents were placed in the wall or the cloth wounded too badly."

"I haven't had a chance to look at the books yet. But I somehow had the idea that business wasn't as good in the last few years."

"People didn't want to get involved or maybe be caught in a bad situation, so they started staying away, going other places," Terri said quietly. "Gossip isn't good for their community standing, or their businesses."

"I'm going to get Nine Balls up and running like Mallory wanted," Rachel promised.

Sally Mae laughed aloud. "Now that sounds like the girl I grew up with. You haven't changed at all since high school. You were always a crusader."

Rachel smiled briefly. "Better sew me a cape, because Nine Balls is going to be very busy and very profitable."

Against the wall, a long rack of cues gleamed, perfectly tended. A row of high stools sat beneath them, an easy place for observers. At one end of the airy room with its slowly rotating ceiling fans, there were tables for the checkers and chess, and several dart boards hung on the wall. A small self-help minibar held a humming refrigerator filled with bottled water and soda and candy bars. Tiny packages of assorted salty chips lay in a large basket beneath a sign that read "Included with fees. Please keep food and drink away from the billiards tables. Thank you. Mallory."

Rachel walked around the long, spotless room, taking in the lists of eight-ball and nine-ball rules posted around it. A big-screen television set, radio and CD player dominated one corner. A quick glance at the DVDs said that Mallory had stocked up on billiards and pool tutorial programs. Spread across one wall were diagrams of billiard balls with dotted paths demonstrating the shots.

She opened a door marked Private, and found a small broom closet, scented of lemon and lined with cleaning bottles, mops, and brooms. Everything was too neat, even the cleaning rags were folded.

Another door marked Office opened to a dark musty room. A flip of the light switch and the impersonal and very neat office seemed to hold Mallory inside it. A small desk, one chair and file cabinets seemed all to reflect the woman who had used them, almost as if she had waited for Rachel to come in and start working.

"Tomorrow, Mallory. I'll do a good job." Rachel closed the door softly.

Sally Mae James looked at the big sign on the wall. *No Smoking, No Drinking, No Gambling, No Cursing, No Rough Stuff. Owner reserves the right to refuse anyone who breaks these rules.* "We always had a few drinks on Ladies Night. Mallory understood. I guess she'd understand tonight."

Mallory's whisper seemed to echo around the row of billiards tables. *I want my place to be clean and good enough for women and kids to come play and enjoy the sport.*

Sally hefted the insulated cooler she'd been carrying onto a long wooden bench. "Wine coolers. Everyone's favorite kind. Drink up."

The rest of the women placed their chips and dips and sandwiches on the bench, grabbed a wine cooler and opened the lid. Terri handed Rachel a bottle and then lifted her own. "To Mallory. May she rest in peace. May we all keep her in our hearts and remember what she gave us."

"To Mallory," the women said in unison, then lifted their bottles. Terri took another drink and took her cue from its case. She moved toward the nine-foot table, Mallory's favorite. "Let's play."

Sally Mae chalked the tip of her cue and studied Rachel for a minute. "Are you going to play, or what? Your mom is a good shooter, so is Jada. By the way, where is she?"

As if signaled, the ice cream wagon slid by the front windows of Nine Balls, the music a tinkling sound. It stopped in the side parking lot, and Jada rounded the corner, carrying her cue case and a small thermal cooler. Inside, she said, "Ice cream on me, ladies—

fudge bars, popsicles, ice cream bars, what have you. Eat up, don't let it melt on the tables, and put the wrappers in the trash."

"Wait—I'll be right back." Rachel ran up the stairs and returned quickly, carrying Mallory's cue case. She carefully put the cue together, slid it through her hands, and again noted the new tip. Mallory had wanted to leave her equipment in good shape. . . .

The women paired off and Rachel slid the smooth wood through her fingers, getting the heft and balance of the cue. "It's been years. I've played a little when visiting Mom, but we usually end up just sitting and talking."

*She hadn't really played since that night she'd been attacked as she walked home from playing pool with her girlfriends. . . .* Rachel placed a cue ball on the felt, trying to remember the stance, front hand down, fingers in a bridge, right arm at a 90-degree angle with the cue, leg back, body low and leaning into the table. She slid the cue back and forth in the bridge of her fingers, getting the feel of it.

"Mallory just loved running this place, or did until a couple of years ago. You don't want to break those balls, do you? Because Mallory probably racked them—she was really careful about getting a good tight rack, the one ball in perfect position, the nine ball in the middle. . . . Okay, if no one wants to make the virgin break since Rachel has taken over, I will. Break." Terri bent to place one hand on the table, the other hand back on the stick, her elbow raised. She leaned into the shot and the cue ball hit the number one ball in the diamond shape of balls. "Your turn. I never could get a good break," she said quietly as the balls spread, but left a compact core formation.

Someone had placed a country music CD into the player and the music cruised softly around the room, punctuated by the slight click of balls hitting each other.

Between shots, Rachel studied the women—married, mothers, housewives, and those with occupations, such as Terri, the attorney. Terri watched her. "You're wondering out of all the women who came here, sometimes only to show support for their kids, why we're so special, aren't you?"

Rachel angled her shot, banked it, and the nine ball rolled into the pocket, winning the game. "Nice shot," Terri commented. "Smooth, good spin. You're a really focused player. Mallory wasn't."

"It's been a while. You were saying?" Rachel took another bottle of wine cooler that Jasmine had just handed her.

The overhead fans were rotating slowly, the balls clicking against each other on the other tables, and Terri took her time answering.

"At one time or another, Mallory sent our wayward husbands home to us. Some stayed faithful and others didn't, like my ex. We had a deal after that, we came here, let off some womanly steam and gripes and generally settled life with a few hours away from house and kids. In return—not that she had to, but Mallory settled a few, ah, womanly territorial issues—our men weren't in her bed."

"Maybe Kyle Scanlon was keeping her busy."

"He liked her. Everyone knew that. She stayed with

him a couple times. Maybe they were making a test run for the real thing, but they never really lived together."

Rachel stopped racking the balls, the nine ball in the center, and looked over her shoulder to Terri. The attorney shrugged. "I don't know what happened, but she closed up for a month each time. I guess it didn't work out. Kyle usually has people hanging out at his place—some big bald wrestler-type and some down-on-their-lucks. Maybe Mallory couldn't take that. Did you meet Iris and Patty? They're lucky they've got him to help them out—not a clue about making it on their own, either one of them. They had something in common with Mallory, I guess. Good hearts, but not the usual defenses to protect themselves, like children inside women's bodies. Some men really go for that, you know. Makes them feel good."

"Did you ever wonder exactly where he gets the kind of money to support two ex-wives?"

"He works, I imagine. He's gone once in a while, to see relatives or something. What are you going to do with Mallory's things?"

"I've thought a lot about that." Rachel met the other woman's eyes and walked to the CD player, stopping it. In the silence, while the other women looked at her, Rachel said, "Mallory left everything to me, personal stuff included. I do not want anyone else sleeping on her sheets, lying on her mattress, or wearing her clothes. I want to burn everything that made her look trashy. Let's take this party out to some field and finish it."

"Woo-hoo! New player in town," Jasmine hooted. "I've got my husband's pickup outside."

"That won't do it all. The couch and chair, too. And

that round bed is massive. Everything that—" *That Mallory used to entertain . . .*

"I'm driving the funeral home's hearse, that should take care of something," Dorothy said as she lifted her bottle in a toast.

"And we'll use my husband's garbage truck," Sally Mae added gaily. "I've been dying to drive it."

"We can burn her stuff out on our farm," Jasmine offered as she placed her cue into its case. "Just bring the booze. We'll toast Mallory."

Terri took a deep breath. "We should have had an intervention for her. We should have done more, but I guess we were all locked into our own little secure lives and didn't want to raise problems by—" *By chumming around with the town tramp in our spare time, by sticking up for her when gossip condemned her. . . .*

"Don't feel bad about that. Mallory wasn't letting anyone into her life, including me," Rachel stated carefully. "Let's just do this."

The highway leading to the Parker farm passed Scanlon's Classics, and at night, the big Hummer sat behind the locked gates.

Sally Mae caught Rachel's stare and said, "Sometimes he comes back, dragging some old clunker on a trailer and looking like hell. I guess he does pretty well on the sales of the restored classics. The buyers are usually upscale-looking when they stop in town, like guys who don't want to get their hands dirty, but who want to look cool."

"Where does he go?" *Partying in Las Vegas, gambling, running illegal weapons to foreign countries, supplying drugs?*

"No one knows. He just shuts down the business and he's gone. He buys some kids clothes every once in a while before he takes off. My sister, Ronnie, checks at the discount store and says they're for a girl. Sometimes it's a trinket or two, girl-stuff."

"His next wife probably has children. Or maybe he has his own stashed away from here. It must be tough, spreading himself around between his ex-wives and girlfriends."

Sally Mae giggled and pulled the dump truck away from the ditch. "That's harsh, coming from you. Just think, Jada says he's agreed to be the sperm donor for her baby if she can't nab someone in four years. You'd be related to Kyle, DNA-wise, I mean."

"That's disgusting. And stay on the road, will you?" Jada apparently wasn't keeping her sperm prospect a secret, and Sally Mae understood Rachel's ongoing dislike of Kyle.

"Mallory liked him," Sally Mae teased in a singsong.

"She didn't always have the best taste."

At the Parkers' farm, the women struggled to heap things onto a pile. When it was soaked with gasoline, the women stood silently, holding hands, their minds and hearts filled with Mallory. "Light it, Dorothy," Rachel whispered.

The pile exploded into flames that crackled and sent blue smoke up into the night sky.

Each woman murmured a tearful goodbye.

Except Rachel. She'd noticed the big wide headlights at the crest of the small hill overlooking the burning. They switched off and she knew Kyle was up there, watching the private ceremony to erase Mallory's darkness. She was moving up that hill to Kyle before she realized it.

"What are you doing here, Scanlon?" she demanded as she topped the hill.

He was leaning against the Hummer, his arms folded across his chest. Pup sat beside his boots. Kyle slowly took her sweat shirt and jeans. "Quite the little caravan went by my place a while ago. Thought I'd come out and see what was happening."

"It's a private party. You're not invited, Scanlon."

"You've always been able to stir things up, haven't you? What if that fire gets out of control?"

"It won't." She edged her tennis shoe away from the long spindle of drool Pup had just released.

"I'm just doing my job, honey . . . I'm on the volunteer fire department, rural and Neptune's Landing. You've always had style, and Mallory would have liked this little bonfire party. Maybe that's what she didn't like about you, too—that she could never live up to your style and expectations."

Rachel had to know: "Did Mallory actually tell you that?"

*You're so righteous, telling me how to live . . . I'm not you, Rachel. I'm not strong like you. . . .* Mallory had said once. *You know all the right things to do and say. I'm a mess and I'll always be just that—a mess. So stop coming around, trying to make me feel bad. I'm doing the best I can, and it's just never good enough, is it? Don't you get it? I'm not you and I never was. . . .*

Rachel swiped at the drool running down her shin, and Kyle reached into the rig and brought out paper towels. He handed the roll to her. "Sure."

It was so like Kyle to lay bare hurting truths, to remember them so clearly. Rachel briskly scrubbed a length of paper toweling against her leg, until she noted that Kyle was studying her breasts, the way she was bending and the V-neckline provided a provocative view. She crumpled the towel and fired it at his face. "You should get out of here now—"

He'd moved and the paper towel hit the windshield, deflected, and rolled to the ground. Kyle grinned at her. "See? Lot's of 'you shoulds'."

"You should do something about that dog's drooling."

"More shoulds." The smile had stopped and he asked quietly, "What's driving you, Rachel? You're all worked up and it isn't only me. Most people would be sleeping off that long trip from New York now, not housecleaning."

*She owed Mallory . . . her sister with the fear of flying, who had come at a moment's notice to draw her from the darkness—*

Pup was barking loudly, answered by the Parkers' beagles in the distance. The women were shouting up at Kyle to come down and toast Mallory. "I did that already. Had a private party with Rachel," he called back. "Good job."

"You knew exactly how that would sound—'private party' with me."

Kyle shrugged and lifted an eyebrow. "So? True wasn't it? You were with me the night of her funeral."

While she was dealing with Kyle's skillful nudge, too-perceptive question, and with the drool Pup had just thrown against her leg, Kyle lifted the dog up into the Hummer. In a lithe movement, he swung up and closed the door. "You're set to make her dream come true, aren't you? You show more than you know, Rachel."

"Get out of here."

"I was just headed out of town anyway. Don't get too worked up while I'm gone, honey. I like the thought of you saving all that fire and brimstone for me." He grinned again, slowly, as if he approved of her and that nettled.

Rachel decided to keep the roll of paper towels and let Kyle suffer Pup's drool. "Headed off for another girlfriend, Scanlon?"

"Hey, I'm a guy in demand." He took a long promise-filled look at her, then started the vehicle, reversed and eased across the field, leaving her all charged up and no finalization, last-word fight with him.

"I've got to get better at this. He knows that he sets me off and that is irritating," Rachel promised herself darkly as she walked down the slight hill to the other women. She was used to controlling her temper, to carefully monitoring what she said, but with Kyle, perhaps her first blast of dislike should be voiced— "I do not say that many shoulds."

Several hours later, on the return trip back, the Hummer was gone, but Rachel's need for revenge to take Kyle down and make him pay was still simmering.

Terri dropped her off at Nine Balls to collect Harry, then walk home. While there, Rachel checked on Mallory's hidden treasures. There was some reason she'd tucked them away like that, keeping them safe, and Rachel would discover why. . . .

* * *

*Had he gotten everything that could tie him to Mallory, to what they did together? No, he hadn't found the doll she'd used against him, casting spells, driving him into his addictive activities that made him feel like a god. . . .* Worry that his secret pleasures, his life would be exposed, changed into fury at Mallory. His addictions weren't of a chemical nature, rather a relief that kept him functioning normally. He was her master and she'd defied him by taking an exit that stirred the community—his community.

First, it was only sex . . . then only sex while he was hurting her, then sex after he'd seen her with other men, performing for them. . . . He'd worked for years to hold Mallory, to shape her, to make her obedient. "She had no business taking her life—it was mine. It's her fault that she lured me into evil, tempted me. It's her fault that she needed more money for her habits. None of this is *my* fault. If she hadn't been so weak, we could have gone on for years. . . . Only she could satisfy me, knew what I needed."

He built his rage, feeding it as he drove slowly past Nine Balls. Through Jada's running dialogue about her sister, he knew that Rachel was set to run the billiards parlor, and Rachel was pure trouble—unmanageable, driven by her own desire to succeed.

*What had Mallory told Rachel?*

Three years ago, Mallory had once again decided to make a new life for herself, leaving the pleasurable evil she'd drawn him into. He couldn't have that happen, and he'd made good on this threat to harm one of her family—he'd enjoyed planning Rachel's attack, telling Mallory about it, threatening her with another, perhaps on Jada, until she was compliant again. But after her first defiance, threatening to expose him, she'd decided to self-destruct and that wasn't in his plan. Nothing could bring her back from that edge, because she simply didn't care anymore—

He looked outside to children playing in the field. Mallory had loved him at first, trying to please him, and she'd been so sweet—he'd loved her, too. He loved how she made him feel—and then she was out of his reach. . . . "If you hurt my family, I'll haunt you forever," Mallory had said during those last two years. *I'll haunt you forever. . . .*

"Well, dear Mallory, if Rachel poses a problem for me, I will hurt her, and that is a promise. . . . I have to find that doll . . . it wasn't anywhere when she died. Maybe she got rid of it before she died—sneaky little witch, killing herself that way. I couldn't find it after they took her away, the month before Rachel arrived. I've been through everything—She actually used my hair, took it right from my brush, and cut up my shirt to make it. It exists, I know it does, because she showed me the shirt, the patch cut from it, the missing button— She cast a spell and I couldn't perform anymore. Everything is Mallory's fault, not mine."

But the hair on the back of his neck lifted as he thought of Mallory's fierce threat—"I'll haunt you forever. . . ."

# Five
___

AT ELEVEN O'CLOCK AT NIGHT, RACHEL STOOD ON THE
sidewalk in front of Nine Balls and slid the key into the
front door, locking it.

Fog had rolled into Neptune's Landing, settling
damply around her, blurring the lights of the businesses
down Atlantis Street. Just two days after the burning of
Mallory's dark past at the Parkers' farm, Rachel sat in
the small neat office and set to work on forming a real-
istic picture of her sister's finances. She'd started late in
the morning—recovering a bit from the wine coolers
and late-night girl-talk with Jada, who was worried
about their mother. Needing to walk, Rachel had taken
Harry in his carrier to her mother's used-car sales office
and had shared a sweet roll and coffee that somehow
had run into lunch at Fast Eddie's Diner.

She'd worked all the next day, transferring Mallory's
handwritten accounts into her laptop. In the evening
she had accepted a ride on eighty-year-old Francie
Alexander's golf cart back to her mother's house. Francie had long ago lost her driver's license, but she'd been
approved to drive a golf cart down certain streets during designated hours in good daylight. Everyone along
Francie's route waved to her and a police car prowled

behind her as usual, making certain that the elderly woman was protected from speeders.

At six o'clock, Bob had been barbequing as usual, and the delicious dinner eaten from the backyard's picnic table had been relaxing. Rachel had taken Harry and some tidbits back to Nine Balls, and there she'd worked until eleven, when she'd started to make too many mistakes and had decided to walk home.

The bygone elegance of Atlantis Street settled around her, the shops closed, Natasha the Fortune Teller's pink neon hand sign seemed almost welcoming. In the distance, the waves pounded the shore almost like the heartbeat of Mallory that had always seemed very close while Rachel worked. Mallory's presence seemed so real, as if Rachel could reach out and touch her, talk to her. Mallory had taken her life—why had she been so desperate?

"I owe you, Mallory, and I am going to make Nine Balls a success." Rachel picked up Harry's carrier and he struck out a claw, scratching her lightly. "Hey. Jada is allergic to you. It's either come to work with me and stay in the guest bathroom at night—or it's the garage. And you should really be declawed. And you will be, the first time you scratch those pool tables. Taking your bad mood out on my couch is one thing, but you're not ruining Mallory's things."

She began walking the three quiet blocks to her mother's home when a lowered car cruised by, the rap music pounding at the damp silence. Homes bordered the streets to her mother's house, their front porches and sidewalks lined by shrubs and flowers.

As she stepped off the curb of the first block and was crossing the street, a cold tingle hit her, as if someone was watching her. Three years ago, after leaving the pool hall, she'd had that same full-bodied chill and should have paid attention to it.

"It's just spending the day in the place where Mallory died, Harry. I'm not being stalked. No one is after me," she said to reassure herself.

Her heart stopped when she heard a sound behind her, like footsteps that stopped when she did. She walked faster across the damp red bricks and they gleamed from the streetlight, contrasting the black pavement of the next and newer street.

In the middle of Mermaid Lane, she walked slowly and listened to the sounds of the night: the ocean, a car passing on another street—and to the footsteps slowly, surely following her. . . .

She turned suddenly and a shadow crossed from the night into the pool of light from the streetlights. She couldn't move, transfixed by the man coming closer. She wouldn't run again, only to be run down and attacked. "Who is it?"

Shane Templeton's narrow face appeared to loom over her. He was dressed in a sweatsuit, his unshaven jaw giving him a tough appearance. "I didn't mean to frighten you. I was only out walking and I guess we happened to be going in the same direction."

Rachel breathed slowly, trying to calm herself. "Hi, Shane."

He studied her quietly. "You're nothing like Mallory, are you? I'd heard that you were stronger, more focused, that nothing could stop you, once you'd set your mind on a task. Jada confirms that you're going to run Nine Balls. Good luck."

He lifted his head and looked around. "It's very quiet here now, isn't it? You can hear the dampness dripping off the leaves, cleaning them. That's what I'd hoped would happen with Mallory—that she would find the courage to start a new life. I prayed that would happen."

Then suddenly, Shane's pensive expression was gone as he stared at her, his voice hard. "You'd tell me if you found that Bible or anything that might—that might be something I'd given Mallory? But then you burned everything, didn't you?"

This time, Rachel paid attention to her warning senses. For a supposedly mild mannered man, Shane was too harsh. "Just how well did you know Mallory, Reverend?"

He frowned, and an almost savage expression compressed those full, feminine-like lips. "She was one of my flock. A poor misguided woman who needed me, to become a better person."

That remark struck Rachel's temper and she resented the image he presented of Mallory as less than a "better person," which of course, made him the superior in the relationship. "According to whose standards?"

Shane's smooth, controlled tone flipped into a curt, bitter one. "You could do with some humility, Rachel Everly. Perhaps your arrogance is why you've never married. I've heard that you had a certain attitude. Mallory spoke of you often, of how strong you are. She said that you had to be, because you were the oldest and had to help your mother, who was deserted by her husband at a young age. That's so typical of the women with mothers like that—they are either too tough and make decisions for everyone, or too clingy and can't make decisions for themselves. You, and this according to Mallory, are the make-decisions-for-everyone type. It's not always a positive factor in a woman, you know. It's not—attractive in a woman."

Rachel didn't like Shane's condemnation. Her mother had struggled desperately to support her family. Rachel had done whatever she could to make things easier for all of them, taking over household tasks, delegating them to Jada and then Mallory. Keyed into his reaction, sensitive to his threatening body language and his tone, Rachel used the probing skills she'd learned in human resources training courses. "Whew. I guess you go for the submissive type, then. Was she? Was Mallory submissive? Did you like that?"

His eyes flared and Rachel noted the way his fists curled at his side. He'd leaned forward, his stance threatening. "You're inferring—"

"I'm inferring nothing. I'm going home now." Rachel wasn't up to going rounds with an obviously athletic man at the edge of his temper. She shook as she turned and moved away, half expecting him to come after her.

She took a deep breath and inhaled the cool fog. One thing was for certain: Shane was very concerned about what she might find that would link him as a man to a woman of questionable morals. She heard the click of a heel on the bricks and walked faster.

She wouldn't turn to see if Shane followed her; she wouldn't expose the old fear that swallowed her now, her body chilling, her mind racing back to another time as she hurried across the next street and to her mother's front door. Her hands shook as she inserted the key into the lock.

The door opened suddenly and Trina's bright smile at Rachel died instantly. Her mother drew Rachel into the house, the familiar hallway lined with a refinished antique table, the wooden floors gleaming beneath the wall's artistic fern and leaf prints. Rachel shivered slightly, trying to wrap the familiar safety around her; she wasn't in a park and she wasn't being held down and—

Trina closed the door. "What's wrong, honey? You look scared."

She didn't want her mother to worry. No one but Mallory knew of the other time she'd been so frightened, afraid of footsteps, of the men who had come out of the shadows, holding her down—but then, attacks at night in a New York park were pretty common, and the police had said she'd been "unwise" to take that short-cut at night. They'd questioned the regulars at the pool hall that her friends and she had been using; they'd pushed the young toughs who had played and lost to her. But she couldn't positively identify any of them.

Rachel worked to climb out of her terror. . . . She was in Neptune's Landing now, where she'd grown up safely, and she was in her mother's house. . . .

"I'm just out of breath. In his carrier, Harry gets pretty heavy for any distance. And I should have brought my laptop home, but I didn't want to carry them both. It's only a short distance, but I think I'm going to get the Caddie fixed."

"You've always loved Buttercup. I don't mind picking you up, or I could get a car for you—there's a beauty coming in tomorrow, a sweet little compact, and gets good gas mileage." Trina smoothed Rachel's hair. "What's really wrong, honey? Is it because Mallory died there? I know it would bother me. I can't stop thinking about her."

"Mom, you did more than anyone, went the extra distance to try to get her to straighten out."

Trina smiled sadly. "I just feel I should have done something more. But I didn't understand what was happening to her. It was like Mallory wanted to self-destruct. We all offered to help her. Bob and I were going to use our connections to get her a regular job and paycheck to cut down her responsibilities. But she wouldn't have any of that. Nine Balls was her dream and she held on to it to the last. I wanted her to stay here, you know, to—to get off drugs and drinking, and I said I'd help her. But she just laughed like it was some insane joke. I couldn't help her. My own daughter, and I couldn't help her."

"I know." Rachel looked around the familiar comfortable living room, the long soft sofa, the fireplace with an insert, the recliner where Trina often sat going over figures for car sales. The other recliner was larger to accommodate Bob's portly body. Rachel shivered just once, forcing her terror back into the past. . . .

Trina studied Rachel. "I guess you're not going to tell me why you were so shaken a moment ago. You were always very competent and independent, Rachel. It's not like you to be afraid of walking home a few blocks at night. But then, maybe Neptune's Landing's growth has changed things since you were younger. If you want Buttercup fixed, Kyle Scanlon is the best mechanic in town. I call on him sometimes when the regular garage can't fix a vehicle. He's good. He's got quite the reputation for fixing classic cars. You could ask him for a tune-up."

Rachel knew exactly what the word, "tune-up," coming from her would mean to Kyle. "Scanlon isn't touching Buttercup. She isn't charging. That probably means she just needs a battery, or maybe she's just sat in the garage for too long."

"I can have Leon, our mechanic, come over and check her out," Trina offered.

"That would be great, and I'd like to be here when he does."

"Honey, Leon knows what he's doing. He just doesn't have Kyle's magic touch."

The memory of the attack three years ago kept Rachel awake for hours, and back then, Mallory had helped her recover with reassurances. *You'll be okay, kiddo. You moved into a security building with a doorman. I promise you that this won't happen again.*

*How can you be so certain?* Rachel had cried, shattered by the attack.

*Yeah, well. I just know things. It isn't going to happen again. You have to believe that. . . .*

The bedroom Rachel shared with Jada was too quiet, the echo dying away into the night's shadows. . . .

"I owe you, Mallory, and you had no right to die before I paid you back. I am so angry with you—" Rachel punched her pillow into shape and forced herself to relax and gradually sleep came . . . and so did the nightmare of being held down—she awoke with a cry on her lips, stifling it to prevent her mother and sister from hearing. "I love you, Mallory. Don't leave me," she whispered shakily, and listened for the answer that Mallory had given years ago.

*I love you, too, kiddo. Go to sleep now—I'll be around. I'm always around, and nothing is going to happen to you again, I promise. . . .*

"That should have been locked."

In the predawn light, the streetlights provided a backlight to Rachel's silhouette, casting it upon Nine Balls huge windows, the old glass yielding an imperfect, rippled reflection. Rachel slipped Nine Balls' key into her tote bag and gripped the heavy brass handle of the front door. She tested the door again, and it opened easily. "I locked this last night."

Inside the dim recesses of the billiards parlor, a dim slice of light came from the opened office door. "And I turned that off last night."

Rachel eased open Nine Balls' big heavy front door and stepped inside. She placed Harry's carrier on the floor and stood still, listening. . . . The building was too quiet, seeming to wait for her; she'd had that same sense last night, as if the rooms were silently waiting for her. As if Mallory was waiting for her. . . .

"This isn't funny, Mallory," Rachel whispered, as she bent to open Harry's carrier.

Harry streaked under a pool table. He didn't like Nine Balls yesterday, and from the looks of it, he wasn't going to like it today. In fact, Harry hadn't liked anything or anyone, except Jada, since they'd arrived three days ago. "Coward."

Taking a deep breath, Rachel slowly walked toward the office. "I might as well start taking care of my property right now. I can't run to the police at the first sign of problems. And I was pretty upset last night, just maybe I didn't lock up as I should have. . . ."

If someone had unlocked the front door, they'd used a key. "It's four-thirty in the morning now, and that means they had over five hours to come in here. Maybe. Or maybe I'm just stressed and tired and thinking of Mallory too much. On the other hand, if she'd passed keys around to her midnight callers, I'm getting new locks."

She placed the flat of her hand on the office door and it creaked as she pushed it open.

Everything looked the same—Mallory's handwritten ledgers stacked at one corner of the desk, the one Rachel had been feeding into her laptop's spreadsheet lay beside it; her place marked by an envelope. But the stamp of the opened envelope, an electric bill, had been showing. The envelope was still inside the ledger, but now the stamp was hidden. Rachel had purposely left it in that position because the bill was dated and payment was overdue—she'd planned to give that priority.

Rachel sought to reassure herself. The envelope could have slipped down. She was probably just tired last night and hadn't turned off the light or locked the door. It had been closed and off, but the yellow note pad she'd placed beside the laptop had been moved to the top of the bank statements. Rachel sat down, opened the laptop, turned it on, and waited for it to come to life.

She keyed to where she had been working on spreadsheets. Rachel sat back in the chair and stared at the screen that yielded nothing. In a flurry, she opened her other programs, looking for evidence of someone prowling. Everything seemed untouched.

Except that yellow pad wasn't where she'd left it, placed on the left side of the laptop, when she'd left it on the right. That small telling thing caused the hair on her nape to lift. "I can't prove anything, Harry, but I'd say someone's been through this desk—I worked on that drawer with files, sorting them yesterday, and they were all level, not at different heights."

Harry came to rub around her legs and she lifted him onto her lap. His claws dug into her jeans, a reward for the petting she was giving him. "Very interesting, Harry. I think we have a prowler. And he used a key. There was an empty envelope in Mallory's desk yesterday—I pitched it—but she'd written 'Keys for Kyle'—Mmm. Why Mr. Scanlon, apparently you have keys. What were you looking for?"

The trash basket looked different, the crumpled yellow paper beneath the others when she'd tossed them on top before leaving.

Tucking Harry under her arm, Rachel carried him up the narrow stairway to Mallory's barren apartment. The heavy maroon damask drapes had been burned with the rest and the windows let squares of dawn onto the gleaming varnished floor. An antique sewing rocker that Trina had given Mallory, a family heirloom that

Mallory had loved, had been moved slightly, making way for someone to leave by the apartment door.

Rachel slowly walked to the bedroom, and noted the mirrored closet door had been closed.

It was empty now, but the can of air freshener she'd used, placed in front of the closet on the floor was now inside the closet. One glance at the cedar board told her that Mallory's hiding place was still safe.

Rachel smiled grimly. She'd taken very good care of Mallory's scrapbook and personal effects. "Looking for something, Kyle?"

When she came down the stairs, Harry thump-thumped down after her. "Speaking of the devil," she murmured as she discovered the man playing pool. . . .

Kyle Scanlon's tall body leaned over the nine-foot tournament table, poised at the "head rail" for a shot at the triangular shape configuration of the eight-ball game. His stroke was smooth, hitting the cue ball. It hit the one ball, breaking the "rack" perfectly. Two solid-colored balls rolled into pockets. He straightened, glanced at her, and moved into pocket another solid-colored ball.

Rachel leaned against the wall and watched Pup and Harry go through their growling, hissing thing before Pup dropped his jowls to his paws and settled for staring at Harry, who was beneath an eight-foot table, rubbing against the legs. Then Harry rolled over on his back, confidently teasing the dog, and Pup growled softly.

"Stay." At Kyle's order, the dog gave a disgruntled "whoof" and settled for staring at the cat.

Kyle's silvery and deep shadowed eyes studied Rachel. In a black T-shirt with a torn pocket and greasy worn jeans and battered work boots, he looked as if he hadn't slept. His jaw was dark with stubble, his hair mussed.

"Having fun?" she asked.

"I thought you were open for business. The door was unlocked, and I've paid for a full year." He methodically circled the table, finishing off the solid-colored balls.

"Yes, well. Anyone could come in then, right? Say a prowler? Someone looking for something? Someone with a key who could come and go as they wished?"

"If you say so." He shrugged and placed his left hand on the table, using his thumb as a bridge for the shaft, his right "back hand" with a perfect grip on the butt, his forearm in a 90-degree angle to the cue. A striped ball banked on a rail and rolled into an opposite pocket.

When he placed his left hand on the table again, Rachel noted the raw places on his knuckles. "Been in a fight?"

She circled him to get a look at his right hand, and there was a long scratch on it. Kyle glanced at her and there was a dark bruise on his cheekbone; the whites of his eyes had a distinct bloodshot appearance.

"Nope." He moved around the table, angling for a shot that took the five and six balls into opposite pockets. "What makes you think so?"

"Your knuckles are skinned. That looks like a bruise on your cheek. And your eyes say you've been drinking. You smell like smoke and oil."

"Why, I didn't know that you cared. You smell really

good, by the way. I like that getup—tight jeans and T-shirt, flip-flops, no makeup, your hair in a ponytail. You look cute and sexy, just as you did when you were doing charity car washes during college vacations. I used to come to those things, just to see you bend over. Then, if I was lucky, your shirt would get wet and— well, you've filled out more since then."

Rachel remembered his "nipple" remark on the night of Mallory's funeral. She fought the blush rising up her cheeks and faced him squarely. She refused to be embarrassed by him. "That happens. No need to elaborate."

Kyle smiled easily as he bent into the next shot and finished the striped balls before he spoke. "Always ready to believe the worst, huh, Rachel? Like maybe I was in a bare-knuckle fight, or worked someone over because they didn't pay up? Something low and back-alley type that you'd expect from me?"

She had long suspected that Kyle enjoyed fostering her notions that he moved in the underworld and crime, and he definitely enjoyed stirring her temper. He pointed his cue tip to a pocket, then leaned down to angle for the shot, stretching out that long lean body. A smooth powerful stroke and the eight ball rolled into the designated pocket.

He picked up the chalk and rubbed it over the cue's tip. "Care to play?"

"I'm busy. What were you looking for here, last night?"

He frowned slightly, carefully placed the square of chalk onto the table's rim, and looked squarely at her. "I wasn't here."

"Sure . . . I don't believe you. I locked up when I left and the door was unlocked this morning. You look like you've been on an all-nighter, and there was an envelope in Mallory's desk drawer marked 'Kyle's key,' but there's no key in it."

He took his time walking to the cue rack and replacing the one he had used. "You don't waste any time, do you?"

"Not with you." She watched him walk toward her. "I want that key and your promise that you won't prowl around here at night. It's business hours only."

He was too close now, forcing her to look up as she backed against the wall. As he braced his body inches from hers, Kyle's hand flattened beside her head. His eyes followed his finger as it smoothed a tendril behind her ear, then strolled down to where the dimple hid in her cheek. Then those blue eyes locked with hers. "What are you going to do, refund my year payment? People would ask why, wouldn't they? You'd have a hard time explaining that, wouldn't you? And I did not, repeat, did not come in here last night."

He was too close and that old fear moved in to twist her gut—"Back off, Scanlon."

Kyle was lazily studying her lips. "Mallory gave me a key. . . . You can call me at any time, honey."

His eyes moved up to hers and he frowned, that lazy sensual look replaced by an intent concerned one. "You're shivering and you've just gone pale. What's wrong?"

"You . . . you're too close. I . . ." Rachel couldn't tell him about the rape, about the panic that tightened around her now, that caused her to go ice-cold.

His expression was fierce and hard, his voice low and primitive. "What happened to you, Rachel?"

Her lips moved, but she couldn't speak, her throat tightened by the old fear that always came when men came too close. Her heart raced as her trembling hands tightened into fists at her side—"Step back," she whispered breathlessly and thrust out her hands to protect herself.

The palm of one hand hit the torn cloth over his flat stomach and he tensed, scowling down at her.

"Your hand is ice-cold, Rachel." Kyle studied her for several thundering heartbeats and then pushed away, backing several feet from where she stood. "I know fear when I see it. Your eyes are huge now, filling with me, and that isn't how I would ever want a woman to look at me . . . any woman. I may want to push you, Rachel. Hell, I really enjoy seeing you light up, because I know that you're not all smooth cream and manners. I like to see the lid come off and all that passion come out."

He ran his hand across his chest. "But I wasn't here last night. I wouldn't try to spook you. I like coming straight at you too much, watching your reaction. Do you really think someone was in here last night?"

Rachel crumpled onto a bench, her arms folded around herself as she forced the familiar panic away. She believed him; Kyle had always enjoyed a head-on confrontation, watching her react to him. "Yes, I do. Someone rummaged through the desk, tapped into my computer, and moved around upstairs."

Kyle's expression hardened, the lines bracketing his mouth deepened. "Someone is looking for something."

She understood perfectly: Mallory had affairs with married men, and someone might have been looking for evidence linking them to her. . . . "I know what Mallory was, but she was still my sister and I loved her."

She explained briefly how she'd been so careful to lock Nine Balls, downstairs and upstairs, and Kyle asked, "What do you think they were after? It wasn't cash. Mallory never kept cash here. She made a final deposit the day she died."

"How do you know that?"

"She trusted me with her money. I always took it to the bank and brought back the deposit slip. I knew something was wrong then, but she wasn't talking."

"Did she—did she ask you that day to mail a letter addressed to me from out of town?"

Kyle shook his head. "No. Why?"

"Someone did. Mom and Jada said Mallory had given up driving. . . . I got it on the day of the funeral. She mentioned you."

Rachel watched his reaction intently, but Kyle's sadness appeared genuine. "She would. She was thoughtful."

"I don't know why someone would want to come in here at night. There's nothing here. But don't you tell my mother or Jada. I do not want them to be worried." *There's nothing here except her scrapbook, the things that were precious to her.*

"Oh, you don't? Now you're starting to sound like Mallory, only she always included you in her don't-worry-them list."

"What do you mean? We were terribly worried about her. These last two years—"

"I know. The year after she came home from visiting you, she was fighting something, but she lost—she just gave up," he murmured grimly. Kyle walked out the door, opened the Hummer's door, and returned with a thermos bottle. A slice of morning sunlight cut through the opened door as he sat beside her on the bench and poured steaming hot coffee into the plastic cup, handing it to her. "Drink."

Harry left the safety of the pool table and hurried to the bench, leaping up beside Kyle. The tomcat purred loudly, rubbing against the man, and instantly Pup was on his three paws, hurrying to growl at the cat. "Down," Kyle ordered quietly and the boxer plopped his bottom down, but showed his teeth at the cat.

Harry lay down, his front paws on Kyle's thigh. When Kyle petted him, he leaned into that big hand and purred louder. Pup whined softly, inching closer.

"I do not want your dog to drool on me," Rachel stated as she eyed Pup.

Kyle reached to ease the dog away, to the side where Harry was lying on the bench. Pup stuck his muzzle in the cat's face, then as if disgusted, walked out the open door.

The coffee was bitter and the memories of Mallory too strong, causing Rachel to shudder slightly. She couldn't believe she was sitting next to Kyle, actually drinking from a cup that he had probably used. Intimacy and sharing something Kyle's disturbing lips had touched weren't on her list of planned activities . . . nor was letting him see the fear that had stalked her for three years since her attack. "Okay, you can go now.

You've probably seen that there's nothing personal here that might interest you."

He shrugged lightly. "Maybe it interested someone else. You wouldn't like the men she entertained, and they're certain to be around, wanting to come upstairs. Do what you have to do and sell this place. You weren't cut out to be a small-town girl anyway."

"I promised Mallory that I would do my best to take care of something she loved. I'm going to insure that it isn't turned into the tavern atmosphere she didn't want. I'm not leaving, Kyle. I'm moving in upstairs and I'm running this place."

Kyle stared at Rachel; her chin was lifted defiantly, her eyes narrowed at him. He'd seen that look before, admired it, but now he didn't trust where her stubbornness could lead her. "You mean it, don't you?"

"I do. I promised Mallory that—"

His throat tightened with fear; Mallory had lived a hard life, and Rachel knew nothing of the details—the abortions, the beatings. He'd been frustrated, angry with Mallory, because she wouldn't listen, and now the same thing was happening all over again—but not if he had anything to do with it. . . . "She's dead, Rachel. You don't owe her anything. Do what you have to do and settle down to raise kids, join a bridge club or something."

"I . . . owe . . . her. And I loved her. So I'm moving in upstairs and running this place," she repeated.

Kyle's curse boiled out of him, then he said, "Hell bound and determined to do whatever you want, regardless of the danger. You were always like that—a crusader against all odds. It doesn't look like you've changed, but this place cost Mallory, and it could cost you, too."

She smiled tightly. "And you think your opinion matters, do you? Someone like you who's been out drinking and fighting in a bar all night?"

He thought about the hard drive to that Idaho farm house, his hours at welding the stock car's frame, lowering a new engine into the speed demon, and working with a too-tight timing chain that had scraped his knuckles. He'd been too tired before he even began the long drive home, because he couldn't wait to see Rachel again. *You sick, son of a bitch,* he labeled himself grimly. Rachel Everly had looked down that pretty nose at him for years—and maybe he wanted that, because he knew he wasn't what she needed. "If you say so, honey," he drawled, watching her.

She stood abruptly and faced him, her cheeks rosy with anger, her eyes flashing with that passion he loved to nudge—"Why didn't you marry Mallory? You married everyone else. She lived with you. You should have married her, too."

Kyle leaned back, his arms crossed behind his head and allowed his legs to stretch out, framing hers as she stood in front of him. Mallory had needed his protection two special times, because she was afraid of who might come visiting at the apartment when she wasn't up to "taking it." But she always went back to the apartment and Nine Balls as if it had a hold on her, as if she knew her life would end there, an obsession she couldn't break. "I offered. Mallory wasn't buying."

"You're pitiful." Rachel looked pointedly down to

where his legs had closed against hers. "I'm not going to ask you to let me go."

"Well, then, just how long do you think you can stand there?" It was always the same, Kyle decided wryly, he just enjoyed seeing Rachel's composure skitter and change into real emotions. When he purposefully studied her breasts, she shivered and blushed and Kyle couldn't help grinning up at her. He touched her hot cheek where that enticing dimple lurked. "Now, that is some reaction for a woman who isn't interested."

"Stop leering and stay away from here."

"Sorry. Paid for a full year, compliments of Mallory. Deal with it."

"I'll refund."

"Read the rules, honey. You have to have a real reason to kick someone out of here. Drunken or unacceptable behavior, that sort of thing. To my knowledge, I haven't done any of that. What are you going to say, that you can't trust yourself with me?"

He stood slowly, allowing his body to come close to hers, watching her reaction. Rachel shivered just once, and then she took a step back. She'd gone pale and that flashing anger in her eyes was gone, replaced by wide-eyed fear.

Had she been raped? Kyle asked himself for the second time in over a month.

He didn't like that dark glimpse into what Rachel hid so well by her competent, independent disguise. Stepping into Mallory's life was certain to bring Rachel real trouble. "Don't stay in that apartment, Rachel. You can't help Mallory now. Why don't you go back where you belong, find some rich guy and join a yacht and country club? Do what you have to do, and put Nine Balls up for sale."

He wasn't prepared for the fist that shot out to grip his shirt, and after hesitating, he obeyed her tug, leaning down to look into those dark brown eyes. "Yes, dear?"

"Stop telling me what to do, Scanlon. I'm a big girl—"

"Oh, I know that," he agreed, looking down to where her breasts were almost touching him.

Maybe it was because he was raw from guilt about Mallory. Maybe it was because he'd driven across a state, and had worked hard before that, but Kyle had to put his hands on her, to know that she was safe—

His hands opened on her waist, slid just a fraction to lock onto her hips, and the air between them stilled, then seemed to quiver with electricity. She was soft and curved in the right places, and she smelled like freshly mowed grass and flowers. Those wide brown eyes were filled with him as the heartbeats pounded silently by—

Kyle couldn't stop his fingers from digging in, locking onto her, kneading that softness. He'd never been this close to her and his instincts were humming, his body hard. She'd always gotten to him since the first day he'd seen her, wearing that mermaid outfit with the shells covering her breasts. . . .

Just that thought caused his hands to move slowly higher to frame her rib cage.

He was just bending to taste that slightly opened mouth, to taste her that first perfect time, when the nudge of something hard and blunt touched him in a very vulnerable place.

Kyle looked down to see the butt of a cue placed between his upper thighs. "Mm. Interesting."

"Yes, isn't it?"

"You think that could stop me from kissing you?"

"I think it might."

He smiled at that; Rachel was back in form and she wasn't afraid of him and that was very good. "I've got to hand it to you, Rachel. You sure know how to spoil a mood."

She looked down meaningfully. "The mood looks like it's still there, Scanlon."

She was right; his body was humming, taut and full with the need to feed upon her, to taste her in every way—to make Rachel his. . . . Strange, Kyle thought distantly, that he'd never wanted to test a woman like he did Rachel, to call all that raw passion out where he could taste it. . . .

Kyle knew he could disarm her, but instead he lifted his hands away. He stripped Nine Balls' key and the apartment one from his ring, tossing them onto the pool table, then he walked out the door, closing it behind him.

He frowned as he lifted Pup into the Hummer. He'd seen that obsessive look in a woman before, in Mallory as she talked about how Nine Balls couldn't fail, how she'd kill herself to keep it alive. Now Rachel had that same look, and she wasn't listening to reason from someone who had been with Mallory down the whole horrific road to suicide.

Harry hopped up on the running board and then into the front seat beside Pup. Kyle didn't hesitate; he got in, started the vehicle, and drove in a U-turn, heading back for his shop. If Rachel wanted her cat, she'd have to come and get him.

The thought of Rachel coming to him, all fired up, caused Kyle to smile.

Then he glanced in the mirror at his reflection, unshaven, dirty, and eyes blurred from welding and exhaustion. "I'm going to have to make myself more appealing," he said to Harry and Pup.

He settled into thinking about Rachel, about Mallory's obsession with Nine Balls, about those well-traveled steps to the upstairs apartment.

"Why Rachel Everly, dammit? Why some high-nosed woman who can make my life miserable by making me jump through her hoops? Getting too close would be like walking over glass to toss myself on a bed of nails."

Kyle looked at where his dog and Rachel's cat sat together on the seat, as if they were old chums. "Well, then. I guess the game is on," he said as he reached to punch in Nine Balls' autodial number.

"Nine Balls. We're not open for business yet. Please leave a message." Rachel's professional tone caused him to smile.

"Message machines beep, and then you leave the message. How about dinner tonight? You know, dinner out, or an intimate candlelight one at my place? I'll move the carburetor I'm rebuilding on the kitchen table, open a can of beer and grill some brauts and onions."

Her slight gasp caused his smile to widen. "No, thanks. Goodbye," she said and then the line clicked off.

"Always a lady," Kyle murmured dryly as Harry came purring onto his lap. "And one with an attitude."

He rubbed the cat's ears. "Gotta appreciate a woman with attitude. But she's a hardhead and likely in trouble, because Mallory's regulars just might think that one sister is as good as another."

"What did you say about Shane?" Jada looked up from the shot she'd been studying.

Rachel placed her cue aside and cradled her mug of tea. Life passed slowly by Atlantis Street, Nine Balls' old bluish windows serving wavering images of people and cars. Advising Jada to stay away from the man she wanted to marry wasn't going to be easy. . . . "I think that Shane is a dangerous man and that you should be more careful of him, maybe stop cleaning his house."

Jada took the shot and missed; instead the cue ball rolled into the pocket. She straightened, leaned back against the pool table, and folded her arms. "I'm going to marry Shane. You're out of bounds, Rache. You may have told me what to do when we were younger, but we're both adults now. Just maybe you need to get your own man and stop worrying about my life."

"He had a relationship with Mallory—"

"Of course he did. Shane was just doing his job and he's a compassionate man. He told me that he tried to help her."

Rachel took a deep breath before she pressed on—"I think they were more than that."

Her expression furious, Jada threw the cue down onto the table. "You're so full of it. Just stay out of my life."

Jada marched out of Nine Balls and leaped into her ice cream wagon. It tinkled merrily as she pulled out onto the street, tires squalling.

Rachel watched the wagon swerve and tilt precariously. She ached for Jada, but feared for her, too. Last night on the street Shane had been threatening, and Rachel could feel the violence, his anger in the damp air. If that temper would turn on Jada—Rachel shook her head and didn't look forward to future discussions with her sister about Shane. "Well, Mallory. I think that went well, don't you?"

Kyle Scanlon had interfered too much with Mallory, and now he was putting the moves on Rachel. Kyle had always been a complication, supporting Mallory in her attempts to leave the master of her life. She'd stayed with Kyle while she was recovering from her abortions, and she'd later sworn that she hadn't told Kyle about the secret man, the master of her life, the one she obeyed. . . .

Rage, hot and burning as lava, flowed through the man who had owned Mallory for years. He could feel his obsession with Mallory, for the sexual thrills she had given him, sliding to her sister, Rachel. But Kyle and Rachel were probably already intimate—his Hummer was parked in front of Nine Balls early this morning. Kyle's relationship with Mallory was well known, and now he was having her sister.

"I should have had Rachel that night in the park, had her first. She'll pay for bedding Scanlon—a low-class mechanic. I don't know why I've let him live this long. . . . Mallory had been holding out on me. She hadn't given me all of her money . . . I saw that in her ledgers, once Rachel had transcribed them. Mallory had written monthly checks to Kyle. Now why would she do that? She knew I couldn't stand him, and yet she disobeyed me, seeing him, calling him to help her— You've made another mess, haven't you, Mallory? Rachel is going to be prowling in your life—and therefore in mine—and I will not tolerate anyone looking at my life. . . . *What did you do with that doll?*"

In the silence, he thought he heard Mallory whisper, "You'll soon see, lover. Feeling a little under the weather? A little headache? A little heart pain? A little malfunction when you're trying to be a man?"

Suddenly chilled, he thought he heard Mallory's voice, "I'll be waiting on the far, still side of tomorrow. . . ."

# Six

—

**"YOU STOLE MY CAT, SCANLON. SINCE YOU LEFT THIS** morning, no one but the locksmith has been in Nine Balls, and I was careful to open and close the door for him. If Harry had been around, he would have tried to run out then. I was just too busy to notice then." Rachel drove the Caddie through Scanlon's open gates and noted the muddy Hummer sitting beside the garage.

In the hours between Kyle's early morning visit, a hard and fast telephone row with Jada about Shane, and five o'clock in the evening, Rachel had been working hard, leaving Harry to hide and explore as usual. At ten, the locksmith from Bob's Handy Hardware came to replace Nine Balls front lock and the one on the apartment, adding another dead bolt to each. Bob had dropped by to check on his man's work and had helped move the refrigerator, so that she could clean beneath it.

Since Harry didn't like intruders, Rachel had supposed that he was hiding when several other people stopped by, including Terri, who had noticed the locksmith's van. "That's a good idea," she said quietly, her eyes meeting Rachel's in quiet understanding; Mallory's keys could be on several men's key rings. . . .

At eleven, Leon had called and she'd met him at her

mother's garage. "Scanlon specializes in these old cars. You should have gotten him, but I think a new starter and battery, cleaning off the cables, and changing the oil and antifreeze will get her up and running for now. She could use some new rubber and that'll cost you. You got all greasy, helping me."

Leon Smith, a fifty-year-old mechanic, had reached down to wipe a greasy rag over her hip. Surprised that he would touch her, Rachel had frowned and stepped back. For just that moment, she recognized the lust on the mechanic's face before he concealed it and mumbled, "Just trying to help. No offense."

Leon had worked on and off for Trina's Used Cars for many years. A reclusive, quiet man, he lived alone in a small ramshackle house surrounded by junked cars. Jada hadn't liked him from the start, and now Rachel had to agree that Leon was "scary."

That scenario had troubled Rachel as she showered and dressed, feeling refreshed in a white long-sleeved sweater and gray slacks. Used to dressing professionally, she took a few minutes with her cosmetics.

She had held her breath as she turned the key in Buttercup's ignition. The yellow Cadillac had coughed a few times, then she was gliding down the road, her big steering wheel turning easily. More difficult to parallel park than Rachel had remembered, Buttercup had stalled a few times in the process. After stopping at the electric company, city hall and other places to change Nine Balls' bills to herself, Rachel returned to find that Harry had not touched the food she'd left for him. His litter box remained clean and unused and not a hair ball in sight.

The last time she'd seen him was early that morning—when Kyle had left the door open. . . . She hadn't hesitated to call him as she kicked off her black business pumps and slid into her comfortable thongs. He had answered after a few rings and sounded distracted above the metal clang in the background. "Have you seen my cat, Scanlon?"

There had been the slightest pause before he'd drawled, "Sure. He's around here somewhere."

"I'm coming to get him. And I'm in no mood to play games."

"Suit yourself," he'd said, then had added softly, "I'll be waiting, honey."

"You just do that."

Rachel eased Buttercup in next to the Hummer and walked into the office. It was empty. No one responded to her knock on the apartment door. She circled the big weathered building to find Kyle's recognizable backside and long legs. The rest of him was tucked under the hood of an old black car. On a fender beside him was a thick cloth with an array of tools. Harry sat, sunning on the other fender.

Pup came running around the car, barking loudly, and planting himself in front of Kyle protectively.

"Pup, hush."

Kyle looked over his shoulder, glanced at Rachel, then went back to work, ignoring her. Harry leaped off the fender and ran deep into a neat streetlike arrangement of old cars.

"Harry!" she called desperately.

After a half hour of calling and chasing Harry, who

wasn't going to be caught, Rachel returned to Kyle, who was still bent beneath the hood. "You should have called me right away."

"Your cat walked all over my cars, and he dug up some flowers that Patty planted, and he doesn't know that the sand in the ashtray is for cigarette butts. Clean that out before you leave. . . . The threads are stripped on the breather—Here, hold this."

Rachel looked down at the grimy big round metal part in her hands, and then Kyle was straightening, wiping his hands on a greasy rag and looking down at her with those sky blue eyes. He'd changed, shaved, smelled like soap and male, and her mind stopped as he slowly took in her ponytail, the pink pearl studs in her ears. The lines crinkled beside Kyle's eyes, his lips curving only slightly. His gaze moved downward to her white sweater, gray slacks, and pink thongs with the plastic flowers. She watched as in slow motion, he bent to kiss her, just a brush of his lips across hers.

"Hi," he said softly, watching her. "You changed clothes from this morning and you smell sweet, like flowers. You looked great in that mermaid outfit, riding on back of that convertible when you were Miss Mermaid in the Neptune's Landing's parade."

The moment clung and warmed and terrified. Then her mind started clicking, adding and comparing dates. . . . "I was seventeen then, Kyle. You weren't even in town yet. Did Mallory show you pictures?"

He looked down to where she was holding the grimy breather protectively against her. "Nope. Just passing through back then."

He eased the breather from her tight fingers and looked down at the twin grease stains on her sweater. "You'd need bigger shells now."

She buried any small quiver of softness for Kyle Scanlon. "You are so crude."

"It's true, isn't it?"

She let that one drop into the hard-packed, greasy dirt at his boots. "Just how did you come to have my cat? Stole him, did you?"

He placed the breather on the fender, and leaned back against the car, crossing his arms. "Your cat jumped into my rig. He wasn't invited, and he seems to like it here. You've been calling and chasing him for a half hour. Seems like he comes easily enough to me. What did you do to him anyway? And why did you change clothes?"

Since she'd had Harry neutered, he didn't come as easily when she called, his grudge obvious. "I was helping Leon, and—it does not matter why I changed my clothes, Kyle. Harry gets the best cat food and lots of love. He just has his moments, that's all. That's quite typical for cats."

"Leon—Next time call me. Leon has—private interests you wouldn't approve of. Stay away from him." His blue eyes locked onto her lips and darkened. "You liked kissing me. Want to do it again?"

After that brief moment in her mother's garage, Rachel's instincts agreed with Kyle's assessment of Leon's "private interests."

Kyle's offer of a kiss lingered on the oil-scented air between them and Rachel wondered what those hard lips would taste like—in a real kiss.

Then the lines beside Kyle's eyes crinkled even more, that slight curve of his mouth lifting. "You're blushing, honey. You know what that does to a man, to know a woman reacts to him, getting all hot and sweet?"

Kyle was back in form, tormenting her as usual. "I don't have time to stand here, talking with you. I expect you to deliver Harry to me when you catch him. And I want to know, right now, why Mallory was writing a four hundred dollar check to you at the first of every month. She wasn't making enough money at Nine Balls to barely live, and yet, her checking ledger says she wrote a check to you every month."

Kyle's expression closed and locked, his voice grim. "That was between Mallory and myself."

"I'm good at research and I'm going to find out just why she was making those monthly payments to you. What's the matter? Don't you want people around here to know that you take money from women? That you don't work enough to make a real living for yourself? What did you have on her?"

He ran his open hand across his chest, those eyes silvery slits now, the planes of his face dangerous. "Think what you want, but don't move into that apartment. That place is already getting to you, like it got to Mallory."

"Tell me how it got to her. Explain. I don't understand."

"She had a chance for a different life. She didn't take it. In the end, it swallowed her. And if you don't leave it alone, it will do the same thing to you."

"Nothing or no one is making me leave that place, not before I do the job I intend to do."

"Have it your way. You always do." Then Kyle walked from her into the big garage.

She needed a place to think, away from her family and from Nine Balls, where so much needed to be done. Rachel pulled into the wooded parking area for picnickers just off the shoreline highway. As teens, the three girls would often park in the same place, then take the narrow rocky path down to the beach.

The crimson sunset lay over the swells, the big black rocks jutting into the layers of color, seagulls pristine white against the water. In August, the sea lions would be mating and their barking would shatter the air. Occasionally, a gray whale and her calf would blow out in the ocean—just a white spray amid the wide blue expanse, and thrilling enough to stop a person's heartbeat. On the hillsides, blackberry briars would be lush, and deer and elk would come to water at the tiny creek that wound from the hills above to the ocean below.

Rachel removed a blanket from her back seat and carefully worked her way down the rugged path to an open expanse of sand. The waves slid upon it, and when the delicate froth slid away, it left small worn pebbles in the smooth, wet sand.

The beach was empty now, the waves crashing against the timeless huge black mountains of stone. Was that how Mallory felt in the end? That she couldn't change her life? Why?

The wind tugged at Rachel's hair, pulling it from the sleek ponytail, and she shook the rest of it free. The cold crisp salty air matched her mood as she spread her blanket and sat, wrapping the ends around her. Memories slid by her, the wind tugging at her hair, lifting it. She remembered the first time her mother had brought them here as a family with a new sister. "This is going to be my special place," thirteen-year-old Mallory had declared, as she'd spread her arms wide to the Pacific Ocean and the world.

As teens, they'd come to lay and sunbathe, or to huddle together on a driftwood log, sharing a sandwich and chocolate cookies, and talking—but then Mallory had slowly started to ebb away, to distance herself from Jada and Rachel.

"Oh, Mallory, why?" Rachel asked the salty air.

A small herd of deer had come to water at the creek, and Rachel gave herself to the past when her sister had sat quietly beside her, watching the same scene.

The sun was only a bright arc sitting upon the water when she heard a sound and saw a big man moving down the path. Terror ripped through her—she knew what could happen to a woman alone. . . .

Fear drove Rachel to her feet and running across the sand in her bare feet. She ran until her heart and sides pounded painfully. No heavy footsteps followed her as they had that horrible night and she slowed, looking over her shoulder.

The man sprawled on her blanket waved lazily at her, then settled back onto his elbows, watching the setting sun.

She instantly recognized that big long body and his arrogance. "Kyle Scanlon."

Rachel walked back to the blanket and he looked up at her. "You're fast. Is that why you never married? No one could catch you?"

"Get off my blanket."

She nudged his thigh with her bare toes, and instantly Kyle's big hand circled her ankle. His thumb stroked her flesh. "Afraid?"

"Of you? No."

His hand slid higher to massage her calf lightly. "If you're not afraid, then you won't mind sharing this blanket with me, would you?"

The challenge was in his soft drawl and Rachel wouldn't have him thinking she was afraid of him. She circled those long legs and sat beside him. In a worn flannel shirt and jeans, Kyle's muscled body was relaxed and his heat spread to her, despite the Pacific's cool late April wind. "Okay, there. I'm sitting."

He rolled on his side, bracing his head on his hand. "You look good this way, your hair soft around your face, the flush on your cheeks."

"You scared me and I've been running." She looked out at the rolling waves, pushing away that instant, surprising terror. Kyle's intent study caused her senses to quiver, very aware of him, those silvery eyes taking in her profile—and her body.

"I've been watching you for a time from up there. It's dangerous for a woman to be alone here. This is where Mallory came to brood, too. I'm not in the mood for a replay, watching another woman come apart, Rachel," he stated firmly.

She leveled a look at him. "I don't come apart."

Those silvery eyes turned cold. "But then you're not

Mallory. You're tougher, aren't you? You always were, and that's what she admired the most about you. She wanted to be like you, maybe she was trying to prove that, to succeed at something the way you can so easily. She knew that Trina had dragged herself out of hard times with two daughters in tow, and I think Mallory admired your mother even more. I know she loved her. Jada always went with the flow, whatever happened, happened. You and Trina were hard to live up to, but Mallory tried."

The need to know Mallory's trials, what drove her so relentlessly, caused Rachel to grip his hand. "Tell me about her. I couldn't help her," she said urgently. "I need to know. I need to understand."

Kyle's hand turned slightly, warm and calloused, his fingers interlacing with hers as he lay down, his eyes closed. Linked, their hands rested on his flat stomach, his big broad hand, rough against her own, the fine glistening hairs on the back. Pressed between his stomach's heat and the strength of that very masculine hand, her own seemed so feminine, narrow and pale and delicate. The fascinating difference between her own smaller one and his caused her to breathe slowly, wondering what it would be like if their bodies tangled intimately, light and dark textures, male and female. But then, it was the season of odd sensations. . . .

"It's getting cold. Here, put on my sweater," he said as he took the rolled pad from beneath his head.

"I can manage. Tell me." She was cold and shivering and to hide that, she picked up a white smooth pebble and toyed with it. She didn't understand why, but Kyle's hand linked with hers gave her a sense of safety.

Had Mallory felt that, too? The safety in Kyle? Was that why she kept so close to him?

He turned her hand to lay palm down on his stomach, his hand over hers and he rubbed gently. She could have pulled away, but fascinated by all that raw power and heat beneath her touch, Rachel wondered if Kyle somehow needed her touch to soothe him.

Odd. She'd never thought of Kyle as needing soothing or tenderness. He'd always been so cocksure, tormenting her with a look or a soft, drawled remark.

His thumb stroked the back of her hand and the friction caused her to hold very still. She hadn't expected his gentleness and understanding, the friendship that hovered between them, two so different people who shared a common bond—Mallory. "You're a difficult woman, Rachel. Just make this easy, okay? No big deal? Everything with you has to be a big deal, doesn't it? All the rules defined?"

Just to prove him wrong, Rachel wouldn't make a big deal of taking a sweater on a chilly night. She eased into the sweater and was surprised when Kyle lifted her hair free, smoothing it over the garment that held his warmth and scent. She could have dived into that erotic, spicy scent of his aftershave, that all-male scent of his body. Little kept her from nuzzling the sweater with her cheek. "Did you know Mallory had married?"

"Uh-huh." His big hand smoothed her back. "You could lie down here beside me. The wind wouldn't hit you so much then."

The impulse to do just that terrified her. Very aware of the warm hand cruising her back, the pleasure of it on her body, was too tempting. Once she crossed that sexual line with Kyle Scanlon, there would be no going back, and she'd regret a momentary weakness. She looked out at the ocean and relaxed slightly against his hand. "Did you know she had divorced?"

"Sure. The louse beat her. He didn't like getting a taste of his own medicine," Kyle stated darkly and his hand paused briefly.

"How do you know about that?"

"I just know."

Rachel took a deep breath and wondered just how much Kyle knew about Mallory. Mallory had promised never to tell anyone about Rachel's attack in the park. Had she told Kyle? "What else? If you know that much, you know more."

He nodded and tugged her down to his side; Kyle turned to her, his head braced on his hand as he looked down at her. "Don't get all rattled and scared. Maybe I can keep the wind from you. Three times now, I've seen you act terrified, and all of them had to do with me—or the fact that I'm a man. You were never that way, Rachel the crusader, Rachel the bold. Never afraid, but something changed didn't it? Something that happened about the time Mallory borrowed money to fly to you in New York—after that you were different, more guarded. I know more . . . everything but why she wouldn't leave Neptune's Landing and start a new life somewhere else."

He smiled slightly and brushed a strand of hair from her cheek, his finger returning to her lips, tapping them gently. "What's the matter, Rachel? You're looking all panicked and uncertain. Can't you handle a little one-on-one with me? You ask, I answer. And then to be fair, I ask and you answer."

"My feet are cold, that's all. How was Mallory going to finance this new life?"

"She could have sold Nine Balls for a little profit. There were people who would have helped her. I could rub your feet, make them warm," he offered in a deep tone that curled intimately around her.

"No, thanks." She didn't like Kyle's knowing smile.

Mallory had told her of the babies she didn't want and Rachel had to know if Kyle was the father—"Did you know about Mallory's . . . medical problems?"

"Specifically?" Kyle sounded distracted as he watched the flow of his hand down her shoulder to her hip. His leg lifted and fitted over her feet, warming them as he turned her to him. "Better?"

Rachel lay quietly, assessing Kyle and the slow way he'd looked down at her body, as if he were fitting them together, intimately and without clothing. . . . His hand slid up her hip and over her back, and somehow, she was lying close to him, his heat steeping into her. "That's close enough," she whispered, bracing her hands on his chest.

"Okay, you're nervous and flushed, Rachel. Now why would that be?"

*Because I'm wondering just how warm you'd be, covering me. . . .*

Too aware of Kyle's impact on her body, the softening of it, the ache to touch him, Rachel tried to focus on the information she wanted from him. "She—didn't want children and she—"

"Got pregnant?" His expression hardened and he jackknifed into sitting position. Kyle picked up a stone and hurled it into the ocean, then drew up one knee and locked his hands around it.

He'd moved so fast that she took a heartbeat to adjust to the loss of his touch and his heat, the wind cutting at her without the protection of his body. Rachel sat up slowly, and studied Kyle's furious expression, there was no questioning the validity of his emotions, how deeply he felt about Mallory. "Whoever the bastard was that got her pregnant should have helped her and not sent her to some back-street abortionist. If she just had to, Mallory could have gone to some clinic for those abortions and had good medical attention. I'd have taken her. But then, I guess a badly beaten woman isn't a good candidate for that, and there would be questions. In bad shape already, Mallory might just have answered them, and that wouldn't do—not with this bastard. Then, he'd worked on her mind so much, gotten her feeling like a piece of dirt, like something that didn't deserve good medical care. And the whole thing was weird—she was so far down that she actually wanted to please this jerk, afraid if she didn't. Hell, who knows? Maybe she wanted to go, to end it right there, to die on that butcher's table."

Kyle took a deep unsteady breath, the muscle in his jaw working. "She was half dead when she came back both times and wouldn't let me take her to a real doctor. I'd like to meet that son of a bitch sometime. I think he played the hell out of her, sucked her dry in some sick way. I've been hunting him for years, and Mallory protected him. We fought over that—how she could protect him after what he'd done to her. I think he had something over her, some hold she couldn't break and she wouldn't let me do that for her."

Kyle sucked in breath and his words exploded, vibrating his frustration into the night air. "I never want to feel that helpless again."

His violent emotions were too stark, vivid with rage, but Rachel understood and shared them. She placed her hand on his bare forearm, aware of the taut muscles, the heat and the textures of the hair there, so different from her own. She slid her hand down his arm and eased her finger into his locked hands, and then wondered why she had reacted to comfort him. Rachel had to drag her eyes away from the contrast of male and female, her hand on his, to look at Kyle. "You mean the two times she stayed a month with you was because you were taking care of her?" she asked carefully.

Kyle scrubbed his face with his open hands as if trying to erase a horrible scene. "No woman should go through that. There was blood everywhere, and she wouldn't let me call a doctor. I was going to anyway, and then she came around. There's something about a woman threatening to kill herself that can—I guess she did in the end, anyway."

Rachel drew up her knees and pulled his large sweater around them down and over her feet. "And I wasn't there. I should have been."

Kyle looked out at the last sunlight skimming the ocean. "She wouldn't go to Trina, and she was really down. She knew Jada couldn't keep a secret, and she didn't want you to see how low she was. She wouldn't see a psychiatrist. . . ."

He looked over his shoulder to Rachel. "You thought

I was the father of her babies, didn't you? You're probably not going to believe me, but that's how it was. She came to me when she needed me. Or she called me to come to her when she hit that last wall and couldn't take care of herself. The rest of the time she was locked in surviving her nightmare, whatever that was. It might shock you to know that past those first years when we were kids, we were just good friends. . . . So what happened to you in New York?"

She was unprepared for his shift to her, prowling in her life, searching for things she didn't want to relive. "We were talking about Mallory."

"Let's change the subject to you."

"No." Rachel stared out at the black waves, shutting him out.

"It was bad then. Because Mallory was pretty open about your news, your achievements. She loved you. But she never said a word about why she went to you, other than to visit. I always thought something had happened, that you needed her, and that you didn't want Trina and Jada to know—that you thought only Mallory could help you. She was scared of flying and of the big wide world, and suddenly she was in a plane and headed for you."

Rachel continued to look out at the ocean and couldn't help shivering as a myriad of images swept by her: She'd been almost broken, huddled upon her apartment couch, feeling dirty; the rough touch of the men's hands had left bruises. . . . Mallory, angry as Rachel had never seen her, shaking with it . . . then tender as she held Rachel and told her she was just as good as ever, that the men demeaning her were "lower than snakes." "But he didn't rape you? You're sure? He didn't rape you?" Mallory had asked furiously.

The man had worn a knit ski mask; he'd pawed at her, held her legs apart, told her what he was going to do—but he hadn't. While the other two men held her naked body to the ground, he'd positioned himself over her—and then other than a few slaps, nothing had happened. One of the other men had laughed, and then he made the odd rough comment, "That's enough. You get the point, don't you, bitch?"

*Point? What point?*

"Wherever you went just now, it wasn't pleasant." Kyle looked down to where Rachel's bare toes had dug into the cold sand. He dusted away the sand and studied her nail polish. "Pink suits you. How's the boyfriend?"

"In New York. I'm here. Who are you, Kyle? You just landed in town one day, started to work for Mac, and sold that red job on consignment at mom's used cars. When he retired, you bought him out. Didn't that garage make enough money? Did you have to lean on Mallory?"

"You're not going to believe anything I say, are you?" Kyle stood abruptly, the wind tugging at his flannel shirt, the sleeves rolled up to his forearms, as he looked out into the night. "It's dark. That trail could be dangerous. Are you coming or not?"

"You're right. Truce time is over." She rose slowly to her feet, pulled his thick sweater over her head and handed it to him.

Whatever had lingered between them in the cold salty air still remained, and Kyle inhaled roughly. "You looked good wearing that sweater."

The wind pushed his hair back from that stark face

and in the shadowy light the hard lines had softened into genuine grief. At the funeral, he'd straightened Mallory's collar like a loving brother. Were his feelings for her that tender? Enough to see her through her pain, to tend her? Had he come to this beach with Mallory to help her fight her demons, or to give them to her? "Tell me about the money, Kyle. Why did she write a check to you every month?"

"Handyman stuff."

"I don't believe you. I've seen the other receipts. Mallory had her dependables and called them when she had a problem with repairs. Mom and Bob helped her sometimes, until Mom couldn't take it anymore. Mallory wrote you a check for something else. What was it?"

When Kyle shook his head and that jaw locked, a taut cord running down to his throat, Rachel pushed harder, "Then tell me who you are. Where you came from."

He smiled at that and leaned down to whisper in her ear. "Makes the investigation that much easier, doesn't it? If you have those little details?"

She refused to move, and lifted her face to return the whisper. "Much easier. I'm going to nail you, Scanlon. No one knows much about you before you came into town. I guess no one has ever been curious before, but I'm going to dig out every little detail about you. I'm going to find out why you were taking money from Mallory."

His lips brushed her cheek and his deep drawl packed a sensual punch. "I'm flattered that you care, honey."

"Don't be. As owner of Nine Balls, I'm going to demand repayment. I haven't added it up yet, but you're going to owe quite the tab." The friction of his rougher skin, the heat and scent of it, struck her with the need to place her hand on it, stroke it, and feel the man inside, the gentle one who cared for Mallory when she needed him most. "Did she pay you for taking care of her?"

The thought that Mallory had almost died twice before, and hadn't asked Rachel to help, hurt her.

"No. We were friends."

"I was her sister."

"She wanted to protect you." Her body tensed as he moved against her. "Just blocking the wind, Rachel. Afraid?" he asked again in a deep raw tone.

"Not a bit," she lied . . . because she feared what ran inside her, the primitive need to turn her head just that bit and taste those hard lips, to bite them slightly. Kyle was pushing and she knew it, because he expected that she'd move away. But she wouldn't give him that pleasure.

His face shifted, the curve of his smile against her throat. "That's my girl . . . fearless. If you want to know why I stayed in Neptune's Landing, it was because I thought I'd found a home. I drove through town one day and it hit me that this was where I wanted to live. Just that easy."

"If I was seventeen, you were nineteen when you came through town that first time. And it would take a lot of money to own that car you had at twenty-two when you started to work at Mac's garage. The question is: How did you get the money to buy Mac out?"

"Why, honey, I sold my pretty little car. Then I worked my butt off."

"How did you get that 'pretty little car' in the first place?"

"The same way I get everything, by using skill and patience. I rebuilt a wreck someone didn't appreciate. Took me two years of working odd jobs to pay for the parts and working in body shops for the rest."

"So you sold your baby to stay in Neptune's Landing. That's hard to believe, Kyle."

His gaze moved down to her lips. "Maybe I saw something here that I wanted more than moving on."

Her body was taut and warmed by his, but she wouldn't step back. "I bet you know how to hot-wire cars and do a few other things. Or maybe you learned them in juvie hall?"

"If you say so." His voice was deep and richly sensual, his face warm against hers. "You're trembling and hot, Rachel. I can tell when a well-tuned motor—or a woman—is humming. Are you going to kiss me or not?"

That quick unexpected question took her back a step, and Kyle grinned. "You'd get me greasy anyway. This shirt is clean and yours is full of grease from that intake breather you cuddled. Or you could take yours off."

She tilted her head, studying his confident smile, that cocky tilt of his head. Then her fist shot out and grabbed his shirt, tugging him down to her. "Back off, Scanlon. I know exactly why you make those remarks and spoil any inkling that I might have that you are anything but one big gland. You're afraid of me."

His silvery eyes flashed at that, the first sign she'd ever seen of any temper in their clashes, and she intended to nudge and use it.

"You seem to like grabbing me. Be careful with those fists. I outweigh and out-muscle you, honey, and I'm no gentleman. I wouldn't push my luck, if I were you, sweetheart."

"You won't do anything. You had your chance, and you didn't use it. I use mine, and I know that every time you drop one of those low-class, sexist remarks on me, it's just after you show some human emotion. You're afraid to show too much. But I saw it when you talked about Mallory. If you lied about her abortions, about being the father of her babies, I'm going to find out and I'm coming after you. And I'll run you out of town, Kyle. That's after I take everything you have."

"Oh, God. Women think they know every—"

Then her other hand gripped that mass of thick hair and tugged his face down to hers. "Just to give you a little something to think about, and keep your hands where they are," she murmured before lifting her lips to his. . . .

She'd just tasted that wild hunger inside him, the banked storm when Kyle stepped back, glaring at her. "What was that about?"

"Just to prove my point. You're afraid of me. I don't know why exactly, and I'm tired of this conversation," she said as she picked up the blanket and shook it deliberately in the direction the wind would carry the sand to Kyle.

She was shaking as she started toward the path, still shaking as she tossed the blanket onto her floorboard. Because the big Hummer had parked behind her, she had to wait until Kyle stalked by, slammed the door, and started the motor. When he reversed, she backed onto the road, slid Buttercup into drive, and pushed the powerful V-8 engine down the highway.

The Hummer came up behind her, but Rachel wasn't afraid. She was too wrapped up in the taste of Kyle, in the discovery of how she could have devoured him. Rachel opened and closed her hands on the big thin steering wheel. She was just really, really tired, and Kyle had always set her on edge. "He intends to do that. And I let him. I hope that—"

The hard jut below his belt had said that Kyle had wanted her badly, instantly, his face hot against hers. If he wanted to play games, she was ending them, right there on the beach.

She adjusted her rearview mirror to cut the glare of the Hummer's headlights. "I'm going to find out why she paid you every month, Kyle."

While she was zinging Kyle, she might as well finish the job, Rachel decided as she hit the right-turn signal and braked hard, turning onto the shoulder of the road. Rachel didn't wait until the Hummer had fully stopped before getting out of her car and walking back to Kyle. He was already out of his vehicle and waiting for her, his hands on his hips. "That's no way to treat a good car."

Because telling Kyle off wasn't going well, she decided to take the offensive. "I want my cat."

He leaned down to her and frowned, those silvery eyes studying her face as if trying to understand her.

"Have I upset you?" she asked sweetly, because she was winning a game that Kyle had started years ago and she was elated, flying high on victory. She'd pinned a truth on him that he hadn't wanted, that he was afraid of her. For some reason, she had a real advantage in their skirmishes; she'd tagged him, and she'd won.

"Let's just say I wasn't prepared. With you, I'm usually not," he said, moving suddenly to pin her back against his vehicle. "Just to even up," he whispered softly before bending his head to kiss her. . . .

Kyle was very careful with her, framing her fine-boned face with his hands, feeling the heat beneath that smooth flesh. He wanted her to see him coming, moving slowly, so that she wouldn't be frightened. Wary of him, she wasn't backing down or moving away. Instead, those dark eyes met his as he studied the texture of her hair, silky in his fingers, webbing sensually against his skin, binding him.

With a deep breath to steady himself, and a sense that he was free-falling off a cliff with no parachute, Kyle brushed his lips against hers, tasted the corner of her lips, one then the other. When Rachel inhaled sharply, he tasted her with the tip of his tongue, inserting it gently against her teeth. Those sharp teeth caught his tongue, biting with enough pressure to stop him.

Against his chest, her hands flattened, the fingers digging in, and then she sighed and closed her eyes, freeing him. She tasted incredible, soft, sexy, sweet, warm. "Open," he whispered as he nuzzled her cheek and found her ear, nibbling it gently.

She breathed unevenly. "Scanlon?"

"Hmm?"

"What's going on here?"

"Mm? What do you mean? The usual, I guess. You.

Me. Us." Her pulse was racing beneath that soft skin, her throat arched for his access.

"Do you really think you can use sex to keep me from finding out whatever you don't want to come out?"

He smiled at that; it was typical of Rachel to distrust him and think about alternative motives at a time like this. With another woman, he'd have moved on and they'd both be satisfied by now. With Rachel, he enjoyed the game, the unique way she played it. "What makes you think that?"

"A. You're very hard and that says you have intentions of a sexual nature. B. You're taking your time."

Her voice was husky and uneven, and she'd just lifted her hips against said hardness. Kyle moved his foot between hers, nudging slightly until her legs opened just that bit. "I'm a thorough sort of guy."

Her arms were around his shoulders now, her hands gripping his hair. He studied her expression: unpredictable, mysterious, setting her terms. Just to see how far he could go, Kyle let his hands wander downward, over those soft curved breasts, testing the warm weight in his hands.

"You're all hot and shaking, Scanlon. Too bad, because you're going to regret getting all worked up later," Rachel murmured huskily, and he realized that she was testing him as much as he was pushing her.

She didn't move when he smoothed her hips and cupped her bottom, kneading that softness gently. She tensed and looked surprised as he suddenly lifted her against him. Then face-to-face, Rachel studied him and her lips curved at just that one side as if she were confident and in control. "A little macho, baby-I'm-so-strong, demonstration?"

The rock-hard ache below his belt proved that she was winning. It took all of Kyle's willpower to carry her to her car and let her slide down his body. "Nope. Just trying to pry you off me and send you on your way, before you embarrass yourself."

Rachel's confident smirk died, replaced by a quick frown and a snappy, "Don't think that you interest me, Scanlon. Not in that way. But like I said, I'm going to find out everything about you."

"Liar. You're hot for me. But because you're no sweetheart, I'm going to play hard to get." He opened her car door and held it, waiting for her to slide inside. "Next time, bring a picnic basket. You can feed me, romance me, and then you just might get lucky."

Before she revved the engine, Rachel's frustrated groan pleased him. From inside the Caddie, she scowled up at him. Then she smiled prettily. "FYI, Scanlon—you're a real rat. Don't count on any picnic baskets from me. . . . Buy the Hummer for some kind of compensation symbol, did you?"

With a knowing grin, he let that one pass and the Caddie's tires spun as the big V-8 dug out, swinging onto the highway again.

Kyle shook his head and grinned as the taillights disappeared softly into the night. Rachel caused him to feel alive and fresh, emotions he hadn't felt for a very long time, the need to share his life, to have a real home with a few kids in the mix. They were old dreams, rusty and forgotten, and that hot kiss had proved that Rachel wasn't out to make his life easy.

At least she wasn't thinking about whatever had happened to her, reliving that time when Mallory had flown to her side. . . .

He inhaled the damp night air and watched a big elk move from the brush to cross the highway. He'd promised Mallory that no one would know her secret, that he would keep it safe.

And Rachel was set to examine everything in Mallory's life.

She just could get caught in Mallory's nightmare, in her obsessions . . . she was probably right about someone coming into Nine Balls last night. Mallory had a lot of late-night visitors.

Maybe new locks would stop them, maybe not.

Kyle got into his rig, started it, and sat for a moment while the motor idled. With a shake of his head, he put the Hummer in gear—and realized that with Rachel in town, he was in for trouble.

The man eased back into the shadows of the trees and watched the big Caddie's back lights float through the fog and into Trina Everly's driveway. Rachel moved out of the car and hurried into the house.

*Where was Mallory's private stash, the little pieces of herself that she kept intact and private? If she'd left anything that could tie her to him to what he was, it could ruin him!*

Mallory had somehow gotten into witchcraft and creating spells. He'd stripped away her how-to books whenever he found them, but he couldn't erase her insidious small remarks here and there, just enough to make a sane person wonder. She'd fashioned a voodoo doll from his hair and shirt; though he'd never seen it, he didn't doubt the pleasure she took in tormenting him with its existence.

Cleared of Mallory's things, the apartment should have felt different, but she was still here, waiting, watching. . . .

In her office last night, the laptop had sprung into life and showed that Rachel had been transferring Mallory's neat handwritten ledgers into electronic spreadsheets. Rachel's notations on the yellow pad revealed nothing, no damning evidence to show that Mallory had "after-hours pleasures" that paid very well—or that he had taken that money from her.

Mallory had been paying Kyle Scanlon four hundred a month—holding back that money from him, the man who owned her. He'd always left her enough to pay the business bills, but not enough to run away from him. "And she held back on me. If she were alive now, and I knew this, I'd—"

He breathed in the salty fog, and a chill wrapped around him. "I'll haunt you forever," Mallory had said.

Just one bit of evidence, tying him to Mallory, and he'd be ruined.

"Where is that damned doll?"

*Where?* Mallory's sultry laughter seemed to curl around him. *Why are you so worried, lover?*

Chilled by the eerie sense that Mallory's curses could come true, he shivered. *What's the matter, lover? Worried that someone will find out our little secret? I'll be waiting for you—on the far, still side of forever.*

# Seven

**"MALLORY?"**

The next morning, the overpowering sense that her sister was near caused Rachel to stop just inside the apartment door. "Mallory?" she repeated and waited for an answer that did not come.

She looked at the bare apartment, the small towers of boxes, as yet unpacked. Stripped of their heavy drapes, the windows were open to let in the fresh May air. The bare varnished floors gleamed in the sunlit squares. In a canning jar serving as a vase, the bouquet of fresh flowers that Rachel had bought were fragrant and perky. They stood on the kitchen table she'd found at the used furniture store; of chrome and Formica, it was small, serviceable and perfect, a marbled red to match the four chairs.

Rachel inhaled slowly, preparing to face a day of cleaning and moving, and hoped to stay in the apartment that night.

"I don't like the thought of you staying at that place. I wish you would reconsider, maybe stay with us for a while, or maybe rent a place, some little house away from Nine Balls," Trina had said earlier.

"I'll be working odd hours to get the business up and running, Mom. I wouldn't want to disturb you—"

"Disturb me? *Disturb* me? You think I'm not afraid that what happened to Mallory will happen to you? That you'll become as obsessed with that place as she was— oh, I can see that you've made up your mind. In some ways, you're just as headstrong and stubborn as I am."

"It works for me," Rachel had said with a smile. "And you, too."

"I just want you to be safe. What about installing an alarm system?"

Rachel had started to say that she'd lived in a big city and she'd managed . . . but that wasn't true. She'd been attacked while walking home at night . . . she knew the dangers and the panicked aftermath of fear that occurred after an attack. "New locks should do it," she'd said.

She looked around the small kitchen that hadn't been cleared and cleaned. Apparently, in the last years, cooking and eating weren't a priority with Mallory. The apartment-size stove seemed new and unused, the instruction booklet still inside the oven. The refrigerator was also new, empty but for a few frozen dinners that Rachel quickly tossed away. After turning on the local radio station, she scrubbed the refrigerator's shelves thoroughly, planning to fill it later.

The announcer moved from the weather to sports, and then back into the soft rock portion of the program and the music filled the stillness of the apartment, the DJ a talkative companion as Rachel worked. Ricky Timberlake's friendly voice announced a sweet ballad-like song, not his usual choice, but something that fit the day—*I'll be with you forever, till the tides no longer flow, till doves no longer fly and roses no longer bloom, till time comes no more. . . . I'll be with you forever. On the far, still side of tomorrow. . . .*

Rachel paused and closed her eyes, remembering how well Mallory had liked the song. "Oh, Mallory. There was so much we could have done together, so much life—how could you? How could you?"

When the music returned to soft rock, Rachel shook her head. "You left me owing you, dammit. Why?"

She forced herself to continue, opening the cabinets over the counter and studying the few contents. Mallory's dishes were inexpensive and haphazardly stacked, then something odd about how the cabinet looked caught Rachel. Her finger traced the outside of the cabinet, nearest the window, and she looked inside. . . . "They don't match. The outside is larger than the inside shelving. . . ."

She held her breath as she measured the three-inch discrepancy with her fingers. Rachel slowly removed a stack of dinner plates and paused, holding them as a thin block of wood fell from the side of the cabinet onto the shelf.

A miniature cloth doll, sewn and stuffed, tumbled onto the countertop. The pins sticking from it gleamed eerily in the sunlight, like tiny swords.

Rachel slowly placed the plates on the table and lifted the doll. Something shivered coldly within her, a sense that a door was opening, an insight that Mallory had withheld. . . . "Mallory?"

The doll was obviously male, and the clothing was hand stitched. The crude shirt was pinstriped, tacked by a single button, and a short length of hair was fastened to the cloth head.

Rachel stood very still, studying the doll, sensing the true, bitter darkness that was Mallory's. The pins were those used by florists' corsages and boutonnieres. One slid through the doll's heart, and the other between its legs. "That message is pretty clear, Mallory . . . whoever this is, you didn't like him."

She held the doll, turning it, trying to imagine what her sister had felt. The eyes, stitched black Xs, stared back at her. The blue pinstripes of the shirt showed other perforation marks, and the doll seemed soft and worn. "You handled this a lot, didn't you, Mallory? Why? Why did you place one portion of your life in the closet—that good warm safe part, and this away from it?"

A chill shot through Rachel, despite the apartment's comfortable warmth. The dusty collection of small beach shells seemed to catch the slight breeze from the open window, rattling slightly before one tumbled into the sink. . . .

Instinct told Rachel that Mallory had dissected her life, keeping the mundane and good away from the darkness that had eventually killed her. The kitchen had been basically unused, and probably the safest place from searching eyes. Rachel carefully replaced the doll, this tiny insight into a Mallory she hadn't known, and looked at the next shelf above this one; it bore the same three-inch discrepancy. "Okay, Mallory. Give up whatever you hid when you were alive. I'd really like to meet this guy."

She eased the heavy casserole dish from the side of the next shelf and lifted away that block of wood. A cassette tape clattered onto the shelf.

As Rachel reached for it, her fingers trembled; she feared that it could reveal more darkness in Mallory's life. "You were so careful about your other things, to hide what you were, the precious moments in your life. Did you forget these?"

Rachel carefully inserted one tape into the radio's player and an eery moaning floated through the kitchen. She clicked it off immediately, and hurried to close the windows so that no one might hear.

When played, the tape was that of a woman moaning, and a man's voice was in the background, too low and indistinct to understand the words. He was angry and demanding, his rage filling the room. . . .

Rachel recognized Mallory's voice, the pain in it, the cries, and the anger. "You even come close to my family, and I'll kill you. *I'll kill you! You better not have raped Rachel, you bastard—*"

After the sharp crack that sounded like an open-handed slap, there was silence punctuated by whimpering . . .

"Oh, Mallory—" Unable to listen to more, Rachel turned off the tape, and silence again filled the apartment—the waiting heaviness of something that had passed and something that would happen. . . . She crumpled into a chair, wrapping her arms around herself, and shivering. "You were afraid for us. Raped me? Did you think that whoever this—this man is—would rape me?"

Mallory had used past tense—"raped." "When? In

New York? You knew whoever attacked me? That's why you were so furious? Mallory? Who is he? Oh, my God. . . . You never went anywhere since that time nine years ago, that five months vacation, before you opened Nine Balls. The attack on me was three years ago. This is a new type of tape. . . . Is it someone here? Is he here in Neptune's Landing? *Who is he?*"

Rachel rubbed her face and her shaking hands came away damp with tears. "Who is he? What did he do to you? Oh, I'll get him, if it's the last thing I do."

She replaced the doll and the tape, but the horrible sounds of Mallory being hurt echoed in the apartment and couldn't be erased from her mind. *What had she gone through? To protect Rachel? Why?*

"I know what everyone thinks, that you were too far gone at the end to be reliable. I don't believe that. I'm going to find out who hurt you and I'm getting his voice matched with that tape. I'm going to handle this very personally, Mallory."

Rachel held still, breathing quietly. "This is what you wanted, isn't it? For me to find these things? That's why I'm the new owner, right? Okay, then you're going to have to give me something to work on, Mallory. . . ."

But the apartment was silent and haunting—

That evening, Jada stopped by the apartment after completing her initial ice cream route. After swearing her sister to secrecy, Rachel showed her the doll. There was no reason now for her mother or Jada to know what Mallory went through during the making of that tape.

As they sat on Rachel's cream-colored designer love seat, the only furniture she'd shipped from New York,

Jada propped up her feet on an unpacked box and studied the doll. "You're after this guy, aren't you? Think this scary doll worked?"

"I think it gave Mallory some sense that she was not entirely helpless. It's only guesswork and not something to take to the police. They'd only put it down as a druggie's weird life-style."

"So all we have to do is to look for someone with heart problems and penile dysfunction, right?"

When Rachel nodded, Jada carefully removed one pin and placed it in his head. "Whoever he is should be getting a headache about now."

"I think whoever that doll is supposed to resemble was the man who threatened to harm us, if Mallory didn't do what he wanted. I think he blackmailed her into doing what he wanted," Rachel stated softly and watched her sister's stunned reaction. Jada didn't know about the attack three years before, but Rachel had linked that timing to Mallory's sharp decline. *You get the point, don't you?* he'd said to Rachel back then.

Rachel closed her eyes and settled back on the love seat, her arms around her cold body as she relived that nightmare. . . .

Her attacker couldn't perform, his erection soft against her, and then he'd gotten really mad, slapping her. But when she'd cried out, begging him to stop, he'd hardened again but had pushed away when the other two men had begun laughing. . . . *You get the point. . . . What point?*

Jada stared disbelievingly at Rachel. "You really think that Mallory was doing whatever she had to do to protect us? How did you get that idea?"

"We were the only people who mattered to her. I think she allowed what happened to her, because she was protecting us—and what she had built. I think someone was involved with her."

"Not my sperm donor. Not Kyle," Jada stated firmly. "In the end, she pushed him away like she did us. But Kyle still came here, checking on her, and filling in with lessons when she—when she wasn't feeling good. At that stage, Mom couldn't bear it anymore. He kept an eye on Mallory—or as much as she'd let him. This doll represents someone else, and she sure hated him. She always said she loved Kyle—as a brother and sometimes as a father, but always as a friend. He brings that out in most women—not you, of course."

"Is that why Kyle came to Nine Balls so often, to take Mallory's place, help her with her business?"

Kyle had cared for Mallory, that much was obvious by his stark anger and frustration last night on the beach. . . .

"He sure wasn't doing anything else with her, not since they were so hot years ago. All that died a long time ago. If she was seeing anyone in particular, she was hiding it from him—he would have gone after the guy. Kyle is very protective."

"Whoever it is, I am going to find him, search every detail of his life and make him miserable."

Jada stared at Rachel. "I've seen you like this before, a hell-be-damned attitude. You mean it, don't you? You're going to catch him and make him pay."

"I will. I swear I will."

"That could be dangerous. Count me in."

After Jada had gone, Rachel carefully replaced the

doll and settled onto her bed. She studied the scrapbook and mementoes, looking for any clue to indicate the man hurting her. . . . There were so many pictures, ribbons, flattened corsages, each preserved with intricate, loving care.

All legs and thin arms, young Mallory, Jada, and Rachel grinned impishly at the camera. There was Trina, holding her cue in one hand and her arm wrapped around Mallory who was holding a trophy.

In another picture was the usual collection of high school friends at a car wash, Mallory and Rachel soaked after spraying each other—Rachel's finger traced that photo and then moved to the next, Mallory sitting in Kyle's small red sports car, waving at the camera. . . .

The telephone rang and when Rachel answered, there was silence. "Probably a wrong number," she told herself and tried to believe it.

The next ring jarred her. If it was someone trying to scare her, it was working. That fear flipped into anger, because the same thing might have happened to Mallory—she grabbed the telephone and stated quietly, fiercely, "I know who you are now. And I'm coming after you."

"Anytime . . . I'd like that," Kyle drawled softly.

After a few heartbeats in which she recovered, Rachel said, "Maybe I just will, Scanlon."

She smoothed the picture of young Mallory in Kyle's red sports car. Rachel thought of the doll, of the hair that matched the color of Kyle's, but not his crisp texture and waves. "You wouldn't happen to know any of the men who visited Mallory after hours, do you?"

"Maybe."

"Like?"

"Men," he answered briefly, seriously. "Just men. But most of them liked her. She was a good listener and a good heart beneath all the crust. She also had pretty good survival instincts from scrambling around before your mother adopted her. Then something happened to her, and she didn't care anymore."

*You get the point, don't you?* the man had asked during the attack on Rachel. Whoever it was wanted to frighten Rachel badly enough that she would summon her family to her side—not her mother, or her younger sister, but someone who could understand a man's dark side—Mallory. . . .

"The money, Kyle. Why was she paying you each month?"

"That was between us."

"How's my cat?"

After a moment, the loud purring told her that Harry was quite happy. "Shall I bring him over to visit?" Kyle drawled.

"I'd rather just come pick him up."

"Like I said. Anytime he wants to come with you, it's fine with me. He eats a lot of food, Rachel. I had to get a litter box to keep him from digging up the girls' flowers."

Rachel smiled, and found herself enjoying Kyle's dilemma. "Oh, really?"

"He only eats sardines. They get expensive after a while. I'll have to charge you a boarding fee."

Harry would eat dry cat food if he were really hungry. But he knew how to wait and play his keeper into giving him more expensive fare. "Then bring him home."

"He likes it here."

"He's *my* cat."

The purring increased and Kyle said, "That's questionable now, honey."

"Kyle? Did you call just a minute ago and then hang up?"

After a brief pause, Kyle answered curtly, "No. Is someone calling you?"

"Probably a wrong number . . . don't say anything to Mom or Jada."

"That says you don't think it was a wrong number. Do you want me to come over?"

"In your dreams."

"Oh, I have them all right. Be careful, Rachel. And don't go to the beach alone. Call me."

She traced the photograph that had just slipped from the front cover of the scrapbook. It was of Kyle standing next to a girl about eight or so, who was proudly holding a small bike. The picture had been hidden between the cover and the backing, carefully taped inside, and that said it was precious and private. Rachel had to know the girl's identity and how she fitted into Mallory's life—and Kyle would know.

Rachel tapped the picture in her palm. She was very good at research and it was only a matter of time before she tracked down the girl. And Kyle was a definite link to the girl. . . . He definitely knew more about Mallory's life than anyone. And Rachel had learned more about her sister's adult life in a few moments with Kyle than she could have ever guessed had occurred. . . .

She might be packing that picnic basket after all. "Okay. Thanks. Good night, Kyle."

* * *

Three days passed in the first week of May, and each time Rachel looked at a man, she wondered if he'd known Mallory, if he'd hurt her. She noted those men with fine brown hair that might match the cloth doll's. In her trips to the print shop for Nine Balls' advertising flyers, in the grocery store, at the drugstore, Rachel talked about her excitement about reopening Nine Balls. If a man looked wary, she dropped in Mallory's name and watched his reaction.

There were too many reactions, including Leon's stunned expression when she asked him about Mallory's car, why she had sold it to him. "Uh—it needed a lot of work and she said she wasn't going anywhere . . . needed the money to pay bills. And I ran errands for her."

"Just before she died, did you take a letter from her to a post office away from here?" Rachel had asked, still puzzled about the last letter Mallory wrote to her, received on the day of the funeral.

"Yeah. She was in bad shape, but still sweet, you know. She always was a sweet person. I liked her," Leon had answered with a genuinely sad tone and Rachel noted that his thinning hair was red and coarse with curls, not fine and brown as that of the doll's.

Bob had looked sheepish when Rachel had asked him if he'd helped Mallory. "Some," he finally admitted. "She wasn't handling the business end of things very well at the last. She said some creditors were leaning on her. I told her not to get mixed up with loan sharks, and I didn't tell your mother, but that's my guess."

After going through Mallory's payments again, Rachel had called Kyle. "Know anything about loan-sharking, Scanlon?"

He had sounded distracted and the metallic click of tools sounded in the background. "Sure. How much do you want?"

"Not me. Did you ever loan money to Mallory? Tack a nice hefty interest on it, did you?"

He had chuckled at that. "You miss me. That's sweet, Rachel. Got that picnic basket ready for the beach? Just you and me?"

"I'm not sweet, Scanlon, and the basket is empty."

He chuckled again. "You really should try to be a little nicer. Then maybe you could keep a boyfriend and get a ring on your finger. If you do, let him wear the pants sometimes. You're pushy, Everly. Men don't usually like a woman who shoves them around."

"This from someone who's been married two times. You're giving me advice?"

Rachel had disconnected the line, but not before she'd heard Kyle's chuckle. "Glad you're enjoying yourself, bud. You may not later."

Four days of promotion and preparing later, and Rachel opened for a one-day test. She hoped to regain Nine Balls's customer base with an advertised special of free pool, and gain experience in handling business.

The busy, hectic day gave her more experiences than she'd planned—including a motorcycle gang who brought their own beer, despite ad work that designated no alcohol. An eight-year-old boy, accompanied by his parents, decided to throw the cue ball, instead of hitting it with a cue. A bag of chips spilled onto the floor and was tracked onto the playing area. One couple wanted their favorite playing table, which was also another couple's favorite table, and someone drew back their cue, hitting someone else in the eye with the butt. But Rachel did gain experience in sorting the serious players from those who were just taking advantage of a freebie, and those who were curious about the new owner—like the men who flirted with her.

Rachel closed early at five o'clock to recover with her mother and sister, who had helped throughout the day. Jada grinned at Rachel. "Harry has been at Kyle's for over a week now. So whose cat is he?"

Rachel frowned at Jada. She'd been too busy moving into the apartment, and preparing Nine Balls for the test day of free billiards, to deal with Kyle and retrieve her tomcat. Kyle's ex-wives had reportedly arrived, probably spoiling the tomcat until he might never come back.

When she had answered the telephone and loud purring was the only sound, Rachel had no doubt that Kyle was really enjoying himself.

"Bring him home," she'd yelled at an oddly quiet moment, when everyone in the billiards parlor had suddenly stopped talking. She'd heard a distinct, recognizable chuckle before hanging up the telephone.

"I enjoyed my little fifteen minutes of fame, and the money I won from taking bets was good," Trina murmured as she lined up for a trick shot. "And I'm out of practice . . . it's been a while since I've concentrated on anything but paperwork, sales, and car titles. This is called 'around the world.' "

Rachel leaned against an opposite table and sipped a

bottle of water as she replayed everything that had seemed so compressed into that one test day. . . .

Some of Mallory's regulars had been put off by her suicide and responded coolly to Rachel's invitations to reserve table times. "Bad karma," one had said.

Then there were the novelty seekers, wanting the "dirt" on why Mallory had finally decided to "off" herself. With the help of Trina and Jada, Rachel had quickly gotten rid of anyone inclined to rummage through Mallory's darkness.

One look at the wary preteens and teenagers who had turned up, and Rachel had seen why Mallory had felt good about her work; she understood why Saturday mornings were "teen time" at Nine Balls. The boys and girls were excited and dead serious about playing. Familiar with them, Trina had settled them into a game.

Several women, apparently friends, came in the early afternoon, wishing her well; they were eager to return to schedules. Terri and the others stopped by, and Tommy James had stopped to ask if he could help "tote and carry" anything, to "help out." The only male in a covey of women and children, he seemed uneasy as he played a quick game of stripes and solids with his wife, and was soon gone.

Rachel had decided to keep Mallory's basic schedule for now: designated week-day mornings for classes and women-only, Saturday mornings for youths, and then two in the afternoon until ten at night for regular customers. A grueling schedule for one person, Rachel's family had already offered to help, once she was ready to open permanently.

"You can do that shot, Mom," Rachel murmured.

When she was younger, she'd seen her mother put on exhibitions many times for charity events. Then, as a retired pro nine years ago, Trina had helped Mallory's Nine Balls off to a good start by helping with youth and women's classes.

Trina took a deep breath, poised for the shot by putting the cue ball on top of the rail. Three balls were lined up in front of the side pocket closest to her.

"Go for it, Mom," Jada said.

"I'm older now, you know, girls. Don't expect too much," Trina said as she placed a piece of chalk on the rail to keep the cue ball from rolling off. "You should be practicing this, not me."

"It takes too much time to concentrate. I just like to shoot," Jada said. "Big sis has the touch, that dead calm when you isolate everything from you. I don't."

"Hush," Trina murmured and shot the cue ball with enough power to hit the middle and the last ball. The first ball, poised in front of the side pocket nearest Trina, dropped into it. The middle ball rolled down table into a side pocket. But the shot was named for the last ball's path; it shot diagonally to a corner side rail, hit the opposite rail, then hit the rail just down from where it had started and rolled diagonally to the other corner, dropping into the side pocket.

Trina shook her head. "That was an accident. I've got to practice if I'm going to do much exhibition shooting for you, Rachel. I helped Mallory teach the basics after Nine Balls was going well, so I really haven't tried any of this for a long time."

"You've still got it, Mom. That was skill, not an accident. I never doubted you at all." Jada racked the balls in a triangular shape, the eight ball in the center. "Let's play until Bob calls to say he's got supper ready. Gotta love a man who knows how to keep us fed during busy days. You lucked out on him, Mom. Maybe you'd better take him up on that marriage offer. Your kids are grown and almost out of the house. Make that a big white wedding, will you? You deserve it since dear old Dad wasn't up to par. . . . I'm tired and going home. Someone else can break."

"Your father is gone now. He died a few years ago. Let's just forget about hard times now, shall we?" Trina replied.

"You were the one with hard times, Mom," Rachel said. "And you crawled out. I remember."

"I think I was down so low, financially and psychologically, that there wasn't anywhere else to go, but up. I kept going for you kids, and having some skill at pool, getting recognized, did something for me inside, as a woman, apart from being a mother. My pride came back, something I'd lost gradually—it's not worth talking about really."

The three women were quiet for a moment, because there was another way a woman could go—and Mallory had taken it. Then Jada said, "It's like she's still here. I mean Mallory, before she—before she just seemed to give up. She was always good about business, though, keeping this place running well. She was great with kids. She should have had several. She might have had that little house with the picket fence she always wanted, with a flower garden to tend and a swing in the backyard."

After Jada left, Rachel's mind was on Mallory, and

the children she had decided not to have. Who was the father of that girl in the picture? Kyle? Did he and Mallory have a child?

He'd denied that. But Mallory and he had been close for years. Could Rachel believe him?

The girl in the picture was maybe seven or eight years old, and Trina would have mentioned Mallory's pregnancy. But whoever the girl was, she was special to Mallory, enough to be hidden between the cover and front paper of the scrapbook.

Rachel listened to the building, the tiny creaks that were unfamiliar. Jada was right: Mallory's presence seemed almost palpable, not as she had become, but soft as she had been early in life.

Rachel chalked her cue, and moved into play the game with Trina. "It's been a long time. I only played when I came home to visit."

"Didn't you play in New York?"

Rachel leaned toward the table, and hesitated as her mother adjusted her position, a touch here and there, moving her right leg back just that fraction, lifting her right arm higher. "A few private games at the brass's houses. And at one time, friends and I had regular after-work games. It helped relieve a lot of negative stress."

*That had stopped after her attack three years ago.*

"Easy on your stroke, honey," Trina advised. "You've been gripping your cue really tight. How's the apartment? If you decide you don't like it, you can always move home."

Trina stepped back and critically studied Rachel's posture. "Okay. Just remember to keep that leg back and your elbow higher, ninety degrees to the stick. I've been watching you today. Lean down in, stretch out. . . . You're punching the ball, honey. Smooth stroke—"

She paused to adjust the "rack," placing the one ball directly on the "footspot."

At Trina's nod, Rachel made the break, but didn't pocket a ball. In the game of nine ball, the first shooter to pocket a ball would then play the lowest numbered ball on the table, the nine ball as last. Trina shot next and sank four balls in succession, before Rachel took out the five and six, then missing her shot to the seven ball. Trina finished all the balls and shook her head as they collected the balls from the pockets and Rachel racked them. "I don't feel much like playing, if that's okay with you, Rachel," Trina said tiredly.

"Fine. Thank you for helping today. I just needed the experience and I really got it today. It's been a long first day, but a good one, I think."

Trina's eyes shimmered with tears. "Things should have been better for Mallory. I just couldn't bring her out. She got worse and worse—"

Rachel held her mother tight. "Mom, it isn't your fault."

"But it is. Mallory always felt inferior, that she couldn't do things right. I tried to reassure her, but somehow that darkness was always there—like she wasn't up to par, and I knew it—I recognized it from what I'd gone through. Bob and I got her this really nice car—used, one of those little-old-lady-type things— well tended and easy on gas. I thought she'd take some pride in it, but she ran into a wall—a one-car accident on an open road. She'd been drinking and—I wonder now if she wanted to kill herself back then."

Within Rachel's arms, Trina's body shivered. "Before that, I thought maybe when she got this place, something of her own to build from, to succeed, it would make her turn that corner. For a while, it seemed to be working, and then in the last few years, she did turn a corner, the wrong way—and I could only watch. I didn't want to go to the apartment after she—left. I couldn't bear to see what others were talking about."

Rachel eased away and reached for a tissue, handing it to her mother, who suddenly looked so helpless. In some remote corner of Rachel's mind, she'd hoped that Trina had come to Nine Balls for closure. "You didn't come into the apartment in the month that I was gone? I left the key with you."

Trina stepped back and shook her head. She separated her cue and placed the two pieces into the carrying case. "No. Why do you ask?"

"I thought maybe you'd come in at some time during the month—or maybe while I was out with the others, burning Mallory's things."

"But, honey, I would have told you." Trina frowned slightly. "She'd planned for her death, they say . . . like the letter to you after her funeral."

Her cell phone rang and Trina smiled. "Jada says Bob has dinner ready."

"I think I want to stay here, Mom. I'm exhausted and have some things to do for a 'Grand Opening.' If I'm going to make a profit off this place, the money-people in this town need to feel comfortable. They're edgy now, not wanting to be connected with gossip. Your exhibitions should help . . . they'd like to be able to make those shots. Did you notice how many teens came today?"

"Mallory really worked with them. 'Focus on the balls and on your life and you can become anything you want,' she'd say. In the end, she wasn't focusing on the balls and she rarely played. But she really had worked with those kids. . . . I don't like you staying in that apartment. If you don't want to stay with us, then there are lots of nice houses for rent. I always felt that if Mallory would only have balanced her life more, taken some time away, maybe hired someone to help her, that she wouldn't have been so driven."

"You may be right."

Trina smoothed Rachel's hair back from her cheek. "Don't let this place get to you, honey. Promise?"

"Promise."

# Eight

**"ONCE UPON A TIME THERE WERE THREE SISTERS. . . ."**
Rachel ran her hand along the smooth driftwood log.
Unable to settle down after working so hard that day,
she sat and looked at the ocean, the sunset touching
gold on the crests of the waves. But in her mind, she
saw three young girls, romping and splashing each
other, building people of sand, covering each other and
forming enormous breasts on their budding bodies.
"Mallory, you've got to help me understand. I can't
leave you like this, not thinking about what I could have
done, leave me owing you—"

Rachel picked up a smooth white pebble, one just
like those she'd collected long ago on this same beach,
amid girlish laughter and dreams. "Don't you dare
leave me without giving me a chance to pay you back. I
miss you so much, Mallory."

The seagulls cried, flying white against the graying
sky; the waves crashed upon the rocks, the surf with the
same endless sound, the same smells—

She frowned slightly, listening to the seagulls, and to
a girl's cries of terror. Rachel stood, following the cries,
running toward that strip of sand above the driftwood
line, near the trees.

In the shadowy light between sunset and night, two teenage boys were holding a girl on a blanket while a third stood above her, unzipping his jeans. His intent was clear as he bent to position himself upon the sobbing girl. "You will stop that now," Rachel ordered fiercely as she stepped up on a log and then back down to walk up to the boys, the girl sobbing at her feet. "Let her go."

The boy who had unzipped his pants, stood leering at her and a whiskey tang mixed with salty air. "You willing to take her place, pool hall lady?"

"I said, 'let her go,'" Rachel ordered the boys still holding the girl.

"Hey, Jimmy. Maybe we'd better—" one of them cautioned as they released the girl whose two-piece bathing suit had been cast aside. She scurried to collect it, and Rachel briskly picked up the blanket, shook it and tossed it to the girl, whose heavy mascara lines streaked down her pale cheeks. She edged behind Rachel and her voice was hoarse and uneven. "They said it was a party . . . that other people would be here," she said as she huddled beneath the blanket. "They . . . they . . . wanted me to drink and I didn't want to and then—"

"I know about what happened then," Rachel stated curtly as the other two boys started hunkering away. She recognized them from earlier in the day, when they'd come to check out Nine Balls. "What are your names, hot-shots? I'd like to remember the names of three boys it took to handle one girl."

The leader stood his ground. "Don't say anything. She'll turn us in."

"You've got that right. Underage and drinking, trying to rape a girl." Furious with the boys, fearing for the girl, Rachel held her cold hand. She knew exactly how the girl was feeling. "I'm taking her with me."

"Like hell. We're not finished with Angie yet. You're next." Jimmy moved toward her and suddenly Rachel was beyond fear, burning with anger. She clenched her fists and stood her ground, though the youth was much bigger. "You should know that I detest bullies. One step more and you're in for trouble."

"Hey, Jimmy . . . maybe you'd better—"

"Shut up, chickens." He watched the others run into the woods and then, his expression turned mean. He took that one step toward Rachel, and her punch in his midsection. He doubled, coughing and grabbing his stomach and when he straightened, he lunged at her, taking them both down into the sand. He was heavy and strong, but Rachel wasn't letting anything happen to her a second time; she knew exactly where to thrust her knee.

With a guttural cry of pain, he fell upon her, taking the breath from her lungs. Suddenly his weight was lifted up and away easily, and Kyle was looking down at her. He held the youth upright by his shirt as easily as if he were a kitten. "Are you hurt?" he asked Rachel.

She was winded and couldn't move. "Do I look like I'm hurt?" she asked glaring up at him. "I'm just catching my breath, Scanlon."

His grin was brief and admiring. Jimmy, clearly terrified by Kyle, was holding his crotch and groaning. "Apologize to the lady," Kyle ordered, giving the boy a shake.

The boy mumbled something and Kyle said, "Louder."

He reached down to Rachel, his big hand open. Rachel took it, letting him pull her to her bare feet. Kyle glanced quickly up and down her body. "You're lucky she didn't beat you to a pulp. But I just may."

"I'm underage, buddy," the youth smirked. "You'd be picking on a minor."

Kyle's expression hardened. "Let's just say that I know that while you'd feel a lot of pain, you wouldn't be bruised at all. They'd think you were faking. Say it."

"Sorry."

"Say it to her, and mean it this time." Kyle lifted Jimmy up until he stood on tiptoe.

"Sorry," he grumbled.

"Well, then. I think we all better go home. Except you. You're going to the police station and you're going to tell them your buddies' names. Can you take the girl home, honey?" Kyle gently asked Rachel.

"I don't want anybody to know," Angie cried out. "I'm not supposed to be here. If my parents found it—"

*I don't want anybody to know. Not my family, not anyone in Neptune's Landing. . . .*

Rachel had told Mallory the same thing three years ago. She looked at the girl's shaking body, her disheveled hair, her pale face, eyes huge and shadowed with the terror that still rocked her. . . .

That image lasted after Rachel dropped the girl at her house, advising her to tell her parents and that other girls could pay a heavy price if she didn't stop the boys. . . .

Rachel had just pulled into her parking lot when

Kyle's rig pulled up beside hers. Because her legs were still unsteady from the anger she'd felt, from the flashback to another time, Rachel leaned back against her car. She wrapped her arms around herself and tried to stop shaking.

Her voice sounded far away, tight with a mix of fear and anger. "Her name was Angie . . . she's a really sweet girl. I don't know if she's going to press charges or not. That's her parents' business. She was just doing what any girl would have done, going to a beach party with what she thought was the in-crowd, a date with the high school sports star. But he had another party planned for her."

"Jimmy and I had a little chat before I turned him over to the police. He and his friends are going to have my special attention. His parents are rich and he'll likely get out of this, so I recommended that he might think about a school somewhere else. If he bothers you, I want to know. Got it?" Kyle stated darkly as he studied Rachel.

He reached to wrap his hand around Rachel's nape, tugging her close to him and tucking her face against his throat. Rachel reacted instantly, locking her arms around him, holding on to his safety.

"It's okay, honey. You've got a right to be reacting now. You were a little outmatched, you know, but you still went for it."

Rachel noted the humor in his tone, but she wasn't up to sparring with Kyle. He was big and strong and she needed him right then. She gave herself to the comforting hand stroking her back, to the deep rumble of his voice and his warmth. At the moment, she could have clawed herself into him, wrapped him around her, if she could. "What were you doing there?"

"That big Caddie is hard to miss along the beach road. I pulled in just in time to see you sprinting across that sand. I wasn't feeling cheerful, not after I'd warned you not to go to the beach alone." He smiled slowly, tilted his head and studied her. "I bet you have sand in your shoes right now and you're so worked up you haven't noticed."

Still locked in her own attack, refreshed by the girl's, Rachel forced herself to step back from him. She folded her arms around herself as she leaned back against her car and tried to draw her shields around her. Kyle smoothed her hair and shook his head as he said gently, "It's not a crime to need someone to hold you, especially not after what you've just been through. You're just reacting now. . . ."

"I was so mad, I could have—"

Kyle's look was perceptive. "Been there, done that. But there's something else going on inside you, isn't there? Want to tell me about it?"

She wasn't telling any one and the one person who had seen her through the darkness was gone—"No. There's nothing to tell."

"Don't believe you, but it's your business."

"Thanks."

Kyle smiled at that. "Always a lady, Everly."

"Now isn't the time to needle me, Scanlon."

"Maybe not. But whatever is riding you is more than what happened earlier and just maybe you need to talk to someone about it. I'm offering." He bent to wrap his fingers around her ankle and lifted away one shoe, shaking the sand from it, then the other. Holding her shoes in one hand, his other hand curved around her leg as he rose to stand in front of her. The trail of his touch warmed up her body and locked onto her waist. "Okay, now?" he asked gently.

She was afraid to move, afraid her legs wouldn't carry her. "You didn't need to check on me. I'm fine. I just want to stand here in the night air for a while before going in."

"Nice night." Kyle moved to stand close beside her, his arm going around her waist as he looked up at the stars. She knew what he was doing, giving her the safety and warmth she badly needed, wrapped in a casual stance, so that she wouldn't find reason to step away. His hand caressed her waist and Rachel found herself leaning against him, tucked into the protective cove of his body. It felt too right and in another minute, she'd—

Rachel moved away, this time trusting her legs to walk away from Kyle and the need to make love with him, to have him in her, around her, tasting him— "Good night," she said as she walked toward the apartment's stairs.

When she'd reached the top, she turned to see him still standing in the same position, watching her. He was still there when she opened and closed the door, looking out the window. Only then did Kyle get into his rig and slowly drive away.

At ten o'clock that night, Rachel awoke from the brief necessary nap and turned slowly from her stomach to her back. She'd had to put the beach incident out of her mind. She wasn't in New York, fighting an attacker; she was in Mallory's bedroom, the ceiling fan rotating slowly, the reflection of it caught in the closet's glass mirrors.

The room held nothing of Mallory now, the muted creams and greens of Rachel's furniture was nothing like Mallory's heavy walnut bookcase, bed, and chest of drawers. The heavy drapes had been replaced by white plantation blinds.

Rachel lay thinking about her sister, the woman who had died in this room. "Are you still here, Mallory?"

*I'll always be here when you need me,* Mallory had said. *I love you, kiddo, and take it from someone who knows, your attack didn't change the person you are, didn't lower you at all. You get back whatever you think they took, and you do your thing. You're tough. You can do it. . . .*

*Then Mallory had planned her death . . . and Leon had driven out of town to mail her last letter. . . .*

"I'm still mad at you, Mallory. You didn't let me help. You're not supposed to close off the ones you love. . . ."

Troubled by her unsettled emotions and exhaustion, Rachel took a long shower, dressed in her comfortable men's undershorts and a worn T-shirt, then padded into the kitchen to heat the casserole her mother had brought that morning. While eating in the living room, her legs extended from the couch to the coffee table, she surfed through television programs and studied her new living quarters.

The apartment had a homey look now, pieced together by Rachel's things, used furniture and discount store purchases, and a contribution of odds and ends from her mother's and Bob's houses. The shells she'd collected with her sisters filled the glass bottom of a lamp, a flat earth-brown pottery bowl on her coffee table held the white smooth pebbles they'd collected on the beach. She'd placed three lavender-scented candles of different heights within the pebbles, the flames throwing eerie shadows on the lamp table's framed pictures of the Everly women.

"Soho shabby," Jada had labeled the apartment as they'd fitted a covering over a couch Bob had said he'd been wanting to discard. The cream color matched Rachel's own designer love seat beautifully. Jada had plumped the stamped-fern-motif sofa pillows, and studied her work critically, taking in the expansive painting that Rachel had taken to New York to remind her of Neptune's Landing—a seascape of the beach, the waves white and foamy upon it and crashing against a mountainous black rock that disappeared into a layer of mist. "Not as nifty as all your contemporary black and glass furniture. And, gee, not a big wrought-iron wine rack in sight—I always thought that was so classy at your place, the bottles of wine poking out of that thing and the different shaped wineglasses you used when entertaining. Your parties had real class—quiet music, fancy dinners, expensive wine. Think your boyfriend will like it?"

"Those parties were more for business than for fun, and you know that Mark and I were over a long time ago," Rachel had said, remembering their furious argument after her attack: Mark Bradburn was certain she'd been flirting at the pool hall before taking that walk across the park, and he'd resented her playing billiards with her friends anyway. Tramping back and forth across Rachel's New York apartment, Mallory had been furious with Mark's assumption that she'd flirted while playing pool. "So the only reason you gave the police was because you beat a few bastards at pool? You actually think whoever he was came after you for that?"

Rachel's assailants words tumbled back into her mind: *He'd known her name, he'd used it while humiliating her, exposing her body—he'd known that she worked in an office, dated and lived with a rising executive, and that she jogged alone. . . .*

She pulled herself back from that awful night and opened the letter that she'd read many times, the last letter Mallory had written: "I know you don't like Kyle, but try to understand that he was my friend, and maybe try to repay him a little for his kindnesses since I can't, will you?"

*Kyle.* The mention of his name brought Rachel to her feet; she stripped away the damp towel from around her head. She walked into the bathroom, spreading the towel over the rack to dry, then returned to the kitchen and poured herself a glass of wine, a little private relaxation at the end of the day.

The candles resting inside the layer of white pebbles were inviting, and Rachel watched them, thinking of Mallory. "You're still here, aren't you, Mallory?"

Her breath caused the candlelight to sway and flicker against the shadows. "What do you want from me? What will it take to make you rest?"

She went to the kitchen cabinet and removed the

cloth doll, taking it to the candlelight. "Who is this, Mallory? Who is he? You were protecting us, weren't you? By sacrificing yourself?"

A slight clatter at the back stairs caused Rachel to go to the window overlooking the parking lot. Tommy James's pickup was parked beside the steps, and he was lifting the trash sacks from the garbage cans, placing them into the pickup's bed. Rachel opened the door and flipped on the porch light. "Tommy?"

The light caught his upturned face, his expression stunned and blank as Rachel moved down the back steps. "Tommy, what are you doing here? It's not your usual run."

At close range, Tommy was obviously nervous. "I noticed that you had a lot of trash bags stacked outside the stairs. Usually those big bins are enough to handle Nine Balls stuff. Business was pretty good today, that free day of pool and all. That's good advertising, Rachel, but maybe you need a Dumpster now. You have more trash than usual."

"It won't be all the time. Some of those things are Mallory's. Just some odds and ends."

Tommy moved quickly to toss the bags onto the back of his pickup and the wind riffled his soft brown hair—hair like that of Mallory's doll. "You need any help tonight, Rachel? I mean any cleaning inside the pool hall, or need anything heavy toted for you? I'd really like to help."

*Was Tommy James the man on the tape, the man hurting Mallory and threatening her family? Was he the father of her unborn babies?*

Rachel gripped the handrail and tried to speak

evenly. Tommy had a loving wife and two sweet little girls; if he were involved with Mallory and that fact got out, he'd be ruined in Neptune's Landing. He would have a lot riding on anything inappropriate left behind that could tie him to Mallory. How far would he go to protect his life? Murder?

She'd known Tommy all her life; he was a community leader, active in church and school, and he had always been upright. She was just imagining his nervousness, that shifting of his eyes and body, that startled expression. Tommy James wouldn't hurt anyone. . . . "No, thanks. I've got a handle on it, I think. Maybe some other time?"

But his hair was the same shade of brown as that of Mallory's doll—and of many other men in town.

Tires squalled as a big beige Ford Taurus pulled into the parking lot. Sally Mae slammed out of it and walked to stand by Tommy. "I got Mom to watch the kids, while I hunted for you. Why are you here?" she demanded hotly.

Tommy seemed to shrink. His glance at Rachel said he was wary and embarrassed. "I was just getting a little ahead. There's more stuff here than usual. Tomorrow is trash day."

Sally Mae was shaking with anger. "You don't have any reason to be here."

She stared up at Rachel and took in the men's undershorts and T-shirt. Her "Don't you look all comfy?" wasn't sweet.

Kyle's big Hummer pulled into the parking lot and parked by Rachel's Cadillac. He got out, leaned against it, and folded his arms.

"Is everything okay, Sally Mae?" Rachel asked carefully. Was it possible that Sally Mae was jealous of her?

Or was Tommy looking for something that could tie him to Mallory?

He got into his pickup, slammed the door, and drove onto Atlantis Street. "He was just getting ahead of a big work schedule," Sally Mae said furiously. "He won't do it again. But you shouldn't go running around, or talking to other women's husbands, without wearing a bra. I didn't think you'd be like Mallory, but maybe I'm wrong."

"I just came out to see—" But Sally Mae was in her car and racing after Tommy. Rachel frowned slightly. "Okay. Have a nice night, guys."

Had Tommy come for a reason other than collecting the trash bags? Was he looking for something?

Had he been involved with Mallory?

With Jimmy immediately released into his parents' custody, Kyle wanted to make certain that Rachel wasn't in danger and had returned to check on her. Sally Mae and Tommy in Nine Balls' parking lot at eleven o'clock at night probably wasn't a friendly social call and Kyle had decided to stick around to see what happened. By the way the Jameses' left, the big Taurus's tires leaving rubber, the meeting hadn't been pleasant.

In the light coming from the apartment's doorway, Rachel looked feminine, small, and vulnerable in her baggy clothes. She gripped the handrail and stared after the Jameses, then as she refocused on Kyle who was walking toward her, she seemed dazed. She had that sick, pale look that said she was adjusting to an unsavory fact. But then Rachel's fine mind was trying to fit Tommy into Mallory's life—and she was just starting to see that Mallory didn't always turn the town's husbands away.

"What are you doing here?" she asked unevenly.

"Just stopped by for the convention. Any problems?" Kyle placed his boot on the bottom step and watched Rachel wade through her thoughts as she studied her wiggling toes in those cute little pink thongs. She was hurting, and feeling helpless wasn't a thing Kyle liked; he'd had enough experience with Mallory.

Rachel looked up at him suddenly and her expression wasn't helpless—it was tough and fierce, the kind of cold mad that didn't go away easily, the kind that ate at a person's gut until they had to do something. And even revenge might not take that burning ache away. . . .

He'd learned to survive as a child and Kyle knew a lot about that kind of frustrated rage, how it could destroy chances for a good life. He ached for Rachel, who was just discovering how badly raw anger could burn, how deep it could go, obliterating life's positive opportunities. . . .

"Yes, I think there is a problem. Did you know about Tommy and Mallory?" she asked briskly with that lift of her head, that attitude showing in the flash of her eyes.

But just that touch of breathlessness in her voice underlined that Rachel was really shaken. He admired her more at that moment than any other—the girl knew how to cover her emotions too well, had taken a bad blow to the heart. "I suspected a relationship. He always liked her. Mallory could never turn away anyone with real trouble, and Sally Mae is real trouble. He wouldn't have hurt Mallory, if that's what you're thinking. Tommy is gentle, like she was. They both have— Mallory had—a special sort of innocence that nothing could take away. That really irritates people who do not have it . . . they need to ruin those with it."

Rachel turned and started up the stairs. Halfway up, she turned and looked down at him. "Are you coming or not?"

He couldn't resist teasing her, hoping to distract her from that slap of harsh reality. "What's in it for me?"

But Rachel wasn't sparring tonight; she was dead serious. "I want you to listen to something."

"Sure it's not too late? I mean, if someone saw me coming upstairs they just might get the wrong idea." Kyle thought about the different cars that had stayed for hours when Mallory was alive; he didn't want her visitors getting the wrong impression of Rachel.

Her jaw had that stubborn set, her tone cool and crisp. "I'll handle gossip. If you're afraid, then go on home. But I really don't see how gossip could hurt you much. A man living with his two ex-wives surely has had some taste of it."

"Oh, she's real mad," Kyle murmured as he moved slowly up the stairs. An invitation from Rachel could only mean trouble, and he should know better. He stood inside the apartment, moved slightly aside to let her close the door behind him. She reminded him of a businesswoman in an office, getting ready for a conference.

Those dark brown eyes were watching him as he took in the living room and kitchen changes, a sophisticated retro look blended with comfort and style. "Nice."

Then he looked down to her breasts and realized there was nothing but soft, sweet curves beneath her shirt. Rachel never stopped studying him; she didn't move as he took in the loose undershorts and her legs, down to those pretty pink thongs with the flowers. "Is something wrong?" she asked as she flipped on a lamp, the glass base filled with seashells.

The movement had tightened the soft cloth across her bottom, and the slight bend of her body had revealed one really nice bare cheek that would just fit in his hand—"Not a thing."

"I'll be just a minute," she said and walked into the bedroom. The heavy scents and dark brooding colors were gone, replaced by light shades and simplicity. Candles were burning in a brown bowl, the flames flickering, casting shadows on the big painting of the beach. Something smelled really good, and Kyle thought of the French dish Iris had tried to cook recently. When she wasn't looking, Pup had loved it.

Rachel's laptop was sitting on the kitchen table, tiny little fish swimming around on the screen, a yellow pad and pen nearby.

Kyle ran his hand across his chest where the sorrow for Mallory lay, cold and hard. The apartment looked clean and fresh and—Kyle frowned slightly. There was something else here that he couldn't define: Mallory's favorite scent, vanilla, before she'd started in on heavy, musky perfumes, seemed to hover close. He held very still and something seemed to wrap around him. It was just the candles, he told himself, his emotions uneasy because he hadn't been in the apartment since before Mallory had died.

Then the air stilled, and he could almost hear Mallory call softly, "Kyle? I need you, Kyle. . . ."

He studied the flickering candles, the shadows dancing on the wall, and they blended with the echoes of Mallory's calls, the times when she couldn't handle business or herself.

Rachel came into the living room dressed in loose black slacks and a silky Chinese-style tunic that probably cost plenty. She moved to the small minibar and looked at him as she lifted a bottle of wine and questioned him with a look. When he shrugged, she poured wine into two goblets and walked toward him. She handed one glass to him and then took a sip of hers, her eyes locked on his face. "Do you like the changes?"

"They're okay." He picked up one of the candles and inhaled its scent. It was lavender, tiny purple buds embedded into the wax. Yet the vanilla scent seemed to linger around him. "Nice," he said to cover his curiosity and replaced the candle.

"So you were up here a lot?"

Rachel was smooth, he decided, taking her time to get what she wanted. "Sometimes. Sometimes she needed me."

Mallory's wispy voice echoed in his mind. *Kyle? I need you, Kyle. . . .*

Rachel's dark eyes locked on him. "Are you certain that there was nothing else?"

He didn't want Rachel to know how badly her sister had gotten at the last, that the images weren't pleasant. "Something smells good. Are you serving dinner?"

"I can get you something. Sit down."

Rachel was being too accommodating and that caused him to be suspicious. Kyle eased onto the big couch and watched Rachel move gracefully into the kitchen. She spooned something onto a plate and in a minute, the microwave sounded. She collected a napkin and a fork and walked back to him.

"Do much of this in New York, did you?" he asked, noting her grace, the way she moved—she'd make love like that, he supposed—smooth, graceful, keeping her poise, and getting what she wanted. He had no doubt that Rachel could leave a man hurting, but he didn't intend for that to happen. . . .

"Enough. I wanted the usual things—that big fat executive chair and a key to a private washroom. Having parties was a way to move up in my career. I did a little hosting for other people. I got what I wanted, a neat little V.P. job, and I wanted more. . . . But that's Mom's casserole, not mine."

Kyle got the point: Rachel was pointing out that their lives were different, that he didn't fit into hers. There was a lot to admire about Rachel Everly, Kyle thought, especially all those soft curves beneath that Chinese outfit. "Well, then, you'll have to cook for me sometime, won't you?"

"I usually have something in mind when I issue invitations, Scanlon."

"Ah. Ulterior motives. I'll keep that in mind." While listening to the soft music she'd started in the small entertainment center, he ate the baked meatball, pasta, and cheese wedge with a spring-greens salad. The wine was a good Napa Valley red, smooth with a smoky cherry bite; it matched Rachel—smooth, full of body and strength, with an underlying nip that could satisfy and excite.

A man could really enjoy playing games with Rachel—waiting for her to deliver what she wanted, Kyle decided reluctantly, as she curled up at the other end of the couch. She sat sipping her wine and studying him and Kyle knew that she had an agenda; he wouldn't be alone with her, in this apartment, if she didn't.

He placed the empty plate on the coffee table, tossed his napkin on top of it, and sat back to look at her. Playing with Rachel was dangerous. On the other hand, Kyle never could leave a motor untuned and humming. The real satisfaction was in the ride, either smooth and long—or a hard drive to the finish. He was starting to get hard just thinking about making love to her—watching her react to each touch—and decided to speed up whatever she had in mind. "Okay, we went through that little routine to get me fed and pliable. Now what's up? What do you want?"

He didn't trust her slight, tight smile. Then Rachel reached to a side table, jerked open a drawer, and withdrew a pad and pencil. She held it out to him. "Here. Make a list of every man you even 'suspect' of visiting Mallory, of being involved with her."

"Now that would be telling." Kyle ignored the pad and she tossed it to the table. He didn't know all of the men who had visited Mallory, though he was pretty certain some of Neptune's Landing's elite businessmen came to her for private pleasures their wives wouldn't supply.

At first, he'd tried to stop them and the outsiders that

somehow found Mallory's door, but she'd been livid, furious with him. *I have to have them . . . you don't understand, Kyle, and you don't have to—just take your do-gooder interference somewhere else.*

And then Mallory had hugged him, held onto him like a lifeline. *I love you, Kyle, but I have to do this. . . .*

With such a list, Rachel could get into real trouble, because these men didn't want their lives disturbed. "Maybe you'd just better let this go, Rachel. Let Mallory rest."

She scooped up his plate and was on her feet moving into the kitchen again. She moved quickly, efficiently, purposefully, and that was the Rachel he knew—set on her goals, determined. "There's something I want you to hear."

While the tape played, Rachel stayed near the entertainment center. She leaned against the wall as she watched his reaction—Kyle didn't like the sound of a woman in pain; he didn't care that his expression revealed how the sounds sickened him and twisted his gut with hatred for any man who would hurt a woman like that. "Turn it off."

The pitiful sounds clicked off and Rachel spoke quietly, bitterly, "There's more, but that's enough to get the idea. . . . I'm going to catch that bastard and ruin him."

He turned to her as she sat on the other end of the couch. "You think I hurt her?"

Kyle thought of the times he'd revived Mallory, the helplessness of taking care of a woman who wouldn't defend herself, who wouldn't let him defend her.

"No—"

"You'd better believe I wouldn't. You're coming

close to insulting me, Rachel, so watch it. There's limits to what a man can tolerate, and being labeled as someone who mistreats women is mine. You may not like me, but I've never touched a woman like that. Back off."

Her voice was cool, precise, a businesswoman briskly presenting a sales package to a prospective client. "I just had to know. No one else knows about that tape. She hated a man, Kyle, and I want you to help me find out who did this to her. I want to keep Mom and Jada out of this."

He was on his feet, pacing across the vanished floors, furious with the men that Mallory knew, who brought her down, who used her . . . furious with himself for not being able to stop them—or her very determined path to self-destruction. "You think I haven't tried to find out who was hurting her? What spineless son of a bitch wouldn't want his own babies? Mallory wasn't talking, not even when she was drugged. Who knows? It might have been anyone, or someone who just stopped by when they felt like knocking her around. It could have been one or a few. Jesus, Rachel. Don't you think I've tried?" he demanded again.

"But it wasn't Tommy?" she pressed.

Kyle remembered the scenes where Mallory had brusquely ordered Tommy to carry out Nine Balls garbage, speaking to him as if he were nothing—and Tommy had been too eager to please. "No. I think he was in love with her and Mallory knew it was no good. She knew he had a wife and children and that his life would be ruined if they were together. In her way, she protected Tommy by turning him away."

Rachel stood abruptly and rubbed her hands together. "Whoever it was, she hated him. She felt powerless, but she took her revenge in an unusual way for someone in this part of the country."

"What do you mean? 'This part of the country?'"

She didn't answer, but leveled a look at him. "The other wives? Did they know? Could one of their husbands have wanted to keep Mallory quiet?"

"I don't know. Mallory wasn't talking. I got the impression that there was only one that she really hated, some guy with a real power trip and a hold over her."

Rachel went into the kitchen and returned with a small ragdoll, evidently meant to be male, and handed it to him. "The Northwest coast isn't exactly voodoo country, but the meaning of this is hard to miss. It was something she needed to try, anyway."

Kyle studied the pins, the different perforations remaining in the worn cloth, several in the heart and head and more in the crotch. "Think it worked?"

"Jada does know about this doll, but not the tape. I don't care if Mallory was a consenting adult. He's got brown hair, Kyle—fine, brown hair. I think that shirt and button belonged to him. And I want him."

All this time, and Kyle had no idea that Mallory practiced voodoo. "So do I. You know this could represent several men, not an individual."

"I don't think so. But I think this was a special man, one who threatened her with the safety of people she loved. I think that this was something she held over him, some part of her that he couldn't reach, some private pleasure of her own."

Kyle thought of the little girl that Mallory loved more than herself, and perhaps even more than her family.

"Just for curiosity's sake, how do you know that isn't my hair? It's the same shade."

"Too soft and fine. Yours has a crispness and a tendency to wave."

"So you noticed. Should I be flattered?"

"No. It's just a fact. I felt it. Why else do you think I'd touch it?"

"At the moment, you had your reasons. So did I . . . Jada can't keep a secret and you know it. You deliberately told her, didn't you? To start things rolling so that you could get this guy to come out of the woodwork, to show himself? I thought you were a smart woman, honey, but you've just asked for it."

"I'll handle it." Rachel replaced the doll and walked to the door. She opened it slightly. "Okay. Thanks for coming. You can leave now."

Kyle rose slowly; he didn't like the way she dismissed him. "Just business, right, Rachel?"

Her jaw lifted. "That's right. The only other thing you can do is to tell me why you were on Mallory's monthly payments."

He smiled and let that drop, but Kyle wasn't done with her. "You stay here, get obsessed with this place and revenge for Mallory, and you could be in real danger, especially when he finds out about the doll. He'll be coming after it."

"It's been a long, long day. Good night, Scanlon."

Rachel had set her mind to driving this guy out of the woodwork and making him pay. Kyle worried that her obsession could kill her. "I'll buy this place from you. Name your price."

"You don't have enough money and I promised Mallory. I'm going to get this place up and running, turning a profit, and draw in the money crowd. This isn't going to be the local tavern with a few pool tables added for boy-girl games. You're not getting Nine Balls, Kyle."

"You think I'd do that? To something Mallory wanted to be high class?" Rachel was getting to him, putting him in his place, and she was pretty damned irritating. And right now, he needed to push her buttons, testing her. . . .

Just that flickering of her eyelashes as she looked away from him said that she was aware of how close he stood. Just to push her for a reaction, Kyle reached to curve his hand around her nape. At that, her eyes lifted to his. "Easy. . . ." Kyle murmured. "You're getting all nervous and jittery. Now I wonder why."

He stroked his thumb along that smooth throat and felt the electricity in her, between them, sensing that it could strike at any moment. He held his breath, because pushing Rachel could result in anything.

After a heartbeat, she looked away. "I'm too tired to spar with you."

"You're all keyed up. You won't sleep. I could help you to relax."

She eased from his hand and opened the door wider, indicating that he should leave. "Maybe I am a little tense, but that's not your concern, is it? Don't you have ex-wives waiting for you?"

"Women usually do. It's that anticipation thing, making them wait."

She didn't hesitate, moving into getting what she wanted—information. "You buy clothes for a girl. You've got a girl's bike at your garage. There was a picture of you in Mallory's scrapbook with a girl around seven or eight. Do you have a daughter, Scanlon? Another ex-wife tucked away somewhere? Or a girlfriend you never married? *Do you have a daughter with Mallory?*"

That picture was a year old and that very special girl was nine now, but Kyle wasn't giving Rachel any tidbit to work on. He smiled then, because Rachel was back in the ball game, hunting for something she could use. "She's just a little girl, no relation to me at all. Mallory liked the picture, and I gave it to her. I'm saving myself for your sister, Jada, honey. I thought you knew."

Rachel reacted immediately, her eyes flashing at him. Once again those slender capable hands gripped the front of his shirt and Kyle allowed her to haul him closer. "Don't you dare."

"But I promised, and like you, I always keep my promises. You just have to have your hands on me, don't you?" He placed his hands over hers, smoothing them with his thumbs. He loved nudging that hidden emotional side of Rachel, momentarily distracting her from tracking down the men in Mallory's life.

But she'd be watching for anything that might tie a man to Mallory, and she was definitely going after whoever was on that tape, whoever Mallory hated enough to try black magic.

He studied Rachel's face, the candlelight framing her hair in a reddish tinge. He smoothed it, held that silk in his fingers, and studied the different shades, warm against his skin. "Don't go after them, Rachel. It's dangerous."

"You could help me. You seem to know more than anyone about Mallory."

"And watch you get tangled into the same mess? No. That would be a real shame for a girl who looked terrific in a mermaid outfit," he added to lighten the mood and bent to brush his lips across hers.

"Scanlon?"

"Mm?"

"Tell me more about the girl. Who is she? Where were you when that picture was taken? There were fields in the background, and a horse, so it was at a farm, right? Around here somewhere? No, somewhere else, because those are pine trees . . . the mountains maybe?"

Rachel wasn't moving away. She was still gripping his shirt in her fists and Kyle leaned closer to nuzzle her cheek and taste her ear with a flick of his tongue. "Scanlon?" she breathed against his ear. "I'm going to find out anyway. You might as well make it easy on yourself."

"Or you could," he suggested and let his hands wander over that sleek satin covering her bottom. He deserved a little feel-good action, he decided, enjoying that softness as he squeezed gently.

"You're in for trouble, Scanlon," she whispered against his lips, her hands slipping up his chest. Her arms locked around his shoulders. "I'm good at research, really good."

"Promises, promises," he returned and slanted his lips to hers.

She was all there, everything a man could want—

heat, hunger, strength, and softness combined. But she was dangerous, withholding, keeping just that edge from really opening up, and he knew that she was on the hunt for answers he didn't want to give.

His body aching now, Kyle eased away from her. "Nice try."

Rachel crossed her arms and her tight smile didn't reach her eyes. "I thought so."

He had to admire her control and promised himself that he'd see her break it, watch the passion darken her eyes, feel her body let go of that slight tension and release itself to him. He placed his fingertip beneath her chin and lifted it for a brief hard kiss. "Good night. By the way, I would have thought you'd have a different perfume. You're wearing the same vanilla scent Mallory liked, aren't you?"

Her confident cool slipped momentarily. "No, I'm not wearing any perfume. There's just the candles, and they're lavender scented—Vanilla was Mallory's favorite scent. . . . Do you . . . do you feel that Mallory might still be here? In this apartment?"

He didn't want to admit that his senses were telling him that there were two women in the apartment—one was Rachel, sharp, strong, and in control, and the other one was waiting. . . . But then, listening to that tape, seeing Mallory's cloth doll, the pins in it, and combining that with a woman he wanted badly, could do strange things to a man. . . . "She died here, that's all. You're letting this place get to you, Rachel, and that's not smart."

"Don't ever underestimate me, Scanlon." Rachel

wasn't the kind of woman to toss idle threats around; she knew how to back them up—but then, so did he.

"Oh, I won't." Kyle studied her, their gazes locking. "I'll be around."

"Yes, that would be nice."

"Because?"

"You know why. You have something I want and I'm going to get it."

"Harry likes it at my house."

"I'll get him—and whatever else I want," Rachel stated confidently.

He smiled at that. Because Kyle knew what he wanted—Rachel—and he knew other things, too. She liked the hunt, and all he had to do was to wait. . . .

"I'll haunt you forever. . . ."

He wiped the sweat from his forehead, his skin clammy and cold. Rachel was up in that apartment, burning those candles and focusing in on him. She had Kyle with her, probably explaining how to use the pins—

"Kyle, always Kyle. They were together and sinning long before you got tangled up with Scanlon, Rachel. Now you're following your sister's road straight into hell, Jezebel. You're going to see that it isn't a pleasant road, dealing with me."

He looked up at the lighted squares of the apartment and pictured what they were doing—Kyle Scanlon and Rachel Everly.

He stepped back into the shadows as the door opened, a slice of light in the darkness, and Kyle's tall body stood outlined in it. He'd be so easy to kill, standing like that.

Rachel came to stand beside him, male and female silhouetted against the flickering candlelight, and the man's anger leaped, full blown, furious with them both. Mallory's witchcraft wouldn't protect them, not when he was ready—

The door closed and Kyle, an athletic man, came down them two at a time.

Then a song floated through the open windows, a song that tortured the man, because it was Mallory's favorite and she'd promised to wait for him in hell—

*I'll be with you forever, till the tides no longer flow, till doves no longer fly and roses no longer bloom, till time comes no more. . . . I'll be with you forever . . . On the far, still side of tomorrow. . . .*

# Nine

MID-MAY'S COOL EVENING MIST SWIRLED AROUND ATLANTIS Street's lights and settled on the cars in the Nine Balls parking lot. The first official Ladies-Only Monday night was in session, the players a mix of housewives and businesswomen who were oddly quiet, as if wary of the new owner.

Trina pocketed the eight ball and looked around at the other players in Nine Balls as she chalked her cue. "Business is picking up. You've only been open for a week, just a month and three weeks after Mallory— left. You've been very busy herding business back."

She lined up a ball parallel to the end rail and positioned the cue ball between the ball and the rail, angling her cue high. The trick shot called for "a massé" in which the shooter plunged the cue down, skimming the one ball and causing it to jump over the others on its way to an end pocket. "I used to be able to use more than one ball as an obstacle. Let me see if I can try something else."

Trina placed six balls in a row leading off an end rail, positioned a cue ball near the rail and took her time studying the shot. "The cue ball is supposed to—if hit right with enough english—spin around that line of balls on its way to the opposite pocket. . . ."

When she missed the shot, Trina shrugged and sighed. "I'm way out of practice. I used to make a lot of money taking bets on that shot."

Rachel racked nine balls into a diamond shape, indicating a game of nine ball on the tournament-size table. "I haven't had much time to practice or to play either."

"I know. You look really tired and we haven't seen much of you."

Rachel chalked her cue and looked at the tables. She had decided that her mother didn't need to know about Mallory's tape or the doll, and was choosing her moments to ask questions. "I've been going over Mallory's things, her scrapbook and pictures. Did she ever talk to you about anyone in particular?"

Trina studied her daughter. "That's it, isn't it? You're looking for some reason Mallory took her life. Haven't we all blamed ourselves enough?"

"Scanlon. I'm looking for information on him."

"Kyle?"

"He changed his name legally when he was twenty-one. The question is: Who was he before that?"

"If I know you, you've got your business connections working on that one. I blame myself, you know, for your need to succeed. Your guard is always up when it comes to men. As a child, you saw me working too hard, desperate to make money to survive and wishing I had that college degree behind me to make a better living for us. I think if you'd have had a better father image—"

Trina looked at Rachel's raised eyebrows. "If you'd

have had any kind of a good father image, your take on men might have been better. I blame myself for that. It seems like Jada went one way, marrying a man like your father, and you went a totally different direction, not really trusting one at all."

"Okay, Mom. You opened this conversation. . . . Tell me again why you never remarried. You're pretty sexy still, Mom, and I've seen men's heads turn toward you more than once. You dated and you were asked to get married a few times through the years. Jada and I are grown now, so if you waited, that's no excuse."

"I have what I want—a comfortable relationship. And you may be right, that deep down, I still don't trust enough to marry . . . I did love your father, though. But now, I'm worried about *you*, that my experience with your father may have wrongly influenced you. You're pretty, you're smart, and you could be pushing away love. Life cheated me when it came to love and that isn't what I want for you girls."

"I'm a career woman and I like it, Mom. Please don't worry. You first."

As Trina lined up to break the balls, Rachel watched a boy on a bicycle ride by the window. *Who was the girl with Kyle in Mallory's scrapbook?* And *Why was Kyle with the girl?*

Then: *Who did that cloth doll represent?*

*Was that man somehow connected to the child?*

The first answer came back as Any Man. After a week of getting used to Nine Balls patrons, their preferred times and keeping the minibar stocked, Rachel had learned that deals were made at Nine Balls, the businessmen scheduling for afternoon games. Other men put in a fast game after five-thirty with a sly request that they be "invisible" for "anyone who might ask," which translated to wives with dinner on the table.

They were no more curious about Rachel than she was about them. She dismissed the usual morning checkers crowd, the older retired men, needing a place away from wives, who wanted to do their cleaning without husbands underfoot. After realizing Tommy's involvement with Mallory, Rachel was careful to note men who were looking at her with sexual interest, as if she might replace Mallory. Too many of them had fine brown hair. . . .

Trina's arm went around Rachel. "Honey? Where did you just go off to?"

"I'm just enjoying the first Ladies-Only tonight. Are you staying?"

"No, Bob and I are watching a movie, a western, at his place. He's cooking Italian. I'll see you tomorrow and bring leftovers. So Kyle still has Harry?"

Rachel thought of the phone calls that consisted only of a cat's purring sounds. "I've been too busy to deal with Harry, but I am getting him back."

"I heard that Harry is getting fed well—Iris has been checking out the fisherman's catch—"

Rachel turned to her mother who was placing the cue in the wall rack. "You mean that they might be feeding my cat fish guts?"

Aware that Rachel was furious, Trina said lightly, "Oh, I have no idea."

"I'll kill him, Scanlon, if he lets anything happen to Harry." That young tom had come from the park's bushes after Rachel's attack; he'd licked her face and had lain close to her, warming her stunned, icy body. She'd carried him home that night and he'd stayed near as if he sensed that in her trauma, she needed a friend. . . . "I love that cat. But Harry isn't exactly happy with this place. He tried to run out of the door from the minute I put him down on the floor. Either that, or he hides and won't come out."

Trina kissed Rachel's cheek. "Cats choose their people, remember? Got to go. If Jada turns up, tell her I'm at Bob's, okay?"

At eight o'clock Nine Balls' tables were filled with women. Rachel knew some of them from her previous visits. Several twenty-ish women were lively, adding whoops and catcalls to the steady hum of gossip, all of which Rachel listened to as she moved around the room.

They were all curious about her, cautious about what they said about Mallory, about when Rachel would sell the billiards parlor, and about the details of Mallory's death. Apparently gossip of the burning of Mallory's things had reached all of them. Whatever the case, Nine Balls was packed with women, and while watching the tables' reservation schedules, refilling the minibar's supplies and promoting the upcoming children's Saturday morning lessons, Rachel listened very carefully to the gossip about their husbands and boyfriends.

As arranged, Terri, Sally Mae, Dorothy, and Jasmine arrived on their usual nine o'clock schedule for an hour of playing time that Mallory would sometimes let extend into a late-night girl's session without paying for the tables. At nine o'clock on a Monday night, the other women were leaving and Rachel made the rounds, encouraging them to come back and handing out free one-night courtesy passes.

When Rachel turned back to the four women who usually played after nine o'clock, Sally Mae seemed embarrassed; she looked away from Rachel and chattered nervously to the other women. She played briefly, then left because "the kids both have a cold and Tommy just isn't good at taking their temperatures."

Rachel methodically played each woman, listening to her talk about her family, the everyday stuff. But she focused on information about their husbands. Terri Samson had a new boyfriend and was excited about him. She wasn't ready to give his name, because they "weren't in really solid yet."

"I'd like to know more about Mallory's boyfriends, more about her life," Rachel said and noted that Jasmine Parker missed an easy shot.

"She had a few, I guess . . . sounds like," Dorothy said quietly and avoided looking at anyone else. But her fingers, formed around the cue, gripped it too tightly. She jabbed at the ball, rather than her usual smooth, easy stroke.

"I've heard a few husbands were involved," Rachel said quietly at the next table and noted Sally Mae's indrawn hiss of breath, her furious expression.

"Leave Mallory in peace," Terri said quietly, almost defensively as she moved around Rachel to line up for a shot. She bent, positioning for the shot and called it, "Eight ball, corner pocket. Don't stir up Neptune's Landing on a witch hunt that could hurt too many people."

Terri missed the shot; Rachel made it and said, "I'd like to talk to you privately, Terri."

The attorney's expression hardened. "Sorry, no can do. Mallory was my client and what she said stays with me. Let her rest, Rachel."

Rachel met the attorney's cold blue stare as she racked the balls for a new game. "I owe her, Terri, and she deserves more than the way she died."

Terri didn't wait; she lined up the cue ball and shot, breaking the "rack." She moved to sight in on the one ball, aiming for the corner pocket. "Rebuild this place. That should be enough."

When she missed, Rachel lifted her cue. Terri gripped it, studying the inlaid design. "That was Mallory's."

"It was and it should be used. As her attorney, you should know that everything she had is now mine."

"You're not exactly making friends by asking so many questions." Terri released the cue and Rachel shot, hitting two balls, each rolling into separate pockets. "You dig up dirt and someone could get hurt," Terri warned quietly.

Rachel hadn't really played in years, but she intended to win this game, and the other silent one. She finished the "rack" quickly and turned to see the women studying her. "I want the names of any man involved with Mallory, and I'd appreciate your help."

After a static silence, Terri put her cue into its custom case and snapped it closed. "Game is over."

In her apartment later, Rachel worked on her laptop on the kitchen table until the figures started to blur. With her own savings invested, Nine Balls just might get back on a paying basis—it would take expensive radio ads, promotions, freebies. . . .

Tired and aching from the routine nightly cleaning,

Rachel lay down on her couch and watched the candle-light throw shadows on the wall. "You're still here, aren't you, Mallory? You want him caught, don't you? But you want to protect those you love? Is that it? Help me, Mallory. Give me something to work on—"

*If you do anything to my family, I'll haunt you forever. . . .* That eerie light in Nine Balls' upstairs apartment reminded the man of another woman and her endless chanting.

He could almost see Mallory now, her long red hair tight with natural ringlets, bending over her candles, her eyes green as a witch's amid that pale angular face. She had rocked as she chanted to the candles. She'd fashioned a doll from the hair from his brush and from a blue-striped dress shirt, and no matter what he did to her, Mallory would not give it to him.

Instead, she had chanted the words damning him, and he could never erase the curses that clung to him, even after her death. He'd taken her charms as he found them, partly to take away something she seemed to need, and partly to make certain nothing was in them that could lead to him.

"In a way, only I know of what you did, and that makes me special, doesn't it, Mallory? You only revealed to me that part of you that you didn't want the Everlys to know about?"

Rachel's long yellow Cadillac sat next to the apartment stairs, gleaming alone in the streetlight. The mist that enfolded and hid him had settled onto the waxed finish and sparkled like jewels as he thought about Rachel. She was up there, burning candles, just as Mallory used to do. "Sisters beneath the skin, witches the both of them. . . ."

But Rachel was steel to Mallory's pliability, and intent upon piercing the secret that bound him to Mallory. . . .

In the shadows of Atlantis Street, the damp ocean air settled into his clothing, causing a chill to settle into his bones. Or was it the echo of Mallory's chanting?

She was dead now, mourned by a few, and he wasn't one of them. Mallory had known too much and eventually, she would have exposed him, and ruined his life.

The woman in the apartment now was asking too many questions and that meant Rachel knew something, too. But Rachel already had a taste of what he could do . . . he might just have to do it again. . . .

"None of this is my doing. Mallory lured me into sin. It was all her fault."

The steady drip of water from the tree branches onto his head had created a headache and each drop brought echoes of Mallory's litany—*If you do anything to my family, I'll haunt you forever.* . . .

"I wondered when Rachel would get around to my girls."

At nine o'clock on Wednesday evening, Kyle entered his home and looked at the women who had just stopped line dancing. Patty and Iris let out delighted squeals and came running toward him.

The third woman stood in the center of his living room, her hands on her hips and her stance pure attitude. Rachel was dressed in a tight pink sweater with a cord barely keeping the edges of the bodice closed, and tight jeans rolled up to the top of western boots; it was the kind of look that would appeal to Patty and Iris, both fond of tight, revealing clothing.

Rachel's lips were glossy, her hair was in a spiky-looking ponytail, and her cheeks were flushed; her dark eyes burned him from within heavy layers of shadow and mascara. The big flashy hoop earrings were a real surprise, shimmering a little to tell him that she was holding back a brewing temper. And that tapping foot wasn't keeping time to the music. . . .

"Hi, honey," Kyle murmured directly to her as Patty and Iris stood on either side, hugging and kissing him.

He handed each woman a gift-wrapped package and wallowed a bit in their excited, "Ooo . . . you never forget. Thank you, thank you, thank you."

The woman standing in the middle of the room looked grimly disgusted and he gave her a big grin that he knew would irritate. "If I'd known you were waiting for me, I'd have brought something for you, too."

Rachel's "Spare me" was flat and hard.

"Something big with a bow wrapped around it, too." Kyle enjoyed the slow perfect flush that his sensual remark brought to her cheeks; her anger spiked in the tight set of those glossy lips and her jaw, the way her eyes nailed him.

Kyle let his grin widen as the other women gushed about their sexy thongs and stuffed teddy bear gifts. Road weary, his back hurting from bending beneath a racing motor's hood and running on a lack of sleep because Rachel's kiss had left him simmering, Kyle was in a perfect mood to tangle with her.

Or make love to her. The cord zigzagging down her

front exposed her rounded breasts. "That hot sexy look is good on you," he stated, just to start the ball rolling.

"So you've been gone for three days, huh? You look like crap."

"Thanks. Always good to hear those sweet little nothings." Kyle moved into his favorite easy chair and Patty promptly lifted his feet to the footstool, then unlaced his work boots, taking them off.

"You feel like dancing with us, Kyle-honey?" Iris asked hopefully.

"Maybe later. I just got in. Give me a break, will you?" he asked with a smile and a pat to her bottom. When she giggled, he smiled at Rachel, who looked disgusted and ripe for taunting.

"Get me a beer, will you, Iris?" he asked. "Beer, Rachel?"

"Sure. Love one." She wasn't backing down, a real player, Kyle decided, admiring Rachel as she sat gracefully onto a couch. She crossed her legs and tapped her fingers on the arm as if she were a business executive, poised for a tough meeting. She smiled tightly and asked, "So where have you been, honey?"

He took the beer bottle Patty handed him and thought of the elegant wineglasses at Rachel's home; the glassware marked the differences in their lives, that common didn't mix with elegant. "Thanks, Patty. Rachel might like a glass."

"The bottle is fine," Rachel stated.

"Napkin?" he pushed and smiled as Rachel took the perspiring bottle and wiped it on the arm of the large couch.

"I'm fine."

He lifted his bottle to toast her and their eyes locked, both understanding the purpose for her visit. Rachel was here to get information, and she wasn't running. A man had to love a woman like that—The thought stunned Kyle and he sipped his beer to recover; a man had to be a fool to get tied up with a woman as headstrong and independent as Rachel. "You are truly that—fine. Learn anything useful?"

"You weren't supposed to be back tonight, you know," Rachel returned sweetly and lifted her bottle to drink. "So where have you been?"

"We didn't know, honey, or we would have told her," Patty said.

Kyle decided that with Rachel around and obviously prowling for information, he needed to caution Patty and Iris about his privacy.

He settled down to place his head on the back of the chair and enjoyed watching Rachel on the hunt. He'd been hunted by women before, but Rachel could definitely raise his body to alert—especially dressed like that, the light gleaming on the wedge of curves exposed by that cord. . . . "I've been gone, now I'm back. Everything okay at your place?"

"Just fine. I had the tour earlier. Your parts room—very neat and organized—the bedrooms, one for each ex-wife. I'll bet that's handy."

Patty and Iris had come to sit on the edge of his chair. "She loved your room, honey," Iris said warmly. "We thought we might show her your racing pictures later."

He wasn't surprised. Rachel wanted to know about that young girl in the photograph, and she was looking for damning information about him. "It's boring and in the past. I was a kid. That can't interest any one. I'm better looking now."

"Racing, hmm? Now that's interesting." Rachel smiled and lifted her eyebrows. Anyone who didn't know her better wouldn't notice that narrowed intense look.

"That was a long time ago." Harry chose that moment to come from wherever he'd been hiding and leap up onto Kyle's lap. Just to up Rachel's brewing temper, Kyle stroked Harry and the tomcat's purring sounded loudly.

The cord confining her breasts lifted as Rachel breathed deeply, apparently controlling herself as she calmly sipped her beer. Kyle appreciated that: the way Rachel kept focused on what she wanted, those dark brown eyes locked onto him.

"Oh, I'm interested," she said. "I like old jock stories. But if you're not talking tonight, there are always other times. I'd better go. And I'm taking my cat with me."

"Ohh," Patty and Iris cooed in disappointed unison.

"We were having so much fun. We were just talking about how we met you and how you're always so good to us, Kyle. See if you can't make her stay longer," Patty said.

"I would, if Kyle is telling stories."

Kyle lifted his beer bottle in a toast; Rachel was still in there, angling for answers. "Pass. I'm tired."

"Oh," Rachel's feigned unhappy sigh matched the other women's. "That's too bad."

"You missed me, huh, Rachel?"

"I wouldn't exactly say that."

Kyle noticed Patty and Iris's quiet, alert interest, the

way they watched Rachel and then him, then back again. "She's hot for me," he explained. "Can't leave me alone."

The other women giggled knowingly, but Rachel was on her feet, her eyes flashing. Then she smiled slowly. The smile didn't reach her eyes as Harry rolled over to have his belly scratched and his purring sounded even louder. "He wishes. Patty and Iris, make sure you come into Nine Balls when you can. I'll give you free lessons, but not on Saturday morning, because that's time I'm reserving for children and youth sessions."

"But that's what Kyle does. Or he did, when he was helping poor Mallory."

"Rachel hasn't asked me to help her yet. She hasn't had a room full of kids, some of them thinking that the balls are for throwing, the others wanting to play swords with the cues."

"Oh, he's so good with kids, honey," Patty stated sincerely.

"Any special ones? Little boys? Or little girls?" Rachel asked smoothly.

"Both," Iris said. "You know, your sister, Jada is hoping that she'll get married, but if she doesn't, Kyle will—"

"And either one of you? No kids with Kyle?" Rachel interrupted as though she didn't want Kyle's "sperm donor" job outlined.

Both women stared at each other. "But we thought you knew those stories of Kyle and us. I met Kyle when I was dancing in a strip joint—" Patty began.

"Let's keep our romance private, okay?" Kyle asked quietly. "Just between us?"

Patty and Iris frowned and looked confused. "But she thinks—"

"Uh-huh, and that's what I want her to think," Kyle said.

Rachel smiled warmly. "But I'm so interested in everything about your 'romance.' Was it separate or together?"

"But you're leaving now, aren't you?" Kyle asked. "Things to do and all that? You probably don't have time."

"Maybe I'll come back when you're not around," Rachel said smoothly. "Just to get the full flavor of the romances and weddings. Girl stuff, you know, all the little details."

She bent to take Harry from Kyle's lap and the cat immediately leaped up and ran out of sight. Kyle deliberately lowered his gaze to where that cord held the deep V of her pink sweater together and her breasts pressed together.

"Real nice," he drawled softly and enjoyed the flash of her eyes before she pushed away.

When she went outside, Kyle stood at the doorway. The Cadillac's starter clicked, but wouldn't turn over, and behind the windshield, Rachel frowned at him. She opened the door and stalked to him, all curved and hot and—

"What did you do to my car?"

Kyle tried to look innocent. Removing the distributor cap was just a little safety plan to keep Rachel long enough to find out what she was doing and what she had learned. Whatever games he enjoyed playing with her, he'd promised Mallory to protect the little girl, and

Rachel could unknowingly endanger her. "It needs a tune-up."

"It runs, doesn't it? And how do you manage to keep two ex-wives happy?"

"Hey, I'm a lovable kind of guy. Consenting adults and all that." With that, he bent to kiss Rachel lightly. "Did you miss me?" he asked again, softly as he watched that pink tongue flick over her bottom lip.

"You know, I did. I wondered when you'd turn up and give me that list I wanted."

"That's not happening."

Rachel stood close to him. She framed his face with her hands and tilted his head toward hers. Her hands smoothed his chest, his ribs, and flowed down his waist to his hips. "Isn't it?"

Kyle knew what she was doing, but he was so far gone that he let her go all the way, pulling his keys out of his pocket. His body pounded as Rachel looked up at him, fluttered her eyelashes, and murmured, "You want me bad, Scanlon. You're all revved and hot."

She was as right as a piston engine pumping away, timing-gear smooth and ready, but Kyle managed a cool, "Like I said, it's all in the anticipation, the build up."

"I'd say you're warmed and ready right now, chum." She tossed his keys in the air and caught them. She walked to the Hummer, climbed into the driver's seat, and started the engine. Through the open window, she said, "The list, Scanlon, and I want to know who that girl is. If you'd come clean about the payments Mallory was making to you, you'd make it a lot easier on yourself. Just one little tip to the IRS boys, and you'd be swimming in investigation."

She was right, of course. "But then so would Mallory and whoever took over her business, right?" he countered.

Rachel was ready to trade barbs— "Racing, huh? If you took awards, they'd be on record somewhere, wouldn't they? Under the name of Scanlon, or something else? You were twenty-one when you changed it, so all I have to do is follow that paper trail. All I need is a few free hours and I'll have what I need."

"Always nice to know a lady is interested," Kyle returned, but Rachel could make a man uneasy, especially if she were on the hunt for information he didn't want revealed—that Mallory had hidden for years.

When Rachel backed out of the gate, the big Hummer barely missed a side post before shooting forward and Kyle released the breath he'd been holding. "Busy girl. Smart one, too. You know about my name change, but that's all you'll find."

Rachel stood still inside her apartment. "Mallory?"

She'd momentarily forgotten about her adopted sister's death, or she'd wanted to forget it and wanted to see Mallory alive just once more. . . . But the shadows were too quiet, and Rachel's senses were uneasy. The fine hair on her body had lifted, just as it had that night she'd been stalked three years ago. At the doorway, she turned to look at the parking lot. Atlantis Street was quiet, the streetlights casting shadows around the squarish Hummer. Natasha's big neon fortune teller's sign was pink in the mist, the street's bricks gleaming, the trees surrounding the houses draped in night shadows.

She closed the apartment's door and locked it, turning

the new dead bolt. She was uneasy, but then everything had a cause, she justified. "I've just finished sparring with Kyle again. He's enough to set anyone off."

Rachel sat on the couch to tug off her western boots, then noted the slightly different position of her left jogger, which had been placed exactly parallel to the right one on the floor. She'd kicked them off, too, before leaving the apartment and the left shoe had been a little—The shoelaces had been tied in neat bows, when she had left them untied.

Rachel shook her head. "Maybe I did that. I was all revved up about getting to Patty and Iris after work. Sometimes I'm thinking too hard, focused really hard, and do things automatically. Then I forget that I've done them—I'm just imagining things. No one has a key to this apartment except my mother. And she would have left a note—"

She scanned the coffee table and then walked into the kitchen. There was no note on the table, but the cotton rug she'd placed in front of the sink had been moved slightly aside—or was she imagining that, too?

She opened the cabinet door to see the stacked dishes standing tightly against that first protective block of wood concealing the tape, and the heavy mugs held the concealment for the rag doll and pins.

She moved through the apartment and then opened the locked door leading to the billiards parlor. Downstairs, Rachel opened the cleaning closet and flipped on the overhead light bulb, noting the contents. A damp mop she had used that evening leaned slightly in its holding rack, the long absorbent cords neatly straightened. While closing Nine Balls, she'd been in a hurry and had mopped a sticky area by the minibar; she'd almost tossed the mop into the closet.

The cues on the wall rack were neatly arranged as always, but something about them caused Rachel to study the cues more closely. Mallory's inventory had a mix of maple wood and graphite cues with different shaft designs, single and two piece, larger or smaller tip, with a variety of leather or nylon wraps on the butt ends. The various styles had all been arranged neatly, separated into one or two-piece cues. "I do not like this, Mallory. Stop playing jokes. There's no one here. There couldn't be. Not with all the different locks I've just had installed."

On impulse, she picked up the telephone and dialed Jada's cell phone number. "So you were out at Kyle's tonight, huh?" Jada promptly asked.

"Only because—" Rachel waited for Jada's burst of laughter to stop before she continued, "Never mind. I've got his rig . . . it's in my parking lot, so if you hear any gossip, just say it was a loaner while he fixed mine. And don't ask any questions. And how did you know that I was out at the garage?"

"The highway goes right by his place, you know. A few people saw your Caddie parked out there, namely Shane. I cleaned at his house today and he called late to say I'd forgotten to leave my bill—I never leave a bill. I don't know where that came from, unless he just wanted to talk with me. He's a sweet, lonesome guy, and I could use a dose of that after Wussie-boy. Then Shane mentioned that he'd seen your yellow monster parked out at Scanlon's. Plus, you closed early and Wanda Schmidt said you looked really sexy when you stopped to gas up Buttercup. You don't usually dress in a tight pink sweater and western boots. That's not you at all. You're more the designer duds girl. So what were you doing with Kyle, hmm?"

Shane Templeton had been checking on her, following her. He wanted that Bible and whatever else linked him to Mallory. A minister linked with a woman with Mallory's reputation wouldn't do. . . .

Jada cleared her throat nervously. "Um—Rache? I accidentally mentioned that voodoo doll to Shane. I didn't mean to, but it just came out. He won't say anything."

"It's okay. But just watch who else you tell, okay?" Rachel said. Perhaps Jada's little slip might cause Shane to make his own mistake and say the wrong thing about his relationship with Mallory.

She glanced around the apartment. She hadn't found the Bible or anything about Shane, except his picture, taken with the women serving the church dinner—and Mallory was one of them, looking aglow and young and in love. With Shane?

"Don't get any wrong ideas about my visit to Scanlon's. I was visiting with his ex-wives, Patty and Iris."

"Oh, yeah. They're really nice, aren't they?"

Jada did that snort-thing that signaled she was enjoying a joke and stifling a giggle, and Rachel asked, "What do you know about them? What's the story?"

She walked to the closet that held Mallory's private things behind that block of cedar. The clothing that Rachel had stacked beside it remained neat and untouched. She slid the closet doors shut, then opened the other side to look at the chunk of cedar nailed into place.

The phone's steady scratch-scratch sound said Jada was filing her nails. She made a slurping sound that said her braces had caused her to drool slightly. "You had a reason for going there. Patty and Iris aren't your usual social set and your outfit was picked to fit in with theirs, to make them comfortable. See? I'm not so dumb. . . . I think Kyle is a born collector of the helpless and needy. I mean, he's a real nurturer of people who aren't exactly on track with life, or the victims of it. That's why I think he'll make a good dad for my baby—should I miss out on Shane, who seems off track lately, by the way. You know, Mallory had a definite thing for him—"

"Tell me more about that, Mallory's relationship with Shane."

"Well, she wanted him and did the good church-goer role for a while. A lot of single women do that, and some of the married women are in love with him, too. But I think when she realized that Shane wasn't returning the man-woman interest like she wanted, she dropped out. I asked her why once, and she said he was a nice guy and that they just didn't fit. Shane probably thought he was helping Mallory, doing his ministry work, and she probably took it for something else—like patients who fall in love with their doctors. Women sometimes do the same thing with their ministers. Why all the questions?"

Rachel traced her finger around the nails that had been hit several times, indenting the wood. It seemed

like her sister had a penchant for hiding things behind
blocks of wood. "I get lonesome over here, you know.
You're always good for news."

"You mean, I know a lot of gossip. Yeah, I suppose.
Cleaning houses, you get a lot of inside info . . . for in-
stance, there are a lot of invitations to women's homes
on Shane's desk . . . all sorts of trumped-up reasons for
him to stop by their places. He's a nice guy. . . .
Thoughtful . . . It's easy to be nice to him. The Ladies
Circle keeps his refrigerator filled, but they're not going
to swab his toilet bowl or scrub his floors."

Rachel retrieved a butter knife from the kitchen and
slid it between the cedar and the side of the closet.
Looking down at the inside of the closet to its end on the
floor, she noted that it measured more than the top shelf.
"Now back to Kyle's ex-wives. You were saying?"

"I think they're strays that he's collected. Like Mallory."

"He ruined Mallory. She wasn't like that before he
arrived in town."

"Says who? You? Rachel, you were usually so
wrapped up in causes and your success, getting schol-
arships and good grades in college that you had tunnel
vision. Except when it came to Kyle. What's that noise
I hear?"

"I'm rearranging furniture." Cradling the telephone
to her ear, Rachel stood up on a chair and carefully
nudged the wooden block until it loosened the nails.
"Do you know anyone who wears size fourteen double
wide, custom-made high heels?"

"Probably someone does somewhere. Don't have a
clue. Why?"

"Just curious. Did you know that Kyle races? Or did?"

"Oh, jeez. That's likely. He used to rev that little red sports car up and Mallory and I just held on hard while he laid rubber. He was probably good enough to drive professionally then, but he's running that garage now."

Rachel wiggled the butter knife, wedging the nails farther out from the wall. "It's not a common, fix-it mechanic's garage. He's custom rebuilding classics, or stripping the wrecked ones for parts. His actual inside garage is so clean it looks like a surgery room. He's got shelves of itemized parts. That messy front office isn't anything like the rest of the place. Even the old cars—classics, I guess—are lined up neatly. While his ex-wives were showing me around, I managed to flip through his books—just interested in his computer programs, you know. Or so they thought. He's making a killing on restoring those classics, and he'd better not paint Buttercup any other color. I wouldn't put it past him—"

The cedar block came free to reveal a flat rectangular box. Fearing what was inside, Rachel lifted the lid.

"Are you okay? I just heard you gasp," Mallory asked anxiously.

Rachel stepped down off the chair and then sat on it, studying the contents of the box. The book of Elizabeth Barrett Browning's poetry was bound in white leather and several dried flowers were inside. A small plain gold wedding band was inside a carefully folded envelope. Rachel tried it on her left hand and it fit perfectly, just as it would have fit a hand the same size— Mallory's. The inside of the book had been inscribed, "To Mallory. From Shane."

Just how friendly were Shane and Mallory? Rachel wondered. "I'm okay. Tell me about Kyle's ex-wives. You said they were nice."

Jada snorted again, then released her bawdy laughter. It ended in gasps of breath, and when she could finally talk, she said, "I knew all that about his neat cataloging of parts and his garage. The guy has style. They're not married to each other. Never have been. Patty and Iris need a place to crash periodically and have someone pay a few bills for them, and Kyle likes helping them. He's never married—the whole 'ex-wife' thing started as a joke and just continued. I get the idea that he doesn't think he's material for that scene. Patty and Iris were married, several times, I guess, to losers who kept bothering them. Kyle ran off the losers, put Patty and Iris under his protection, sort of. He's like that—sweet, kind of a knight in shining armor. You're the only woman whoever gets upset with him."

"Uh-huh, he's a real Prince Charming."

"Despite your sarcasm, you sound distracted. Are you okay?"

"Um? Tired, I guess." After hanging up, Rachel carefully replaced the poetry book, easing the wood block back into the same nail holes. She looked at the opposite end of the closet where the cedar block had not been nailed. "This was even more precious, wasn't it, Mallory? You really loved Shane, didn't you? This is what he was looking for, a link to him, and now I have it. He didn't want people to know that you were involved, did he? What else didn't he want people to know?"

At midnight, Rachel still couldn't sleep; she tossed off the blankets and decided to go into the living room to lie on the couch. In the dark, she thought of Mallory, the cloth doll, the girl in the scrapbook, and Shane Templeton who did, or did not, realize Mallory's love. "I'd say a book of poetry and pressed flowers generally meant that you and Mallory had something going, Shane. Add that wedding ring, and I wonder exactly what."

She listened to the familiar muffled sounds of traffic passing on Atlantis Street, the building creaking, settling—and she drifted asleep, only to awaken again to the sound of the stairs creaking.

Rachel held her breath as a man's tall silhouette appeared on the light miniblinds covering the door's window. "Who's there? Kyle? If that is you, I am really not happy now. Just leave Buttercup's keys—oh, yeah, you probably hot-wired her, right? Just go on your way—hot-wire your own rig—and take your full-of-it self back home."

Heavy footsteps pounded down the stairs and Rachel frowned and reached for the telephone. "Just when I was getting ready to call the police, too. You would have had a hard time explaining that one, wouldn't you? As it is, you're in for an ear-burning, Scanlon. . . ."

# Ten

—

**"IT'S KYLE. OPEN UP." AFTER RACHEL'S FRANTIC CALL, IT HAD** taken Kyle exactly fifteen minutes to tug on his jeans, race the big Cadillac from his place to Nine Balls, park it, and run up the stairs.

Kyle waited until Rachel peeked through the mini-blinds and saw him standing beneath the porch light. Then the sound of furniture scraped the floor behind the door, the dead bolt clicked, and the door opened to reveal the apartment's brightly lit rooms. Rachel was in the same pink top and tight jeans as he had last seen her. Only the pink sweater wasn't tucked into her waistband and she was standing in her bare feet, her face scrubbed clean of everything but wide-eyed fear.

"I thought it was you earlier," she whispered unevenly. "I thought you might have brought Buttercup back and some man was standing in front of the door—"

Kyle moved inside and closed the door, locking it. She was staring at the big semi-automatic in his hand. Kyle placed it on a side table and spoke quietly, "Take it easy, Rachel."

She was shaking and cold when he tugged her into

his arms, tucking her face into the curve of his throat and shoulder. "You might not like this, but I've got to hold on to you—"

Kyle lifted her into his arms and walked to the couch, sitting down with her in his lap. To his surprise, Rachel didn't struggle. Her body still shook in his arms. He tilted her pale face up to his. "Tell me about it. What happened?"

For a moment words didn't come and then she said, "I was lying on the couch . . . I tried sleeping, but I couldn't. Someone was at the door. I thought it might be you with some smart-ass comment about Buttercup. I . . . I think he might have come in if I hadn't been awake. . . . The door knob rattled—"

She gripped his bare shoulders, her fingers digging in. "I thought it was you," she repeated. "I said a few things and then he ran down the steps. So I called to leave a message on your machine to tell you off—and you answered. You had been asleep. You couldn't have been whoever has been prowling—"

"Wait a minute. 'Whoever has been prowling'? Some one has been in here?"

"It's just small things. Nothing specific, but I feel that someone has been in here, looking for something. . . . But I had the locks all changed, so no one else *could* have gotten in. Mallory hid the doll and the tape and—"

"And? What else?"

"A scrapbook, mementoes, things like that. The sweet things a woman would keep, pictures—"

She'd stopped speaking too quickly . . . there was more, and Rachel didn't trust him enough to tell the rest. "This place is getting to you, Rachel. Get out of here. Live somewhere else."

"That's not going to happen. I made a promise to Mallory and I'm going to keep it," she stated fiercely, the wide-eyed fear gone. "But I know there is potential danger in stirring up things, so I'll be careful. I'm going to find that son of a bitch and ruin him. I'm going to find his weak spot, or find evidence that he was hurting Mallory, or—What are you looking at?"

Her hand flattened over her breasts where the cord had come free. "You're a dog, Scanlon. Here I am scared and—"

His hands were open now, smoothing gently, his fingers gently pressing into the outer softness of her breasts. "No bra, huh?"

"Oh, I get it. It's take-advantage time, right? FYI, Scanlon: Heroes don't do that when women have been—and you know what? I don't remember inviting you over here. You just said you were coming."

"Suspect the worst, why don't you, Rachel? It seemed the thing to do when a lady calls—and she's so scared that her voice won't come. For a minute, I thought someone had you by the throat." Kyle leaned back and put his hands behind his head, leaving Rachel with the option of leaving, or staying on his lap.

Instead, Rachel leaned her head back on the couch's arm and studied Kyle. For the moment, he felt strong and safe and she wasn't going anywhere. She resented the feeling that she could always depend on Kyle, that she could trust a man she'd always disliked, and that he actually had good qualities. She'd almost told him about the poetry book and the wedding ring.

At Mallory's funeral, Kyle's dislike for Shane had been evident and he'd been furious with whoever had been beating her. If he knew about the ring and the poetry book, he'd make a direct connect to Shane, the man who had wanted to reform her, and the outcome could be bloody.

Rachel's planned chat with Shane would be less straightforward, but might get better results. . . . For now, she would play Kyle's game, flip it over, and distract him. "I don't like you, you know."

He lifted an eyebrow. "You've been working on that one for years. You think that matters with what we've got going on?"

Rachel followed her instinct and smoothed his cheek, sensing the wariness that Kyle immediately pulled around him. Her fingertips followed his broad cheekbone, traced a tiny half-moon scar there and she lifted to kiss him lightly, to give him the gentleness she sensed he had missed along life's way.

Kyle's head went back, breaking the kiss. Beneath his lashes, those silvery eyes were wary. "What was that?"

"Just a little something I thought you needed," she whispered unevenly.

"I'll choose what I need. But thanks for the offer." He'd reverted to that sexy drawl, the one he used to protect himself when she came too close to his private emotions.

"Have it your way." She was wary, too, because this Kyle was new to her, his compassion revealed, though he would hide softer emotions. He'd cared deeply for Mallory, mourned her as a brother, that much was obvious; that he cared for Trina and Jada was also clear as well as Iris and Patty. Kyle might try to bury his humanity from Rachel, but now she knew. . . .

This new tenuous bond between Kyle and herself was chock-full of potential disaster. She'd loved Mark, or thought she had, and when she needed him most, he'd failed her. . . . Kyle wouldn't do that.

Uncertain of the more tender emotions within her, Rachel opted for another approach, a game she enjoyed very much playing with Kyle. She moved her hips, rolling slightly toward him so that her breasts were against that flat stomach. Rachel placed her hand on his bare chest, smoothing the hard planes. Kyle's long body tightened and his nostrils flared, his expression hard. "Having trouble dealing with me, Kyle?" she asked softly.

"Lay off." The words came tight and grim and his hand clamped to her hip, his fingers digging briefly.

She circled his nipple with her fingertip. "What was your last name before you changed it?"

He shifted uneasily. "I thought you were scared about your visitor. Let's stick to that, shall we? And you said you couldn't put your finger on it, but that something was different in Nine Balls?"

His chest was hard, his heart thumping solidly beneath her palm, the lines etched around his lips. Rachel considered those lips and how much she wanted to taste them. . . . "Things have been happening. A. I feel that Mallory is still here. I was close to her once, before she pushed me away, and I am going to get some closure. . . . *I need it.* And B. I think that someone wants that tape and that doll. C. And when I find out who it is, specifically, his butt is mine, because I'm good at paper trails and digging out what this guy probably doesn't want to surface."

He trapped her hand as it moved to his other nipple. "Stop that. Any ideas as to who?"

Kyle's brisk, frustrated tone said she was getting to him—and just maybe herself. He was definitely exciting, a raw blend of heat and power, of textures she wanted against her bare skin. Rachel looked down his chest to where the V of hair narrowed into a thin line to his navel. Her fingertip followed that line across that six-pack stomach. "It's just a matter of time until I find out all about you, Scanlon. Make it easy on yourself."

Those lines beside his eyes crinkled and his lips softened as he looked slowly down the length of her body. "You can try. What did you do with that mermaid costume?"

"It's somewhere."

"I bet your toes curl when you make love."

"And I know that your 'ex-wives' aren't really that. I have to hand it to you—it's a very funny joke. Your little harem out there in the garage is just because you like feeling like a sugar daddy."

"Every man should have a harem. I can't help if you believe everything you hear at face value. Having fun? Seeing how far you can take this? Pushing me?"

In a quick movement, Kyle flattened her beneath him and lay between her legs. "Push now," he challenged softly against her lips.

"You wouldn't." He was heavy and aroused and very warm, and dammit, she trusted him not to force her.

Kyle was a player and so was she, and he'd make her come after him—

She'd always held just that bit within herself, never releasing it to Mark as they made love—smooth, automatic movements, coming to a gentle climax, just enough to keep her mildly pleasured. But her body was already responding to Kyle's, warming, softening, moistening, and sensed that "mildly" wouldn't suit the explosive storm she expected with this man.

Just to push the limits, and because she felt safe enough to test him, Rachel lifted her hips slightly and Kyle's eyes immediately narrowed and darkened warningly.

"You wouldn't," she repeated huskily as she inhaled his dark arousing scent and shivered with the challenge that being near Kyle always brought. Warning bells started echoing inside her head, even as her hands opened to stroke his shoulders, tensing on the hard width of muscle and bone. While her hands were moving, her mind was warning: *Step over the line with Kyle Scanlon and there's no going back. . . .*

Kyle's lips slid along her cheek to her ear. "You're right, I wouldn't. But I like the invitation. What else are you holding, honey? The name of who you think was at your door earlier? Who do you think that doll represents? And what happened to you in New York that took Mallory flying off to be with you?"

Rachel looked away, guarding that horrible moment, but she couldn't prevent the tear from slipping down her cheek. *The attacker had held her down. He had muttered her name, where she had lived and worked and where she liked to jog and eat. . . .*

After a ragged sigh, Kyle eased to her side, lying full length on the sofa. "Okay, sorry. Wrong question, wrong time."

Rachel sat up slowly. She'd experienced almost every emotion possible tonight and she was drained. Someone had come right to her door and would have come in. . . . Kyle's Hummer had been sitting in the parking lot. If the man had known Kyle was inside the apartment, he would have had more sense than to tangle with him. Whoever the man was, he had known that she had driven Kyle's noticeable Hummer, parking it and walking up the stairs. That meant that he had been watching. . . . Cold again, Rachel shivered lightly, the night she had been stalked three years ago, blending with tonight. "Sure. You can leave now."

Kyle's hand flattened on her back, smoothing it. "Get some sleep. I'm not going anywhere tonight. In the morning, you're going to report this."

She looked at him over her shoulder. "And do you know what the police would probably say, after poking around a bit and scribbling a report? That it was just one of Mallory's men friends who didn't know that the management—and the services—had changed. I don't want the police in here again, going through my things this time. From what I've heard, Mallory's male friends might have included some city fathers. I want to catch that special bastard on my own and nail him so badly that he can't wriggle free."

"You're asking for real trouble, Rachel."

"You're not going to stop me, Scanlon. Don't try," she said as she shoved to her feet and walked into her bedroom.

\* \* \*

"Rachel Everly is just the same as Mallory—a tramp."

As the man drove by Nine Balls, the big Hummer and the yellow Cadillac, standing side by side, gleamed beneath the streetlights. "I handled Mallory and I can do the same with Rachel, if she pushes me."

The bricks on Atlantis Street were wet and shiny after the rain, and driving slowly he thought of how Rachel had looked earlier—tight pink sweater, tight jeans rolled up to show western boots, those big flashy earrings and all that makeup.

"Rachel has class and if she's dressing like that, she's after something." If she managed to link Mallory's voodoo doll with him, Rachel would be digging around in his private life. *She could ruin him, and he had to stop her.* "Just maybe she needs another reminder to watch her step and keep out of my business."

His body squeezed tightly as he thought about how she'd looked in that getup, standing by that big Cadillac at the service station, waiting for the attendant to fill her tank. Rachel might be even better game than Mallory, resist more, and the thought of a woman fighting him, being terrorized as he used her, fascinated and aroused him.

"Yes, Rachel would fight well. But she would lose."

He remembered the feel of her beneath him—before the men holding her had laughed at him. . . . They wouldn't laugh at anyone again; he'd seen to that very efficiently in a dark quiet alley. . . .

The light in the apartment clicked off and fury raged through him. Kyle Scanlon was having her now—Rachel was letting a low-class mechanic have her, debasing herself with him . . . she was just as sinful as Mallory—all women were when their true base natures were revealed.

The man's hands gripped his steering wheel so tightly that it creaked. He closed his eyes as he tried to control his body, his mind picturing Rachel beneath him. . . . "I'll move slow, getting to you, making you fear that you're imagining this or that, nothing big really, just enough to let you notice—then you'll be vulnerable and I'll know if you found that damned doll. Or maybe Jada could be used to get my point across. You'd recognize the trademark technique, I'm sure . . . a lonely place at night, alone, say an invitation from you to meet her at the beach. . . . There are lots of tourists partying around now, and she was just at the wrong place at the right time, that's what the report would say after an intense investigation. . . ."

He thought of how he'd seen Rachel drive the big Hummer into the parking lot, of how she'd raced up the stairs.

He'd wanted to look at her—just look for now, but she'd been awake, calling out, "Who's there? Kyle? . . ."

There was more, but in flight, he couldn't hear the distinct words. They were probably lover's words, sexual come-ons. . . . He breathed harder, aware that he needed sexual relief soon, and that he'd have to arrange a trip out of town, easy enough to do for a man in his profession.

"So you've taken up with that greasy-hands mechanic, have you, my dear? You really shouldn't have done that. On the other hand, if anything happens to you, he'd be a perfect suspect. A lover's spat, maybe?"

He liked the idea of framing Kyle while getting rid of Rachel.

But then, he wouldn't get to play, would he? And he'd missed playing very much. . . .

*Rachel had been terrified, shaking and cold in his arms.* Kyle lay on Rachel's couch and tried to push away that heavy, painful sexual ache, because very little kept him from joining her in that creaking bed. In purposefully distracting Rachel with a frank sexual come-on, he'd also set himself up for a whole lot of pain.

And Rachel knew it; she knew she could get to him, and she wouldn't be making life easy. Kyle shook his head and tried to divert his mind, and hopefully his body away from sex with her.

He started with a big fat, obvious question—who had come to her door?

Whoever had appeared to terrify her could have been any of Mallory's men, who hadn't known about her death and had stopped by for a "visit." Obviously, her local "friends" already knew about her suicide.

Or it could have been someone who wanted the evidence that would connect him to Mallory and whatever he did to her. The pins stuck in the doll's chest and groin indicated Mallory's thoughts about him—she hated the man who had hurt her.

Kyle frowned slightly and thought of Mallory. In those early years, she had been one of those unguarded delights in life: who didn't doubt, who could be so easily snared into other's wills.

Then suddenly, her innocence was totally stripped away; she'd believed in nothing, became careless with herself and, finally, at the end, with the business that she'd struggled to build.

The bed creaked once and then the floor, indicating that Rachel wasn't having an easy time going to sleep. The building's old pipes groaned and water began to run, and Kyle shook his head. The image of Rachel, naked in the shower, wasn't helping his "No" Factor.

On the other hand, he decided, as he lurched to his feet, nothing was helping, not since Rachel had deliberately turned him on. He looked at the clock and shook his head. "Three o'clock and hours to go."

Fastened to each sound in the bedroom, and damning himself for letting Rachel arouse him, Kyle waited for the bed to creak again.

Instead, Rachel walked into the living room, dressed in sweats. She plopped her running shoes on the coffee table and sat in a chair.

Kyle looked at her; she was maddening, and she knew it. Unpredictable, sexy, and he resented the surge of frustration and anger that she could raise so easily surfacing in a hard demand. "What the hell are you doing?"

She slid on one shoe, propped her foot on the coffee table, and tied the laces briskly. "Going for a run."

In a single sweeping motion, Kyle sat, stood up, and lifted Rachel from her chair. "Like hell you are."

She wasn't fighting and that caused him to be suspicious. "Ooo. My master speaks," she singsonged. "You can run with me, if you can keep up."

"Oh, I can keep up, honey, but you're not going anywhere alone, not for a while."

Her eyes widened slightly and she frowned. "Just what do you mean by that?"

Kyle had to get her out of his arms. Either that, or—
He walked into the bedroom and tossed her on the bed.
"Cool off. We'll talk about this in the morning, over a
cup of coffee when we're both not ready to tear at each
other."

For an answer, Rachel tightened her lips, glared up
at him, and kicked off her one shoe. "If we talk, I want
answers."

"Good enough," he said grimly and jerked open the
door to the bathroom.

Kyle took off his jeans and stepped into a cold, sting-
ing shower. He used Rachel's fragrant shampoo and
soap, and fearing that she might leave without him,
dried himself quickly. The steam in the room shifted
suddenly as the door opened and Rachel entered to lean
against the doorway; she tilted her head and coolly
looked him up and down.

Kyle tossed the towel over the shower rod. "Like
what you see?" he asked tightly.

"You're determined to play this bodyguard bit, aren't
you? I bet you did it a few times with Mallory—she
trusted you implicitly."

"I never touched her after that first bit. But you're
not her."

"No, I'm not. She was special and she was my sister,
and I'm going after that bastard. You're not going to
stop me."

"Are you going to tell me what happened to you that
caused Mallory to run to New York?" Offensive was
usually good, but that statement—now—disgusted
Kyle and probably every male on the planet. Was that

the best he could come up with, while standing nude in front of an appraising, sexy woman?

When Rachel continued looking, but didn't answer, he tried a threat, which seemed a nice offset. "You can see I have a little problem. Any lady would leave."

"You do have a big problem."

Kyle forced himself not to move as Rachel studied his jutting erection, then walked slowly around him. "Are you about finished?" he asked her.

"No, and neither are you," she said as she came to stand in front of him. Rachel slowly drew away her sweat shirt and stepped out of her pants. "Let's finish this."

"Just that simple?" he asked roughly, not trusting himself to touch her. "No strings?"

Rachel had that dark, edgy, challenging look that could set him off as she said, "A. Let's get this out of the way, and then we'll both know, and B. after this is done, I want your promise that you will not, repeat not, think of supplying Jada's sperm cup or even doing it the natural way, and C. are you going to kiss me or not?"

"That's pretty clear cut," Kyle stated as his hands framed her waist and he tugged her close to him. "Jada won't be happy with the news."

"You're complicated, Scanlon, and I'm going to find out about that four hundred Mallory gave you every month. According to your books, you didn't deposit it, because you're meticulous about bookkeeping, something I wouldn't expect."

"Thanks. I'm very careful about deposits," he said, letting her know that he wasn't talking about bookkeeping, rather that he would use protection as they made love. He slid his hands upward, brushed his thumb across her nipple and prayed that he wouldn't embarrass himself. "So this is how you're going to play detective?"

"Let's play," she whispered huskily as her arms circled his neck.

*She'd always known that Kyle Scanlon would be her lover.* That tidbit came prowling into her mind as Rachel opened herself to the rough, primitive possession of a male demanding everything.

But Kyle was only taking what she allowed, drawing her close, standing with his legs braced, his body hard, thrusting between her thighs, blunt tip already seeking entrance to her body.

His big hands moved down to press her bottom, easing her closer, until he entered just that bit. "You're all tense, honey. If this isn't right for you, don't—"

In and out, slowly, just that bit until Rachel could feel her inner muscles relax slightly. Kyle leaned his face down to her throat, nuzzling it. "If we get serious about this, I'm prepared. What about you?"

She leaned her head to one side, enjoying the slow movement of his open lips against her skin. She moved her breasts against his chest, slowly, side to side. His rough sigh and the shudder of his big taut body said that Kyle was right on target, right there and ready. Rachel smoothed his shoulders, his upper arms and absorbed that controlled power. "You're holding back, Scanlon."

"And maybe you are. Tell me what happened to you in New York . . . why Mallory hurried to you."

"We had things to do . . . shop, girl stuff, and some pop-up little vacation and I asked her to go." She smiled against the lips cruising hers. "You'd use sex to get what you want?"

This time it was his turn to smile against her cheek, then his teeth gently bit her earlobe. "Sure. You were engaged, weren't you? What happened to that?"

"Things. You talk too much."

"According to Jada, that breakup came a little after Mallory visited you."

"Jada talks too much."

His open hands smoothed her body, flowing over her. "Career woman is married to her job, right?"

"I was engaged, and that said I wasn't totally about business. And you like to play, don't you?" she managed as heat began to slide over her.

"Same as you. But with you, it's different."

Rachel ran her fingers through his hair, testing it on her skin. "And you don't like it?"

"Not a bit. If you wanted, you could ruin a man. You're getting all hot and damp and fragrant, Everly."

"Then you'd better do something about it, Scanlon . . . because you've got that desperate tight look and your body is hard and quivering."

"Men don't 'quiver,' honey." Kyle picked her up and walked into the bedroom. "The first time, a man likes to be a gentleman and take it slow. Then, just from this— test run—I'd say you haven't had sex for a while. And that—" he said as he dropped Rachel onto the bed, "means that I'm going to be very careful with you."

"How sweet," she commented dryly as he walked into the bathroom to retrieve his jeans.

He was gorgeous and definitely prime, Rachel decided as he returned to flip a small opened foil package onto the bedside table. "Anything else, other than your appraisal of my lack of sex lately? And it's a little early for wearing that, isn't it?"

Kyle looked down her body and Rachel fought shielding that intimacy. A dangerous man, Kyle Scanlon could rip away any pretense, and that irritated. He smiled briefly. "Never hurts to be prepared ahead of time. You want this your way, don't you?"

She drew up a sheet to cover her body. "I don't know what you mean."

"You will. Yes or no?"

She wanted to keep this sexual game on a level that wouldn't get to her, not deep inside where it really mattered. Kyle understood that there was nothing between them, no softer emotions, and sex with him would clear the board of that distraction—she'd know all there was to know about him before she was done. "Yes."

Rachel wasn't prepared for the gentleness that Kyle gave her, the slow thorough study of her body with his lips, his hands. She wasn't prepared for the earthshaking need to lock him to her, to have him quickly. "This is taking too long," she whispered unevenly as he held her just that bit away from him and when she moved to capture him fully, he moved away.

"Is it?" Kyle asked grimly.

His body was heavy and slick upon hers, hot, full, tense to the point of release, but yet he wouldn't—His hands ran down her thighs, stroked the back of her knees and raised them. "What's the matter, Rachel? Getting a little involved now?"

For an answer, she tugged his head down to hers and fed upon his mouth, seeking that wild dangerous primitive streak beneath the control. Kyle eased into her, still gently, then rested, watching her as she shifted her hips and adjusted to him. "This is nice," she whispered when she could breathe. "What do you think, Scanlon?"

His smile tight and brief, his heart pounding against her own. "Sure. Nice."

She had to push him, to make him take them further than just that bit of pleasure shimmering on the edge of true orgasm. "Sweet, don't you think?"

For an answer, he began to move. . . .

Kyle sank the eight ball in the side pocket, but his mind wasn't on the shots. The morning sun slid through the front windows of Nine Balls as Rachel's last drowsy words echoed in his mind: "You're not sweet, Scanlon."

He'd dozed briefly with her body tangled around his, her breath gentle on his throat. She'd been soft and warm and he wanted her again, but as tight as Rachel was, he'd reined in his need. She'd been shocked when her body climaxed, fighting him on the very edge of release, holding him until they both opened and flowed into one another. . . . .

Kyle sipped the coffee he'd made earlier and brooded his emotions; Rachel had gotten to him a long time ago, and he might as well admit it.

When a woman cries out in her sleep, sounding like a frightened child, something was eating at her, and he didn't like it. When the muffled cry became words, "Don't! Don't touch me! You're hurting me. . . ." and her body threshed as if it were being held, Kyle didn't like his conclusions—that Rachel had been raped.

That would have been enough to send Mallory running off to take care of Rachel.

That would explain her reaction to him at first, that brief tenseness, that flash of fear.

That he'd made love to her said one of two things: that Rachel trusted him some small bit, or that she wanted her answers about Mallory enough to use her body. But Rachel had always depended on her quick mind for answers, and the physical honesty with which she'd met him spoke of hunger and a demand to equal his.

Kyle fought the impulse to return to her bed, and instead picked up the misting bottle; he sprayed the ferns that Rachel had repotted near the front window. While thinking of how the sisters had loved each other, he meticulously picked away discolored fronds and worked at the facts:

*Mallory was different after that trip, sinking quickly. . . .*

*Was there a connection between Mallory protecting her family and whatever had happened to Rachel?*

*If there was, that meant someone in Neptune's Landing knew of Mallory's love for her family and they were making a point that she had better obey—* "Maybe Rachel was right that Mallory was protecting her family. It adds up."

Shane Templeton jogged on the sidewalk in front of Nine Balls. Mallory had had a thing for the minister, who was now frowning. He strode purposefully toward the front door and knocked on the glass.

Kyle decided that he might as well let everyone know that he'd spent the night with Rachel, to let whoever came to her door last night know that he had a stake in protecting her. So what if that bit of macho possessive streak had surfaced where she was concerned? If the good minister was woman-hunting, Kyle wanted him to know that Rachel was off limits. Kyle smiled briefly at that as he walked to the door and opened the locks. "Come in."

The minister glanced at Kyle's bare chest and his jeans, then looked around Nine Balls. He looked at the opened door at the stairway leading up to the apartment. The door wasn't that noticeable and yet the minister had spotted it immediately. Kyle wondered how many times Shane Templeton had gone up that stairway to see Mallory.

"I was just—"

"Sure. You just dropped by to see how Rachel was. I'd offer coffee, but Rachel is still sleeping," Kyle stated, as he studied the minister and wondered if he could have been last night's caller. "Jog at night, do you?"

Shane seemed flustered. "Sometimes. Are you running this place now?"

Kyle let that nudge pass. "Like I said, Rachel is sleeping."

"Is she okay? I mean, why are you here, this early in the morning?"

Kyle answered with a shrug and let the minister make his own conclusions. He glanced at Bob Winters who had just parked his car in front of the parlor. Bob walked around the big black Lincoln and stood peering into Nine Balls. He walked through the opened door and found the two men instantly. He seemed immediately concerned. "Is there a problem? I mean why are you two here? Is Rachel okay? What are you doing here, Scanlon?" he asked pointedly.

"Night shift," Kyle said slowly and waited for that innuendo to sink in.

Bob recovered quickly, his face reddish with anger. "I don't want you hanging around Rachel."

"Now, now—" Shane interrupted. "Things aren't always as they seem. I'm certain there's a good reason."

"Reason for what?" Rachel asked too quietly as she walked through the doorway leading from the apartment.

# Eleven

---

AFTER A NIGHT SPENT WITH KYLE, FEELING WARM AND WILTY and satisfied when she first awoke, Rachel had heard the rumble of male voices downstairs. She had been alone, and it had been only six o'clock in the morning. The indistinct sounds of the men said that Kyle was ominously quiet, while the other man's loud tone had belonged to Bob. Another man's tense voice had blended with the others, more soothing, but still tense.

Rachel had splashed water on her face, brushed her teeth, and dressed quickly before hurrying down the stairs. Then she had stopped near the doorway, priming herself to meet the man who was almost like a father to her, and Shane, who had given Mallory the book of poetry—and just maybe that wedding ring.

But Rachel's priority now was Kyle. She'd heard the "Night shift" remark and recognized the bald inference that they were lovers. Wearing only his jeans and moccasins, his jaw dark with stubble, Kyle watched her walk toward the men. "'Morning, Sunshine," he murmured quietly.

Low and deep within Rachel, her body clenched, remembering Kyle's, the heat and strength of him, and the tenderness that had followed. But his blatant acknowledgment of their lovemaking to Bob and Shane was unnerving and embarrassing.

She shot Kyle a warning look. She knew exactly what she looked like in a sweatshirt and jeans and her pink thongs. And Kyle was looking at her feet as if they were dessert.

Then his gaze rose up her legs, slowly tracing her body up to the heat rising in her cheeks. Without moving, he reached out, snared her nape and drew her close for a brief, but thorough kiss. When he released her, Kyle kissed the end of her nose and patted her bottom. " 'Morning, honey."

When she recovered, Rachel didn't return his grin; she knew exactly what Kyle was doing, demonstrating his possession. She moved unsteadily away, putting the distance of another billiards table between them. She picked up the cue ball and tossed it lightly, catching it a few times to let Kyle know how much she wanted to throw it at him. He acknowledged her "I'll talk to you later" look with a nod and crossed his arms over his chest.

Rachel dragged her eyes away from him; Kyle's chest was too fascinating, too fresh in her body's memory, that crisp wedge of hair had rubbed erotically against her breasts.

She placed the cue ball onto the table, rolled it into a pocket, and pulled herself away from the sensual tension and irritation between them.

"What is this, a convention?" Rachel asked lightly and forced a light smile, when she could have killed Kyle. "A little early, isn't it?"

Bob's reply was short and darkly accusatory. "What

will your mother say? You know that Mallory took up with Scanlon and you know what happened to her? He's a womanizer and he'll ruin you. We expected more of you than this."

Shane's reply was soft and concerned. "We were only concerned. His car was parked next to yours this morning. He came over to see Mallory at odd times, and we just thought that maybe you—were having trouble."

"Oh, I know what he was here for," Bob stated darkly.

Kyle set up another eight-ball rack and began shooting expertly, apparently ignoring the scenario and leaving Rachel to defend herself.

Bob frowned at her. "I will not have you involved with him. I care for you girls and I warned Mallory off him, but she wouldn't listen."

Kyle's next shot clicked forcefully and he stood up to chalk his cue. His stare locked with Bob's. "He's right. We did have quite the conversation years ago."

The crisp morning air was heavy with shadowy tension that Rachel didn't understand. Then Kyle shrugged and started shooting again. His body was stretched into perfect position, the morning light coursing across his bare back, flowing over the ripple of his muscles, his arms—

Shane breathed heavily, glancing at her and then at the men. "I suppose I'd better go on my way. The ladies are having a meeting this morning and I've been asked to speak."

"Get rid of him," Bob stated tightly to Rachel and scowled at Kyle.

Kyle straightened and tossed his cue onto the table. His braced legs and that cord moving rhythmically in his jaw indicated a dark temper. "I guess that's Rachel's call, Winters."

"Rachel will have nothing to do with you. She knows what you did to Mallory."

"Well, I'd better go," Shane stated briskly and hurried out of the open door.

"I'll see you later, Rachel." Bob kissed Rachel's cheek and then raised to frown darkly at Kyle, who returned a steady impassive expression.

When Kyle picked up his cue and starting shooting as if nothing had happened, Rachel closed the front door and locked it. She felt like yelling and maybe killing Kyle who seemed intent upon lining up the cue ball on a tricky shot. She turned to him and crossed her arms as she leaned back against a pool table. "Thanks for making coffee," she said, keeping a leash on the need to yell at him.

He shrugged and slid the cue through the bridge of his fingers several times.

"What are you doing, Scanlon?"

"Lining up a shot . . . After last night, you could call me Kyle. Seems more intimate somehow."

He made the shot, pocketed one ball, and Rachel picked up the other as it rolled toward a pocket. "Game time is over."

"Sure." Kyle looked at her face and then slowly down her body. A muscle in his jaw clenched and he shrugged. "Anything you say."

He tossed the cue onto the table and walked to the door.

"You are not going out that front door on to Atlantis Street, dressed like that. People are starting to go into their shops. There are people walking and jogging now before going to work."

He turned and lifted an eyebrow. "It was what I was wearing when I came here last night."

"Fewer people will see you if you go upstairs and out the apartment door. And we haven't had that talk yet. I want those answers."

"So you're inviting me back upstairs, honey?" he questioned softly as he walked to her. Kyle's body blocked the view of anyone looking in the window as he ran a taunting finger down her cheek and her throat, down to the center of her chest.

Rachel's body instantly started humming, but she wasn't giving into his tormenting. "Suit yourself. You seem to do that easy enough when you were making certain that everyone knew you had been with me last night. What was the point of that anyway?"

Kyle watched his finger cruise across the tip of her breast. "First of all, it's impolite to leave a lover in the morning without some kind of sweet talk. I was just killing time until you woke up."

She snorted a little at that and tried not to focus on that prowling finger that had crossed to her other breast, circling the perimeter before tapping a nipple that was already peaked. Rachel gripped the table's rail at her hips tightly—in another minute she'd be touching Kyle, going for him, and he'd avoid the answers she wanted by making love to her once again. "You're no gentleman. Bob warned you off Mallory years ago, didn't he?"

Kyle's lips tightened slightly. "He did. But you knew that, didn't you?"

"I guessed. Who is that young girl in the picture?"

Kyle smiled briefly, then bent to nuzzle Rachel's cheek, the stubble arousing against her skin. "You're really warm, honey. And you smell really, really good. Has Shane been making a play for you? He seemed quite concerned."

He moved slightly, enough to bring his erection against her stomach, to nudge her gently. " 'Morning, honey."

"You're really good at this, aren't you? Getting what you want, and around what you don't want? You think you can push me into sex or into yelling at you and writing off that little chat you promised, don't you? You're very, very wrong. I'm not buying this time." Rachel pushed him away and her legs were unsteady as she crossed the room and went up the steps. She could feel Kyle behind her, the heavy attraction sizzling between them, growing with each step.

In her apartment, she turned to Kyle. "Your little display downstairs could have just been pure ego, or just maybe you were making it clear to the town that I was under your protection. . . . That is so outdated macho-bull, Kyle—"

Kyle had framed her face with his hands, lifting her lips to his. "All I said was that you smell great," he repeated. "Sexy."

Her hands were already at the snap of his jeans, locking him to her as Kyle slowly walked her backward into the bedroom. "Answers, Scanlon. Give me something I can work on. . . ."

"Oh, I intend to," Kyle returned as his hands began to move knowingly over her body.

*Dangerous woman,* Kyle decided later as Rachel lay

soft and sleeping against him. He already knew that trust came difficult to her, a fact that Mallory had placed on the father who had deserted their young family.

Rachel sighed softly and her hand rested, palm upward on his chest. It was a trusting gesture, that lightweight slender hand, the elegant fingers with practical short nails. Kyle brought it to his lips, and then to his face. He studied the softness of her skin against his darker skin, the fragility of woman's hand to man's larger, stronger one. The moment was bittersweet for him, there in the quiet shadows, when Rachel slept so quietly against him.

While she settled the haunting darkness inside him, he feared for what Rachel could uncover—and the danger she could bring to herself, and just maybe to Jada and Trina—and the girl.

He'd sworn to protect the girl, and he would, and that just might cost him the one thing he wanted for himself—Rachel. . . .

At three o'clock in the afternoon, traffic rolled quietly by the windows facing Atlantis Street. Nine Balls was quiet, except for the music Rachel had chosen and the steady click of balls against each other.

Mallory's favorite song curled around Rachel. . . . *I'll be with you forever, till the tides no longer flow, till doves no longer fly and roses no longer bloom, till time comes no more. . . . I'll be with you forever. On the far, still side of tomorrow. . . .*

Was that how Mallory felt, waiting for her? Waiting?

In her office, Rachel tossed down her pencil and drifted back to the earlier hours when Kyle had taken his time making love, "Making an impression that lasts," he'd said, holding her at the peak, taunting her until the last minute before releasing both their pleasures. . . .

His last kiss had been fierce and hard, demanding. "Don't open that door tonight and maybe you'd better consider moving somewhere safer, like my place. You've already got some idea of what Mallory went through. I don't want that to happen to you. I'll call you and you'd better have everything locked tight tonight."

"I'm not moving in with you."

His knuckles had lightly brushed her nipples, causing them to peak. "Then I could move in with you. Think about it."

Her senses had told her that Kyle wasn't coming to her tonight, but then she hadn't invited him. "I don't like firearms. Take that big gun with you."

"What big gun?" he'd taunted before pinning her to the bed, holding her wrists. "You have nightmares, you know. You don't like being held like this, do you?"

Kyle was right; pinned against her will reminded her of that attack. His orders about locking the door and the gun hadn't sounded like he was coming back that night, and that meant he was leaving town. Rachel had intended to find out where he went, what he did, and the identity of that young girl. "I don't believe that story about the girl—you know her, and I want to know what she was to Mallory."

At that, Kyle had pushed away and had slid into his jeans. "Did anyone ever tell you that dogging a man isn't polite?" he asked coolly and hadn't waited for an answer before leaving the apartment.

A list of emergency numbers, including police and

fire department and unfamiliar names of men, printed in Kyle's precise block letters, had lain beneath the big deadly semi-automatic. But it wasn't the list Rachel wanted—the one with the men in Mallory's life.

She already knew about Shane, who evidently did not want to be linked to Mallory, fearing that Rachel would find the poetry book he'd given to Mallory. Then someone wore size fourteen double-wide, custom-made high heels, and the cloth doll represented a man who Mallory hated very much, someone who might be using her family as a prod—

The men in Mallory's life could include Tommy James and Fred Parker and whomever Terri Samson was seeing.

The women were playing pool now, "taking an afternoon break," and Rachel left her office desk to watch them.

Just entering the billiards parlor, Trina smiled warmly at Rachel and placed her briefcase on a stool. She removed her navy blue business jacket, kicked off her high heels, and walked to the cue rack. With an expert eye, she selected one, hefted it, and rolled it on the nearest pool table to test for warping.

She smiled briefly at the women, slid the stick on the bridge of her left hand and shot, hitting the cue ball and creating a perfect spread in the break.

At a side table, Rachel sat with Anthony Cornelia, a small, aged Spanish immigrant who created custom-made cues, but he had also maintained Nine Balls' cues. Anthony had several sons who had their own businesses, but who sometimes picked up and delivered the cues. Rachel wanted to review the bill with Anthony, but also make it clear to him that if a before- or after-hours visit was necessary, that he or his sons must first call to arrange the time. But Anthony's attention was locked on her mother, the aged Spaniard enjoying the movements of a sensuous, long-legged woman and thinking of his youthful romantic adventures.

Rachel studied Terri, Sally Mae, and Dorothy. They were shielding their glances at Trina, but their expressions held guarded, fierce jealousy. Had they been so jealous of Mallory that they would hurt her, that they would send someone to do their dirty work, warning her off their men?

In a white business blouse and navy blue skirt that showed off her long legs, Trina Everly held the men of Nine Balls attention. The table of elderly men who were playing checkers stopped and watched the woman who had fascinated them for years. Two young male executives, wearing slacks and dress shirts, designer glasses and neat haircuts, had been apparently networking, sharing confidences as they shot a game of eight ball. They stopped playing and considered the older woman with the lithe body and froth of soft blond hair around her still attractive face.

"Excuse me, lady," Anthony said as he rose slowly. "I must see your mother. She was so good as a professional. I made her first sticks, you know, that is how I got my start in business that grows every day—your mother, she go to tournaments, she talk about my work, I get business to support my family. She is the same, always the same, beautiful, kind. Like Mallory with her tender heart for an old man who missed his homeland.

Almost nine years ago now, she bought this place and she have me take care of the sticks."

Rachel watched Anthony make his way past the pool tables, nodding politely to the women as he passed. She finished her notes on his bill, closed the file, and walked to her mother. "Busy day? You look a little tense?"

Trina placed the cue ball in position for a trick shot and missed, sinking two balls of the three. She smiled at Rachel. "It's a good thing I'm pushing calculator buttons instead of entering tournaments or taking bets on games and trick shots."

"You're good. You could play pro again if you wanted."

"Maybe. But I had a lot more drive back then, when I was desperate to support us and make some kind of a real life for myself."

Rachel hugged Trina briefly and said, "You've done that. Now what's up? You look worried. Are your braces hurting?"

"As if you didn't know my problem, sweet pea," Trina returned easily. "My braces are fine, if irritating when I speak to a customer. At fifty-two, I'm a little old to be wearing them—but I've always wanted straight teeth, and they aren't going to fix themselves. . . . I just finished speaking at a luncheon for businessmen and several people asked me about how you were doing here at Nine Balls. Bob was there. He feels almost like a father to you girls, and he's obviously concerned. He thinks Kyle Scanlon spent the night here last night and that Kyle is no good."

"I know that Bob thinks Kyle had a lot to do with Mallory's problems. I don't. I think Kyle probably kept her going longer than she would have without him—but not even he could stop her," Rachel said gently. She decided not to worry her mother; the unidentified man at her door just could have been anyone. "I trust Kyle, Mom."

"That's something, because you've very cautious. . . . I know Kyle took care of Mallory and I'm grateful. There were times I couldn't understand—" Trina smoothed Rachel's hair. "Miss Mermaid of Neptune's Landing," she murmured lovingly. "You're old enough to choose what you want to do, the relationships, I mean. After all, you're thirty-three and you almost married Mark Bradburn, that's the closest you've ever come to a commitment. I'll talk to Bob, but know that he loves you and wants the best. But you handle your life as you wish . . . I just want you to be safe, and living here—"

She looked around the billiards parlor at the women playing there, the young businessmen smiling back at her. "I worry that something can happen to you. I couldn't bear to have another daughter—"

Rachel wrapped her arms around her mother and leaned her forehead against Trina's. "Nothing is going to happen, Mom."

Trina held her daughter tight, her blue eyes locking with Rachel's. "Something is already happening. I feel it. I have the oddest feeling when I'm in here, like—"

"Like Mallory is here? Waiting?"

"Yes, just like that. I feel that she is very close and that she needs something. It's like when she was so young and sick and scared, but she wouldn't ask me to hold her. Do you think I'm—"

Rachel shook her head. "No, I feel that way, too, like

Mallory needs something to rest, and I intend to give it to her."

"It's just grief and the closure we didn't have, the things we couldn't make right for her. Don't let this obsess you, honey, please don't. If anything happened to you—"

"It won't. You're going to have to trust me on this one, Mom."

Trina's smile was tender. "Sometimes you're too much like me. You just decide you're going to do something and you do it."

Rachel kissed her mother's cheek and returned her smile. "And that's a bad thing?"

"You were too young, taking on too many responsibilities while I was working two jobs and traveling to tournaments. You don't have to do this. You can't be responsible for everything and everyone. You can't take the blame for how Mallory died, or for how she lived."

"I owe her, Mom. And I'm going to repay her."

"What do you owe her, Rachel? Why?"

Later, working in her office, Rachel shook her head. She hadn't answered her mother's question, because her debt to Mallory was very private; it would only hurt Trina now to know that she wasn't included back then. "I know what that humiliation feels like, Mallory, and I'm going to get whoever used our family as leverage to get what he wanted. Don't you dare leave until I get this worked out."

Rachel tapped a pencil on the desk. *Who was that girl in the photo? And what did she mean to Mallory?* She had an impish look that reminded Rachel of young Mallory, but her hair wasn't red and curly, it was light brown and straight, fine enough for the slight wind to pick it up, just like Shane's. . . .

"And Kyle knows. That girl meant something to Mallory and I'm going to find out just what it was. . . ." She listened to the office telephone ring, to her recorded answer, then to the deep rumble of Kyle's voice.

He was using his cell phone, the same as when he'd left two messages upstairs on her private line, but this time the rumble wasn't smooth and sexy—"Dammit, Rachel. Pick up or call me back."

The curt sound and brief call said his temper was fraying, and that was fine with her. She wasn't obeying his orders. . . .

Would he have called her at all, if she had not left a message on his brand-new answering machine?

Was he in another woman's arms?

One night with Kyle didn't make her an expert, but Rachel didn't think that his sex drive could equal two very busy nights.

But then, she didn't really know Kyle at all, did she?

And perhaps it was time to find out more.

And the best way to change that was to invite his "ex-wives" over for a private game of pool and girl-talk. But soothing Bob's ruffled feathers was first on her list.

Bob Winters' Handy Hardware was quiet at closing time; the store was small and stuffed with an old-fashioned mix of small appliances, basic hardware, pest controls, lawnmowers, and yard tools. Rachel, Jada, and Mallory had often worked part-time in the store, sweeping floors, sorting nuts and bolts, and stacking new items, gift-wrapping irons and mixers at Christmastime.

Bob's balding head gleamed beneath the fluorescent lights, his expression guarded as Rachel walked to where he was arranging a display of camp cookware. "Hi, Bob."

He placed an aluminum coffeepot onto the small camp stove. "Hi, yourself."

"How's it going?" Rachel didn't know where to start, to ease the tension created by Kyle's display that morning.

"Oh, pretty good. How about yourself?" He nodded to Jason Frederick, the clerk who was just leaving the store.

"Good." Rachel handed him a sack of his favorite bakery sweet rolls. "Sweets for the sweet. Jada is watching Nine Balls for me, so I can't stay long."

"Thanks. These rolls are my favorite." Bob wasn't looking at her, his usual warm smile gone, and he was obviously uncomfortable.

This wasn't going good, Rachel decided. She moved close to hug him, felt the safety that had always been there, the comforting softness of his belly, the familiar old-fashioned aftershave he preferred. "Are we all right? I mean you and me?"

"Sure, why not?" But his body was stiff, his words curt, and the air was cold between them when she stepped back.

Bob placed the bakery sack aside, when he usually opened it with delight. He walked past a key-making machine to the display of doorknobs and locks and started to tidy them.

He was obviously upset, and Rachel felt like she was

thirteen years old, awkwardly explaining why she had eaten a second helping of his homemade ice cream when no one was looking. "About this morning—"

His expression darkened as he opened a box and took a dead bolt from it, placing it into an empty place in the display. "I don't want to talk about that. Just don't see Scanlon again. He ruined your sister, and now you're asking for the same thing."

Uncertain how to handle a scolding she sensed was coming, Rachel didn't want to defend herself against a man who had been almost like a father. "Bob, I don't know what to say. I thought the same thing, but Kyle took care of Mallory when she needed someone."

"Mallory could have come to you or her mother or Jada or me. I know she stayed with him several times. You girls aren't mine, but I feel just as though you were. Now here you are, an intelligent, competent, educated woman, going down the same road as Mallory with the same scum. I can't tell you how disappointed I am in you, Rachel."

Feeling guilty and censured and young, Rachel was uncertain of what to say. The words came out unexpectedly, "I'm sorry, Bob. Really, I am, but Kyle isn't what you think he is—"

"I know what he is. Years ago, when he started fooling around with Mallory, I tried to stop her, too. But she wouldn't listen. I tried to give that—that mechanic— money to leave town and never come back. He laughed at me. I've tried to protect you girls the best way I knew how. It would break your mother's heart to see you going down the same road as Mallory did. My poor wife and I came to town years ago, and when Alissa passed on, I came to be a part of your family, caring for all of you. Think of your mother, for God's sake, girl. You think she wants to see you relive the hard life with a no-good like she had? Think of the consequences. Think of how she had struggled to take care of all of you, of how you were doing more than a girl's share of house and home. What happened to that nice boy you were engaged to?"

"That didn't work out." Mark Bradburn hadn't been nice when she couldn't respond to him after her attack. While she'd been sexually traumatized, he'd expected her to go on as if nothing had happened—

Rachel kissed Bob's cheek. "I know you love us and that you worry. But don't—"

"I want your promise that you won't see Scanlon again," Bob stated firmly.

"I can't do that," she returned honestly, and decided that their exchange was probably the usual, the father figure challenged by a younger man's entrance into his daughter's life. Patience and soothing usually settled these interpersonal irritations, and Rachel decided that everyone just needed that adjustment of time.

"Very well. Don't say I didn't tell you so. But think about your mother, what she's gone through and how this will just make her life more difficult. I wanted Mallory in a business she could be proud of, something that would take her away from the likes of Scanlon, and that's why I encouraged her."

Rachel studied the man who'd been like her father, at every holiday meal, fixing little things around the house, and said gently, "I know you gave her money to get started in Nine Balls, because you cared. This will work out. I love you, Bob."

With that, he reached for her, his hug familiar and safe.

Unsettled by Bob's adamant dislike of Kyle, Rachel was in no mood to chat with Shane Templeton whom she met on the street in front of Handy Hardware. She had the feeling that he'd been waiting for her, just as he had that night in the fog. He smiled pleasantly, "Ah, Rachel. So nice to see you again."

"Shane." While she would work to repair her relationship with Bob, Shane was another matter.

He fell into stride with her. "Visiting Bob? I know he's been like a father to you and he was quite upset this morning. I worried about his heart. Such trauma can't be good for a man of his age, you know."

"I'll worry about Bob. I really didn't appreciate your input this morning. The days of the scarlet letters are over, you know."

His smile wasn't nice, his full lips stretched back to reveal those small sharp teeth. "Yes, but some of you never learn, do you?"

Rachel wondered just how much effort Shane had put into teaching Mallory about life's righteous ways. Had he hurt her? His hair matched the color of the doll's and that of the girl's. Could he be the father of that girl?

A quick conversation on the street would allow him too much room to escape, and when Rachel pinned him, she wanted no place for him to run. "I've got to get back to my business. But I'd like to discuss this further with you. I'll call when things slow down a bit and we'll get together."

His hand locked onto her forearm and Shane leaned close. "Did you find anything that should be returned to me?" he demanded coarsely. "Tell me the truth—"

She looked down to the fingers biting into her arm. "Don't touch me—"

Bob stepped out onto the street and frowned at them. "Is something wrong, Rachel?" he asked in a tone that said he'd defend her.

Shane smiled as he released her, but the warmth didn't touch his eyes, slitted down at her. "There's nothing wrong at all. I was just telling Rachel that I knew how much Mallory meant to her."

"No, we're just chatting, Bob. . . . I'll talk to you later, Shane. Bye, Bob. Have to get back to work."

When she looked back, Bob remained standing on the sidewalk, alert as any father for a potential threat to Rachel. She waved to him, caught Shane's dark menacing look, and wondered if he had hurt Mallory, if his voice was rumbling in the background on that tape. . . .

*I'll haunt you forever.* . . . Mallory's threat echoed in his mind.

But now Rachel was asking questions and she just might find that damnable voodoo doll.

He chewed the tablets for indigestion and paced his home, building his rage. "Tramp. It appears that Neptune's Landing doesn't know you very well, Rachel Everly. You're sleeping with Kyle Scanlon, just like your sister did, and you're evil just as she was, driving me to hurt you. None of this is my fault, none of it.

Mallory tempted me, just as you do. And when I'm finished satisfying myself, I'll let the others have you. You'll learn to respect me, to want me . . . but first Kyle has to pay."

He smiled briefly, thinking about how he would enjoy killing Kyle, for taking what wasn't his. "She's mine, Kyle, just as Mallory was. Mallory ran to you for protection, but I'm giving Rachel nowhere to run. She'll be mine, just as Mallory was. . . ."

*I'll haunt you forever.* . . . He shivered as Mallory's promise rang through his mind once more, and the scent of vanilla seemed to curl around him. . . .

# Twelve

**"REAL NICE." JOHN SCANLON JR. GAVE A LOW WHISTLE AS** the yellow Sedan de Ville pulled onto the country racetrack. The men gathered around the stock car watched the big Cadillac coming slowly toward them on the unpaved country racing track.

In the bright late-afternoon Idaho sunshine, miles north of Boise, the narrow paved racing track seemed tiny against the backdrop of the surrounding fields and mountains. A child could grow and be safe in the white two-story house a few yards away, surrounded by flower and vegetable gardens. In the pasture was an easy tempered mare, perfect for a young girl to ride and to love, as well as the new kittens in the barn.

Kyle put down the wrench he'd been using and wiped his hands on an oily rag, tossing it aside; the younger man gave a low wolf whistle at the woman stepping out of the Cadillac.

"You better hope your wife didn't hear that," Kyle warned quietly as he walked to the weathered barn, employed as a garage. There, he used the basin, soap, and clean towel that John's wife insisted the men use before entering her spotless home.

*Rachel hadn't answered Kyle's calls, and he was on the point of leaving, returning to Neptune's Landing.* Things will have to change, Kyle decided grimly as he dried his hands. Leaving John Scanlon's number would be a lead straight to answers Rachel wanted. She could have used Kyle's cell phone number to return his calls; he'd left it by the semi-automatic and the list of whom to call in an emergency. Rachel could have called him at any time, and he didn't like the fact that he'd waited like a teenager for the sound of that ring, for her voice. She was getting to him, but that was what Rachel did best.

Living with her would be like walking through land mines.

Not living with her was even worse.

Rachel had always raised that something up in him that was more dangerous than sex, a protective, softer side shifted inside him, the need to open doors for her, put his arms around her and just hold her when she ached for Mallory or in her hard times.

Worse than that, he'd never known such peace, not just from sexual relief, climaxing inside her, but the softness after, her hand stroking his hair, his back.

Holding back those sweetheart urges had now become a real war within himself.

When a man started thinking marriage with a woman as headstrong as Rachel, he was definitely in for trouble . . . and yet, that was just what Kyle had done while making love to her—thinking about not using that condom, about placing his child deep within those soft clenching folds. . . .

She'd been right about showing off his macho territorial rights; he didn't want to think of her in another man's arms, much less his bed. . . .

Kyle allowed himself a grim, self-satisfied smile. Unless that condom glove was lying to him, the tightness of Rachel's body proved that sex had been a long time ago for her.

And that proved that she trusted him on a base level, or she would never have allowed him intimacy.

She'd pinned his need to set her off with a crude statement to divert his own emotions, the scars he didn't want touched.

"She's saucy, looks like she has a real attitude and knows what she wants." Younger and happily married John Scanlon grinned at Kyle. "She's locked onto you. You're drooling, old man . . . like she's the only dessert on your table. Know her?"

A hard knot tensed low in Kyle's body as he remembered Rachel moving beneath him, over him, that aching helpless sound as her body left her control and skyrocketed, convulsing around him. "A little. She's trouble. Where's Katrina?"

John, a protective father of the nine-year-old girl, frowned. "She's with her mother in the house, baking cookies. Why?"

"Tell Nola to keep Katrina out of sight for a while, will you?"

"Has this got anything to do with Mallory?" John asked warily.

"Plenty. That's her sister and she's not like Mallory."

"That's why you came out here last night, wasn't it? To warn us? You usually call, but this must be really serious. . . . It's Rachel, isn't it? I remember Mallory talking about her, wishing she could be more like her—sharp, intelligent, strong. . . ."

"Just call." When John picked up his hand unit to call his wife, Kyle leaned back against the red stock car, a nice fast number in the local weekend warrior races.

Dressed in loose flowing blue slacks and a blouse that the slight wind pasted against her curves, Rachel lifted her hand to remove the long leopard print silk scarf from her head. She threw it into the driver's seat with enough force to show her anger, as unsmiling, her eyes locked with his. There was just that tilt of her head, the edgy posture of her body—one hand rested on the Cadillac's open window and the other on her jutting hip—that spelled pure attitude. That silent message said she wasn't going to make the encounter with him easy, that she'd come after answers. Rachel lifted her head and shook it slightly, the wind picking up the strands of her hair.

Then she slowly, meaningfully looked at the girl's bicycle leaning against the garage. When Rachel looked back at Kyle, that small smug smile said she'd found what she'd wanted.

And what Kyle didn't want her to see . . . not yet, not until he was certain Rachel wouldn't move in to change things and endanger the girl—

He braced himself for the encounter, which was going to be a fast game; Rachel would bird-dog, pinpoint his every word. She leaned back against the Cadillac and crossed her arms, waiting for him to come to her.

Rachel was all curves, using what she had to torment him, to get to him, to nettle him.

And that said *he* was getting to her, because Rachel

wasn't the kind of woman to use sex to get what she wanted—she'd just go straight for what she wanted. She was enjoying herself now, getting to him, and that meant she was definitely interested. . . .

Kyle didn't hide his slow perusal of her legs, the place between them where he had lodged so deeply, and higher to her breasts, remembering how they tasted, the peaks. . . .

John finished his call and stood beside Kyle. "Now that is a whole lot of woman."

"That she is."

"Yours?" John asked quietly after a perceptive glance at Kyle.

John didn't know Rachel's driving need for independence or he wouldn't have asked that. Just the same, Kyle decided, after a night of passion—some sweet, some hard and demanding on both their parts—he had some small claim on Rachel Everly. A little tough, a little edgy and all woman, Rachel was careful of her relationships and protective of her body, and she'd allowed Kyle both. On the other hand, Kyle understood that she wouldn't tolerate a free and easy relationship, that both were locked in unspoken rules of this game. "Mine, and neither one of us are happy about it right now."

Kyle walked to Rachel and framed her body by bracing his hands on the Cadillac's open window. He reached past her to Pup, who was sitting in the passenger seat amid towels that covered the car's seat. A cannister of wet wipes sat on the floor; a stack of towels were in the back seat. He stroked Rachel's hips with his thumbs and leaned in for a hard fast kiss that she returned, without touching him anywhere else. "You wanted me enough to find me, now let's get out of here," he murmured against her lips.

The shadows beneath her eyes, her tight tense expression said that she hadn't been sleeping, that she was locked onto finding answers about Mallory's life—and death. Rachel wasn't likely to stop until hell broke loose and she'd dug down through the layers of the past . . . and answers that Mallory had made him promise not to reveal. . . .

If Rachel uncovered Mallory's beloved secret, she wouldn't stop there; she'd want more answers. . . .

But what did Rachel owe Mallory? Why had Mallory flown to New York so quickly to visit Rachel? Why had Mallory changed drastically since that visit?

Rachel lifted her jaw, her face slanting with that attitude that challenged him, her eyes dark with it. "Don't get any ideas that you're the only reason I'm here. I'm just delivering your dog. That's the bicycle you were repairing in your office, wasn't it? The same pink handlebar grips with fringes? Who's the girl, Kyle?"

Kyle leaned in close, but Rachel's crossed arms prevented access to those soft breasts. Nothing about the woman was easy access, he decided as he nudged his boot between her feet, then the other boot, until he was pressing intimately against her body. But she still didn't uncross her arms, giving him no evidence that he was getting to her. In the Idaho sunlight, with Rachel against him, Kyle momentarily enjoyed the sense that his life was good and rich. But the feeling was only momentary, because Rachel was on the hunt and she wanted answers from him. "How did you find me?"

"I told you, I'm good."

There was enough huskiness in her voice to tell him she wasn't immune to the sexual play between them. He nuzzled the side of her face, enjoying her scent, taking it into him. "Patty and Iris, right?"

Her smile moved against his cheek. "Mm. We just happened to play pool last night, after hours and chatting as women do. They were worried about charging up too many phone bills while job shopping. I told them I'd take a look at your past bills and see what kind of calling plan you had. Amazing where telephone numbers can lead."

Kyle bent to nuzzle her throat, flicking his tongue over that smooth skin, and the slight quiver of her body said she wasn't immune to his play. He moved to bite her earlobe gently. "You work fast. I only left yesterday. Patty and Iris are supposed to vacate while I'm gone. Time for the kids to grow up someday, and I didn't think you'd want them there when you make those cute little noises, when you're struggling to hold back from coming."

Kyle actually wanted the girls out of harm's way. Whoever had taken Mallory down that long dark road, might not like the trouble Rachel was certain to stir up—and his little chicks just might end up in danger. Protecting Rachel was going to be difficult enough, especially with a midnight caller appearing at her door. . . . "What took you so long, honey?"

"Yes, well. I needed time for Patty and Iris's private lesson with just a little wine later upstairs in my apartment, didn't I? They'll probably tell you about how much fun we had. Then I had to follow them home to the junkyard to review those bills— By the way, I met your buddy, Moses Fry."

"He's helping move the girls. Did he make an impression?"

"A six-foot-seven human wall with no neck usually does. I've seen him in town before, but I didn't know he belonged to you. What's he do for a living? Break arms and body parts?"

Kyle fought a smile and lied, "He grows flowers. Orchids are his specialty."

He'd called in Moses, an ex-wrestler and a contract bodyguard, to help the girls move, and to help protect Rachel and her family—because someone was certain to be provoked by her questions. Someone in Neptune's Landing liked to hurt women, and Rachel wouldn't stop until she found who Mallory's doll represented. . . .

Then, Moses would be a hefty deterrent if Jimmy and his friends decided to make life rough on Rachel.

She angled a disbelieving look up at Kyle and he admired the sweep of her lashes, the way her lips curved and that dimple slid into her cheek. He bent to kiss it briefly, and Rachel braced her hands against his chest to wedge room between them. "Sure. You're lying, Kyle. But hey, what's a little white lie between friends. If I'm looking tired, you could make things easy on me. It was over three o'clock in the morning when I got home. Harry still won't go home with me, by the way. Pup did . . . he can jump into a car, you know. He's not easy to trick, by the way, so he stayed in my car all night. I tried to drop him off at your place on my way out of town at five this morning, but he wasn't buying and I wasn't wasting time. . . . *Who is that girl, Kyle?*"

He let a strand of that soft fragrant hair cling to his

skin, enjoying the sunlit burst of color, reds blending with browns, sparks dancing across the ends. Rachel was tracking, hunting down facts and that quick mind would soon lace them together into a neat package that could endanger Katrina. He had to buy time, to distract Rachel until he could think of a plan to get her away from the girl he'd sworn to protect "Let's go into town for a hamburger, okay?"

Rachel arched a brow. "Will I get what I want? I'd better, or I'm right back here and I won't be put off."

"I know," Kyle agreed grimly as he rounded the car and opened the passenger door to let Pup out.

The dog immediately ran to John, and Rachel watched the dog's happy frisky play with him. "Mm. What do you know. . . . Pup has been here before, hmm?"

Kyle tossed Pup's towels in the back seat and crooked a finger at Rachel to come to the passenger side. Despite the brewing argument coming up, it was always worth the challenge to Rachel, just to watch her light up to a silent order. She smiled tightly and rounded the car, sitting in the passenger seat. "This better be good," she warned. "And you had better not race Buttercup."

He got into the driver's seat, adjusted it and the rearview mirror to his taller height. He started the car, driving it off the small acreage that John Scanlon Jr. had purchased from his father. Kyle glanced at the scrap of paper tucked into the sun visor of the driver's seat. Rachel had written, "Margie's Little Motel" and number for the motel not far from the Scanlons' place. Something that looked like a confirmation number followed. Two and two weren't difficult to add—Rachel was staying at the motel.

The car hurried over the paved road and Kyle was just framing what he should or should not tell Rachel when she said, "That's Scanlon Heat and Cooling on the side of the service truck back there and on that stock car. Scanlon. . . . as in you?"

"As in John's father. John Sr. pulled my teenage butt out of trouble and into his home, a cop's home with love and rules. He was a great guy who didn't need to spend all his time figuring out how to get to me, but he did. He trusted me with his son and everything he had. The Scanlons were the first real family I'd ever had. They put up with a lot while I sorted out why I didn't want to end up in jail. . . . The senior Scanlons are retired in Florida now. By the way, what did you do with my gun?"

"Left it where it was, with that thoughtful note of who to call. What was your birth name?"

He stared at her blankly and thought back though the blanket of years to remember. "Smith, plain old Smith. You just left a fully loaded handgun lying around?"

She returned the stare with a challenge. "What was I supposed to do with it? Mail it to you?"

"You're damned irritating."

"So are you."

She wasn't backing off and Kyle had expected no less. "I suppose we're even, then. Any unexpected visitors last night?"

"For the whole two hours I was home, no . . . no one other than your buddy, Moses Fry, sitting in my parking lot. He was snoring with the car window open and looked like he'd been dragged through quite the day—relocating Iris and Patty, I guess. I took him out a piece of Mom's German chocolate cake and told him to leave or I'd call the police. That made an impression, if you can call a grunt that, and he left. You came out here to warn them about me, didn't you? They—and the girl who you gave that bicycle to—must be very special, or else a simple phone call would have done. The way I read this is that you didn't want to alarm them, but take your time easing into a big fat warning about me, right? What they should say and not say? That sort of thing?"

"You're damned irritating, honey," he repeated slowly, because Rachel was right on target. He'd come to gently prepare Nola and John that Rachel would probably be asking questions about Katrina.

"And the hamburger offer was just to get me out of there, right, Scanlon? Mm. Scanlon, as in Heating and Cooling, stock car racing, a cop, and let's see, there should be more clues to run down. Make it easy on everyone, Smith-Scanlon, tell me what I want to know—all those interesting missing pieces."

"Okay, it's a simple story—I'm a usual run-of-the-mill kid who'd had enough with my boozing parents, and I took off on my own too early. I hung around racing tracks and got into trouble. John's dad took me to his home. John Sr. got me into country racing and I got those trophies, small-time stuff, just enough to make me feel like someone special, a little pride in myself. Somewhere in there, I wanted my own home and my own place. One day I was driving through Neptune's Landing on my way to a race—I could always get work as a mechanic, but I was racking up a few trophies by then—then I saw this mermaid riding a wave on a parade float, and I thought how much I'd like to get my hands on her shells . . . and I wanted to live in a town where I could see the ocean every day and watch the whales blow. . . . Did anyone ever tell you that you've got bullying tendencies?"

Bob Winters had also been a determining factor for Kyle to stay in Neptune's Landing. He'd come to Mac's Garage, found Kyle stripping a car for parts, and had his say. "You'll never amount to anything. You're a punk, a smart-aleck kid with greasy hands, and you'll end up with DTs in some drunk tank. We don't need your kind in Neptune's Landing. You're trouble for anyone around you. Get out of town and save yourself some grief."

But at twenty-two, Kyle had other plans, one of which was to prove Bob Winters wrong and John Scanlon Sr. right. Bob may have been acting as a protective father to Trina's daughters, but Kyle wasn't letting anyone push him back down into that gutter with his parents, if that's what they could be called. . . .

Rachel searched his face. "That's what you and Mallory had in common, wasn't it? The hard times as a child?"

"I knew where she was coming from, what had changed my life, the same thing that should have changed hers—someone who cared. But something went wrong with her . . . she had chances. Trina was a great mother and loved her, but Mallory chose something different. I could have ended up the same way. I . . . think she thought that kind of life was what she deserved, that she wasn't worth anything—but she was. She was the gentlest person I've ever known."

Rachel looked out the window to the passing farmland and her voice was uneven and quiet. "I wanted—I wanted her to be safe and I thought I knew what was best and I screwed up. I probably forced her in the opposite direction by pushing so hard. . . ."

"Get over here." Kyle reached out his arm and pulled her close to him. He kissed her cheek, tasted the tears there, and knew that he cared more for Rachel than he should. He eased off the highway and onto a country dirt road, then parked in a sheltered grove of pine trees. "Come here."

This was the Rachel that few saw, the fighter stripped away, the vulnerable woman inside grieving for her sister, blaming herself for something she couldn't fix or control. Her body shook in his arms and the place where her face rested against his shoulder was damp with tears. "I loved her so much, Kyle. And now she's gone, and I probably didn't tell her that enough."

"You told her," he whispered against her temple. "She knew."

Rachel raised her face and drew his down for a light kiss. She studied each feature of his face slowly, intently, as her fingertips stroked his lips. Kyle let himself sink into the warm feminine softness curled next to him, but at the same time, realized that Rachel could bring danger to herself and others. "You're tired, honey, and locked onto this thing. Not a good combination."

And then Rachel said, "You could use a shave. . . . Is the girl who owns that bike Mallory's daughter?"

From the moment she saw Kyle, standing in a greasy T-shirt and worn jeans, Rachel's body recognized his.

When he'd walked slowly toward her, his expression

grim, Kyle had known exactly how he affected her, his jaw rough, unshaven against her skin, raising Rachel's sexual attention and something else.

There, crossing that bare ground, the barn and the stock car behind him, Kyle looked tall, tough, and fascinating. Rachel's senses had spiked, needing to challenge him, to taste him. Sex, she decided, it had been a long, long time since she'd enjoyed lovemaking, and Kyle was an expert. He'd use sex to distract her, to waylay her, from the answers she wanted—if he could.

The really bad part, Rachel had to admit to herself, was that he had redeeming qualities—enough to make a woman care for him, to trust him.

Worse. At some base level, Kyle matched her need to challenge, to test, to play. Now that was an irritating thing for a woman to discover in a dangerous opponent, that she could really care for him, that she ached to hold him and comfort those raw hurting edges she had sensed.

Maybe that was his appeal—that women needed to ease his darkness from those times before the cop brought young Kyle into his home. In this man's arms, Rachel definitely felt all woman, who could possess and who could be possessed.

Now, in his arms, Rachel drew her fingertip across Kyle's lips, testing him. "Answers, Scanlon?"

He bit gently, humor rising in those blue eyes. Then, before she could take a breath, his hand gripped her hair, holding her as he took in her face. "Nice lipstick. Tastes like cherry."

"Make it easy on yourself, Scanlon." Rachel forced

herself to breathe, her heart pounding, because Kyle had that tight narrowed look of a man with one thing on his mind—her.

"Did you miss me?" he asked rawly. The husky, uneven sound spoke of his uncertainty, of that appealing vulnerability and truth.

"Not at all," she lied; she'd thought about him almost constantly—and his confident grin told her that he knew it, too.

"Sure. You're here, aren't you?"

She placed her hand on his chest, enjoyed the smooth hard surface, the male body beneath it. She tilted her face up to his and studied the way his eyes crinkled at the sides, the slight curve of his lips. "Just delivering your dog, Smith-Scanlon, that's all. And running down answers."

"Sure that's all it is, honey?" His low drawl and look down her body said he was ready to supply her sexual needs.

She'd relaxed, enjoying the crisp texture of his hair in her fingers, the sensual intimacy between them, and Kyle had just shifted it into a woman running after a man for sex. "There you go, saying things like that when you don't want to—"

Kyle raised an eyebrow. "Give you what you want?"

Once again, he'd raised his defenses, not letting her too close, firing a lewd remark at her that would set her off and let him escape an uncomfortable intimacy—lovers relating truthfully to each other. On edge and deeply tired, Rachel didn't want to play anymore. "I've had enough. Just get out. We're both wasting time."

Kyle's expression hardened. "You've got other plans, right?"

She reached for her scarf and tied it around her head with shaking hands. "Get out."

Kyle nodded grimly and got out of the car, closing the door behind him. Rachel slid to the driver's seat, started the motor, and reversed, leaving him standing in the middle of the dirt road. His weight on one long leg, his arms crossed and looking tough and fierce, Kyle wasn't asking for anything.

Which was exactly why she couldn't leave him; Kyle expected nothing, no kindness, nothing but hard times—and that said his boyhood scars weren't far from the surface when it came to her. He didn't know how to relate on the simplest of intimacies and protected himself with those lewd remarks, keeping everything on a sexual level, when it evidently went deeper with them both. . . .

Rachel drove slowly back to him. She parked, got out of the car, and walked to him. She took a deep breath, separated the hurt, vulnerable boy from the man staring down hard at her and asked, "Are you going to kiss me or not?"

His casual answer only irritated her more. "Okay, if that's what you want. Do you think it will stop there?"

"Probably not."

"You wearing that pink toenail polish?"

"Uh-huh." Sensual heat quivered between them as Kyle's lips brushed hers. "Let's go get that burger."

Forty-five minutes later, Kyle parked in front of Margie's Little Motel, a plain tan-colored strip of rooms with doors painted in chipped maroon. In the late afternoon sunlight, several battered farm pickups and older cars parked in front of the different rooms. While Rachel was absorbing her current situation—parked in front of a cheap motel, located in a tiny burg of a town—a big tough-looking, unshaven mechanic was circling the car. He held a sack of burgers and a drugstore sack with a man's basic travel kit and a big box of condoms. Kyle opened her door and grinned down at her. "What's the matter? Is this a first?"

The milkshakes she'd been holding were probably melting from all the growing sensual tension between them. As they had made the purchases, Kyle's hand had ridden low on her waist, his body had moved around hers as he opened the Burgers and Fries door and that of the drugstore. Embarrassed by his purchases, Rachel had studied the magazine counter.

"You won't need those," Kyle had whispered as he reached past her to collect one. He had added a couple of candy bars to the sack and had again rested his hand on her waist, guiding her out the door and into the car. It was a possessive gesture of a man who knew what he had coming, who was familiar with her body, keeping his close to hers. . . .

Now Rachel slid out of the car's seat and stood in the bright Idaho sunlight with the milkshakes melting in her hand and cars passing on the road nearby. A light was out in Margie's high neon sign, and the city limits sign of ChakChak read, Pop. 1500. "Is this where you take all your dates?"

Kyle closed her door and opened the back one to retrieve her overnight bag. "Not a one, honey. They usually cost more. You paid for the room with your credit card," he said with a wide boyish grin that said he was teasing her.

"Very funny. I need to check in."

"No need. I told Amy, the clerk at the drugstore, to call Margie. The door is unlocked, the keys on the dresser. I also had Amy call John and tell him not to expect me any time soon."

"Great. Now everyone knows."

"Probably." Kyle chuckled, a rich sound that took her looking up at him. Then everything inside Rachel stilled and locked onto this man, the textures, the colors, the sunlight glistening off his eyebrows, the wave that just crossed his brow, the sensual curve of his lips. . . .

"Let's get inside." Kyle's voice was uneven and low, his expression taut. With her overnight bag on his shoulder and the sacks in that same hand, Kyle's other hand rested on her waist. Near his body as he opened the door, Rachel absorbed the heat and tension in it. She walked to the tiny table and placed the milkshakes on it, then watched Kyle close the cheap blinds, sealing the world away. He glanced at her and her hands locked together, icy with the fear of this threshold, this new relationship.

Kyle walked to her, took her hands and raised them to his face, warming them with his heat. Kissing each palm, Kyle looked at her. "Be here when I get back."

"I'm not promising that, Kyle." It had been too easy, standing beside him, considering the menu above the fast food counter, aware of his body brushing hers, his hand possessively on her hip, and the stop by the drugstore for essentials where Kyle knew the employees, chatted about the weather and crops, and introduced her simply as "Rachel." And through all that, he'd held her hand, as naturally as if they'd been dating for years.

Kyle rubbed her thumb across his lips. "Honey, the heat is fairly dancing off you, the way you move against me."

"I'm not going to ask how many times you've done this—burgers and condoms routine. You probably have a standing accommodation somewhere. . . ."

His smile curved beneath her thumb, and he bit the pad gently. "Nope. This is a first for me."

"I don't believe that."

"Then, don't."

Their eyes locked and Rachel realized that her hands had gripped the jeans covering his hips. "I've never been in a cheap motel room before."

His eyebrow lifted. "Always a first time."

"I might leave, Kyle. I might just go back to the Scanlon ranch and talk to that girl."

He bent to kiss her jawline, running his tongue along her skin, flicking it. "You could, but I'm asking you not to."

She was warm, melting, vibrating, hungry for him. "But can you trust me not to?"

Against her ear, Kyle's breath was warm, his tongue busy. "She's just a little girl who's safe and loved. . . . I'm so hard, I don't know if I can wait, and I've been working all morning with motor oil."

Rachel inhaled that underlying pure male scent, and wanted him then, her hands moving up and under his shirt, smoothing that hard, hot chest, his pounding heart. "Down and dirty might not be too bad."

His eyebrows lifted. "We're still in the courting stages. I'm trying to be a gentleman."

The challenge was there, to have her way, to push him. Those flickering silvery eyes darkened as she stood on tiptoe and kissed him, biting his bottom lip, enveloping herself with his textures, the hunger pouring out of him, that taut body jutting against hers. "What if I want you now?"

Only one night with Kyle and she was addicted, wanting more. . . .

"Too bad. You'll have to wait."

"It's not nice to keep a lady waiting."

"Anticipation," he murmured as he held her hands away; he walked into the bathroom, leaving her the choice to leave, or to stay.

Rachel picked up her strawberry milkshake and sucked the straw. Her insides were quivering, clenching, hot, aching for Kyle, and he knew it. She eased into a chair and studied the bag of burgers on the tiny table. She should leave him and drive back to the Scanlons. He'd tossed her keys onto the dresser. She could take them and—and she remembered the possessive way Kyle's hand had caressed her nape, his thumb cruising erotically just behind her ear.

Strange that she should have had a long-term lover who had never discovered that tiny spot just there. . . .

Rachel swallowed nervously; she was in a cheap but spotless motel room, and she was paying for the room and dinner was burgers, fries, and milkshakes. If she had any sense at all, she could leave and return to the

Scanlons to find that girl. Once she'd talked to the girl, she'd know if she was Mallory's daughter.

That's what she *should* do. But Kyle had trusted her—

She was still sitting on a chair when Kyle stepped out of the bathroom, showered, shaven, and smelling great. Naked and powerful, a towel slung low around his hips, Kyle crossed the room slowly, kneeling beside her, taking her cold hands in his, taking them to his lips. "Hungry?"

"Yes."

"Afraid of what's happening between us?"

"Yes."

He smiled against her fingertips, rubbing them against his newly shaven jaw. "Then I guess we should eat before those burgers get cold, right?"

"That's logical." The brisk scent of the drugstore's cheap aftershave mixed with that of soap and shampoo and man; his skin was damp to her touch, his hair wet, uncombed and standing in odd peaks. She smoothed Kyle's hair, locked her fingers in it briefly, before stroking the hard planes of his face.

Hunger danced across her skin, heating it and making her ache for him, for the press of his body deep inside hers. The knowledge that soon they would be wrapped in each other, pleasuring each other, caused her to breathe raggedly.

Rachel wouldn't deny that her body needed his, that heat simmered between them, her hunger building. . . . She tried to breathe as his hand slid over her thighs, resting open on one as his thumb stroked her intimately, and heat flooded her body, her sensitive folds opening with the slight pressure. "It's just five o'clock, Scanlon. Your hand is very busy down there."

"You're damp, Everly. And hot. Don't you think we should do something about that?" He reached for a milkshake, took a long draw, and kissed her with cool lips and eased his cold tongue into her mouth as his hands moved over her breasts, caressing them. His fingers started loosening the buttons of her blouse, slowly undoing them. He looked down at her breasts, and she wanted him to see her body, to watch his reaction, that primitive flaring of his nostrils, that heat skimming across his broad cheekbones, the burning intensity of his eyes. "You taste like strawberries. Ever made love while drinking milkshakes?"

When his mouth lowered to take her breast, sucking gently, Rachel cried out softly.

"No, I don't believe I ever have. . . ."

*I'll haunt you forever. . . .*

In his study, the man paced back and forth. Jada didn't know where Rachel had gone. Rachel was after something, prowling around Neptune's Landing, digging into private lives, and pretty soon she just might stumble onto something incriminating.

"I can't afford that. . . . She could ruin everything, my whole life of hard work, my standing in the community. . . ."

Rachel had closed Nine Balls with a simple sign on the door—*Closed For Repairs.* She'd called Jada early that morning and had told her and Trina not to worry, that she was taking a "little drive" to relax, maybe staying out of town overnight.

"She never relaxes, and she always has a purpose."

He continued to prowl in his study, furious with Rachel's interference. A methodical woman, she'd scour Nine Balls and the apartment and she'd find the connection he didn't want discovered. If the doll was still there, the doll with the needles that had caused him to be impotent. . . .

He rubbed his forehead where the headache had lodged and imagined the pin piercing his head like a sword. . . .

Rachel had burned candles, the same way as Mallory, the vanilla scents lingering in the apartment. "Witches, the both of them, deserving what they get. Rachel is no more than the evil harlot her sister was. She's out there now, doing something she shouldn't be, poking around in other people's business. Just maybe she needs a lesson, right here in Neptune's Landing. I'd prefer to do it away from here, but if I have to—"

The sunset slid through the window and shot straight into his brain. He reached into his desk drawer, found the headache pills his doctor had prescribed, and swallowed two of them with a full glass of water.

Until Mallory's death, he'd had a means to find pleasure, either watching her with other men by the video camera he'd installed or by punishing her for the evil seductress she was. Mallory had drawn him into her web, caused him do things he didn't want to do. Only when she was groveling, practically strangled, could he successfully use her. "Because she actually liked it, knew that it was her punishment for being a sinner, a whore."

He'd removed the camera, just a tiny device hidden behind Mallory's headboard with a perfect view to the activities on her bed. It wouldn't do to have anyone else find it, because technology could have traced it to him. Rachel had stripped the apartment, burned Mallory's bed, and replaced it with her own, one that Kyle Scanlon had obviously shared.

"Where is that damned doll?" Forcing rage under control that few had seen, he sipped his cup of tea and brooded about Rachel and her lover. "Scanlon should have taken the hint, but he didn't. Now it looks like I have Rachel and Scanlon to deal with. Not a good combination, but one that I am perfectly able to handle," he murmured confidently before going back to his paperwork.

A car passed by on the street bordering his office and soulful music slipped through his open window. *I'll be with you forever, till the tides no longer flow, till doves no longer fly and roses no longer bloom, till time comes no more. . . . I'll be with you forever. . . .*

Shaking, his hand knocked over the teacup, the brownish liquid spilling onto his paperwork. "Mallory. . . ." he whispered, because the song was her favorite, and in his way, he'd loved her.

# Thirteen

---

**"YOU'RE GOING TO TELL ME," RACHEL WHISPERED FIERCELY,** her fingers digging into Kyle's shoulder as she pressed her hips down upon him, moving slowly to feel him deep inside, filling her.

"I am?" Kyle's hands were busy cupping her breasts, his mouth tormenting them, the edges of his teeth applying just enough pressure to keep her on that peak without releasing her.

Rachel's thighs slid against his, her hips lifting, withdrawing that tight moist heat gloving him. "Tell me, Scanlon."

Her hair clung damply to her cheeks, her muscles taut with the physical pressure of demanding everything from Kyle. Her skin burned with every touch of his hands, of his belly, hard against hers, of the place where his body locked with hers.

Riding on the edge of her passion, fiercely needing to match Kyle's raw, honest hunger, Rachel pushed herself—and him—and reveled in the wide-open freedom, holding nothing back. . . . She smiled briefly into his silvery slitted eyes, testing the beast within him, the control of those big hands moving on her possessively.

He clamped her to him and she loved moving within the power of their lovemaking, holding her own, demanding as much as he. . . . She'd never been so alive, prowling through her sensations, her hunger, feeding on it—

She tasted the perspiration on his jaw, nipping him lightly to feel the rock-solid jolt of his body within her, the strain of holding back nudging him.

Once more, she dived in to feed on his lips, to taste the hot dark depths of his mouth, her tongue matching his, the slant of their kiss as tight as the joining of their bodies. She pushed down hard, felt the resulting inner pressure and held still, feeling his breath upon her face, gauging that dark savage look on his face, the stark primitive look that said he'd be coming soon, that he needed relief.

"You're not sweet, Scanlon. You're holding out in more ways than one."

"That's my charm, honey. Keeps 'em coming back for more."

Rachel grasped his head and took his mouth again. "You know that's not true. The girls and I had a little chat about you. You haven't had sex for years."

Kyle's hands slid down to cup her butt, hiking her closer, moving her body faster, rocking her above him. "What would they know?"

"They aren't exactly sweethearts, Kyle. They just know. You're sweaty."

"So are you, and you're close to it—"

"No more than you. . . ."

"Oh, no?" His hand curved around her hip and eased down low on her, his thumb pressing, rubbing just there—

Rachel closed her eyes as the tightening within her started to pound, racing through her bloodstream, burning her mind. Amid her pleasure, swimming in it, resenting letting it go, Rachel couldn't think, arching back as Kyle took her breast into his mouth, sucking in rhythm to the pounding of their bodies. She tossed against him, fighting to control the tide of heat and pleasure overtaking her. . . . But Kyle held her tight, moving relentlessly amid the storm enfolding them.

On that high edge of release, Rachel held herself tightly, going inside herself for the pleasure that ran on without her control.

Kyle turned her quickly beneath him, moving deep inside, holding them both on that edge. Rachel gripped his back, dug her fingers into the powerful, flowing muscles, her feet braced to lift her hips higher to his. When her pleasure burst, she cried out and supported by his forearms, Kyle's muscled body arched bow-tight.

After a long sweet fall into a pool of pleasure, Rachel summoned her strength to look up at Kyle, still locked in place, his body quivering with his own release. His expression was no longer primitive, but tenderness and uncertainty moved around the hard planes, something that caught and bound her.

Rachel lifted her hands and smoothed his face, drawing him down for a soft kiss. She felt more for this man than the passion that rose too quickly, the burning flame too hard to control. She was half in love with him, needing him, enjoying their game. She floated amid the small, gentle kisses across her face, the tenderness soothing after an almost savage lovemaking, and gathered him down upon her, stroking those quivering muscles of his back in a leisurely play she'd never wanted, never had. . . .

"I'm heavy," Kyle breathed against her throat as he prepared to ease away, his muscles tensing.

"Stay . . ."

She ran her insoles up and down his legs, cherished the difference of male and female textures, her thighs rubbing against his. "Mmm. . . . Is that all you've got, Scanlon?" she whispered dreamily. She didn't want this moment to end, the weight of Kyle upon her, the safety and warmth she felt with him now, the barriers gone. . . .

He nuzzled her throat, kissed the edge of her jaw and smiled against her lips as his hands moved gently over her. "Having fun?"

Rachel drifted amid her soft, glowing cloud, luxuriating in the aftermath of their passionate struggle. She sighed and when she forced her eyes to open that bit, she caught Kyle's closed expression, the way he watched his hands flowing over her breasts, over her hips and thighs. "You're so pale, so soft," he whispered unevenly.

"You're not," she returned gently, as she sensed Kyle wading through his emotions. Whatever was being forged between them, apart from sex, shimmered and warmed. He'd held her so possessively, touched her so reverently, almost in awe.

When he looked back at her, Kyle frowned and eased away, lying beside her. Rachel curled against him, placed her thigh over his, her hand running across that damp, intriguing chest as she kissed his shoulder and listened to his slowing heartbeat. His fingers slid the damp strands from her cheek and replaced them with his kiss.

The air-conditioner's steady hum enfolded them, sunset lighting the closed blinds, people talking, yelling as they entered their cars, the beep of automatic locks being opened and closed. Enclosed in their private world, Rachel slid into much needed sleep.

She slowly surfaced to Kyle's warmth moving over her, his knee easing her legs apart, his sex stroking her up and down, dampening her to slide within, filling her. Dreamlike, they made love, a gentle contrast to their first desperate hungers and later, lay tangled amid the sheets, hands lightly caressing each other's bodies, a kiss given and one taken as the hours slid by.

"Mallory's vanilla scent is soaked into everything, even my notepad."

At eleven o'clock, his office was quiet and shadowy, the light of the computer screen lighting his face. He answered a few impatient e-mails, "friends" wanting their old meeting place back—and the girl that went with them. They didn't know who he was, of course, his identity protected by an anonymous e-mailing system. They weren't happy about staying away, but he needed time to get Rachel out of Nine Balls.

Jada's running dialogue as she'd cleaned his house had infuriated him, but he'd pushed away that anger and coldly set to work tracking her sister. Bringing Rachel to heel excited him, and the next time he'd make certain that she fought—and aroused him. He flipped open his notepad to the numbers he'd taken from

Rachel's credit cards. Luckily, she was one of those people who used online banking and her credit purchases could be easily tracked with a password. He had taken down several passwords from the booklet he'd found in her laptop briefcase. . . . "That sloppiness was not typical of her, but then, she was upset about her sweet sister, wasn't she? Mm . . . Mallory . . . that password fits right on target, Rachel. . . ."

He scanned the list of Rachel's online accounts. "Nice investments. Smart, but then, you've always taken care of business, haven't you, Rachel? You've got quite a nice nest egg. You can run Nine Balls for a while without showing a profit, can't you?"

He hunted for her credit cards, anything to show him recent purchases. Rachel had used her credit card just that afternoon, and he quickly clicked to her last charge. "Margie's Little Motel," the 800 number, and the charge was listed.

Confidently, he dialed a number of an "associate" who called the motel asking directions. Within minutes, the motel's location in ChakChak, Idaho, came back. Using the white pages online, he found a John Scanlon Jr. "Very interesting, Rachel. You're with Kyle now, aren't you? That mechanic—letting his greasy hands touch you. . . ."

His own were soft, but strong and he knew they could hurt.

The semi-automatic gleamed on his desk and he hefted it, getting the feel of it. The fully loaded clip was filled with deadly hollow-point bullets. "Mmm. A handy little thing. Left right beside a list of people for

Rachel to call if she felt threatened. Most likely it belongs to Kyle, who wrote that list."

He sighted it out in front of him, supporting his right hand with his left. He'd never really toyed with a gun before. It was heavier than he expected and he chuckled as he thought of the stunned look on the mechanic's face as a bullet took him down—not to kill him immediately, but just enough to disable him. "It is always you, Scanlon, standing in the way of what I want. And then I can have Rachel . . . she'll grow to love me, too, just as Mallory did."

He thought of Rachel beneath him—soft, agile, terrified—and chuckled again, wildly, the sound ricocheting in the shadows. . . .

Somewhere between midnight and predawn, Rachel roused. As she slipped from Kyle's arms, his eyes opened, hunger still simmering within the depths. Her body ached slightly as she walked to the bathroom, aware of his stare, the attraction of his body for hers. Had she returned to Kyle, they would have made love once more.

Instead, Rachel collected her overnight bag and then walked into the bathroom and showered luxuriously, her body sensitive to the pinpricks of warm water, to the soap bubbles sliding down her, to the intimate and sensitive areas of her body that Kyle had possessed. She towel dried her hair and in the mirror found the slight reddish marks of his morning stubble on her skin, the heavy sated look of her eyes, the new fullness of her lips. Kyle's overnight kit—aftershave, a toothbrush and toothpaste, shaving cream, and a blue plastic razor he had used yesterday—rested on the scarred vanity next to the chipped sink.

*What was she doing in this cheap motel room, a sack of cold, untouched burgers on the table and a man sprawled, sleeping in the bed with the sagging mattress?*

*Why did she want more, even now, after making love for hours, the muscles of her body aching slightly from the exertion, pushing the limits?*

Yet there was tenderness between them now, a caring she hadn't expected or hadn't wanted. The attraction could be physical and momentary, soon dying and leaving little self-respect.

On the other hand, now, at this moment, she didn't want to be anywhere else but in this cheap hotel with its cracked mirror and dripping faucet—with Kyle Scanlon, a man she had always detested, a man who she had believed ruined Mallory—but then, he'd cared for her, tried to save her, didn't he? He'd helped her to live. . . .

Rachel combed her damp hair and studied herself in the mirror, a woman who had never spent a night in a motel like this one, never had a brief affair, never demanded or hungered, or felt so much alive—

*I love you, Kyle,* Mallory had written on the mirror.

*Mallory . . . Rachel's sister and the likely mother of the girl. . . .* Rachel frowned slightly and placed her comb inside her designer cosmetic bag, so different from the drugstore's basic overnight kit for men.

She wrapped a towel around her body, tucked the end between her breasts and opened the door to the tall, powerful, naked man on the opposite side. Kyle's hands braced against the doorframe, and those blue eyes stripped her as one hand moved to cup her breast gently, caressing it beneath the toweling. Then his finger prowled slowly across the top of her breasts, hooking into the cloth between them.

"I came here for a reason, Kyle. This wasn't it," Rachel whispered, even as she lifted her lips to his seeking, sensual kiss. All her defenses were slipping away, just like the towel.

"Disappointed?" There was a rough edge to that deep drawl as though Kyle feared the answer. Rachel caught that vulnerability, and treasured it, one of the intriguing tidbits about Kyle.

"Um. Not really," she whispered, only giving him so much so that he would take more.

He smiled tightly and she knew the game was on, the excitement racing between them. "Feeling okay? Not hurting anywhere special?" he asked.

She let her eyes drift downward to where his erection stood hot against her belly. "Feeling tiptop and shipshape."

The towel dropped between them, and Kyle's gaze slowly took in her nude body. Then his hand curved around her nape and tugged her to him; his other hand pressed her hard against him. His kiss was rawly primitive and possessive, and when Rachel's arms locked around his neck, Kyle picked her up and carried her to the bed, dropping her down on it. His body followed, lying heavy and warm over her. "Any complaints?"

Aware of the tenderness now between them, she smoothed back his hair. "Not a one. You?"

"I think you're going to cost me a lot of sleep."

Feeling warm and alive and carefree, Rachel laughed at that and gave herself to the man already moving within her. . . .

Rachel awoke to blinding sunlight, her own protesting groan, and the heavenly scent of fresh coffee. "That's not nice," she said to the man who had just opened the blinds to the morning sun.

"Just getting your attention." Kyle closed the blinds immediately. He sat fully dressed beneath the window, his legs sprawled out in front of him, his stocking feet on one chair. His hair was damp and combed, his face shaven, but he wore the same greasy, torn shirt and jeans from yesterday. He smiled at her and laid the newspaper he'd been reading onto the table. "Breakfast is on the table beside you."

Holding the sheet in front of her breasts, Rachel slowly sat up in the rumpled bed, adjusting the pillow behind her. The retro designed tray held a big plate of bacon, eggs, hash browns and biscuits, a tall glass of orange juice and a small carafe of coffee. Rachel's hand shook as she poured the coffee into a big heavy mug and tried to ignore Kyle's steady, penetrating look. She resented the fact that Kyle looked so awake while she was struggling to place herself in this room, with this man, after a night of loving him. She opted for casual protocol, as if she were accustomed to morning-afters. "No breakfast for you?"

"I ate at Margie's apartment behind the office. She said the room was free of charge, so you'll get full credit on your card. Any regrets about last night?"

Flip comments churned in her mind, but she

wouldn't cheapen herself—or him. Making love to Kyle was unique and something she knew she'd treasure, no matter what happened later. Rachel carefully placed the knife she'd been using to butter the big hot biscuit onto the tray. "Not one regret, and I pay my own way, Kyle."

"You're not paying mine. I tuned up Margie's pickup some time ago, and through the years have helped her with a few chores. She's busting to meet the one woman I've brought here."

"No . . . way," Rachel stated firmly as she sat with the plate on her lap, devouring her food. She angled a look at him. "So, I am special, am I?"

Kyle's lips curved slightly. "I wouldn't say that . . . just the first woman I've brought here. You've got a healthy appetite."

From the few feet away, Kyle's dark intent look was heating her body, making it hunger. "You've got butter on your lips," he whispered rawly. "Hurry up and eat that, will you?"

"Why?" She licked a crumb from her lips and slowly moistened them with her tongue.

"You know why. You're deliberately setting out to provoke me. That's what you like to do, isn't it? Provoke me? Trying to get that upper hand?"

"I think you had that last night, didn't you?" Right now, sprawled back on his chair, Kyle looked like a whole lot of exciting challenge that she couldn't wait to dive into. The words were flowing easily between them in this cheap room, the scent of coffee blending with that of their lovemaking. In comparison, her aftermoments with Mark were cold and businesslike, a quick discussion of their daily to-do lists, each hurrying to dress, to get on with their business day, or running to the gym.

Deep inside her, Rachel knew that if she had been engaged to Kyle when the attack had occurred, he would have treated her gently, waiting until she wanted to make love—Kyle would have comforted her and would have kept her safe. . . . Rachel pushed away the ugly scenes that had occurred with Mark, a man who actually cared nothing for her—she'd been his vehicle to executive success, a utensil to provide the image he needed, nothing more.

Kyle sipped his coffee, cradled the mug in his hand, and tilted his head back against the wall. His eyes closed and Rachel sensed that he was going into himself, struggling to find the words apart from their banter. Then he spoke quietly, "Her name is Katrina . . . named after your mother. I helped bring her into the world, and back then, Mallory wasn't taking drugs, drinking or smoking, not while she was pregnant. Katrina Rachel was a perfect seven-pound, one-ounce pink, beautiful baby. She's nine years old now, and I see Mallory's gentle heart in her."

Rachel's throat tightened and she set the plate back onto the tray. *Mallory's daughter, Katrina* . . . "Who was the father?"

"John Jr. is now. He and Nola took care of Mallory for five months until Katrina was born. She's legally theirs now. Then Mallory went back and opened Nine Balls."

Kyle stood up abruptly, his hands rubbing his face as though to erase the past. "She was afraid for this baby, wanting to leave something of herself, I guess. She took a savage beating at four months, because whoever was doing her really lost it. But the baby wasn't injured."

Rachel thought back through the years. . . . "I was so busy with my own career then, but Mom said that Mallory had taken off those five months, wanting to find herself. She'd mailed postcards periodically—"

"I saw that they were mailed from different places."

Kyle's rage pounded at the room as he started to pace back and forth, the muscles of his arms tight as he slammed one fist into his palm. "If I ever find out who that bastard was, I'm going to—"

His vivid rage rocked the room and Rachel held her breath, uncertain how to help him, how to understand. But she wasn't afraid, because she sensed that Kyle had held his anger for years, letting only her inside. "We're going to find him, Kyle. I promise."

He turned on her, his expression fierce. "Don't you think I've tried? For years, I did what I could, trying to protect her, but Mallory made her own choices when it came to the men she knew. But this one . . . this one, the one who caused her to make the doll—"

"I said, we'll find him." Cold, hard fury gripped Rachel as she wrapped the sheet around her body. On her feet now, she walked past Kyle on her way to the bathroom.

He caught her arm. "How do you know that?"

"Because I'm good," she stated flatly, leveling a hard, determined look at him.

The lines beside his eyes crinkled briefly. "You are, huh?"

"Damn good. And I think he's still around. He's the

jerk who's calling and hanging up on me. He wants me out of Nine Balls, and I'm not leaving—"

Kyle leaned down, his expression fierce again, his other hand locking onto her, turning her fully to him. "I saw Mallory go down that road."

"I'm not her." Rachel tried to stop the tears burning her eyes. "Oh, Kyle. Ten years ago, when Mallory needed me most, I was just starting my career. I was so determined to succeed that I didn't see what was happening to her—"

Kyle cupped the back of her head and pressed her face to his throat. "Don't. I don't know why Mallory didn't choose to just move away. She'd had enough about three years ago and I was going to help her get a new start. She was going to set up a place, get a good job, far away from Neptune's Landing, and make a life for herself—"

Rachel's arms locked around his shoulders. In the storm of their emotions, Kyle was big, strong, and safe, holding her tightly. "I think the man with Mallory on that tape, the one the doll represents, was using my family as blackmail. Three years ago, I was attacked in New York, in the park, coming home after a game of pool. I think it was the same man, and I was the way he kept her in line. He—"

Kyle caught her hair, drawing her head back. "He raped you?" he asked fiercely.

"No, but close to it. I think that doll worked." Rachel laughed shakily. "He was impotent—"

"Three years ago . . . that's when Mallory went to New York. It figures. She never traveled and all of a sudden she needs money to fly to you. She was terrified of flying, had to borrow luggage and was gone the next day." Kyle picked up Rachel and moved to the bed, sitting with her on his lap, rocking her in the shady room, the bed creaking softly beneath their weight. "Mallory was the only one who knew, wasn't she?"

Rachel nodded against his shoulder. "The only one. I didn't want Mom or Jada worrying about me. Jada had just gotten married and Mom was settling into her own life, her chicks all grown. I'm just putting everything together, the doll and tape, and what happened to me . . . and that's my guess—he threatened her with me, the attack. I think they're linked."

Kyle drew her head back again, momentarily stopping her from drowning in guilt. "Got any ideas?"

"A few. He has brown hair—fine texture. We know that much. That shirt and button could belong to anyone."

"You've been setting yourself up, haven't you?"

"Maybe. I thought I'd branch out a bit. I'm giving a program on personnel development and human resources to the Neptune's Landing Businessmen's Association luncheon tomorrow. I should start back now."

Kyle stood so quickly that she tumbled onto the bed. She scrambled to gather the sheet around her as he stood over her, legs braced apart, his hands on his hips. "The hell you are."

Rachel slid her legs over the side of the bed, preparing to stand up and Kyle clamped a hand on her shoulder and pushed her down. "Sit."

"I don't think I like your tone. I've never liked orders, Kyle."

"Too bad. You're going to see Katrina, aren't you?"

"It's only logical that I would want to see a piece of Mallory alive. I'm her aunt."

He shook his head. "Don't do it, Rachel. Katrina is safe and in the home that Mallory had always dreamed of for herself. Katrina is happy and so are John and Nola. You want to know why Mallory never came to see her daughter, why she burned the pictures of Katrina that I brought to her? Because she didn't want anything touching her beautiful daughter that wasn't good—and she wasn't good. Mallory gave me that four hundred a month because she was proud that she was able to put it into Katrina's support and college account—so she could be smart and independent like you."

Those words hit Rachel like a blow—she leaned back against the headboard and absorbed what Kyle had said. "And she was afraid he'd find out about Katrina—Katrina," she repeated, tasting the name on her lips, Mallory's daughter. . . .

"I would have done it—put away money for Katrina. There's just something about bringing a baby into the world—in the back seat of an Edsel—that you don't forget. I might never have kids of my own, but Katrina comes close to that. She calls me Uncle Kyle," Kyle said more softly as he sat on the edge of the bed. "Mallory didn't want me to build an account for Katrina—she wanted to do it, giving her daughter something. That monthly payment was on time and in full, no matter how much she had to scrimp. She was proud of that. . . . That was the agreement with Nola and John, that Mallory would help with Katrina's expenses, anonymously."

Rachel sat for a moment, pulling her thoughts together. Then she poured another cup of coffee and sipped it leisurely as Kyle lay down beside her, his hand stroking her bare leg. "Don't do that talk, Rachel," he said quietly.

"I'm scheduled. It's good for business if I want the upscale crowd to come back to Nine Balls."

"You're hunting, not promoting a pool hall."

"I'm not arguing over this, Kyle. A. I'm going to find this guy and make him pay, and then . . . then, B. I'm going to meet my niece."

Kyle took the coffee mug from her and placed it on the tray. He tugged Rachel beneath him, and looking down at her, toying with her hair, he asked, "You expect me to stand by and watch you get hurt, too?"

"No, I expect you to help me."

The telephone rang beside the bed and Kyle reached to retrieve it. "This better be an emergency."

He stilled, his body tense as he slowly eased up and away from Rachel. She sat up beside him, putting her arm around him. From Kyle's grim expression, she knew that something had happened. . . . "What's wrong?"

But Kyle was intent on dialing. "Margie? Do you know who that was—the call you just put through?"

He nodded briefly and replaced the telephone. "Well, honey. It looks like someone knows where you are. And now he knows you're with me."

"I didn't tell anyone where I would be staying—I didn't know."

"You used a credit card. Margie already put the charge through when I asked her to cancel it this morning. He's probably tapped into your accounts."

"Then I'd better get started—"

"Oh, no, you're not."

Kyle recognized Rachel's look, those eyes dark with anger, the tilt of her head, that stubborn set of her jaw. It was just his luck to be half in love with this hardheaded woman, whose single-minded determination could just kill her—and maybe endanger others.

He didn't want to point out that she could have endangered Mallory's daughter. He needed time to access Margie's telephone records, to question her and to try to identify the caller—and Rachel was impatient and determined, a reckless volatile commodity all wrapped up in one curved, feminine package that he couldn't keep his hands from touching.

Kyle smiled and forced himself to back up from a head-on confrontation with Rachel—it would only lock her more into a dangerous position. "Look, honey. Why don't we talk about this? Take some time and—"

Rachel shoved past him and on her way to the bathroom, she said, "I'm not wasting any more time with this. Apparently I've gotten to this guy, enough for him to trace me, and I'm going to push his buttons until he comes out of the woodwork."

The bathroom door lock clicked, echoing loudly in the room.

Kyle looked up at the ceiling and shook his head. With a sigh, he stood, walked to the door, tested it, and then put his shoulder to it until the lock broke. He'd fix it later, but right now, he focused on the naked furious woman facing him. "Get out."

"This is not good for my ego, honey. I'd like to think we had somewhat of a relationship now. You know, one of those give and take things. Yin and yang. Let's talk this over and come up with a plan." Kyle decided that he was being very logical and patient, while Rachel wasn't. "Let's get married. Now. That will give me some rights and make it easy to keep track of you."

"You think I need someone keeping track of me? You think that little old me can't take care of myself? Out!"

Kyle folded his arms across his chest and leaned his shoulder against the doorframe. "This isn't going well, dear. I'm only saying that you jump into this thing too soon and you could get hurt."

*And your mother, and Jada, and Katrina . . .*

"Don't worry about me, *dear.* Just stay out of my way."

Kyle's forced patience was slipping, but he smiled anyway. "You could screw this up."

"I won't."

Then he did something he'd promised that he wouldn't—reached for Rachel, held that squirming naked curved softness against him and kissed her hard. It was a possessive kiss and one that rocked the tiny bathroom, that shot down his body and bolted it into rock-hard need. He needed to be locked with her, to feel her as a part of him, keeping her safe, all emotions mixed with his sexual need of her—whatever happened between them when they made love, that fierce truth, male and female.

In the recesses of his mind, Kyle knew that taking her now was the rawest, least civilized action he could have taken—but somehow that didn't matter as heat poured out of her and she dug in to hold him, those hungry noises deep in her throat curling around him, her hands busy with his jeans, stroking him over the denim.

He was rough and disliked himself for the savageness of the taking, pushing down his jeans and shorts, pushing himself up into Rachel's damp, hot body. She moved against him, pushing him to the limits and Kyle lost himself in a haze of passion, aware of her nails digging into his back, clawing at him as they drove higher.

At the summit, Rachel stared blankly into his eyes, her body clenching his as he came, pounding into her—

Even as he calmed, Kyle was furious with himself for losing control, for handling her roughly, quickly. "I didn't use—"

"I know." When he withdrew, Rachel was leaning against him, her hands locked to his shoulders.

He glanced in the mirror to find them—her naked and flushed, the curve of her breast showing against his dirty shirt, his shorts just below his butt. Her look at him was perceptive. "You're worrying, aren't you?"

"I've never taken a woman like this. Yes, I'm worrying. I was rough and you could get pregnant. That would make me no better than—"

Her fingertip rested on his lips, stopping him. "I'm not complaining."

He looked down to the red marks of his hand on her pale bottom. He released her and stepped back. "Dammit, Rachel. You're going to have bruises. I didn't mean to—"

"I did." That edgy, cocky look was back; Rachel was flushed and smiling up at him as she moved up close and personal. She ran her hands over his chest, then slid them up under the T-shirt, rummaging in the hair there, tugging at it gently. "Stop complaining."

Kyle let himself touch her, trying to replace his earlier raw hunger. He smoothed her back and up her sides, then his thumbs caressed her outer breasts. "So did I make enough points to settle this? You'll cancel that program and stop pushing so hard? You'll marry me first thing—"

She frowned slightly and the fences were up. "What is this marrying-thing with you? We're nowhere near that point."

He looked down their bodies, where hers flowed softly into his. "I am."

"Let's stay on the subject here. You offered to marry Mallory—"

"Because she was pregnant and I wanted to take care of her. Later, when she was in such bad shape, I wanted to marry her to take guardianship, to dry her out—"

"But dear, I can take care of myself," Rachel stated too patiently.

"This whole relationship-whatever, is going to be one of arguing, isn't it?" he asked warily.

She patted his bare butt. "Only if you don't see things my way, chum."

"Dammit, Rachel—"

Then she turned and bent to adjust the shower's faucets and Kyle stopped thinking. . . .

# Fourteen

**"RACHEL...I'M SO GLAD THAT YOU CALLED,"** SHANE Templeton said as he opened the door of his home and extended his hand to her. He slowly took in her tight red sweater, tighter short skirt and high strappy heels; his eyes glittered momentarily before his reserved smile concealed that brief lust.

She'd dressed to kill, to see how Shane responded to the flashy, sexy clothes that Mallory had preferred. From his quick hungry look down Rachel's body, she'd definitely scored a hit. If he was the man who had hurt Mallory, Rachel would soon know.

"Nine o'clock is much too late for a call, but my hours start and end late, I'm afraid. I thought you would want to have this back, the picture you gave Mallory." If Shane were the anonymous caller, Rachel wanted to push him into a corner and tear him apart. After a furious argument with Kyle that morning—he'd wanted her to back off until he could warn the Scanlons and come to protect her—irritating one more male wouldn't matter.

She let Shane take the framed picture and draw her into his home. The exterior of the home the church had provided for Shane looked like a warm cottage, set amid well-tended shrubs and trees, with a winding stone walkway to the front door. Inside, it was as neat and sterile as Jada had described, but the colors were heavy with browns and maroons, just as Mallory's apartment had been, and the temperature seemed too warm. As Rachel looked around the room, Shane closed the door; in his white dress shirt and black slacks, he stood too close and towered over her. Shane was freshly shaven, scented of soap and aftershave, his fine brown hair neatly combed—Was that his hair on Mallory's voodoo doll?

Rachel sensed Shane's anger, his eyes bright with it, and his cold smile raised the hair on her nape. In odd timing, she suddenly noted how small and sharp and long his teeth appeared and compared them to the strong, blunt shape of Kyle's. She knew the shape of Kyle's teeth; he'd certainly nibbled enough on her body. . . .

"Are you in trouble, Rachel?" Shane asked gently, smoothly, the words evidently used often. "Here, come sit on the love seat while I get the tea tray. It's a wonderful calming tea, and you look as though you might need that now—and maybe a listening ear, a caring heart?"

*Could Mallory really have been drawn into Shane's superior treatment of women?*

"It's so difficult. I don't know where to begin," Rachel said, playing into the part of a woman who needed a strong shoulder to lean on, advice to guide her. Helpless Female wasn't a role she'd ever played—except that horrifying night when she'd been attacked and shattered—and she hoped that Shane would take the bait.

Apparently, he did. His smile warmed, those full lips curving as he patted her shoulder. "I'll just be a minute and then we can talk."

Rachel waited, her large tote bag at her side, the contents certain to get a response from Shane. She just had time to enter his study and glimpse his computer—the screen was lit, his notebook on the desk—before he returned with the tray. When he removed the teapot's quilted cozy, the elegant china pot matched the gilt floral design of the cups and saucers.

"Very nice," Rachel said as she sat on the love seat and he sat in a chair opposite from her, pouring the tea with delicate, almost feminine movements. His hands were long and pale and smooth. In contrast, she thought of Kyle's hands—big, calloused, and lightly flecked with hair. Her body tightened and she shivered as she thought of Kyle, of the night and morning that had passed. Her day-long drive back to Neptune's Landing was filled with sensual memories—and a frantic sorting of what she had learned about Mallory's life and her daughter, Katrina.

She had to move fast, taking Shane to task before Kyle returned, challenging her head-on tactics to cause Mallory's blackmailer to show his hand. She crossed her legs, deliberately letting her short skirt rise to her thighs and Shane tensed, his gaze darkening, locking to them.

Shane was definitely interested in women, but there was something else, too. She studied his features and compared the picture of Katrina to him. The hair appeared to be the same, straight, fine, brown. The resemblance could be just a little in those soft lips. . . .

They sipped tea through the usual discussions of Jada's housekeeping and ice cream businesses to pay off her credit cards with her ex-husband. The weather topic came next, and then the opening Rachel had hoped for appeared: Shane moved to the love seat and took her hand. "Tell me what's wrong, dear Rachel. May I help? Why have you come back to me?"

*Back to me. . . .* She tried to take the phrase apart and couldn't. She suddenly felt drowsy and too tired; the aftereffects of two days of driving and a lovemaking marathon with Kyle, and worrying about the girl called Katrina had caught up with her. Determined to move quickly, she said, "I thought since you knew so much about my sister, that we should get better acquainted."

Shane's fine features tightened and he leaned closer. "That would be so nice."

"I was wondering why you stayed in Neptune's Landing, when it's usual to rotate in the ministry, isn't it? You've been here—ten years?" *Are you the father of Katrina?*

"I found something here that I liked very much. Neptune's Landing is really home for me now, and the board agreed with my decision to stay permanently. I think I might have left my ministry if they had decided otherwise." He touched Rachel's hair lightly and it chilled her.

Unable to look away from Shane's long, sharp teeth, Rachel found her warning senses dimmed by an incredible need to sleep. Shane looked down at her legs as though he were dying to touch them, lust plainly revealed in his expression. "I know that we can be friends," he whispered in an eerie soft tone that both seduced and terrified as he leaned closer.

She knew instantly how a mouse would feel, cornered by a very big, powerful, unfriendly cat with sharp fangs. *Kyle had been right: she shouldn't have come— but she had to see Shane's reaction.*

"You asked if I would return the other things that you had given Mallory. I think I found them," she said, trying to focus as she reached inside her bag.

"I'm more interested in you right now—what you need. What do you need, dear Rachel?" Shane's hand slid around her shoulders and downward, caressing, kneading. He seemed fascinated with her high strappy heels and reached to fondle one lovingly before he looked at her again. "Mallory used to wear that style. I know you've slept with Kyle, the same as she did at first, before I taught her how to be a lady. You can do better than that mechanic. He has a certain raw power, I give him that, but you're too good for him. An educated, powerful businesswoman like yourself needs more. I could help and guide you . . . we could take that trip to Paris—"

Her lips and throat were dry, her tongue felt heavy, but Rachel forced herself to say, "The things I found are on the table."

Shane glanced at the book of poetry on the table, the woman's gold ring gleaming upon it. He frowned and stated flatly, "You found them. Did you find anything else?"

*Did you find anything else?* The words echoed distantly in her brain as Rachel tried to keep her eyes open. But her lids were heavy as she stared at him, trying to stay awake. Shane's hand gripped her thigh, holding her as he leaned closer, pressing her back against the love seat. "You're beautiful, Rachel. Sensual—" His eyes took in her body, the tight sweater she'd worn to test him. "Desirable. We can share—"

Her body wouldn't respond immediately as she tried to move away, and distantly, Rachel knew she had to escape. When she tried to stand, Shane held her immobile, his eyes burning into hers, his hand hard and searching on her breasts. "Let it happen, Rachel. You know you're attracted to me—"

She reached for the tea service, fumbled until she found the teapot's handle and forced her arm to lift and—

Shane's furious shout rocked the room as the hot tea scalded his neck and shoulders, the pot breaking with the force of the blow. Forcing herself to move quickly, Rachel stood and stumbled to the door.

In the fresh air and moving quickly, Rachel's drowsy, heavy feeling eased. She slid off the high heels, grabbed them, and hurried down the rock pathway; she leaped into her car and the tires squalled as she drove away. In the rearview mirror, her eyes were still heavy lidded, but her expression was furious. Hurrying to her apartment, she unlocked the dead bolt and the door, locking them behind her with shaking hands.

Rachel hugged her body. Then, angry with Shane, she picked up the telephone and punched in his number. After a moment, he answered briskly.

"You drugged me. Is that what you did with Mallory?" Rachel demanded.

"I don't know what you're talking about. We had tea and then, because you're a sexual addict like your sister, you attacked me. A woman, coming here, this time of night, dressed as you were, has one thing on her mind."

"You come over here, you bastard, and you'll get more than a few burns—"

"I'm scalded, you witch—"

Rachel was quick to snag that word—"Witch? As in voodoo doll? What do you know about that?"

"I don't know what you're talking about." Shane added a few ungentlemanly phrases about her, and Rachel smiled grimly. At least she'd gotten him to shed his skin to the snake beneath.

"Then go to an emergency ward and explain to them how you got injured—drugging and trying to force yourself on me."

Shaking, trying to calm herself, Rachel brewed a pot of strong black tea, drinking it as she ate a huge slice of chocolate cake on the kitchen counter; Jada had used Trina's keys to bring the cake and had left a glad-you're-back note. Rachel put down her fork, her mind starting to click, reason setting in. After arriving home, she'd been in a hurry to change her online banking and credit card passwords, to dress for her "interview" with Shane, and she'd forgotten the gun. She glanced to the table where Kyle had left his semi-automatic—it was missing.

But then, Rachel reasoned again, Jada or Trina had cleaned the apartment, made her bed, and probably had the sense to hide the handgun. "I'm blowing things out of proportion, Mallory, that's all. No one has been here. I'll call Mom and Jada in the morning and my sister isn't going to be happy—"

At the sound of the ringing telephone, Rachel's anger hiked back up again. She picked it up and stated coldly, "Okay, Shane. All they have to do is to check your telephone records and they'll see that you dialed here. I'm not done with you. I'm going to find out everything—and the next time you tap into someone's accounts, you won't have the right passwords."

Silence pulsed ominously for a moment, followed by a rough scratching sound, and then the line went dead.

Rachel replaced the telephone and tried to control her chilling fear. The calls always came when she was in her apartment; someone was tracking her movements.

There were three new messages on her private machine, ones she hadn't taken time to dump before going to Shane's. Rachel held her breath before pushing the Play button. Kyle's clipped tone said he wasn't happy.

"Hardheaded woman" didn't exactly sound like a lover's greeting, before he continued brusquely, frustration in his deep tone. "You jump into this thing before I get back and there's certain to be trouble. You didn't return my call to your cell phone and that probably means that you're stirring up trouble that you might not be able to handle. Moses is back in Reno, getting the girls settled, out of harm's way, or I'd have him there. You're going to explode this whole thing, aren't you? When you want something, you're too quick and too hardheaded and not one lick of sense. Nola is taking Katrina on a quick trip to Chicago, to see the museums there and to get her to safety. Don't make this thing blow before I'm back, Rachel . . . honey," he added tightly, as if attempting to soften his direct order and threat.

Kyle's second call was curt. "Call me. Now."

His third was accompanied by the rushing sound of

wind on a car, the grind of gears changing. "I'm headed toward Neptune's Landing, about two hours out—nine o'clock now—and I'm not happy. Stay put. I called your mother and she said you'd checked in, so I know you're in town. Thanks a lot for not returning my calls. We're going to have to work on our relationship—dear. Just as soon as I get my hands on you—honey."

After an attack by Shane and an anonymous hang-up, Rachel wasn't in the mood for Kyle's threats. She called his office number, leaving a welcome-back-lover message: "I've been busy and I don't like taking orders. You've already had your hands on me, Scanlon. Rest up. You're going to need it, if you try to order me around."

She sat on the coffee table, tried to calm herself into straight thinking, and mulled the hang-up. Shane had been clean-shaven a short time ago and the sound of scratching sounded like a man's stubble.

"A. Shane had too much to say to hang up. B. Kyle had plenty to say, too. . . . C. There were no other hang-ups, except late this afternoon, when I got back. This guy knew I was at the hotel, used my credit card information to find me, and he knows I'm back in Neptune's Landing. I changed my online banking and credit card passwords as soon as I got home, so he can't do that again. The question is, how did he get them in the first place?"

She listened to Nine Balls' sign swinging outside, creaking in the wind. "Mallory, help me. A daughter—you had a daughter and didn't tell me. I would have kept her safe. Katrina . . . you named her after Mom. I was so tied up in getting a start in my career that I didn't pay attention to you, and you had a baby girl—I should have been there for you."

The stress of the hard day, the clash with Shane, and the heavy knowledge that Mallory had probably been drugged, too, suddenly hit Rachel. She'd been in fast forward, and now tiny pieces of her were falling away. She doubled over, holding herself, and gave way to the tears burning her lids.

Her sobs echoed in the apartment, her throat dry and tight, her face damp. She hurried to tear away the clothing she'd worn to bring Shane out of his professional minister's role and then stumbled to the couch. With shaking hands, she lit the candles in the dish of stones she'd collected with her sisters, and then lay back, curling on the couch to watch the flames. "It's so unlike me to break down, Mallory. But my sister had a baby. My sister—and never told me. What you must have gone through. . . ."

But Mallory had had Kyle, hadn't she?

"Why couldn't you have turned to me?" The answer came back to her immediately: "Because of Jada and Mom, right?"

The apartment was too quiet and the slight scent of vanilla curled around Rachel. *I'll always be with you. . . .*

"You'd better well be. I've got a feeling I'm going to need you. Don't you dare leave me now, not until this thing is over."

"I'm going to enjoy killing that no-good. . . . He's troubled me enough. Everything was fine until he started messing with Mallory, filling her head with rebellion against me. I should have killed him long ago, but with Rachel pushing for answers and him bedding her, I can't wait any longer."

He hated Kyle Scanlon with a fury, the other man in Mallory's life, encouraging her to leave town, to run away and start new. "I would have never let her go, and Mallory knew it. She knew that I'd make good my promise to hurt her sisters if she even thought she could move away from me."

At eleven o'clock, Kyle's apartment was dark and silent as the man moved through it. He carried the semiautomatic, but didn't plan to use it as he set the scene for arson. But if Kyle returned before he finished his business, the handgun was protection against a man who was fit and tough.

Rachel had come back from her rendezvous with Kyle, and that meant he'd be coming after her. "She went to that cheap motel with him, hot for him, just like a whore. He's got family there, in ChakChak, Idaho. I give her that much—Rachel tracked him down. It will be interesting to see what he does when they're hurt—or dead. But he won't be around for that—he'll be in prison for insurance fraud, or he'll be dead, because I'm tired of him interfering with my women."

Headlights flashed in the office window, and the man backed into the shadows. He watched Kyle get out of the Hummer and decided that he couldn't wait any longer—Kyle Scanlon would die tonight. Just then, Rachel's cat zipped by him into the storeroom. "Good idea, Harry."

The cat was retching and Kyle would be certain to look for him. And then he would die. The intruder chuckled and moved into the storeroom, knocking over a few boxes as he moved. "Scanlon will bend to pick them up and when he does, I have him. Problem solved."

He looked at the goo the cat had brought up, the way it clung to his shoe and cursed quietly. A meticulous man, he retched as he waited. "When this place burns, you'll burn, too, cat."

"Stay. You get out of the car, stir up Harry, and I'll never find him." Kyle ignored Pup's soft whining and closed the Hummer door. Cool, salt-scented mist circled Kyle as he lifted one warning finger when the dog barked inside the rig; a spray of Pup's drool landed on the window, sliding down it. "Great. Slobber all you want. You have one minute before I get Harry and take him to Rachel. Maybe, with her cat in my hand, she won't hurt me."

The soft glow of the tire advertising sign appeared in his office, and Kyle briefly glanced around at the garage, then selected the key from his ring. Inside and on his way back to his apartment, he pushed his new message machine's Play button and heard Rachel's crisp tell-off message. "Sweet. That's my girl."

Harry couldn't be seen in Kyle's apartment, but it looked as if he had been having fun shredding the furniture. Kyle ran his hand over the clawed expensive leather of his recliner and shook his head. "In a bad mood, Harry? Didn't like dry cat food for these three days? Come on, come out wherever you are. . . . I'm taking you back to Rachel and let her deal with you."

In no mood to play games with the cat, Kyle quickly

searched the inventoried racks of his storeroom. Harry had left wads of fur along the shelves, and several of the lighter boxes had been pushed to the floor.

Harry meowed loudly, and on his way to find the cat, Kyle stepped over a hair ball. After a second glance, he bent down to look closer. Someone else hadn't seen the cat's vomit, stepping onto it. A shoe print had been stamped into the orangish mess and had carried the stuff for a few more steps.

"Moses wears biker boots and he's about an hour from town," Kyle noted softly, before the world crashed in on his head. . . .

He came to in a swirling red mass of pain, with explosions going off in his head. His face was in something sticky, and dazed, Kyle hoped it wasn't the cat's hair ball. . . .

Razor sharp pain went through his head as he lifted it, and his ribs and back felt as if an elephant were standing on him. He forced one swollen eye open and was almost grateful that the sticky stuff was his own blood. Slowly, painfully, easing himself into a sitting position as a wave of nausea hit him, Kyle listened to the explosions outside the garage. He caught the scent of smoke and saw it curling toward him. The smell of gas burned his nose and his clothes seemed damp.

Harry chose that moment to walk around a shelving unit and onto Kyle's lap. The cat hissed, hackles raised as smoke and heat came nearer. Kyle managed to loop his arm around Harry before he passed out.

Then he was being lifted like a baby, and his head pounded as he was carried from the garage with Harry in his arms. The big body holding him tightened as he was being tilted precariously. The sound of a man retching his guts out was easy to define. "Moses—"

"I can't stand the sight of blood," Moses stated between gagging sounds. "This whole place is exploding. We've got to get out of here."

Pup was barking excitedly, Harry was hissing, and Kyle was being stuffed into a car. One door shut, then another, and Moses growled, "Get the hell off me, cat."

Kyle felt the Hummer rev and heard the crash of metal against metal. He recognized the sound—Moses had driven straight through the gates, not opening them fully—before Kyle gave himself to the dark painful fist squeezing him—

Kyle heard himself talk, but couldn't rouse fully.

Then Moses's arm was around him, easing him from the car. A man and a woman were arguing—but that could have been Rachel and himself this morning, when he was trying to tell Rachel to wait for him, not to start any trouble before he could protect her. . . .

"He won't go to a hospital. The sight of blood makes me sick," Moses was saying seemingly from another planet. Cool mist curled around Kyle and he lifted his face to it, but he couldn't swim through the daze to reality on the other side. . . .

"Tough. Help me get him into my apartment. You just turned white, Moses. Don't you dare faint now. Don't you dare," Rachel was saying furiously. "He's a mess . . . here, let me get on the other side and we can get him up the stairs—"

Moses cursed briefly, then his voice was indignant.

"I can bench-press a whole lot more than Kyle weighs, lady. Don't try to take the cat away from him. He won't let you."

"You let him fall and you're dead," Rachel threatened as Moses picked him up and began the slow, painful journey for Kyle up the stairs. "He should go to a hospital. Maybe we should—"

"He said to bring him here."

"He's just passed out again—"

For Kyle, time tumbled into rousing slightly, feeling pain crash over him, hearing himself say something, and then slipping back into the darkness. And then it began all over again. In the distance, Pup was barking.

Kyle heard Rachel say furiously, "My sister died in this apartment, and if you do, too, I'll never forgive you!"

He tried to smile, but couldn't. He heard himself saying something and then Moses translated between rounds of gagging. "Kyle said he loves you and that if he has any cat vomit on him, he wants it off."

"Get him into that bed. He smells like gas."

"Yeah, well—" Moses grunted as he lowered Kyle onto something flat. "He's wearing a lot of it."

The level surface didn't stop Kyle's head from spinning, then he recognized the feel of Rachel's hand gripping his, the scent of her leaning over him, her soft touch probing his head gently. "I don't like this. He needs a doctor."

Kyle tried to argue and failed, but Moses growled, "He just wants you."

Something big and thick pulled back each of Kyle's eyelids, and Moses stated, "Slight concussion. I figure a few bruised ribs, too. Just clean him up, will you? Put a compress on that cut on his head and get some ice in a bucket. But first, get the blood off him, and I'll work on him."

"Oh, I don't think so. You're not qualified to be a doctor." Rachel leaned close enough again for her scent to carry through that of gasoline. "What's that, Kyle?"

Moses translated again, "Lady, you need experience with guys with smashed lips, like boxers, to understand what he's saying. . . . He says for you to shut up for once and stop giving orders. Get a scissors and cut his clothes off, the bloody ones. I'll handle the rest. I gotta go wash it off me—"

"You can't just leave me here with him. You stay right where you are, Moses. Oh—are you sure he isn't dying? I really need him, Moses, and I'm not going to be happy if he does die."

*Rachel needed him.* Kyle wanted to smile, but his effort hurt too much; Rachel sounded desperate, like just maybe she cared. Of course, she did, he reasoned woozily. He'd finally had his hands on Miss Neptune's Landing's shells and she was very particular.

"He's too tough to die," Moses stated.

"He'd better not. Don't you go anywhere while I get something to clean him. You look like you're going to faint. Put your head between your knees—"

Kyle felt the bed beside him depress deeply and knew that Moses had stretched out beside him. "Well, fine. Now there's two of you," Rachel said after a moment.

On his other side the bed depressed slightly and Rachel bent over Kyle, dabbing a damp cloth over his face. "I've never done this before, you jerk," she was saying amid sounds that sounded like crying. "I'm not trained for this and I'm scared. What if you really are dying, and that bozo over there doesn't know what he's doing? I should call nine-one-one right now. If I had any sense, I would."

Sirens sounded outside, a fire truck passing by, the red lights flashing in the window, and Pup started barking again. Moses yelped, cursing, shaking the bed as he left it. "Ouch. Damn cat got me in the balls."

Harry purred loudly and settled against Kyle's side. He managed to place a hand on the cat and mumble.

"What did he say?" Rachel asked softly as the cool metal of a scissors slid up Kyle's chest and she cut away his shirt.

"That the cat is worried about him and to let him stay where he was," Moses answered.

"The bleeding has stopped. Get over here and help me undress him, you big ox," Rachel ordered and Kyle almost smiled. "What?" she asked sharply.

Moses translated: "He said, 'That's my woman.' "

"Ohh—" Rachel's voice crooned before she bent to kiss Kyle very lightly.

In his pain, Kyle flashed back to when they were making love, and Moses chuckled softly, another man, recognizing the hard thrusting erection. He imagined Rachel's flush when she whispered, "You stop that right now, Kyle Scanlon."

"Let him think about it, Rachel," Moses advised softly. "It'll keep his mind on you and not on the pain while we undress him."

"What did he say?"

Moses chuckled again. "He said, 'Later.' "

Kyle drifted in and out of pain and then Rachel was

sitting beside him, holding his hand. His other hand was on Pup, whose body rested against him over the sheet. From the feel of the sheet on Kyle's body, he knew he was naked, and the gas stench had settled into an antiseptic scent. His ribs were tightly bandaged, a cold ice pack was on one cheek, and he seemed plastered with Band-Aids. Two uniformed policemen were standing near the bed, and to one side, Jada was holding Trina's hand; both women looked worried. While the officers took notes, Moses was laying out a time chart of when he'd last spoken to Kyle, and when he'd arrived at Scanlon's Classics and what he saw at that time.

Kyle noted that according to Rachel's bedside clock, it was now one o'clock in the morning. He pressed Rachel's hand and she instantly looked down at him, her expression concerned. "They're investigating the fire—oh, Kyle, the whole place exploded. There was gas in all the cars and the fire pretty well gutted them. There's an officer there, making certain that looters don't carry off what is left of your inventory."

Kyle recognized Cody Michaelson's serious tone; it was the same one he used when he was bidding on a good poker hand. "Major explosions, Kyle. Some of the stockroom was saved, the apartment has a gaping hole in one wall where a car exploded, and the office is smoke damaged and water soaked. All the tires and oil out there are still on fire—"

"Do we have to do this now?" Rachel asked tightly. "He's injured, can't you see that? Now, I want you all out of here this minute."

Cody apparently didn't know Rachel well and continued, "Ma'am, we need to—"

"I know, I know. Insurance investigations, et cetera, et cetera. I'll call you as soon as he gets some rest. Do not—repeat do not call me. Nothing can be done right now but assess the damage anyway, is there?"

"It looks like arson, ma'am," Cody pressed boldly on, and Kyle almost felt sorry for him.

Rachel's head tilted to one side, and her shoulders straightened in pure attitude. "Are you saying that Kyle Scanlon would deliberately set fire to his own business for insurance purposes?" she asked tightly.

*She was defending him, his own little fearless crusader.* . . . While he could speak now, Kyle decided to let Rachel handle the moment, because he wasn't up to arguing with her, too.

"No, ma'am, I'm just saying that—" Pup growled softly, and the other officer asked, "Does that dog bite?"

Rachel stood to her feet, and Kyle watched through the slit of his one eye. She gathered her body up, went hip shot with her other hand on her hip, and leaned her head back, studying the officer, sighting in on him. "Yes. He's a trained guard dog. Now he's protecting Kyle and I don't blame him. I don't like your tone, or your accusations and I wouldn't say anything more until Mr. Scanlon can recover, if I were you," she stated coldly, fiercely, as her hand gripped Kyle's. She glanced down at him; her narrowed eyes told him to shut up, that she was handling this now and wouldn't stand for his interference.

It was an odd feeling, a woman defending him so fiercely, going toe-to-toe to protect him, when it was usually the other way around. He tried to sit up, and

Rachel bent to put her hand flat on his chest. "Stay put. I'm handling this. Play hero some other time."

Moses started to laugh. "Kyle just said that he wasn't letting a woman handle his business."

"Oh, he did, did he? Well, get this, Kyle Scanlon— right now, you are my business."

"Ma'am, you've got this all wrong," Cody hurried to say. "I take it you're friends with Kyle?"

"More than that. We're in a relationship. A very close relationship. He's in my care now, and you're in my home. Please leave."

Cody, apparently the senior officer in the investigation, wasn't being put off. "Kyle Scanlon is my friend, too, Ms. Everly. I just want to know that he's in good hands."

"Are you saying that I will not take good care of him?" Rachel asked very carefully.

When Cody looked at Kyle, he managed to shake his head, and motion for the policeman to back off.

After the officers left, Jada said, "Whew. I'd leave, too. You were furious, Rache."

Rachel pushed back her hair. "I've had a hard day, that's all. And I'm worried about Kyle. I still think we should call a doctor."

"No," Kyle managed and the word rattled around inside his brain, hurting it.

"Is there anything we can do?" Trina asked worriedly.

"Moses Fry, isn't it?" Jada asked moving closer to the ex-wrestler and peering up at him. "You grew hair. Last time you were bald."

"Yeah? So?"

"Hair is good." Jada's appraisal ended with an approving nod. "I like the look—black, wavy, thick. Do you use volumizer?"

"What are those things on your teeth?" Moses asked warily, flattening against a wall as Jada stood on tiptoe, looking up at him.

"Braces and rubber bands. Hot pink for spring and summer. Do you like them?"

Moses didn't answer and Rachel sighed tiredly. Jada, definitely interested in the ex-wrestler, was too much to handle at the moment. "Mom, you look like you've had a long day. Jada and Moses will help me with Kyle. Maybe you could call Bob to take you home?"

"He's waiting outside. We called him right away, but he wouldn't come in. I hope you're okay, Kyle. Please call me if I can help, Rachel."

"Okay, what's this about?" Jada asked after Trina had left, and Rachel sat on the edge of the bed.

"Can I talk now?" Kyle asked warily.

Rachel waved her hand as if she'd had enough of everyone. "Me, first. I just had a little go 'round with Shane tonight. It wasn't sweet, and he just could have gotten mad enough to do something rash—"

Jada exploded. "Like setting the garage and cars on fire? No way."

"Someone did," Kyle said as he eased himself upward. Rachel quickly bent to prop a pillow behind him as he sat up in bed and waited for the world to stop spinning. He leaned into the icy cloth Rachel was patting over his face, and drank the water she handed him. "Nice patch job, Moses."

"Thanks. Once after she got all the blood washed off,

I went to work. You learn a lot of stuff in wrestling. Made a few butterfly bandages, but didn't sew up anything. Nothing broken, just bruised pretty bad. Someone kicked the living daylight out of you."

"Did what?" Rachel and Jada asked in shocked unison.

"I thought it was an accident, that something fell on him," Rachel said unevenly.

"Something like kicks. Those bruises are spaced too regular along his side and back and they just fit the shape of a shoe. It was meant to look like an accident, like that scooter motor was supposed to have fallen on him from the shelves. Supposedly, the sparks from a barbeque grill in the back caught on fire and it knocked over close to a can of gasoline—my size fourteen foot, it did. Someone is real pissed."

"Now, I wonder who? And what the hell were you doing with Shane, Rachel?" Kyle asked darkly, because he already knew that she would be pressing buttons as soon as she got back to Neptune's Landing, and not listening to his cautioning argument, or his request that she wait for him.

"Visiting. You tried to get Mallory to see what Shane was, didn't you?"

"He wasn't going to marry her. He couldn't afford what she was, her bad reputation. Shane would have been kicked out of the social circle he loves. What does 'visiting' mean exactly?"

"I took some of the things he gave Mallory back to him." As she sat beside Kyle and looked at her sister, Rachel ached for Jada. "A romantic book of poetry and a wedding ring."

Jada stiffened and frowned. "Are you certain those were from Shane?"

"Yes, and he has hair the color of her doll, Jada. I'm sorry. Don't tell Mom about any of this. Please. And Jada, could you please ask Bob if he would stay over at Mom's tonight? I just want to know that you and she are safe."

Evidently trying to deal with the discovery that Shane had actually had a role in encouraging Mallory's romantic ideas about him, Jada agreed. "I don't know if he'll stay or not. . . . Mom and Bob are having some disagreements now. It's over you, Rachel. Bob is really mad about you seeing Kyle. He says the same thing will happen to you as did to Mallory, and he just can't stand by this time and do nothing. He says your judgment is skewed right now, that Kyle has that effect on women. Mom really went after him when he said that."

"He was here for her tonight and I'm glad of that. But I'm sorry—they've always been so good with each other. I'll try harder to let him know that nothing has changed, that I still love him."

There was more to Rachel's "visit" with Shane, but Kyle decided to save his questions for later. He sensed he wouldn't like her answers. He also had a feeling that they were going to have a hell of an argument, one that would test their "relationship," when he felt up to it.

Moses yawned hugely. "Where do I sleep?"

"Not with me," Kyle answered.

"On the couch."

Kyle managed a leer at Rachel that really hurt. "And who are you sleeping with, little girl?"

\* \* \*

"Nothing to worry about. Just a little bump in the road. Rachel is just as much of a tramp as her sister, and I'll soon have this all worked out to my satisfaction. She'll soon be my private entertainment, just as Mallory was. Everything will be just as it was, only better, because Rachel will be harder to break and that will make a better game."

He wondered what he could do to insinuate that Kyle was probably the arsonist, and the possible recipient of a hefty insurance check.

"If that ex-wrestler hadn't rescued him, Kyle would have died, as he should have long ago—for meddling in my business, in my private pleasures."

He picked up the semi-automatic and hefted its unfamiliar weight, his hands gloved, of course, to retain Kyle's fingerprints. When the time was right, someone would die, and Kyle would be out of the picture. He studied the deadly weapon, the filled clip, and aimed it at a picture of Mallory with her sisters. "One . . . two . . . three."

Mallory had been very malleable, until she'd decided to leave him—and then he'd had to make good his threat to hurt one of her family.

Three years ago, he'd felt Rachel's naked body beneath him, and he needed to finish having her. She might have to die—or she might not. But it had been a long time since he'd had the satisfaction he needed, hurting a woman, listening to her beg.

All he had to do was to wait until the right moment and get Kyle out of the picture, one way or the other.

# Fifteen

---

**"WHAT WAS THAT YOU WERE SAYING ABOUT SHANE GIVING** Mallory a book of poetry and a wedding ring?" Kyle asked Rachel at three o'clock the next afternoon. She had just entered the apartment after presenting an "Employees—Your Best Assets" luncheon program to the Neptune's Landing's businessmen. After her Shane-experience, Rachel had wanted to see if any of the men overreacted to a woman dressed to kill in a short skirt and heels. Several of the men had chatted with her later, and she'd taken time with each one, noting his hair and the sound of his voice.

Rachel had been focused on that grueling, tense time when she had arrived home. But a lean, muscular man wearing strips of her best white sheet around his ribs, low-slung jeans, and standing in high strappy heels, was the irrelevant topping on the past few earthshaking days. Kyle's hands were on his hips, and one swollen eye had opened more than the other, but both were blue and fierce, pinning her. His eyebrows were drawn together in a scowl that must have hurt.

"Nice shoes," she managed while stifling the need to giggle. Since she wasn't a giggler, Rachel knew she'd reached a last-straw limit and anything could send her into an insane laughing fit, a release of tension. She tossed her briefcase to the couch, kicked off her own high strappy heels, and closed her eyes, locking in the sight of a six-foot-four male standing in high heels; she was certain she would need a good laugh when Kyle launched the questions he would certainly ask. She didn't have long to wait—

"And what did you give me to knock me out, anyway?" Kyle added darkly. "When I last looked, you didn't have anything for pain in your medicine cabinet but aspirin."

Seated on the couch, hiding behind the newspaper's sports section, Moses glanced up at her. If the tight crunch of his face, the tears rolling down his cheeks, indicated anything, it was that he, too, was seeing the humor of the situation. "They were too small for me," he said amid gasps that evidently suppressed roaring laughter. "Kyle only has size twelves. They're women's fourteens and they fit."

"What the hell are you doing with custom-made high heel shoes big and wide enough to fit me?" Kyle exploded fiercely.

"Hi, honey. How are you feeling?" Rachel managed to ask with a serious expression as she walked to sit on the couch beside Moses. She ducked behind the paper that was shaking in front of his face, and grinned at him. "Anything interesting in there?"

Moses let go of a huge snort, an eruption of smothered laughter. Kyle sprawled into a chair; he grimaced, pain etched on his pale face, and Rachel forgot everything but hurrying to him. "Get these things off," he ordered between breaths, his face pale and damp with perspiration.

"I found those high heels when I went through Mallory's things. I'd forgotten them until I was looking for shoes to go with this suit. I must have left them out, huh?" Rachel bent to undo the buckles, then knelt between his knees, rested her hands on them. "How's it going, champ?"

"I am not in a good mood. I went out to the garage this morning—rather midmorning. I overslept and had to meet the insurance guys and police at the garage. It looks like a war zone. All my cars were burned to hell."

"Look on the bright side—your office files are in good shape, if damp and smelling like smoke, and most of your inventory on the shelves was saved by Neptune's Landing's finest rural fire department."

"Uh-huh . . . 'bright side,' " Kyle repeated gloomily.

Moses folded the paper and slapped it on the coffee table. "Thanks for unplugging the telephone when you left this morning, Rachel. We needed the sleep. It started ringing as soon as I plugged it in. Your mother and Jada both called, and the police are sending over men to collect Kyle for his formal statement. The insurance investigating team is going over his garage now, checking for salvage."

"Uh-huh. It's a whole day's lineup of answering questions. But let's get back to the question of what you gave me, and it wasn't aspirin."

She'd never forget lying beside Kyle, watching his pain, even while he slept, worrying about him. "Moses and I went through Mallory's stash—I decided to keep the bag of her pills instead of throwing them away. I thought the pharmacy labels and a good drug identification book might lead to something or someone.

They've been in Buttercup's trunk the whole time. Moses picked out a little pill cocktail for you,"

When Kyle's scowl swung to Moses, the big beefy man held up his hands. "You didn't want an emergency room, and we had to do something to keep you down."

Kyle was studying her navy blue business suit and short skirt. "I asked you not to do that program. You're out hunting Mallory's—the men who visited her, aren't you? Didn't I tell you just yesterday morning that the lid could pop right off this thing?"

Rachel nodded contritely. "Yes, you did, dear— honey."

"Didn't I tell you to wait for me? You've set yourself up as bait, haven't you? What a dingbat, empty-headed, irresponsible idea."

She'd done exactly that, and her presentation to the businessmen's club—women included—had led to some very unpleasant conclusions. She was looking at the potential consequences of going after Shane—cuts and bruises all over Kyle, his face swollen, his ribs tightly bound. "I am so sorry this happened to you."

He smiled lopsidedly, the effect of his swollen lip. "Sorry doesn't cut it."

"I know, but I really am." Rachel knew she was going to cry and she bit her lip to prevent it.

"With Kyle and me here, we need more groceries, Rachel. I'll haul some back here," Moses interrupted as he stood, and Rachel had the feeling he wanted to escape the brewing argument. "I'll be right back. Call me on my cell if you need me. Kyle should be flat on his back. He's passed out once already. By the way, if any of the investigators call, the clothes Kyle was wearing last night are under your outside stairway. They smelled too much of gas to leave inside."

"Okay. Take my keys to the apartment. We're not going anywhere. And, Moses, would you mind taking those heels to Shane Templeton? I think they just might fit him. And he seems to like women's shoes."

"Shane? Wearing heels?" Kyle asked, his expression blank.

"Men do that sometimes," Moses said with a bland shrug. "Have no idea why."

"Mallory must have ordered them for Shane and kept them here for his use."

When the door closed behind Moses, Rachel stood and walked to it slowly, locking it. She needed time to package her thoughts, giving Kyle the truthful answers he needed. "I'll make a deal with you. Let's go lie down, and I'll answer all your questions."

Kyle's deep voice was raw with anger and it vibrated in the quiet apartment. "Where's the damn gun?"

This wasn't going well, and Rachel felt almost as bad as Kyle looked. He could be obstinate, pass out, hurt himself—she ran all through the could's while walking back to him. She recognized that dark furious look; Kyle was set to battle, and neither one of them was up to it. "I'll tell you what you want, but I am so tired, Kyle."

"Then go to bed."

"I can't, not without you." *I need you, Kyle . . . I need to know that you're safe beside me, that I can watch you breathe when you sleep. . . .*

Kyle noted Rachel's uneven tone, the tears gleaming on her cheeks, the way she looked as if all that attitude and power had been sucked out of her. She looked as if she would break down with her next breath. She seemed to hang in the shadowy apartment, and he wanted to pick her up, to carry her to bed.

In bad shape, he'd probably drop and hurt her. Kyle fought frustration and anger and the need to hold Rachel, to bind her close and safe to him. In his present shape, he doubted that he could protect her and that terrified him. . . . And he knew she wasn't going to bed without him. "Okay, let's go to bed and take a nap, but you're not getting off the hook. You've got a lot of answering to do."

Kyle let Rachel maneuver him into the bedroom and onto the bed; he watched her as she slowly undressed, tossing aside her suit. He waited while she went into the bathroom and closed the door. Minutes later, she slid into bed beside him, naked and warm and fragrant. She sighed deeply as if she'd come a long, long way and looked at him across the distance of their pillows. "I'm so sorry, Kyle."

"So am I. Get over here. Don't make me come and get you," he added with a smile to soften the order. Rachel eased close, careful not to touch him; her arm rested high over his chest, as she smoothed his hair.

Not one to lose an opportunity, Kyle moved his arm against her breasts and rubbed against them slowly. He opened his hand on her thigh and met her kiss, lingering in the softness of it as Rachel kissed his shoulder and eased her leg over his.

While cuddling and reassuring each other that they were safe, Kyle tried not to focus on that little furry nest between her legs heating his skin. He moved his thigh slightly, and Rachel adjusted easily, that spot on his leg hotter now. He started a rhythmic nudge against her and his body launched into hard overdrive. "The gun, Rachel. What did you do with it?"

She was soft and rubbing her cheek against his shoulder, looking up at him with drowsy eyes and her hand was wandering in places that waited and leaped to her touch— "Mmm?"

"You wouldn't try to sidetrack me, would you, Rachel?"

He didn't believe her sweet "I wouldn't do that, Kyle," but gloved and stroked in her hand, he really couldn't focus on straight thinking. "Rachel, you're very busy there. I seem to remember something like this happening last night."

Her hand smoothed his chest and Rachel lifted slightly, bending over him to kiss his lips, his cheeks, his aching head, and nibble on the portion of his jaw that wasn't bruised. The combination of her body, naked and hot against his, the glove of her hand, and those tempting kisses caused Kyle to get lightheaded. Rachel brushed her lips lightly across his and whispered, "You said something very nice, and you were like you are now—very big—and I thought it might help you to relieve a little pressure."

If "swoon" was in a real man's vocabulary, Kyle might have used it—he remembered her kisses all over him, those soothing whispers, and the—"So, I didn't dream that."

When she grinned impishly, that cute little dimple on her cheek deepened. "Oh, no, you were right with the project. I hope you don't mind. It seemed to be the thing to do with—with your condition."

Kyle tried to work through who said what in the previous night. "What did I say that deserved that kind of special treatment?"

"Nice things. Do you have to talk so much?"

Kyle forced himself to return to the questions that Rachel evidently didn't want to answer. He moved her hand from his really, really want-to bad, and held it in his own, lacing their fingers. "You talk now. . . . Where's the gun and what happened with Shane?"

Rachel sighed and flattened to her side of the bed. "The gun was gone when I got back. I haven't had a chance to talk with Jada yet, but she or Mom probably hid it somewhere."

An unaccounted for, semi-automatic with a clip of hollow points wasn't something that Kyle dismissed, neither was Rachel's meeting with Shane. As soon as Moses got back, Kyle would ask him to find that gun. "What about Shane? What happened last night with him?"

In the shadows of the room, Rachel's face closed and she stared at the ceiling fan slowly rotating above them. "You were right not to like him. I'm worried about Jada. She cleans his house every other day and she's got him lined up to marry her."

"That's not good enough, Rachel. You're avoiding the question. . . . What happened?" Kyle sucked back the rage building in him—from Rachel's tight expression, he guessed that she'd probably been attacked.

"We talked. It wasn't good. He liked my heels,

though," she said shakily. "That's why I thought those custom-mades were his, and I remember Mallory talking about how he liked her high heels. I thought it was odd then, but I didn't make the connection."

"And did he *like* you?" Kyle pressed darkly and held Rachel's hand when she tried to get out of bed. "You're not going anywhere until I have some answers. Someone just tried to kill me. I think I deserve those answers, don't you?"

Not only did Kyle's body and head hurt, but his heart ached because Rachel didn't trust him. They'd made love for hours in that motel room, and he was in her bed now. She'd fussed and worried over him, cared for him, and she still didn't trust him. "Tell me about Shane. The whole story, and we'll work from there."

Rachel's reluctant sketch left Kyle with an ugly deduction. "And you think those are his high heels—the ones you sent Moses to deliver? Do you know what that means?"

Her bare shoulder gleamed as she shrugged. "That he's a cross-dresser with definite tastes. Mallory probably catered to him, because she loved him at first, and later, well, maybe she felt sorry for him. For his part, he probably worried that she'd expose and therefore ruin him. I think he seduced her with things like that poetry book and wedding ring—who knows what happened there—and he had a nice safe place to come for whatever games they played."

Tears glittered in her eyes as she looked at Kyle. "I'm so sorry you were hurt—that your place was burned, and that the cars you loved and brought back to life are gone."

His inventory of classic cars wouldn't be easy to replace, but Kyle had built his business from the ground up and he knew the route to travel. Because Rachel looked like she'd been dragged through hell, Kyle pushed down his frustration and hurt. "Come over here, lady. That's enough talking."

But Rachel shook her head. "No, it isn't. You were probably hurt because I've been pushing and asking a lot of questions, trying to get that list of men who saw Mallory, who might have hurt her. You deserve to know everything, Kyle."

He held her hand, the smooth, soft skin over the fragile bones, and from her expression knew that she was going inside herself to another time, recalling a darkness that she'd opened to few people. Rachel slid from the bed, and dressed slowly. In a black tank top and jeans, her midriff was a pale strip as she moved to open the plantation blinds. She looked out the window at the buildings in the distance; they seemed to be stacked against the Pacific Ocean. "Mallory came to see me in New York, because I called her. You didn't hear all of the tape. Maybe you should."

She turned, a dark shapely silhouette with horizontal strips of bright sunlight behind her. "Are you up to this, Kyle? It isn't pretty."

Despite the pain in his ribs and head, Kyle eased to sit upright. Whatever Rachel had to say, she was taking her time framing the right words to serve him. "Sure."

A half hour later, Kyle shook his head. Rachel sat across the table from him, looking down at the untouched slice of chocolate cake. Her hand shook as she lifted her coffee cup to her lips, her face pale in the kitchen's afternoon sunlight.

Neither of them were hungry, but it seemed to give Rachel something ordinary to do, in an unusual time, settling her somewhat.

Echoes of Mallory's taped voice ricocheted in the tiny room: "You even come close to my family, and I'll kill you. *I'll kill you! You better not have raped Rachel, you bastard—*"

Rachel wrapped her arms around her body and rocked on her chair. "That's what you didn't hear, why I think there's a connection to the man who attacked me. Now here's the rest—"

Kyle tried to fit Mallory's threat into the full story Rachel unwrapped slowly as she meticulously cut her slice of cake into tiny pieces. "At first, I thought it was some guys, peeved that I'd won a few silly little games of eight ball. . . . Whoever intended to rape me—couldn't perform. So I guess Mallory's stick pins did their job, huh?" she asked shakily as her fingers dug into her arms.

Kyle took a sip of the burning hot coffee, the pieces of the puzzle that was Rachel, coming together painfully. All the pieces fit—the way Rachel went after those punks on the beach, pitting herself against them, the first few times he'd moved too close, that fear in her eyes, the way her body had stiffened. He saw her alone, shivering in the park, hurrying to put on her clothes, hugging the tomcat to her as her only friend—and then Mallory, livid that whoever had used her was now moving on to hurt her family. . . .

"She came to you—"

"I couldn't tell Mom or Jada. I just couldn't."

Kyle heard something creak and he'd bent the fork in his hand. He tossed it onto the table. "And the boyfriend, the guy you were living with? What happened there?"

Rachel shook her head and the sunlight caught on the tendrils around her face. "Mark couldn't take it. I couldn't bear for him to touch me. I didn't want to go out at night any more. I added extra locks to the apartment . . . it was like a fortress—"

She laughed shakily, the kind of empty sound brought on by a nervous reaction. "I started wearing a lot of clothing, even in the heat—protection, I guess. The only time I felt safe was when I came back to Neptune's Landing. Funny isn't it? That I would feel safe here, when Mallory was in such pain?"

The flat of her hand hit the table and she stood, hurriedly cleaning the table, the dishes clattering into the sink. "I owe her. Mallory came to me when I needed her, and all that time, I never knew what she was going through—that she had a daughter. I don't know why she gave me this place anyway, challenged me to get it up and running—"

"Maybe I do. . . ." Kyle said softly.

Rachel leaned her hips back against the countertop, crossed her arms and rocked slightly. "Why?"

She looked as if she'd been torn in pieces. Kyle's instincts were to hold her, but just then keys rattled in the door's locks. The door opened and Jada flounced into the living room. She tossed a variety of sacks on the couch. "Clothes for Kyle, just like you said, Rache. Socks, jeans, undershorts, and shirts," she explained curtly. "At least if I don't have a man, I can shop for one."

Behind her, Moses moved more slowly, locking the door carefully behind him. He came to the kitchen, tossed the keys on the table and sat down, hauling the two-layer cake to him. Rachel dug in a drawer and handed him a fork. "Dig in."

"Your sister is in a bad mood," Moses muttered warily.

Jada came into the kitchen, pulled out a drawer and got a fork, sitting down in the chair Rachel had vacated. She reached for the cake platter, started to pull it toward her but Moses held it tight. "I deserve this."

"Listen, you big wall of muscle with gorgeous hair, I need it more." Jada looked from Rachel to Kyle and back again. "You're both too quiet. . . . What's going on?"

"Things." Rachel shrugged and frowned slightly at Kyle. He caught the meaning—*Don't tell my sister about the attack.* . . .

"You were right about Shane," Jada stated fiercely around a huge mouthful of cake. "I ran down your errand boy here and found out he had a delivery to make—he asked me where Shane lived. So I took those super heels from him . . . delivered them to Shane, and he lost it. He's got some kind of burn-looking stuff on his throat and he laid into me so hard about the shoes that hey—what's that about methinks the rat protests too much? Anyway, I told him that I thought he'd look really sharp wearing a garter belt and fishnet stockings, maybe a bustier with those heels. He went nutso. Yelled at me . . . called me a 'ditsy airhead.' I was ready to go for him—because how many times have I scrubbed out his toilet bowls anyway? Then Muscles here, must have heard me yelling back, because he came into the house and asked if there was any problem."

"I didn't give Fly-Weight here, anything," Moses grumbled. "I was minding my own business when she pulled over to the curb in this ice cream wagon. She gave me a tub of More Berry ice cream and a spoon. I should have known something was wrong then—or when she started asking questions about where I was going—well, I had to ask directions from someone, didn't I? Anyway, while I was digging in, she grabbed the shoe box and drove off in that wagon. All I had to do was to follow the sound and it was parked outside this guy's place. She was yelling at him."

Jada scowled at him. "I could've have handled myself. I was all set to marry the guy and bear his children—"

"Poor guy," Moses mumbled. "I almost feel sorry for him, all burned like that and being attacked by a woman throwing things at him—looked like expensive things, too. Your sister has a good aim. Got him a couple of times with fancy cups and saucers with gold and roses on them. I'd say that Chinese vase cost a pretty penny, too. I've never seen a woman that small topple a full-size china cabinet—never would have believed it."

Kyle studied Rachel's raised eyebrows, "who-me" innocent expression. "Would you happen to know how Shane got burned, Rachel?"

She blinked a couple of times. "I think a teapot may have fallen on him."

Jada finished the scenario: "Shane said she hit him with a teapot for no reason at all—my ass. There were tea stains all over the love seat."

"You were on a love seat with him?" Kyle asked carefully. He didn't like the image of Rachel being attacked.

"I—wanted to see how he reacted to—um. . . ."

"To things Mallory might wear? Short skirts, tight sweaters, those kinds of things?" Kyle filled in slowly.

When Rachel pressed her lips together, that dimple showed again. "Um . . . maybe."

"That's even dumber than taking Mallory's stuff back alone," Kyle exploded.

"I . . . am not dumb."

Kyle listened to the telephone ring and when neither he nor Rachel moved, Jada asked, "Um . . . should I get that?"

"That would be nice. Thank you very much," Rachel said, her eyes still locked with Kyle's.

"Maybe you'd better think about telling your mother and sister," Kyle suggested while Jada was talking on the telephone. He took the insurance investigator's call and opened the door to two police officers, motioning them to come in. He spoke quietly with them, and then as Rachel came to his side, her arm around his back, Kyle said, "I need to go with them to make another statement. They want a doctor to look at my bruises, take some pictures, that kind of thing. They just might be agreeing that someone actually did work me over. It had rained and it wasn't likely that the barbeque grill still had live coals, or that it tipped to start the fire. Moses needs to come, too. And Rachel, think about what I said, okay?"

"I'm going with you," she said as she began to take the new clothing out of the packages. Kyle almost smiled. Rachel the Fearless, champion of the downtrodden was set to protect him, and the feeling was pretty damn good.

"I thought you would want to be in on the excitement, but I'd rather you stayed here and rested. And think about how to tell your mother about Mallory—and other things. Trina could be in danger, too."

"I will. It just may be one of the most difficult things I've ever done." She shook the short-sleeve summer shirts, choosing one to slip onto Kyle. She stood in front of him and buttoned his shirt. Kyle realized briefly that no one had ever buttoned his shirt, or straightened his collar.

Funny how a man noted things like that, amid the terror that the woman he loved was probably on someone's hurt-and-kill list.

"Kyle shouldn't have left the gun on the table in the first place. What was I supposed to do with it? And I am not dumb." Rachel frowned as she parked Buttercup in Bob's Handy Hardware parking lot. In talking to her mother and Jada, Rachel discovered that her sister had been the first one into the apartment after Rachel had gone to Idaho. She'd cleaned, but saw only Kyle's handwritten list of names on the table where the semi-automatic should have been.

Rachel collected the box of Bob's favorite candies from the front seat and walked into the hardware store. Bob was behind the cash register, tapping in the purchases of a woman standing in front of the counter. He looked tired and drained, but familiar and loved.

He smiled at Rachel, took the woman's money and placed a receipt into the sack of mouse traps and door hinges. When she left the store, he moved around the counter. "Are you all right, Rachel? I was so worried, and your mother—"

"I've talked with her this morning, and I'm going over to her office right after this."

Bob shook his head. "Terrible thing. I didn't like Scanlon, but I wouldn't want to see him financially ruined—or put away for insurance fraud. That's what I hear around town, that it was arson and he'd just upped the insurance on his place. You should know that he's being investigated now. Rachel, it doesn't look good for you to be associated with him. Surely he can find some-place else to live—and not with you. I'm worried, Rachel. Think of your mother."

"He didn't set that fire, Bob—"

"Arson and insurance fraud are serious criminal actions, and you could be involved."

"I am involved," she said softly. "I think I love him."

Bob let out an exasperated sigh. "It's the same thing as always. You find a cause and you fight for it. He's down on his luck, so naturally that makes him the un-derdog, and you're going to stick by him. That isn't love, Rachel."

"Maybe not. . . ." She handed him the box of chewy fruit and nut candy. "But he's in my life, and I want you two to be friends."

"You want me to invite him over to my barbeques, actually do that?" Bob asked savagely. "He's a punk, Rachel. He's got women all over the place, criminal types staying with him, and some big goon running his errands now. Jada told me about this guy—Moses Fry."

"Did she tell you about Shane Templeton?" Rachel

asked carefully, uncertain of Jada's temper and her fast mouth when angered. The childhood nickname of "Freeway Mouth" sometimes still applied to Jada, the adult.

"She said he was on her 'poop-list' or something like that. She's mad at him. Jada is always having boyfriend problems. . . . I warned her not to marry that one—Larry Something—but she wouldn't listen. She probably just fixated on Shane and—"

"He was involved with Mallory, Bob, and it wasn't always sweet."

Bob was fiercely adamant: "I do not believe that. He's respected in our community. You know how Mallory was, just like Jada in a way—always running after men."

"I found something that linked them together. Shane seduced Mallory."

Bob shook his head. "You've got to be wrong," he stated fiercely. "He's in Neptune's Landing's finest social set, comes from a good family—I've known him for a long time. When it came to men, you were always the sensible one, independent, on your own, a smart thinker—now you're tied up with this Scanlon character. He's just plain trouble, Rachel. Look what just happened—he's probably involved in some drug trafficking that went wrong, and who knows what kind of criminal activities he's into."

Rachel had expected Bob's adamant rejection of Kyle, but it saddened her. She understood that years of Bob's negative opinions about Kyle wouldn't change easily, and that it was best not to push him now. She hugged him and kissed his cheek. "I think this will work out for all of us, given time."

Bob caught her close and nuzzled her hair in the familiar way he'd done with all of the girls. His next words reminded her of when her sisters and she were going down to the beach, when she was finally taking the car out on her own. "Be careful, Rachel. Promise?"

"I promise. I love you, Bob."

"I love you, too," he returned in the old familiar way. *Or was it?*

His embrace, his soft paunch against her, triggered warning flashes that she didn't understand. Unsettled, Rachel couldn't pin down her emotions, but she eased away. "Better go. Mom is expecting me."

"Give her a kiss for me."

"I will. Bye." Rachel left the hardware store, aware that Bob was watching her.

It was an uneasy sensation, and one she couldn't understand. . . .

# Sixteen

"BOB? WE'RE OKAY WITH EACH OTHER," TRINA STATED. "HE'S just worried about you, that's all. Jada heard us arguing about you letting Kyle stay at your place overnight."

"Kyle is staying longer than that, Mom. There are things people don't know about him. Good things."

"I've already suspected that. He helped Mallory as much as she would let him. I'll always be grateful for that. If Kyle hadn't stayed with you, he was welcome here. I would have taken care of him, so would have Jada. As it is, he came to you, and I'd say that is for a very good reason—because he loves you. He said so last night, didn't he?" Trina slowly stood up from kneeling and slid her gardening gloves from her. She tossed them down into the carryall of her hand tools, then eased her bandanna away from her hair. In the last week of May, she looked young and slender against the Pacific Ocean. She riffled her blond multi-length cut with her fingers, freeing it to the ocean breeze.

"He doesn't remember that part, Mom. I'm not reminding him. A man on medication and in pain can't always be responsible."

"Kyle is always responsible." Trina's eyes searched

Rachel's. "You've checked on me several times today, and I suppose that is because of the trouble afoot. I'm safe here and Jada, too. I stayed in my house as usual last night. Bob stayed at his."

"Mom, I really need to talk. Serious stuff." Rachel admired the timeless cheekbones of her mother. Trina's clear blue eyes were untroubled, as if she'd met the worst of the world on her terms, and had come to a confident level of much needed peace.

"I've been waiting for this visit. I thought you might come by and I closed the office early. It's about what happened to Kyle, isn't it? Let me get some iced tea and we can sit and look out at the ocean. Beautiful day for late May, isn't it?"

"I'd like that." Rachel looked out at the oceanfront property that her mother had purchased after leaving low-income housing. Trina had repaired and improved the property where the girls had grown up, the back yard familiar with swings and picnic table, and the flower garden she called "Therapy."

Rachel sat in one of the three swings that Bob had made for the girls. She swung slowly and looked out at the ocean's waves. . . . "Once upon a time there were three sisters—"

Trina came outside and smiled at Rachel as she lowered a tray onto the weathered picnic table. The earthen-look pottery teapot and mugs reminded Rachel of the china at Shane's, of the spotted burns he'd been wearing at the businessman's luncheon earlier, of the way his eyes threatened revenge. He'd looked down her suit jacket, short skirt and high heels as if she were touting whore's wares, the same as Mallory. Rachel had smiled at him, the professional cool smile that carried her own threat: she knew what he was now—how he'd snared Mallory and used her for a side that he couldn't reveal to others. And if Shane were responsible for Kyle's beating and the fire, Rachel was determined to find evidence.

"Bob gave me one of those in-a-minute hot-water pots, the latest in his hardware," Trina explained as she poured tea into the mugs. "He knows that I love a cup of tea, sitting here with my daughters. You've been so busy. It's so special to have you here, Rachel. And I know you want to get back to Kyle. You might be having Jada around. She seems to have shifted her attention to Moses."

"What did she tell you?" Rachel held her breath, because Jada, alias "Freeway Mouth" was apt to reveal everything she knew.

Trina's fingertip circled her mug. "This is about Shane, isn't it? I never liked that man," she said quietly. "I don't know exactly what happened, but Mallory was in love with him for a while . . . then Jada, and I knew a little about him—"

Rachel studied her mother. "Mom, did Shane make a pass at you?"

"It's the oddest thing. One day, he was shopping for a car at my place. We were in the office, and he seemed fascinated with my heels. According to Jada, he has his own high heels. And it seems he has a thing about the Everly women, doesn't it, Rachel?" Trina asked tightly.

Furious with Shane now, Rachel decided to skip the details of her meeting with Shane and that of Jada's. "You could say that. I think he is a dangerous man."

"I agree. He came to me, worried about Mallory, and—"

"And? And what happened?"

Trina's blue eyes were dark with anger before she turned to look out at the ocean. A child's kite appeared white and stark against the waves. "I'm still mad when I think of it. He wanted to conduct Mallory's funeral, and I shouldn't have let him. I didn't want to tell Jada that then, but we were all so grieving and she had her sights set on him. I thought maybe there was something she saw in him that I had missed. But I do not like being pushed, admonished, or told what's best for me. There's something else I can't define—something creepy. And he made the mistake of—Let's just say that while arranging Mallory's funeral with Shane, I used a few things I learned about protecting myself while I was playing for dollars in low places."

"He's disgusting, a real letch. I think he may have had something to do with Kyle's beating and with setting the garage and cars on fire. The insurance investigators think it's probably arson. I just wanted to touch base with you that Shane could be dangerous."

Trina tilted her head and studied Rachel. "I've seen you do programs before, and you were always dressed in classical business, maybe slacks, a white blouse over a jacket, practical pumps. Bob said you were wearing tight clothes and a short skirt today. Was there a reason for that? To bring Shane out, what he really is—that old wolf in sheep's clothing thing?"

"The word is slime-ball, Mom."

"Where did you go—really, when you closed 'for repairs'?"

Her mother was way ahead of the game, Rachel decided, as she sipped her tea and tried to think of a way to tell her about Katrina, her granddaughter. Instead, Rachel asked carefully, "Mom, did you come into my apartment while I was gone?"

Trina shook her head. "No, but Jada borrowed my keys and went over to bring the cake and to do a little cleaning. I was tied up with a trade-in, a sweet little Buick. Is there a problem?"

"A big one. Kyle's gun is missing and Jada said she didn't touch it."

Her mother's hard "oh, shit" cut across the late afternoon air. "I mean, oh, dear me," Trina corrected curtly. "You had all the locks changed."

"I did, but anyone with access to Jada's could have made a copy . . . if she were housecleaning and left them around."

"Mmm. She's bad at that, leaving things lying around. She did mark your keys with your name. I saw her."

"She cleans for Shane—or did. He could have used her keys to get that gun."

Rachel briefly explained the Kyle-leaving-gun scenario, which only made it worse, raising Trina's fears. "If he left it with you, that means he thinks there is real rough stuff involved. What would make him think that? You were gone for two whole days, so someone could have—"

Trina rapped out the time sequence and finished with "They came while you were gone and took it. But why would Kyle leave you a semi-automatic unless—?" she asked again.

"Okay, there's a few missing pieces that maybe

you'd better know—" Rachel didn't look forward to telling her mother about the tape and Mallory's threat: *You hurt my family and I'll haunt you forever.* . . .

But Trina was looking past Rachel to Kyle who was walking from the driveway to the backyard, a three-legged dog at his side. Trina moved quickly, gracefully, toward him. "I want you to sit in that lawn chair right now, Kyle Scanlon," she ordered in a no-nonsense motherly tone.

He was pale and obviously in pain, but he grinned at Rachel as she came to his other side. "I must still have it. Two good-looking women running to meet me. . . . Trina, would you mind getting me a glass of water?"

Pup licked Rachel's hand and she patted him before taking Kyle's. She turned his hand in her own, then took the other, inspecting it, before looking at him. "You smell like smoke and you've got soot on your clothes and hands. You were at the garage working, weren't you?"

"They don't build 'em anymore, honey," Kyle stated logically. He was mourning his loves, the old classics, the parts that couldn't be replaced, and Rachel ached for him.

"I'm not using all of our garage. You can store whatever you want there," Trina offered. "Leon would be thrilled."

"You shouldn't be working now, Kyle," Rachel said, concerned for him.

"Yeah, so? I was there anyway, going over things with the insurance investigator."

After her mother had gone inside, Kyle asked softly, "Did you tell her everything?"

"I was just getting to it. She knows that Shane isn't

exactly a prince. I don't know how to tell her about the tape. I just can't—"

Kyle bent to kiss her lightly. "Tell her. She could be in danger, too, and has to be in the loop. Mallory was protecting all of your family—or trying to. I think I could kill this guy if he's the same one who attacked you—and Shane was out of town that weekend, at some retreat."

"How did you know that—? Kyle, did you go to see Shane?"

"We talked," Kyle stated briefly, "and don't ask about what. Let's just say that I didn't sling a teapot with hot tea at him."

Rachel shook her head and walked with Kyle to a wooden lawn chair. She decided not to add fuel to Kyle's dark temper by telling him about the drugged tea. "That wasn't smart. You're in no shape to do anything now, much less take on a man—he's strong, Kyle. How did the interview go?"

"Let's stay on how you know that he's so strong—dear. How do you?" When Rachel didn't answer, Kyle's lips tightened, his eyes narrowed. "That's what I thought."

"I handled it."

"Not by yourself anymore—got that? This relationship thing we've got going—the one you told the police about—requires trust, not you leaping into dangerous situations without me at your side. If you're leaping, you'd better let me know. . . . As for the investigation, I'm at the top—maybe the only name on the insurance guys' list of arson suspects. By the way, I've turned in the handgun as missing in the fire. There's no reason to involve you in that respect, although they asked about our relationship. I said we had one . . . it seemed to be the thing to do, since you said we had one last night when you were telling the officer off. Let's go take care of that right now—our relationship, I mean."

"You're going to use this relationship thing as blackmail, aren't you? Me, running to you every time a lead pops up? My protector, that sort of thing?"

"I am bigger than you, honey. Sometimes you like that." Kyle wiggled his eyebrows, leering at her. But Rachel understood that he was trying to lighten the long hard day and the job ahead of her—telling her mother about Mallory's tape, and just maybe, Katrina. . . .

"Don't even think about staying anywhere but my apartment, Kyle-dear," Rachel ordered.

Kyle frowned slightly. "Gossip can mark a woman. Bob isn't going to like this."

"I need protection, don't I? Isn't that just why you laid that word, 'relationship,' all over me?"

"You're going to boss me around, aren't you?"

"Just watch me."

Kyle's expression was wary. "Now, get this straight, honey. We're in a short-term relationship and I'm just in it for the sex. Which is good, by the way. Right now, it's working—as long as you don't go off half-cocked again. We get this guy, pin some real evidence on him, and everyone is free to go their own way."

Rachel studied Kyle, the man who in his drugged pain had said he loved her, but that she deserved better. "Did I ask for anything else, Scanlon?"

\* \* \*

"I'm feeling better," Kyle murmured against Rachel's throat at five o'clock the next morning.

"Mm. You're feeling something, Scanlon," she returned drowsily as he moved over her, easing into her.

Kyle bent to kiss her, and tried to keep his body from running ahead of the tenderness he wanted to give Rachel. "Hard day, yesterday, huh?"

Trina had been stunned that she had a granddaughter, and devastated as she listened to the tape with Jada and Moses. Rachel had made the connection between her attack and the tape as briefly and coolly as possible. She'd revised the attack, softening it, but the impact still widened Trina's eyes and she'd paled. "You actually think that Mallory was protecting us? You think it was Shane? I'll kill him. I . . . will . . . kill him."

It had taken two hours to settle Trina, to make her believe that waiting was better, pinpointing whoever used Mallory with hard facts that couldn't be denied. Jada and Moses had taken her home, and from Moses's steady look at Trina, he'd found a woman who interested him; he had nodded to Kyle, a silent indication that he would be safeguarding the two women. Later, Rachel had seemed distracted and quiet and remote.

Around midnight, she'd started tossing and her restless murmurs had become screams of terror: "Don't! Don't touch me . . . don't! Mallory? Mallory, are you still here?"

Kyle had soothed her, but she had good reason to be upset, the past leaping upon her—she'd finally fallen asleep, curled next to him with Pup and Harry on her other side.

Now Rachel adjusted her hips, lifting for his deeper access, moving slowly, dreamlike. Her hands smoothed his chest, his shoulders, his face. "You look awful," she whispered, drawing his face down for those amazing light kisses all over it.

"Thanks. A little to the left, Everly."

She complied and brushed her lips against his jaw. "You're a heavy-beard man, aren't you?"

He stilled, not wanting to hurt her and started to ease away. "Hold that thought. I'll be right back."

Rachel arched toward him, her internal muscles tightening, her hands drawing his lips to hers. "Not a chance, Scanlon. You're not going anywhere. I thought we were just in this for the sex, right? Your payment is overdue, Scanlon."

He relaxed, pushing down on her, luxuriating in that tight warm moist clench, the stroke of her thighs moving around his, her insoles rubbing his calves. "You're all nice and hairy and warm and appealing right now."

Kyle looked down to where their bodies met, hers long and soft and pale against his. "Ditto."

"Hey. I shave my legs on a regular basis."

"But you're warm—hot, really—and appealing."

On the aftermath of a hard, stress-filled, emotional two days, Kyle intended to take his time pleasuring them both and placing the problems outside this room, this moment with Rachel. His hands slid down her sides then back up, his thumbs toying with her breasts. "You always sleep naked?"

"When I'm hoping to get made."

"Mm. You just might get your wish."

"Are you sure you're up to this?"

"Feels like it, partner."

Kyle gave her a "please, you doubt that I can?" look, and Rachel laughed softly, the sound catching him. He smoothed away the stand of hair from her face, studying that dimple on her cheek, kissing it. "I like the sound of that—you laughing."

"Well, you've just got it, you know."

"I'm going to get it." Then Kyle started moving and forgot everything but the sweetness of making love to Rachel.

"That was nice, big guy. Sweet," Rachel said as he managed to breathe again and eased from her. She turned her head on the pillow and stared at him in the bedroom's shadows. "Now, why did you think that Mallory chose me to take over this place?"

"You're her sister?"

"Bull. Why do you think?"

"Tell me what you're holding, why you were so quiet last night, and what you were thinking about, and then we'll talk. You had nightmares for most of the night and—"

Rachel jackknifed upright and wrapped a sheet around her. Kyle gripped it in his fist, holding her imprisoned. "Give, Rachel. You're too much woman to let a freak like Shane bother you. You could have reported him, and you didn't. You should have," he corrected, angry with her and with himself for not protecting her.

"You'd better not have pulled any macho stuff about avenging me with Shane. I take care of my business."

She struggled against Kyle's grip on the sheet. "You're still pretty bruised, Kyle. I wouldn't want to hurt you."

"Try." *She didn't trust him enough to tell him everything*. . . . "We're in a relationship, aren't we?" he stated harshly to remind her of her statement to the police.

Rachel turned to him, her eyes flashing. "It's just sex, you said so."

His own words, flung at him in the aftermath of love-making, hurt. "Sure. That's what I said."

She flattened her hand on his chest, and Kyle allowed her to push him down on the pillow while she sat on the edge of the bed. But he held the sheet tight and waited, locking his stare with hers.

Rachel spoke finally, "You're afraid of the picket fence, the kids' swing in the backyard, and the whole picture, aren't you? Maybe you're afraid of commitment, of letting someone take care of you once in a while. You've been giving me hell every time I wanted to help you, tough guy."

No one had pushed Kyle like Rachel; no one had gone that deep into his scars or his fears. Years of his early fight to survive surfaced automatically. "I am not afraid of anything."

"You're afraid you won't fit. Coward. My gosh, what would happen if people found out how much good you do? What would that do for your tough-guy, loser profile then? I had a little chat with Moses—an ex-wrestler who can't stand blood and I just found out that you got him a job as a personal trainer, no blood involved. Iris and Patty adore you, for good reason. They weren't just showgirls, were they? They did a little more than that, didn't they? Before you started playing big daddy and helping them out?"

"Busy girl," Kyle stated darkly as he released her sheet, and lay back, his hands behind his head. "What else do you know?"

"Just that you're probably the one who helped Mallory with her mortgage-down money."

Kyle chewed on that. Only Rachel had been able to piece that bit of information together. "Like I said, busy girl."

"While I was in your books, checking on those phone bills for your girls, I found several big cash withdrawals that matched Mallory's initial deposit. You helped her quite a bit through the years. You helped her with childbirth and every other thing in her life, but you couldn't save her from herself, could you?"

He'd stopped giving money to Mallory when her drug habit had deepened and when so many male visitors had climbed those stairs to her apartment. She'd started buying exotic negligees and sex toys and she'd drawn away from Kyle—except when she really needed him, then she would call. . . .

"Okay, I helped Mallory. John Sr. helped me, and I was just passing it around a little bit. I knew when someone really needed a boost, and not just for the money either—but for pride's sake. Mallory was at the lowest point I'd ever seen her—she'd given away a baby and she'd come face-to-face with what she was, that she might never be a suitable parent—that she could endanger her own child. I saw how she struggled to redirect herself, throwing herself into that business, the pride she took in being able to help with Katrina's support. . . . But what's up with you, Rachel? What are you chewing on?"

Rachel stood and slid into her jeans and Kyle's summer shirt. "I'm going downstairs."

Kyle waited at the open stairway door until he heard the billiard balls click against each other; at her side, Pup would bark, signaling any disturbance. Rachel wasn't playing for pleasure, she was deep in thought and she'd barred him from whatever troubled her. Harry rubbed against Kyle's jeaned legs, purring loudly for his morning food. "So that's how she got you," Kyle said, bending to rub the cat's ears. "You came to her when she needed you, and you probably saw everything, right? Care to tell me what happened, from a cat's point of view?"

Kyle brewed coffee and took their mugs downstairs. He sipped quietly as Rachel shot, coldly, expertly, intently focused on the balls. She leaned down low, formed a bridge, her body outstretched, elbow high at that 90-degree angle and fired the cue ball into the pocket. "Tell me why Mallory wanted me to have this place."

"Because you can handle it. Because she knew that you'd bring this guy out in the open and because you'd get him and keep Katrina safe. Evidence, Rachel. She knew you'd get him and she was too far gone, with a reputation that would damage anything she tried to make anything stick."

Rachel rounded the table, collected the balls and racked them. The morning sunlight penetrated the bamboo blinds she had lowered, catching the ferns, and outlining her body beneath his shirt. Kyle settled into watch Rachel work off steam, fighting something inside her that she didn't want to recognize. She shook the rack grimly, seating the balls against each other. "She's still here, waiting. I feel her. She wants something."

"Maybe."

Rachel suddenly tossed her cue stick onto the table. "I'm going to the beach."

"Am I invited?"

"No."

"I'll be there anyway. I've watched one woman go through whatever it is tearing you apart, and I don't like watching another—especially when I know you are about ready to do something that could mean a whole lot of trouble. Mallory took it, but you're not waiting, are you?"

"No. I just need some thinking space, and when you're with me—" Rachel moved into Kyle's arms and held him tight. "I need you, Kyle. I need you to understand."

He tried to make light of his tumbling, uncertain emotions. Rachel wasn't including him in her thoughts; she didn't trust him, or she'd be forthright. If it had anything to do with her nightmares, it wasn't pleasant. "I don't. But if you need to go to the beach, I'll keep my distance."

She raised to look at him. "You don't mind?"

"Hell, yes, I mind. Just don't make a move without me."

Later, when he stood watching Rachel walk on the beach, picking up pebbles and tossing them into the ocean, a vast backdrop against her body, Kyle ached for her. He reached to pat Pup, whose drool spindled in the wind as he looked up at Kyle and whined softly.

"Stop it, Mallory. Stop driving Rachel," Kyle whispered into the wind as Rachel made her way up to him.

She searched his face and Kyle waited for just that heartbeat before pulling her into his arms, bending his head to hers. "We'll get through this, honey."

Her body was tense against his, her arms locked around his waist. She was shaking and Kyle knew he had to wait for her to speak; all he could do was to try to understand whatever she was mulling. She snuggled her face to his throat, tears damp against his skin. "When you hold me, your hands are open," she noted quietly against the roaring tides and ocean winds.

"That's because I'm trying to cop a feel," he lied against her temple.

"You're smoothing my back, not copping a feel, Scanlon. You're rocking me. That says you care, doesn't it? That there's nothing sexual in this moment?"

"There could be. Give me a minute to work it up."

Against his throat, Rachel shook her head. "When we make love, then you are very careful, too."

Kyle didn't like where this conversation was going and he tried to lighten Rachel's mood. He held her away, cradled her face and smoothed her tears with his thumbs. "Hey, is something wrong with my technique?" he asked gently.

Rachel leaned close and her expression tore him apart. "Kiss the side of my face."

He frowned and complied. "What's going on?"

"That was a friendship kiss, right?"

The question was odd, disturbing him. So was her next direction, "Now hold me, as a friend would do with a hug, and kiss the side of my cheek."

Kyle complied and then took her cold hands, warming them between his own and bringing them to his lips. "I can do better."

"You fold me into you. You care. There's nothing sexual going on," she rapped out as if logging facts into her mind. Rachel shook her head as if to clear it and then leaned her forehead against his chest. "Let's just go home."

Kyle thought of the appointments he had, the calls he needed to make, the repairs to the garage, and said, "Sure."

In the apartment, Rachel moved automatically, preparing sandwiches, flipping through the television channels, and feeding Harry. But she held her body protectively, rocking as she looked out of the windows onto Atlantis Street. Kyle ached for Rachel; he went to stand behind her and drew her back against his body as he kissed the side of her cheek. "This is not good, is it? What you're going through?" he asked.

Rachel shook her head. "Not good at all."

"Can I help?"

"When I'm certain—" She turned to him. "Let's make love, Kyle. I need to feel you against me, in me, the way you touch me."

"I think I can manage that," he said, bending to lift her into his arms. If he couldn't give her support now, if she didn't trust him to explain the darkness that had come over her, he could give her love with each kiss, each caress. . . .

"I'm going to Mom's office," Rachel said when they lay sated and entangled, together and yet apart. "By myself. I need to talk with her . . . privately."

"Sure. 'Privately' says you don't want me there, so this must be good because I know just about everything, don't I? Except what you're holding now? What you've been thinking about constantly since yesterday? Don't ever let me inside, Rachel. Don't let me get too close."

Kyle sat up in bed and looked down at her. Anger blended with pain as he spoke, "And don't ever, ever trust me. Right? Just you, handling things on your own, wading through whatever goddamn mess you're trying to sort out? Want to give me a hint? Is it Shane? I told him not ever to come close to you again—"

"It isn't Shane. It's just something I have to work out."

Kyle jerked on his jeans. "Well, that's just great. You go work it out. Come back when you're ready. Everything on your terms, right?"

"I'm sorry—"

Rachel looked so shattered and vulnerable that Kyle instantly regretted his anger. "Okay . . . okay. I'm just frustrated and I want to help and you're shutting me out. If this has to do with Mallory—"

He knew then, by the quick way Rachel looked away, that it had everything to do with Mallory. And he could only wait. . . . "Be careful. There's someone out there who tried to kill me and someone who drove Mallory to suicide. You're going after him and I know it," he said finally. "Let me know if I can help, fearless crusader."

But Rachel wasn't sparring, her challenging attitude gone as she stared up at the circling blades of the ceiling fan. "I don't think anyone can help this, Kyle. . . ."

Then she turned, curled into a ball and held Harry close to her, and there was nothing Kyle could do, but wait for Rachel to share her troubled mind with him—

He knew then, that the worst war a man could wage was that of waiting, when he wanted to help, wanted to tear out the secret that Rachel held so close.

With a tired sigh, he walked to the kitchen, braced his hands on the countertop and stared out the window into the mist that had come from the ocean.

A fully loaded semi-automatic was out there somewhere, and the man who had driven Mallory to suicide . . . and in the bedroom was a woman, lying awake and wrapped inside herself, not sharing information that could help Kyle find the gun and the man. . . .

And all he could do was to wait.

Rachel walked to the door, paused with her hand on the doorknob, and said, "I'll see you later."

The distance between the kitchen and the apartment's front door was only a few feet, but to Kyle, it felt like miles.

"You'll be at your mother's?" *We've come so far. . . . Why don't you trust me with what's troubling you?*

"Yes."

Kyle watched Rachel get into her car and slowly pull out of the parking lot, taking a part of his heart with her. . . . Pup came to lean against his side, and Harry leaped up to the countertop where Kyle picked him up. It seemed as if even the animals understood the dark cloud enveloping Rachel, and there was just that light scent of vanilla lingering around them. . . .

"Okay, Mallory, I'm worried, too. . . ."

# Seventeen

**RACHEL COULDN'T BEAR THE UGLY IDEA TRAPPED INSIDE HER.**
Insidiously, it nestled and grew; each memory of Bob
with Mallory pinpointed and fostered a sickening image that wouldn't go away.

"Once upon a time, there were three sisters. . . . I
could be terribly wrong, Mallory. I pray that I am,"
Rachel whispered to the wind as she walked up the
well-manicured grounds to Bob Winters' front door. In
the late afternoon light, the porch pillars stood white
and tall in front of the colonial-style home.

With the sparkling Pacific Ocean as a backdrop, the
front of Bob's home seemed pristine.

In the familiar setting, Rachel's memories came
tumbling back. . . .

How often had they played on the manicured oceanfront grounds, running up the elegant stairway inside,
giggling as they slid down the polished cherrywood
banister? How often had they stayed overnight while
Trina had taken business classes away from Neptune's
Landing? How often had they gone on day-trips with
Bob while their mother was working desperately to
grow her used car business?

The three swings Bob had installed in his

backyard—matches to those at Trina's house—had been moving in the wind as Rachel had parked. Now, echoes of the girls' carefree laughter swirled around Rachel. The girls had rushed to the white picket fence at the edge of the cliff, eagerly watching the ocean, where the gray whales kept their calves close, gliding elegantly through the dark water, surfacing only to blow.

Chilled now, despite the mild late May day, Rachel tried to push away images that clung savagely to her. "I've got to be wrong, Mallory. I'm stressed, tired, on edge because of what happened to Kyle, discovering that you had a baby—that you gave her away, and none of us knew anything about Katrina. I'm overreacting, that's all. . . ."

The wind swished through the needles of the stately tall pines around Rachel. Stunted and malformed on the oceanside, the branches grew long and beautiful away from the wind's force. She momentarily studied the shape, comparing it to truth and untruth. *What were the real memories of the past?*

On her regular cleaning day and day off from making her ice cream rounds, Jada's wagon was parked in the driveway behind Bob's shiny black Lincoln. She answered the doorbell, her dusting rag in hand, the fragrance of lemon curling about her. "Hi, what are you doing here?" Jada asked with a grin.

"I came to see Bob, to see if I can patch things up."

Jada frowned and started wiping the dusting cloth over the cherrywood doorframe. "He's pretty upset about Kyle staying at your place. He never liked me talking with Kyle, and every time I mentioned Kyle, the layer of frost was a foot thick. Bob is just a different generation, Rache . . . that old-school gentleman stuff. You know how particular he is about appearances and Kyle, staying at your place, has really set him off. He thinks of us as daughters and he doesn't like the gossip that's going around—especially since you wore that killer outfit to the businessmen's meeting. He was really upset . . . said it's like advertising wares."

"What do you think?"

"That you're after whoever that doll resembles, trying to bring him out. If it is Shane, I get my piece of the action." Jada paused to take the bottle of lemon oil from her multi-pocketed cleaning apron. She poured the oil onto the cloth and glanced at Rachel. "Don't just stand there— come in. . . . This is almost like home and you don't have to be invited in. . . . And Bob didn't like hearing about Shane, how he'd seduced Mallory. I think Bob is really worked up over that. He's been calling the church committees and putting pressure on them to oust Shane. . . . My, my. Those size fourteen custom-made heels sure did paint a different picture about good old Shane. He's lucky I didn't hit him with one of those spikes."

Rachel followed Jada into the hallway while her sister continued dusting and talking, "Now I'm going to have to start hunting for a sperm donor all over again. You've ruined Kyle for me. He was my last resort, and I can't see you sharing. Then Shane was a total washout. He's been seeing Terri—all that came out in our little argument. But that figures, doesn't it? Or does it? Anyway, Bob is upstairs. He'll be down in a minute . . . but by the way, I didn't know you'd given him keys to Nine Balls and your apartment. I just saw them on his key ring on his desk, marked and everything. . . . And here I was worrying that I'd been careless with my keys—I am sometimes—but with that gun missing, I've been super careful."

*Bob had keys to Rachel's apartment.* Of course, he would have keys. He would have had them when Mallory lived in the apartment, because he often helped her—*Helped her?* Was that what he did? He was often there, repairing this or that, taking Mallory some small appliance, helping her move furniture. . . .

As the person who usually tended the Everlys' handyman needs, Bob had used the locks from his store. He would have had the means to make copies of the keys. His clerk had installed the new locks—but he'd said that Bob had personally checked them. . . .

Personally checked them, and made copies. . . . *Did that mean he had Kyle's handgun?*

Stunned by Bob's possession of the keys, Rachel tried to smile at Jada.

"Do you think I could wait for him in the study?" The study where Mallory had sat on his lap, toying with his computer? A fifteen-year-old girl eager to learn about computers should have had her own chair next to the person teaching her, shouldn't she have?

He'd given the three girls heart lockets . . . but Bob had adjusted the locket on Mallory's chest, not the other sisters' . . . and he'd lingered, fascinated with her. . . .

Jada brought Rachel abruptly back to the present. "Okay, but I'm getting ready to leave. Moses has me on a timer, where and when I go . . . I have to report to him every minute."

Rachel thought of Kyle, how he'd watched her leave

the apartment: tall, silent, brooding, and worried about her. But she'd had to make this journey alone, to talk with Bob, to see his expression—

In the study, Rachel noted the keys and sat in front of Bob's desk. The room was elegant, lined with book-shelves and all the fittings of a home office. She tried to breathe quietly, to steady her nerves. *Was it possible that Bob had taken the gun, had come and gone in the apartment as he wished?*

*Was it possible that all those loving touches were those of a sexual predator?*

Rachel tried to shake that sickening image—of young Mallory cuddling close to Bob, evidently want-ing to please him. . . . She'd wanted to please everyone in those first days after she'd lost her fear of the Everlys. . . . And Bob was always there, more often with Mallory than with Jada or Rachel.

Rachel swallowed back the need to run away as the scenes came rushing back—When her mother had been away on business trips, the girls had stayed in Bob's home, and Mallory had always chosen the downstairs bedroom, next to the master bedroom, while Jada and Rachel had slept upstairs. . . .

As a teenager, Mallory had cleaned his house and he was usually there—

Freshly showered, Bob entered the study. "Hi, Rachel. Jada said you were here. How pleasant."

He walked to hug her and Rachel held her breath, comparing Kyle's embrace, open and friendly when she was troubled, to Bob's tighter hold, which pressed her breasts into his soft belly. . . .

She eased away, uncertain of the past, blending with

the present. The man who had attacked her in the park, who couldn't perform when the others laughed, had been soft—The flashing images leaped back at her and she realized she had trembled.

"What's wrong, Rachel?" Bob asked too quietly.

"I just came to talk. Things have been strained between all of us lately. . . . I didn't know you have keys to Nine Balls or to my apartment."

He glanced at the desk and smiled, his balding head gleaming in the light from the windows. "When my locksmith made your extras at the store, I took the liberty of making copies—just in case you might need me, on an emergency basis. Is that a problem?"

"You made them yourself?" Rachel already knew the answer, but she needed to hear it from Bob.

"It's not hard. A machine just makes copies, you know that. You put in a blank and the master key, and you get a copy. Simple. You girls have been in my store hundreds of times, watching my clerk do that, or myself. It doesn't take a genius."

"I'd like them back . . . please."

Bob frowned at her and quickly took the keys from his ring, handing them to her. He opened his desk drawer, hurled the remaining keys into it and jammed it shut, all angry, abrupt movements. "It's that Kyle Scanlon, isn't it? That no-good mechanic has gotten to you. I'll bet he has a key—"

Bob's fierce scowl, his reddening complexion, the intimidating posture of his body, shocked Rachel. He'd always been so gentle, so mild mannered. . . . He reminded her of the trees outside, beautiful and natural on one side; the other misshapen and ugly.

Rachel tried desperately to cling to logic, that Bob's anger only applied to Kyle, a dislike that had always been there. *Because Kyle was competition? A younger man taking Mallory's attention?* "No, Kyle doesn't have a key."

Bob's hand wrapped, tight and hurtful, around Rachel's upper arm. "Scanlon shouldn't be staying in your apartment. It doesn't look right. First Mallory, and then you. You were dressed like a tart at the businessmen's meeting. I told your mother that she really needs to talk with you."

There was no mistaking this message; Bob intended to intimidate her, ordering her to do as he wished. He wasn't going to listen to her—

Rachel had never liked bullies; the words were framed on her tongue and slipping into the study's deadly quiet air before she could stop them: "Didn't you like the way the other men looked at me? Do you consider me to be your private property, Bob?"

Bob's eyes narrowed, his face tight with anger. "Of course not. You're out of line, Rachel. I'm only telling you for your own good. You've always been headstrong and argumentative, far too independent, not desirable qualities—and now Scanlon has gotten to you. . . . Any idiot can see that you need to watch your step, that you have to stay away from any image like Mallory's. Everyone is waiting to see what you'll do, how you'll act and if you turn up in the same mold as Mallory."

"You're hurting me, Bob." Rachel's statement of fact, soft within his study, was more of a notation to herself, that Bob could hurt her.

He almost flung her arm away. "You need to listen and you're just determined not to, aren't you?"

She had never seen this seemingly mild-mannered man angry, but there was no denying his intimidating stance, the way his fists clenched at his side. Sickened by the lurking thoughts that Bob had been Mallory's tormentor, Rachel felt a deadly, fearless calm. "Did you love Mallory?"

"I don't know what you're talking about. I love all of you girls."

Rachel's one word quivered in the heavy silence that followed. "How?"

Bob snatched that word and his lips flattened against his teeth, another menacing expression, challenging her to follow up with an explanation. "What?"

Rachel wasn't backing down. "How did you love us? How did you love Mallory?"

Bob was silent for a moment, then he exploded, "I don't like that inference. . . . You were girls, I was stepping in as a father you didn't have. Get out and when you're ready to apologize, you may come back. You'll be lucky if I don't tell your mother about this. Trina wouldn't like it."

"I agree. She wouldn't like it at all. And you weren't the one to bankroll Mallory for that first down money—it was Kyle. You never denied it and we thought what a nice guy. What a nice guy you are, Bob," she added too sweetly, her stomach churning, her body cold.

"You're going to take that no-good's word over mine?"

"I saw his books and Kyle doesn't lie. I think you do. How easy it must have all been—with Mallory." With her keys gripped in her cold shaking hand, Rachel walked out of the study and down the hallway. She opened the front door to leave Bob's home, then turned to look back at him.

In the hallway, his anger ricocheted against the walls, the elegant gold-framed paintings, the exotic rugs over the polished floors. It throbbed all around Rachel as she dropped one word into the silent, furious storm—"Mallory."

"You get back here and let's finish this—don't you dare walk out that door."

Rachel closed the door softly behind her, sealing away the place where three sisters had come to play and laugh. . . .

"She knows, damn her. I knew Rachel couldn't leave well enough alone. She's putting things together now. . . . She might even have that damned doll. This is her fault—and Mallory's. I can't let Rachel ruin my life. I've worked too hard to build my reputation. I knew Rachel would be trouble. She always was, and she's not going to leave this alone."

Bob watched Rachel stride down the walkway to her yellow Cadillac. "I taught you how to drive, took you to get your license. I took care of all of you, taking you to movies when your mother was working. . . . And this is the payment I get? Accusations?"

*If Rachel had that doll—she would be playing connect-the-dots and they would lead directly to him.*

"I can't afford that. . . . Measures have to be taken. . . . She just isn't listening to reason, and before long she'll be causing real trouble. . . . Everything I do is justifiable . . . none of this is my fault," Bob stated lightly, calmly as he unlocked a desk drawer and withdrew Kyle's gun, aiming it at Rachel. "Mallory asked for what she got and so has Rachel. Not my fault at all. I am stopping this before it goes any further. Rachel won't dare say anything until she has proof—she's too good at details. One murder-suicide coming up—tonight."

Bob smiled as he thought about hitting Kyle in the garage's storeroom, the force behind the blow, the power of his kicks. "A bullet is too clean, but I might be able to make Rachel bend, and that's the game, after all—getting my way. He can watch as she fights me, as I take her. She'll be careful how she approaches Trina and Jada, and that gives me time. . . ."

He frowned suddenly. Since her visit to Rachel's apartment last night, Trina had been pale and distracted. If Rachel had spread her theories to her mother, that might mean—

His feral growl circled the room. Trina provided him with a shield he wouldn't want to lose, but if he had to—

The study was quiet, but in the sudden stillness Bob thought he heard Mallory's voice: *If you hurt my family, I'll haunt you forever. . . .*

He chuckled wildly. "I don't think so, dear. You're dead."

The shadows quivered and Bob thought he caught the slight scent of vanilla. *Am I? Or am I only on the edge of time, waiting for you?*

Trina looked up from packing her briefcase. In her office light, she looked suddenly worn and tired, her expression sad as she looked at Rachel. "Bob's wife? Alissa? I remember her. She was a frail, sweet woman. She was in a lot of pain, and on depression therapy, and eventually couldn't go on. She committed suicide about twenty-two or -three years ago. He'd already had years of coping with her—such a lonely guy. You were about eleven or so when he came over. At first, he was just an older guy, the safe kind, you know—not looking for a 'hot-to-trot' divorcée. I guess you girls filled a void for him. He was great and gradually, I came to trust him—trust was difficult for me back then. I guess we both needed someone. Alissa had been gone maybe three or four years before we became comfortable with each other."

While Rachel waited, Trina locked her office door. They held hands as they walked to their cars. "I'm glad Jada and Moses are staying at the house, but I'm even more glad that Kyle is with you. I was so worried about him—terrible thing."

"Yes, terrible thing," Rachel echoed, but her mind was on the terrible things that had happened to Mallory.

"I can't focus on selling cars and profit. Maybe I should just take some time off." Trina smiled sadly. "I'd so love to see my granddaughter, to see if she looks like Mallory. Do you think we could just take a few days away and drive to see her? I wouldn't want to upset her—but just that piece of Mallory would be so precious."

Rachel thought of the nine-year-old girl with Mallory's face and angular, athletic body, the girl with fine brown hair. In a few years, she would be thirteen, just the same age as Mallory when she'd become a sister. "I think she's on some kind of summer trip with her mother now. We've got to be careful about that, Mom."

"Why would Mallory ever want to hide my grandchild?"

Rachel shook her head, but in her mind, the harsh, stark answer reverberated: *Because she was afraid the same thing could happen to her daughter.*

Kyle's Hummer slid into the parking lot beside Rachel's Cadillac. He got out and walked around the Cadillac, giving the big yellow trunk his usual pat that said he appreciated good machinery.

It was the same kind of pat he gave Rachel's butt.

The similarity was strange, but somehow comforting.

Until she thought of Bob's pats on Mallory's bottom, then the disturbing images came tumbling back again.

In worn blue jeans and a black T-shirt, Kyle looked big, tough, and unlike the battered man of three nights ago. Kyle wasn't happy, and those blue-gray eyes locked onto Rachel said she was in for trouble. She crossed her arms, and tilted her head, enjoying the sight of him and the senses kicking up in her body, that hunger locking low in it, heating—

Still. Kyle could be more than unpleasant and this looked like war.

He nodded to Rachel's mother. "Trina."

"How's it going, Kyle?" Rachel asked softly.

Despite her mother's presence, Kyle tugged Rachel close to him and took a deep, searing kiss. "Fine," he said grimly, still holding her in his arms, looking down at her. "Just fine."

"My mother is standing here, you know."

"I already said hello to her, dear."

"So you did." Rachel's hands were locked onto his belt, because that kiss was pure possession and she wanted him to know that it worked both ways. "Come down here," she whispered and when Kyle warily bent to her, Rachel kissed the bruise on his cheek.

Kyle held very still as if he were uncertain what to do, this man who had had little kindness in his early life, who probably understood Mallory better than anyone, who had cared for her—

"Your daughter has been missing for a little bit. She was supposed to be here and when I called, she wasn't," Kyle stated to Trina, his expression still wary as he studied Rachel.

"I was busy," Rachel noted, allowing her body to lean against his, to absorb the safety there, a contrast to Bob's anger and domination, his bullying.

"And I was worried. Doing a solo number, were you? Where were you?"

She wasn't ready to spread her theories to either her mother, heavily involved with Bob Winters, or to the younger man who just might decide to avenge Mallory. "Walking."

"Liar." That narrowing of Kyle's eyes said he would want the real answer later.

Trina smiled softly. "It's good to see you two together. Let's go to my house for dinner. Since Moses has been around, I've been cooking more. I enjoy seeing a man with a hearty appetite eat—with gusto, to say the least. Jada has him on her sperm donor list and he's run from the few tentative approaches she's made to him. Oh, I am so glad that Shane is off her list. I really, really do not like that man. Bob agrees. He's trying to get Shane transferred. I can't imagine why a man would want to dress up like that, or why Mallory catered to him at all."

Kyle smiled in that dangerous way. "Different strokes, isn't that what they say?"

Trina shook her head, then said, "Dinner? My house? Backyard barbeque? I'll call Bob."

"You just do that," Rachel agreed softly as Kyle stood with his arm around her. She wanted to see how Bob reacted now, with Trina, Jada, and herself—how all the pieces fit. *Or did they? Was she so mistaken about Bob's relationship with Mallory?*

The violence was definitely there, the way Bob had gripped her arm, his threatening stance. How could any of them have missed that side of him, for so many years?

Rachel understood that Trina wanted to soften Bob's dislike of Kyle. But was it possible for a displaced older male, one with bullying tendencies and maybe worse, to accept a young man moving within his private—very private harem?

Within minutes, Trina was back, her expression uncertain. "I'm sorry, Kyle. Bob says he has to work tonight. I guess this isn't going to be that easy. You're elected as barbeque man, I guess. Bob seems upset, but then I didn't think this was going to be easy. He usually comes around. Ah, here comes Jada and Moses. I'm so glad we're all together."

Trina's voice caught and Rachel finished the thought silently: but everyone isn't here. Once upon a time there were three sisters, and now there were two aunts and one niece with fine brown hair. . . .

"Where were you?" Kyle demanded when he closed the apartment door behind Rachel. After the barbecue, and at nine in the evening, Rachel's apartment was dark and shadowy, Atlantis Street's lights piercing the miniblinds in tiny strips. Rachel paced across those stripes as Kyle watched.

Edgy, tight with emotion, she moved restlessly, like a tigress prowling and hunting, her body taut: first she crossed the living room, pausing at the minibar, then into the kitchen that Mallory had rarely used—the place where she'd hidden her tape and that voodoo doll. Rachel paused at the sink, gripping the countertop, her nails tapping on the slick surface.

Kyle recognized that tilt of her head, that slanted look at him, the way her body shifted in that sea foam green sweater and slacks. The air seemed to hum around her, bristling with energy.

There was one way to burn off that energy and get down to baseline answers, Kyle decided as he walked to her. Rachel leaned back against the counter, watching him.

Frustrated that she didn't trust him, even now, not enough to give straight answers, Kyle didn't feel sweet. He leaned in close, his hands braced beside hers, pressing against that thrust of her breasts, nudging her feet apart so that his body nestled in tight and hard.

"You going to tell me where you were at—or not?"

He already knew the answer that came cool and clear with that tilt of her head, those narrowing of her eyes—"Not."

"Now that's confidence," Kyle stated as he nudged in closer, kept the slow rhythm going against her softness as he bent to nuzzle her cheek, taste that sweet spot behind her ear.

"I'm not the only one with confidence. . . ." She leaned back, giving him access to that long, smooth throat.

"Give—" he ordered as she turned slightly, her teeth nipping his ear.

"Make me."

He smiled just that once, admiring her. Then Kyle stopped thinking as he fastened his lips to Rachel's; he opened them and sought her tongue as they undressed in a flurry of hands and hunger.

Kyle filled his hands with her softness, diving into her. Her fingers dug into his back, nails sliding down, her legs strong against his, opening slightly for just that first connection, then back to keep the play within her grasp, her control. Control wasn't something he intended Rachel to keep, Kyle decided as he bent to taste her breasts, a little rough maybe, but taking her right to the edge without pain. She was breathing unevenly, her body hot and naked against his.

With Rachel, it was always a question of who had whom, Kyle decided as he slid his hand downward and found that dainty responsible nub. A few strokes and Rachel arched, crying out against his shoulder, her teeth caught his skin briefly, and Kyle knew he was in the lead—

There would be other gentler times, but not tonight, not when the tigress prowled, seeking her mate—dark and primitive, she needed him as much as he needed her, give and take, not sweet but lovers meeting each other on a plane where everything else had been stripped away and only the truth remained.

Love was buried deep in there somewhere, but tonight

wasn't for lazy caresses and whispers in the dark. Tonight was to burn away everything else, testing the limits—

While Rachel was trying to pull back, getting control of her quivering body, Kyle lifted her in his arms and carried her to the bedroom.

"That wasn't fair," she whispered unevenly as he lowered her to the bed, coming down upon her, settling tight within that still clenching glove of her damp heat. "You're going to pay for that."

"Make me," Kyle whispered, serving her own challenge back to her as her legs captured him, her arms held him tight.

She bit his jaw lightly. "Don't do that move again, cowboy," she warned, arching up to him.

"Okay." Kyle worked his way downward, over her smooth belly, circled her naval with his tongue.

"That wasn't fair," Rachel whispered moments later as her cry finished echoing in the shadows and her body was limp within his keeping.

"Can't take it?" he asked while licking her nipple, toying it into an erect peak. If he held out much longer, he should get a medal, Kyle decided grimly, his body barely leashed.

"Give me a minute."

"Take all the time you need."

Rachel only needed that minute, fiercely moving beneath him, capturing him tightly, pitting herself against him. They were slick with sweat, breaths harsh and uneven, each trying to control their own bodies, challenging the other to give the utmost. . . . In the shadows, she lifted slightly, frowning down at him. "You bastard. This is real, isn't it?"

Kyle knew what Rachel meant. It might not be the sweetest way for a woman to tell him she loved him, but that was exactly how Rachel felt—she loved him and he was a part of her, not only in this fierce lovemaking, but deep inside where she allowed no other man to touch. . . . "Real enough," he admitted, careful not to give her too much, not just yet.

With a cry, Rachel shook her head, threshing against the pillow, her hips braced high as they locked together, met each other, hearts pounding, racing. . . . And then, the world stood still, burning bright and red and exploding—

Rachel sighed softly sometime later and curled against him, her hand stroking his chest lazily. "You'll do better next time, dear," she whispered against his shoulder.

Kyle smiled against her hair; they'd both reached the ultimate limits quite thoroughly. In the stillness of the shadows, he waited. . . .

Suddenly, Rachel tore free of him and went into the shower. Kyle followed, slowly entering the stall so as not to frighten her.

"Water conservation," he explained as he soaped his own body and tried not to notice his marks still on her body.

She smiled tenderly up at him and smoothed a droplet from his eyebrow. It was one of those caring touches that a guy could latch on to, hoarding them, while his woman was telling him off. "You're a real bastard, Kyle," she said softly.

He grinned at her; Rachel understood that he'd made love to her for a purpose, and for their satisfaction. "Yeah. I know."

Friends, he thought, something that didn't go away. All the sweet stuff was going to his head and making him feel a little foolish. He sensed that Rachel would be telling him in different ways, and every one of them were going to make him feel just as dizzy, as boyishly happy. She had him thinking about a home and kids and a lifetime together.

In her robe and cuddled against him later on the couch as they sipped wine and watched the candlelight flicker upon the dish of beach stones, Rachel said, "Kyle, I need you."

*Kyle, I need you.* . . . He waited, because this wasn't about sex, it was about trust and Rachel was preparing to share her troubled thoughts with him. . . .

"I keep seeing things in my mind. Unpleasant things. I don't like them, and they won't go away." Rachel moved slightly away from him, leaning forward to stare into the candles' flames.

Kyle rested his hand on her back, smoothing her, letting her know that he was with her, no matter what.

She looked over her shoulder to him. "These things actually happened, Kyle."

"Okay. . . ." Rachel needed to take her time to sort through what had happened, the disturbing elements she had wanted to ignore.

"Mallory was thirteen when Mom adopted her. Mom was already seeing Bob, casual dating, that sort of thing. He was a regular at our house, and I guess she was lonely, maybe enjoying being a woman after devoting so much time to raising us."

Rachel placed her wineglass on the coffee table and ran her fingertip across the twin flames. "He always seemed to prefer Mallory . . . he did little special things for her. I guess we thought at the time that maybe he thought she needed extra attention, maybe someone like the father she'd never had. . . ."

She laughed shakily. "But then, I don't know where we got that idea. Jada and I never knew our own biological father. It would seem that Bob would treat us all alike, if he were just playing the father role."

"Oh, dear Jesus," Kyle heard himself say as he closed his eyes, stunned at this awakening idea. "It all fits."

Rachel seemed to fold into herself, holding her hands over her face. "He took time tucking her in. . . . The way she tried to please him. . . . The time she spent at his house—cleaning, we thought, or maybe helping her with her homework—she was always behind. . . . As she got older, we just thought they had a special affinity, like what happens naturally sometimes, how one child can link better than the rest with an adult— Oh, Kyle, I don't want to think about this—"

"Neither do I," Kyle agreed as he pulled Rachel back into his arms, holding her close in the silent quivering candlelit shadows that blended memories, weaving them into one ugly conclusion. . . . "That's where you were, wasn't it, Rachel? You faced Bob, didn't you?"

When Rachel looked at him, her face was streaked with tears, her lips moving soundlessly. "The way he looked at her for all those years—a little different from me or Jada. . . . I don't want to think about this anymore. It's only a feeling. I don't have any proof, nothing concrete, nothing at all to string everything together. There's no way to make it right—what and if that actually happened to Mallory—he's a town pillar, always donating to charities, an upright citizen. But I know it happened. I do, Kyle, and I want him to admit it—that he hurt Mallory."

For Rachel's sake, Kyle tried to push down his rage, tried to hold his voice even. "You think he was behind that New York attack in the park?" he asked, needing to feel his fingers close in on Bob's throat, to beat that soft paunchy body—

"It was him. He wore a ski mask, and it was dark, but I felt him, his body. It was the same man who hugged me today, and for all those years. He couldn't perform that night, but he would have if the others hadn't laughed. I have nothing to go on, but just my feelings. You're right—it all fits. Looking back is so easy—it all fits, Kyle. So simple, the way he touched her, those little whispers, the way she sometimes kissed his lips when thanking him—maybe we all did, I don't know. Maybe we all—"

"He picked the weakest one. A bully usually does." Kyle gathered Rachel's shaking body close, rocking her against his own memories that started moving in his mind—Bob was always here with Mallory, "fixing things" or "seeing that she got what she needed."

"There were no pictures of Bob anywhere in this apartment—nowhere in her scrapbook." Rachel's voice was thin, uneven. "He was so much in our lives, that he should have been in something—we took enough pictures with him. . . . But he wasn't in anything. Why didn't I think of that?"

Kyle held Rachel tight and whispered into her hair. "That's enough for now, honey."

"He had the means to make copies of the apartment's keys. . . . It was all so obvious. I should have—"

"Give it up, Rachel. What makes you think you're so special that only you should have seen it?" Kyle chided gently and didn't expect an answer.

Rachel had been right about Mallory wanting something from her—Mallory had known that Rachel would uncover Bob and block him from ever discovering her daughter.

And Bob, as the supplier of Nine Balls' locks, had had the apartment's keys and probably now had that missing handgun. . . .

Bob would be coming after Rachel, the woman who had uncovered his dirty little secret—and that led Kyle to think that there were more things Bob didn't want uncovered. . . .

Kyle reached for the phone and dialed Trina's number. When she answered, he asked for Moses. "Bring Jada and Trina over here, will you? And then, we'll talk."

To Rachel, he said, "You'd better put on the coffee, honey. It looks like a long night. And leave the door to the stairway open, will you? Pup will let us know if anything funny is going on."

"You think this is going to move fast, now, don't you?" she asked unevenly.

"Real fast, and I want all of your family in one place, and safe."

"You don't think he'd hurt my mother?" But Rachel understood the look Kyle leveled at her—Bob Winters would stop at nothing to keep his secret. . . .

# Eighteen

**MALLORY'S APARTMENT, WHERE SHE'D SPENT HER LAST** hours, suited the place in which Trina Everly would discover her daughter's fatal darkness. The apartment's miniblinds were closed, candlelight leaping over the faces of the three women seated on the couch.

Moses was at the kitchen table, tapping away at Rachel's laptop, seeking information about Bob Winters. The strap running across the beefy ex-wrestler's back and chest ended in a holster lying against his ribs. The semi-automatic resting there was big and black and deadly.

Rachel looked at Kyle who stood with his shoulder against the wall; his face was that of a merciless killer, not the man who had protected Mallory's child and others. Kyle would be going after Bob, and he intended to come back alone. He intended to make Bob pay for destroying Mallory, to make him admit to what he'd done, and then he'd kill him.

Trina stared at the doll's thatch of fine, brown hair; her expression was shattered and disbelieving, her face starkly pale. "His hair was like this before it turned gray—I do not believe this. I don't believe any of it. . . .

Not Bob. He's been my friend for years. He couldn't have hurt Mallory—or you, Rachel. . . ."

Rachel ached for her mother, but she had to reveal everything. "Bob was the person who attacked me. I'm certain of it. I've gone over everything. Kyle just checked to see if Shane really was at that retreat—and he was, he's listed as a speaker at their website, and he did hold sessions that day in California. Even on a coast-to-coast Red-Eye, he couldn't have managed to be in New York at the time I was attacked."

Trina's shaking fingertips flowed over the doll's hair, the blue pinstriped shirt with the tiny button. Her lips moved soundlessly and her head shook, denying the possibility of Bob hurting Mallory. "I always thought they had a special attachment—he'd never had children, and he said Mallory's red curly hair reminded him of Alissa. . . . Alissa died of a drug overdose, too. I—I felt sorry for him even before she died and we weren't dating, that came later. He was just always there—safe, comfortable, lonely. . . . I still don't—How could he abuse Mallory in my own home and me not recognize the signs?" she asked in disbelief. "When did it start?"

Rachel shook her head. "At a guess, almost immediately. Those little special presents he brought her—"

"I thought those were to make her feel more a part of our lives," Trina whispered desperately.

"Holding her on his lap, rocking her—"

Trina scrubbed her hands over her eyes, as though trying to erase those images. "I thought it was sweet. She'd never had a loving father and Bob was showing her what a man's love could be—"

"He sure was." Seated on the other side of their mother, Jada's unusually quiet tone was cold and remote, as if she'd stepped into another life and found it hard to bear. "I remember the same things that Rachel does—the way he treated her, the way she responded to him. I don't want to remember, but now I do and I'm going to kill him."

In that one moment Rachel believed her easy-going, usually carefree sister, Jada, was capable of murder.

Trina suddenly reached for her wine; a little sloshed over the rim of the glass and she automatically dabbed it with a napkin, slowly at first and then frantically, as if trying to wipe away truths she didn't want to accept. "He was in my home . . . with my daughters. . . . We—"

She began to tremble, reality setting in. "His hair was like that years ago, and I remember washing a shirt for him and wondering about that piece of missing material—it looked as if it had been cut, not torn, and a button was missing. It was blue, pinstriped, just like this—"

She gripped the doll in her fist and stared at the location of the pins. "He has heart trouble and he's impotent now. Lovemaking wasn't ever that good, but comfortable—then Bob couldn't anymore and I didn't mind. Oh, dear Lord. He was having Mallory at the same time—"

"Take it easy," Moses advised softly.

Trina was all fire and anger, burning a look at him. "Don't you tell me what to do—how to feel. Mallory was my daughter."

She abruptly pushed up from the couch, threw the

doll to the coffee table, and sobbing, hurried into the bathroom.

"Better let her have some time alone. She's tough. She'll handle it. Your mother is quite the lady," the ex-wrestler said in the tone of someone who'd had experience dealing with trauma.

Rachel rubbed her hands together; they were cold and clammy as she studied Kyle, their eyes locking.

His stare slid to the floor, and she knew that he was sealing her off from what he planned to do.

"You're not going without me," Rachel stated quietly. Despite her fury at Bob Winters, she had to protect Kyle. If he killed Bob, there would be no going back, and she could lose Kyle to a jail sentence.

At that moment, Rachel knew that she would have to ask Kyle to give up what he wanted most. Would he listen?

"No?" Kyle's head tilted with the quiet challenge. "Maybe this time, you don't get your way, honey."

"Mom is really upset. I could kill him for that alone," Jada murmured darkly. She reached for Harry and placed him on her lap. "Do that purring thing, cat."

"You're not sneezing, Jada. I thought you were allergic to cats." Rachel was almost grateful for her sister's comic relief in a dark, tense situation where she would have to pit herself against Kyle—If they both lived. . . .

"I'm too mad . . . I will later. Right now, this cat is warm and hairy and comforting."

Trina came out of the bathroom, her eyes reddened, her face pale. "I'm going downstairs to play a game. Anyone want to come with me?"

"Take Pup," Kyle stated and Trina nodded, realizing the danger of a man who had abused her daughter and who she'd let into her home. He'd been her lover, too, years ago, and she needed time to make the transition from the Bob she'd trusted with her daughters to the one who had abused Mallory.

"Don't you dare take him to the police before I get to him," she ordered.

"Oh, he's not going into custody," Kyle murmured when she'd gone down the stairway.

Moses stood and came to stand beside Kyle. "I called in some favors. This guy has been married twice. Once to Alissa, and before that another woman. Both died of overdoses. They were wealthy before they married him, and he inherited everything."

"Now that lends a whole new angle to Mallory's suicide," Kyle noted softly. "That means she got the job done, killed herself, before he could. That probably made him real mad."

Together, the men looked big, deadly, and merciless. Moses glanced at Kyle. "My guess is that dear old Bob probably did the fire at the garage, too. Working Kyle over like that took someone with a real grudge—like having his life and pleasures ruined."

Rachel stood and wrapped her arms around herself. "There isn't much to pinpoint him, is there? Wouldn't it be better to have him actually admit everything?"

"He will," Kyle said quietly. "I know that look. What are you thinking, Rachel?"

"That I'm going with you."

Kyle smiled tightly. "He's probably miles down the coast right now."

"You don't think so. You think he's out there with a real grudge and coming after me, don't you?"

Both men inhaled at the same time and looked at each other. Rachel understood that look: they thought exactly as she did—Bob Winters wanted revenge, and he'd be coming after the person who exposed him. . . .

"No," Kyle said too easily.

"Liar. Okay, go ahead and do your thing. Find Bob."

He frowned uneasily at her. "You don't want to come with me?"

"Is that an invitation?" she asked, and braced herself for an argument.

"No, but I thought you'd—"

"You were right. I'm coming with you," she stated and picked up the doll. She walked to slip the mini tape recorder she used for testing her presentations into her shoulder bag. She quickly made a copy of Mallory's tape and stuck it into her bag, too.

"Smart girl," Kyle said grimly.

Wary of their cars being spotted by Bob, alerting him, Kyle and Rachel ran through the night shadows. Rachel didn't complain about the fast pace, her hours of fitness jogging and exercise paying off.

At one o'clock the interior of the Winters house was too quiet, but echoes of the sisters' laughter years ago circled Rachel, haunting her.

Kyle's misspent youth served them well as he quickly used a credit card to open the side-door lock to the garage, attached to the house. Bob's Lincoln was still in the garage, and Kyle paused a moment to appreciate the Model T Ford that Bob always rode in Neptune's Landing's parades—the sisters had all ridden in it, and Mallory had sat next to Bob. . . .

Rachel held her breath as she opened the door to the downstairs bedroom Mallory had used as a child. She closed it with a sickening feeling, and looked at Kyle who was moving like a big, silent, lethal shadow up the stairs. Several heartbeats later, he returned and shook his head.

"He didn't leave town and you know it," Rachel stated. "He'll be coming after me. That's why you want to get to him first, isn't it?"

Kyle didn't answer, but his expression was grim. "Let's go. Let's try your mother's house."

Rachel was the first to walk out of the back door, Kyle behind her. They stood for a moment, regrouping, and flashes of the past hit Rachel, just as the Pacific Ocean pounded the rocks below the cliff. . . . Beyond the white picket fence was where the three sisters had stood, eagerly searching for the first blow of a gray whale, where they had flown their kites in the cliff's updraft. . . .

"We've got to move fast, honey." Kyle took a moment to gather Rachel against him, holding her face to his throat.

"It's so awful—"

Then Bob Winters moved from the shrubbery, Kyle's deadly semi-automatic in his hand. "Looking for something?"

Hatred cut deep lines in Bob's face, his eyes wild with anger, his thin hair tossed by the wind and revealing his gleaming scalp. "I warned you, Scanlon . . . told you to get out of town, and you didn't. What happens to Rachel is your fault, not mine."

"It's never your fault, is it, Winters?"

"I know what you want," Rachel said quietly. She had to divert Bob from Kyle; Bob looked as if nothing could stop him from pulling that deadly trigger, and Kyle would be his first—because Kyle was tensed to spring at him now. . . .

"Let's keep this nice and quiet on our drive to Mallory's favorite place on the beach, shall we?" Bob asked, motioning the muzzle of the gun at Kyle. "You drive. Rachel and I will sit in the back."

In the car, with the gun against her ribs, Rachel said, "Wouldn't you like to listen to Mallory's tape while we're driving? The one with both of your voices on it?"

Bob's eyes widened. "There's a tape?"

"With Mallory and you. She was cursing you. That's what she did, didn't she? Does 'I'll haunt you forever' sound familiar? I happen to have it right here. You'd like to hear it, wouldn't you?"

"Get it. Play it," Bob ordered fiercely.

Kyle slipped the tape into the car's sound system and Mallory's eerie moaning began, her words forcefully bitter and threatening: "You even come close to my family, and I'll kill you. I'll kill you! You better not have raped Rachel, you bastard—"

"That's enough," Bob ordered abruptly.

"I guess her curses worked, huh? That little doll she used to stick pins in did its job, huh?" Rachel asked moments later when Bob demanded the tape and stuffed it into his pocket. She was careful to position her bag's outer pocket holding her voice activated recorder toward Bob.

His eyes were wild in the car's shadows. "The doll? What doll?"

"You know, that voodoo doll with your hair—when it was brown—and your shirt. You attacked me in New York, didn't you? You had to have help—two men— and then you couldn't perform, could you? Because they laughed? I guess Mallory's voodoo curse worked, didn't it? Heart trouble, headaches, and trouble with manly stuff?"

"Where is it? Where is that doll?" Bob hissed.

"That fire at Kyle's garage. You set that, too, didn't you? After you hit him on the head and beat him?" Rachel was cold with fury, but she focused on getting Bob's confession. The recorder's tiny red light shone in the shadows beside her.

"Rachel—" Kyle cautioned. In the silvery rectangle of the rearview mirror, his eyes cautioned her.

"Keep driving, Scanlon. Yes, of course, I set the fire and kicked him around a bit. He's lucky it didn't happen before, and he should have died."

"Oh, well. You set out to murder him, then?"

Bob jabbed the gun into her ribs with each word. "Yes, of course. He's lucky it didn't happen before, and he should have died. He deserved it. Always interfering—"

Rachel kept focused on getting the taped confession, despite the sharp pain. The tape on Rachel's hand recorder was still running, and she planned to get everything possible—"You started abusing Mallory when she was what? How old was she?"

When Kyle parked the Lincoln in the beach over-look, Bob was silent; he smiled as though he was enjoy-ing the memories. "Get out, Scanlon, and stand in front of the car while Rachel and I get out. And don't forget that one wrong move and Rachel gets it first."

With Bob's fingers biting into her arm, the gun jammed into her ribs, the three walked down the path to the beach, the sound of the tide matching the heavy beat of Kyle's heart. Rachel was pushing too hard, fear-less in her drive to get Bob to confess everything into her recorder.

"Take it easy, Rachel," Kyle warned, moving ahead of Rachel and Bob. If he made his move at the wrong time, Rachel could die. Fear for her overpowered everything else.

On the beach, he turned to Bob. "There is a doll," he said. "You're going to need Rachel to find it."

"You first, Scanlon. She'll tell me before you die." Bob laughed wildly, shoved Rachel slightly away, and aimed the gun at Kyle, mimicking a shot. "Click. Now where is that doll?"

Kyle held his breath. In the moonlight, Rachel had that hand on her hip, angled shoulders, her chin lifted, looking at Bob in that slanted, challenging way. The wind had picked up her hair and her expression said she was going for it all—and she could end up dead. "Don't you want to finish it, Bob? What you started with me? You get the point, don't you?" she asked, repeating what her attacker had said to her, then added a reinforc-ing, "You do get the point, don't you?"

"Clever little girl," Bob stated, admiringly. "Maybe we can work something out. I've missed Mallory's—

services. Yours may start tonight, if you live long enough. You had to ruin everything, Rachel."

"I get the point," Rachel said too quietly as the bag's strap slid from her shoulder and she gripped it in her fist.

Kyle held his breath, willing her not to force Bob into shooting her. "Rachel has a right to know everything, Bob. Tell her about the men that went up those steps. You arranged all that, didn't you?"

Bob's grim smile and the gun turned to Kyle. "I did. Anonymously, of course. I liked to watch—and it provided me with a little extra spending money—"

"Why, you—" Rachel exploded and reached for him.

Bob instantly raised the gun to Kyle's chest. "Back or he gets it right now."

Kyle struggled to keep Bob's attention on him. "What about the abortions and the beatings?"

Bob shrugged easily. "I told that tramp not to get pregnant. She deserved what she got. But I loved her in my way."

Rachel tossed her bag onto the sand, and Kyle knew that look. She was making her move, regardless of her own life. "There's the doll. Don't you want to see it, Bob?"

In the instant Bob glanced at the bag, Kyle was on him.

No match for the younger, more fit man—or his anger—Bob quickly lay in the sand. In an explosion he wouldn't remember later, Kyle pummeled him.

Then Rachel was sobbing in the distance, tugging at Kyle, and he forced himself to stop. On the edge of violence and sanity, he listened to Rachel's pleas and gradually pushed himself away. He stood over Bob, the gun in his hand pointed at Bob and the fever to kill still running hot within his veins.

"Do it," Bob gasped, his eyes wild. "Do it."

"I love you, Kyle. . . . I love you. . . ." Rachel placed her hand on Kyle's arm. Her face gleamed with tears, her eyes shimmering up at him, her voice husky and filled with terror. Kyle realized that she'd seen the worst of him, the part he didn't ever again want to experience. He struggled at that precarious edge of vengeance and sanity, bound only by Rachel. "Don't. That's what he wants, to ruin your life, too. And in doing so, he'll ruin mine. I do not want the man I love spilling blood on this sand, not in a place where I want to remember Mallory as a carefree girl. Do you hear me?"

"He deserves everything he gets," Kyle stated darkly; he needed to see the man who hurt Mallory dead.

"He does. But I think Mom would really like to talk with him first."

Kyle breathed heavily, pulling the anger back into him, controlling it. "I think you're right."

"Have at it, ladies. You've only got a few minutes before the police arrive," Kyle said as he sat in a chair at Nine Balls. Bob, his wrists taped together with duct tape, his expression bitter, slumped against the wall.

Moses stood nearby, his arms folded over his massive chest, his expression impassive. "You want some bones broken, Trina?"

"No, thanks. I want to handle my own garbage. . . . You hurt my daughter, Bob," Trina said coolly as she lined up a trick shot, sighting in on it. "Rachel was right—I do want a little chat with you."

Bob stiffened and muttered, "You're not going to do anything, Trina. You let it happen. You didn't even question my interest in Mallory. Now, does that sound like a loving mother? And you don't have anything on me, Scanlon. No proof at all about anything."

He shouldn't have looked at Kyle just then, not with Pup sitting on the floor beside his master. The dog immediately growled and quickly did his three-legged walk to stand, legs braced, hackles raised and teeth bared, in front of Bob.

"Stay, Pup," Kyle ordered quietly as Bob edged back from the dog.

"Oh, I think there may be some proof." Rachel stood near her mother, who was slowly, thoughtfully chalking her cue stick.

Trina seemed deep in thought and then suddenly, she moved in on Bob with her cue stick. Hit behind his knees, he went down on the floor, Trina standing over him.

Her cue stick was shoved into Bob's groin, much like the pins Mallory had stuck into the doll's. "I'll need a minute with Bob," Trina said to the police who suddenly appeared at the stairway "Close the door, please."

Cody spoke into his shoulder unit, and a squad car's red light cycled though the bamboo blinds covering the front windows. "You're covered, Trina," he said, closing the stairway door.

"Always a lady, like her daughter," Kyle murmured as Rachel came to sit on his lap.

"I was terrified he would kill you. Then, watching you, I was afraid that you'd kill him. I'm proud of you, big guy. I thought for a minute that I'd lost you, but we've got him, don't we?"

"Oh, I'd say so." Kyle looked at the man on the floor, the cue stuck jabbed into his crotch; Pup had changed his position until his head was near Bob's. The dog growled, his teeth exposed, and a spindle of drool slid onto Bob's cheek. He frantically wiped it off and Pup leaned in closer, almost nose to nose with the man.

Jada had a billiard ball in each fist and looked as if she were going to throw them at Bob. Rachel looked appealingly at Kyle. "You've got another knee, don't you?"

"Sure."

"Jada, Kyle says he needs to hold both of us. Get over here, will you?"

"Just tell me one thing: When do I get my chance?" Jada asked when she was settled beside Rachel.

"When you testify," Kyle said quietly as he watched Moses study Trina. The ex-wrestler was locked to Trina, studying the line of her body, and he had just sighed deeply, like a man who had found his dream woman.

"You need this?" Moses took a chair to Trina. "Take your time."

Trina sat gracefully, without removing the cue stick. "Thank you. Now, Bob. You've been naughty, haven't you?" she said.

"There's no proof of anything—" He grimaced and wiped Pup's drool from his face; the dog growled softly, warningly.

"This is just between friends," Trina stated. "That's what we were, right? Friends? How many times did you tell me that when you couldn't perform? And you hurt my daughter and tried to rape Rachel, didn't you?"

Bob's expression of terror changed to sly certainty.

"No one will believe you. I've got a reputation in this town. I'll have you all in jail."

"Will you?" Rachel asked, before she played the tape with his confession on it.

Despite a few noises caused by rustling clothing, Bob's deep voice had recorded perfectly. His expression now was one of speechless horror, his lips moving soundlessly.

"You will apologize to Mallory now, right here, you sniveling little bastard." Trina's fierce order followed the movement of the tip of the cue into Bob's throat.

"But that's insane! Mallory is dead."

"I'll haunt you forever, isn't that what she said, Bob?" Rachel asked quietly. "She's going to, you know—haunt you forever—with each breath you take. Think of it, Mom . . . the headaches, the chest pains, the stomach aches—all that and he's impotent, too. I'd say she got to him."

"I'll kill you," Trina said quietly.

"You don't want to do that." Beneath Rachel, Kyle's body tensed; he understood the cold fury that could cause a blind killing fever, regardless of consequences.

Before the others could move, Moses stood next to Trina. "So, how about a date?"

Everyone stared at the six-foot-seven beefy ex-wrestler, now a personal trainer. He eased the cue stick from Trina's hand. "I've seen these things kill and break bones. Nasty things. It's too messy for a lady, though apparently, you know how they can be used. This guy is going to jail. Attempted murder, arson, maybe statutory rape, prostitution, slavery, whatever is in the book. So how about that date?"

Jada threw up her hands and groaned in frustration. "Another one shot down!"

Moses turned to her and smiled gently. "I've got a lot of friends just perfect for you. You'll just have to sort out the one you want and get busy raising that family."

Kyle tried to smother his grin. Apparently, Moses had his own plans and that required getting Jada what she wanted. . . .

She blinked and recovered instantly. "You do?"

Kyle started to laugh as Trina continued staring blankly up at his friend. Then she said unevenly, "Bob hasn't apologized to Mallory yet. I need to hear him say it . . . please."

"Okay." Moses reached down and hauled Bob to his feet. "You'll do that—now. And make it sincere. She sounded like a real sweet girl, just like my kid sister."

"You can't make me. The police—" The rest of his words ended on a strangled note as Moses moved close, and whispered something that turned Bob's face pale.

Then Bob Winters apologized—sincerely, thoroughly.

In the aftermath of the night's terror and the intense session with the police, Rachel and Kyle, silent and exhausted, settled into the apartment. Lying on the couch, they watched the flickering candles die as Mallory's favorite song floated softly to an end. . . . *I'll be with you forever, till the tides no longer flow, till doves no longer fly and roses no longer bloom, till time comes no more. . . . I'll be with you forever. . . . On the far, still side of tomorrow. . . .*

"She really will always be with us, the good part of Mallory," Rachel whispered softly against Kyle's throat.

His hand stroked her hair. "She can rest now, don't you think, honey?"

Rachel listened to the apartment, to the creaking of the sign outside on Atlantis Street. She heard nothing, but the peaceful beat of Kyle's heart. "Go to sleep now, Mallory. Katrina is safe now. . . . I love you. . . ."

"I love you, too. See you, kiddo. . . ." the silence seemed to say as the last candle flickered and died.

Rachel caressed Kyle's chest, where only hours ago, his heart had pumped with rage, the need to kill the man who had abused Mallory. "Do you think he is Katrina's father? Or do you think Shane—?"

Kyle's hand stopped moving on her hair. "The subject is never going to come up. Ever. Shane left town and Winters isn't going to be free for a long time. For now, Katrina is my niece, a Scanlon, and that's how it stands."

"Mom wants to see her."

Kyle was silent, then his fingers began stroking and playing with Rachel's hair. "Everything takes time, honey. But we'll handle it. Remember the good times, honey. Hold Mallory close in your heart. I think she can rest now. You need to do the same."

"I knew she was here, waiting for me. I felt her in so many ways, close to me, wanting something. I'll love her until the edge of time, until the other side of tomorrow. And someday maybe, I'm going to tell Katrina a story—Once upon a time, there were three sisters. . . ."

# Epilogue

---

IN THE FIRST WEEK OF AUGUST, THE LOCALS OF NEPTUNE'S
Landing were enjoying freshly caught halibut, the gray
whales were blowing in the Pacific Ocean, and three
species of sea lions were barking for mates on the off-
shore rocks.

With the setting sun painting that strip of scarlet between ocean and sky, Kyle lay down on the beach blanket. After a hard day of business, restocking his new
garage, he was ready to relax and enjoy the woman who
fascinated him. Life wasn't exactly easy with Rachel
Everly, but it was fun to see her light up, that edgy challenging look directly focused on him.

He inhaled the salty air and felt a little like barking
for his mate himself. That's what Rachel was now, he
thought smugly—his mate, the woman who made him
happy, the woman he loved.

In the busy weeks that had followed the investigation
of Bob's two deceased wives, his computer activities,
arson, and the attempted murder of Kyle, Neptune's
Landing was abuzz with gossip and speculation. Nine
Balls, renamed Mallory's Place, had reopened with
Moses helping Rachel, and the upscale clientele was
slowing returning. Sally Mae, Dorothy, Terri and the

others were steady players during Ladies Night, each toasting Mallory and Rachel.

As Moses had promised, a steady, appealing flow of single, marriageable men had started suddenly appearing for Jada's inspection. Currently, she was busy with Alvin Sandusky, the sports announcer, while Moses moved in to reassure Trina that she wasn't too old and battered for romance.

Trina was adjusting to what had happened in her own house, with her own child, and the sisters were coming to grips with what had happened to Mallory— why she'd acted as she had, and there had been few carefree moments.

Kyle's "niece," Katrina, was arriving tomorrow for two weeks of playing on the beach before she went back to school in Idaho.

Before Katrina arrived, Kyle intended to make use of the hours with Rachel. It would be a long two weeks without Rachel in his bed, and he'd gotten very addicted to waking her up in very special ways. . . .

Rachel appeared at the crest of the hill overlooking the beach. Kyle watched her carry a picnic basket down the trail. Near him, she placed it on the sand. "Food. Wine. Pink thongs with flowers. Me . . . all as requested."

Rachel had that edgy, smug look as she took off her blouse. She swung it on one finger while Kyle took in her body and grinned. "Nice shells."

"A little small, but I see that they are still effective."

She sat beside him and looked out at the Pacific Ocean where once three sisters had played. "Nice," she said quietly and gave herself to the moment.

At sunset, with whales blowing somewhere in the ocean, with sea lions barking for mates and with seagulls doing their last foraging for the day, Rachel was at peace. Kyle was at her side, smoothing her back, understanding the quiet memories that flowed between them. They would be making more memories together, because Kyle definitely had his mind on "a permanent arrangement, rings, that sort of thing."

Rachel had found what she'd looked for all of her life, a man to trust, one to stand beside her in the good and bad times. A hero of the best kind, Kyle would shy away from that description, but he was the gentlest man she'd ever known.

She smiled softly, because Kyle was getting his dream house with the white picket fence and the kids playing on the backyard swings. She'd make that bet the next game they played, with a wedding ring on the end of the cue stick pointed at Kyle.

Kyle sat up beside her, staring out at the ocean as he placed his arm around her shoulders. "I can almost see her out there," he whispered softly.

"Me, too. She's happy." While Kyle would remember an older Mallory, Rachel's image was that of a girl who had appeared against the dark waves. . . .

Young Mallory, thin and angular, frolicked in the shallow water and grinned back at Rachel.

Mallory lifted her hand and Rachel raised her own.

She returned the wave and the image of Mallory slowly faded. . . .

"See you, kiddo. . . ."

*Great stories, hot heroes, and a whole lot of seduction are coming this November from*

*Avon Romance. . .*

## This Rake of Mine by Elizabeth Boyle
**An Avon Romantic Treasure**

Miranda wants nothing to do with the scoundrel who caused her ruin years ago, but the students of Miss Emery's Establishment for the Education of Genteel Young Ladies, where she is a teacher, are all atwitter at the attraction that crackles between them. So the girls come up with a plan to get them together, and Miranda and Jack don't stand a chance . . .

## The Boy Next Door by Meg Cabot
**An Avon Contemporary Romance**

Melissa Fuller is bored by her life. But then all sorts of strange things start happening when the lady next door is a victim of a suspicious robbery/attempted homicide. This young woman is determined to unmask the criminal. And most interesting of all is the man who comes to "house sit" while his aunt is in the hospital. Could she have found a boyfriend next door?

## Keeping Kate by Sarah Gabriel
**An Avon Romance**

When Captain Alec Fraser takes custody of a beautiful lady spy, the handsome Highland officer must discover information that only she knows—and refuses to reveal. With secrets of his own to protect, Alec never expects the stunning, stubborn girl to cause him so much trouble—nor does he expect to open his closed heart ever again.

## Gypsy Lover by Edith Layton
**An Avon Romance**

As the poor relation to a wealthy family, Meg Shaw is obliged to be a governess companion to their daughter. But when her charge runs away, she embarks on a search of her own to find the missing heiress and clear her good name. Little does she expect that her path will cross Daffyd Reynard, a wealthy and dashing gentleman with the wild spirit—and heart—of a gypsy . . .